Jimmy Grits
Private Eye

ISBN 978-1-62806-425-4 (print | paperback)

Library of Congress Control Number 2024919341

Published by Salt Water Media
29 Broad Street, Suite 104
Berlin, MD 21811
www.saltwatermedia.com

Cover art by Aubrey Brown © 2024

Jimmy Grits
Private Eye

David Cooper

Contents

Jimmy Grits

A Man Who Feels
He Needs No
Introduction

I did more than my part sweeping miscreants from Ocean Mist's streets, and I still found time to deal pleasantries to sun-seeking tourists buying t-shirts, taffy, and ice cream. Even tipped my fedora now and then. I never complained. Our good people needed someone to protect them from the town's slimy underbelly. Besides, the work kept me fed.

Ocean Mist, the kind of town you passed between blinks while cruising the highway half asleep at two a.m., claimed some coastal Delaware real estate just south of Lewes and a bit north of Rehoboth. We had a town hall, boardwalk, drawbridge over the Rehoboth-Lewes Canal, run-down lighthouse, and even a library for those who were into that sort of thing. I knew Ocean Mist, and it knew me; at least, I thought I did until the day the tinker walked through my door and told me the waves had stopped.

The Case of the
Missing Waves

"What do you mean the waves stopped?" I didn't look up from my desk.

"Just like I said, the water is as flat as a lake."

Ocean Mist accepted the disheveled tinker and his wobbly cart of pots, pans, and unidentifiable metal wares as just another small-town oddity, but his ramblings and pacing of my office really tested my patience.

"You're talking about the ocean? No waves on the Atlantic Ocean?"

"Well, no waves around here, anyway. You have to come and see it."

I didn't frequent the sand. A middle age man of substantial build wearing a fedora and sport coat lounging on a beach-chair didn't attract the right kind of attention. Learned that one the hard way.

I asked, "Doesn't the moon have something to do with the waves?"

The tinker ran his fingers through a salt and pepper mange. Shook his head vigorously. "No, Jimmy. The moon can't have anything to do with this!"

"Okay, easy. Just start again from the beginning."

By that time, I had moved a pile of files from the right side of my desk to the left, and now I had to move the files back to the right side. Another busy day.

The tinker prattled on about the waves, just nonsense, while a bottle of Jack Daniels in great need of emptying sat in my desk drawer. Jimmy Grits' Detective Agency didn't run on coffee and cheese steaks alone.

I patted the successfully moved files then folded my hands prayerlike in front of me. "Listen buddy, I think it's about time for you to—."

"So, the mayor sent me."

"The mayor?" The guy really wasn't the mayor, but he had more money and influence than any of our elected officials, or even the past several city councils combined. Everyone just called him the mayor. He hated me. Something about my case involving goings-on between his neighbor and now ex-wife. "Why me?"

The tinker shrugged.

"Okay." I grabbed my fedora from the coat rack.

He gave me a once-over. "You going like that?"

This question from a man wearing thread-bare cargo shorts and a Hawaiian shirt with more stains than flowers.

I tugged at my sport coat and adjusted my tie. "What, is my knot crooked?"

The tinker frowned and led me out the door.

KIDS STOOD AT THE EDGE OF THE Atlantic Ocean holding boogie boards and scratching their heads. Others waded in flat knee-high water, jumped into the air every now and again, and made exasperated woo-hoo noises. Never seen anything like it. Not a ripple.

"No waves, anywhere?" I asked the tinker.

"Plenty of waves down in Rehoboth and up in Henlopen. Just none here."

People spilled onto the sand from the boardwalk. The beach became as close as Times Square on New Year's Eve. "This is sure bringing the gawkers out of the woodwork." I pushed up my hat, wiped my brow with a handkerchief, and unbuttoned my collar.

The tinker turned to me and did another once-over. "Aren't you hot in those clothes?"

I scoffed. "Don't ever let them see you sweat, buddy."

"That's why I asked. You're soaked. I can see your man-boobs through your dress shirt."

"Don't you have some spoons to sell or pots to bang over on Jefferson Avenue?"

"No one will buy anything from me if the waves have stopped."

I looked at him sideways. "That doesn't make any sense."

"You obviously know nothing about running a tinker cart."

"You're right." I shook my head. "Where's the mayor?"

The tinker pointed, waved, and the tallest man on the beach shouldered his way through the crowd. All the mayor needed was a stove pipe hat to go with his beard, lanky build, and pronounced brow to make him Ocean Mist's own Abe Lincoln, in appearance anyway.

The mayor said, "Grits," but didn't look at me.

No reason to fake pleasantries, I thought, so I got to the point. "Isn't the real mayor working on this?"

"She's standing over there with city council."

"What's their plan?"

"Plan? All they've done for the past hour is look confused."

"Well, can you blame them?" I folded my arms. "What about the police?"

The mayor shook his head. "They have their hands full managing the crowd."

"So, why am I here?"

"No other choice."

"And, let me guess, you don't want to be involved?"

"You know how I like to keep things quiet." The mayor handed me a sheet of tablet paper wrapped around an iron key. "This was on my desk this morning."

I opened the paper. Scrawled in large looping script were the words, *Going on vacation! Deal with it!* As if an afterthought, *Edward* had been added to the bottom.

"Who's Edward?" I asked.

"Beats me. Take a look at that key."

The eight-inch hand-forged key rested heavily in my hand. I ran my thumb over a symbol resembling a set of waves stamped into the head by some long-forgotten blacksmith, which stood in stark contrast to a photo key chain of a grumpy-looking cat and the name *Mr. Cuddles.*

"Know what it's to?"

"No, Grits, but I'm sure Edward does. That's why you need to find him."

"Why?"

"This shows up on my desk the same day the ocean goes quiet. You're the private detective. You tell me why you need to find him."

"Alright, alright." I put the key and paper in my pocket. "But tell me this, why put the key and note on your desk and not the real mayor's desk?"

The tinker scratched his chin. "This Edward guy must not know any better."

The mayor scowled.

I made my next question sound like a statement. "You realize I'm on the clock?"

The mayor gave some vague gesture one could say was acceptance and walked away.

I turned to the tinker. "You saw him agree to my contract?"

"Of course. Where do we start?"

"We, huh?"

THE LIBRARIAN WORE HER SIGNATURE HEELS AND black dress. Red hair flowed around a neckline leading a man's eye down and down, and she drifted to the circulation desk, her every step increasing my circulation.

"Hello, Jimmy," she said in her velvet voice, "what can I get you boys? Maybe, a couple periodicals?"

I leaned over the well-worn oak and pushed back my fedora. "I need to call in a favor, Angela."

Her eyebrow arched.

The tinker tapped me on the shoulder. "Your shirt is still sweaty. She can see your man boobs."

"Don't you have somewhere to be?"

"No, not really."

The scent of lilacs crossed the desk. "What do you need, Jimmy?"

"I need to get into the archive."

"Our library doesn't have an archive."

"Come on, doll."

The tinker recoiled like someone jabbed a finger in his eye. "Did you just call her doll? You can't say that. You let him say that?"

Angela tucked some red locks behind her ear. "I like to think he's a work in progress."

"Since when," asked the tinker, "the nineteen-forties?"

I stepped back from the desk. Put my hands on my hips. "Look, Angela, the archive. The *special* collections."

"Jimmy, I really wish I knew what you were talking about." She glanced at the tinker then straightened some books stacked between us.

"Okay, I get it." I reached into my wallet, pulled out a Hamilton, and stuffed it into the pocket of the tinker's faded Hawaiian shirt. "How about you go on down to Java Bob's? Get us some joe and danishes."

"I don't do gluten," he said.

"Then, I'll eat them."

"I'm not much for coffee, either."

"Just, get whatever you want. Make yourself scarce."

The tinker left.

Ocean Mist's streets belonged to me, but the library was Angela's joint. To get the good stuff, you had to be in the know and know how to ask. I leaned over the desk, again. "Now, where were we?"

"You were about to make an offer."

"You really know how to work me, don't you? Not an offer, doll. I was about to call in a favor."

"You sure I owe you a favor?"

"Who doesn't around here?" I took the key from my pocket. "About the archive, ever see anything like this in one of those old books?"

Angela's fingers followed a string of pearls leading my gaze to reading glasses nestled within her black dress. She breathed on a lens, wiped it with a tissue, and studied the waves symbol. "You really want to go down there?"

"I wouldn't have asked, if I didn't."

Angela checked the lobby to be sure no one was watching then led me into her office, shut the door, and pulled out a filing cabinet hiding a crawl space. She tugged at the hem of her dress. "I'm not exactly prepared for work in the archive."

"Why not? I'd let you go first."

She gave me a scolding look over her glasses. "Let's keep this professional, Jimmy."

"If you say so, doll." I knelt and crawled into a tunnel built for much lesser men than me.

"Are you okay?" she called.

"Yeah, why?"

"You're grunting a lot."

I stopped and hung my head. "I'm fine."

The tunnel ended at a small door with an old tumbler lock.

"Combination?" I called back to her. She gave it to me, and I was soon in a telephone-booth-sized shaft with a ladder leading into a basement few knew lay under the library.

"Look for the brown leather-bound books in the back-right corner. Second and third shelves."

I started down the ladder.

"Did you hear me?" she asked.

"Yes, I heard you."

"Well, I didn't know. All I hear is grunting."

The light switch, a big metal lever between copper contacts bolted to the wall, needed a good oiling and resisted my first couple of tugs. A few bulbs among many dangling from the ceiling buzzed to life. Books untouched for generations lay in stacks, peeking from drawers, and leaning to and fro on rickety shelves. I'm sure if I bothered to look, I'd find some scrolls here and there, too.

I reached the part of the archive Angela thought I'd need. She was right. I found a book with the waves symbol embossed on its spine. Flowing handwriting filled yellowed pages. I didn't recognize the language, which left many possibilities, since I only knew English. I was on Edward's trail, though, because the looping and oversized letters looked very similar to the writing on his note.

Despite not being much of a reader, I had over forty years' experience looking at pictures. There weren't many, not my kind of book, but a promising ink drawing caught my eye. I recognized the Washington Avenue Bridge over the Rehoboth-Lewes Canal and what looked like a door at the base of the east bank drawbridge tower.

I don't spend much time under bridges, not time I would admit to anyway, but I was pretty certain there were no doors under the canal bridge. I ripped the page from the binding and stuffed it into my pocket.

The tinker, a cup of coffee, and two danishes waited for me at the circulation desk. "Sorry, the coffee is cold. She said I had to wait here."

A goose egg swelled above his right eye.

"What happened to you?"

"She slugged me."

"Why?"

"Ask her." He scowled over his shoulder at Angela straightening magazines on a squeaky and leaning metal stand. "I just offered to take a look at her old rack."

I studied him for a moment.

He seemed genuinely bewildered.

"I found something, doll. Can you tell me what you think?"

She fished her glasses from her dress and made her way to the desk.

The tinker retreated behind me.

I showed the page to Angela. "Can you read this?"

The tinker peered around my arm. "Did you tear that from a book?"

"Would you back up, please?"

"You could lose your library card for that. She might even put you in a head lock."

"I said, back up."

Angela looked at us over her lenses. "I don't think anyone can read this, anymore. This could be a dead language."

"That old, huh?" I straightened my hat and headed for the door. "I owe you one."

"You owe me more than that, Jimmy."

"Where are you going?" asked the tinker.

"Following a lead."

I KICKED AT THE TANGLES OF VINES and nettles covering the bank under the canal bridge. "You wouldn't happen to have a machete back on that tinker's cart of yours, would you?"

"Are you sure there's a door here?"

I pulled from my pocket the page I had torn from the book and pointed to the picture. "See? Right here."

"What if that's fiction?"

"What?"

"What if that's a page from a story book?"

I stuffed the page back into my pocket. "Just keep looking."

A few minutes later, the tinker reached down and yanked weeds away from some mortared bricks. "Take a look at this, Jimmy." He pointed to an iron plate with a keyhole set into the masonry.

"Fiction, huh?" I pulled the key from my sport coat's pocket. It fit the lock.

Unseen cogs clicked and clanked. Gears ground and chains rattled over sprockets. A rectangular puff of dust preceded the rising of a steel storm door from the greenery at our feet. The door opened easily, which surprised me given its size, and revealed a dark and damp crumbling-brick passage filled with the smells of machine grease and coal smoke.

The tinker peered around me. "What's down there?"

"Only one way to find out."

We followed the passage to a huge chamber. Silo-sized boilers, pistons with rods the girth of telephone poles, crank shafts, hoses you could crawl through, and piles of coal made me feel very small.

I stared like an awestruck tourist. "This room must be as big as Ocean Mist."

"What's it all for?"

"Do I look like an engineer, to you?"

"There haven't been trains in Ocean Mist in years, Jimmy."

All of the machinery sat still. Nothing moved, hissed, or growled. "No, this can't—." The puzzle came together in my mind, but I just couldn't accept the picture the pieces formed. *The waves?*

"Over here." The tinker moved behind a desk, yanked the pull chain to a small lamp with a frilly shade, and held up a nameplate. *Edward Pushwater, Surf Services.*

"The guy on vacation," I said. Charts and ledger pages all written in the same script I had found in the archives covered the desk.

"What language is this?" the tinker asked.

"You don't recognize it?"

He shook his head.

I shuffled through some pages. "Can you do something for me?"

"Sure. What?"

I lifted a travel folio from among the papers and charts. "Tell your friend the mayor—."

"He's not my friend."

"Tell him, anyway, I need an expense account and a plane ticket to Bermuda."

"Bermuda?"

"That's what Edward's itinerary says." I removed the photograph of a trollish man snuggling a cat from a small frame. Mr. Cuddles, I presumed. "I don't think I'll have any trouble spotting Edward Pushwater in a crowd."

"Right, two plane tickets to Bermuda." The tinker ran back through the tunnel before I could correct his math.

"SIR, WOULD YOU LIKE A COFFEE?" OTHER than a silver pot, the lobby boy's hospitality cart looked more like a minibar than a coffee service. Not that I was complaining.

"Sure, kid."

The boy poured black gold into a large mug then added a generous measure of spirits.

Reaching for my joe, I said, "Now, that's my kind of coffee," but jerked my hand back when he took a lighter to my liquid breakfast. Blue flames danced above the mug's rim. "What are you doing, kid?" I grabbed the mug by the handle and waved my hand back and forth trying to put out the fire.

The boy gave me a puzzled look. "Welcome to Bermuda, sir." He pushed his cart to a young couple reclining on a couch.

"Waste of good liquor," I said.

The tinker stepped from the stairwell. His stained Hawaiian shirt seemed a bit more appropriate given our setting. "Any sign of Edward?"

"Nope."

"You'd think we'd have seen him, by now. The hotel isn't that big."

A childlike "woo-hoo" followed by a splash came from the pool just beyond the lobby window. I glanced in that direction. A hunched, long armed little man with stringy gray hair ringing an otherwise bald and somewhat lumpy head pulled himself gleefully from the pool, clapped his hands, and called out another "woo-hoo" before jumping back into the water.

"Found him," I said.

"Are those floaties on his arms?"

"Yep."

We walked to the pool and looked down at the frolicking troll. "Edward," I said, "we need to talk to you."

He pulled apart dripping strings of gray hair covering his face. "You from Ocean Mist?"

"All the way."

"Well, I'm on vacation."

"Vacation, huh? What about Ocean Mist's vacationers staring at a giant salty puddle?"

"I don't care." He got out of the pool, woo-hoo'd, and performed a rather impressive cannonball.

"Edward," I said, "the problem is no one knew you were leaving."

"No one remembered I was down in that hole, either." He motioned for the poolside waitress. "Miss, may I have another?"

The waitress rolled her eyes. "Another Shirley Temple, sir. Coming right up."

I tossed my hat on a table and loosened my tie. "Look, just come back with us, and we'll straighten everything out."

"I've decided." Edward stared off into the sky. "I'm never coming back."

I followed his gaze, but there was nothing there.

He looked back at me. "Unless, I get weekends off and two weeks of vacation a year."

"That sounds reasonable," I said.

The tinker folded his arms. "Who would we ask for that?"

I shot a stern look at him. "This doesn't concern you."

Edward did another cannonball, surfaced, and spouted water from his mouth. "The mayor can change my contract."

"You have a contract?" The tinker asked.

I took the tinker by his shirt. "I said, be quiet."

"And, I need an assistant," Edward said. "A trainee. I can't do this job for another forty years, you know."

"Forty years, huh?" I took off my tie. "Are we talking the actual mayor or *the mayor?*"

"There's more than one?" Edward shrugged. "Not even the guys who deliver my coal come to see me anymore. They just dump it down the chute every three months and leave me to shovel it, by myself, into the bins." He reached up from the pool, took his Shirley Temple from the waitress, and slipped her a quarter. "A little something extra for you."

"Gee, thanks."

The tinker rubbed his chin and thought about as hard as I believed he could manage. "A trainee, you said?"

"Yeah," Edward sipped at his drink, "you interested?"

"Well, I can't give up my tinker cart, completely, but I can work for you on some weekends, though, and vacations."

"It's a deal!" Edward said. "Now, stand back. This one is going to be big."

Another cannonball.

BOILER VALVES RELEASED PUFFS OF STEAM, CAMSHAFTS spun, and pistons chugged-out a throbbing rhythm.

Edward paused his labors and placed his hands on his hips. "Listen to that kitten purr."

The tinker sported a new flowered shirt we had picked up in Bermuda. He watched every turn of Edward's wrench and the adjustment of every gizmo and whizbang in Surf Services.

The mayor— not the real one— stood with me and wore the same slack-jawed expression I had when first entering the cavernous room under Ocean Mist.

I interrupted his awe. "The tinker tells me he has a new part-time job, and you have an arrangement with Edward."

"Something like that." The mayor leaned toward me and lowered his voice, "Who's paying these guys?"

"You're asking me?" I held out my hand. "I just know where my next meal is coming from."

The mayor handed me an envelope.

"Now that we're done here, I need to renew my library card."

The Case of the
Bottomless Shorts

The bottle of Jack Daniels in my desk drawer made it only to sundown, so I decided to take the edge off with a brownie sundae at Scoop and Shake, just off the boardwalk at Jefferson Avenue.

As I was about to lift the first hot-fudge-dripping spoonful to my lips, Officer Eneau of Ocean Mist's finest called to me from the ramp to the boardwalk. "I thought I might find you here."

"Well, you did."

A rather flustered looking lady huffed and puffed behind Eneau, and they closed the distance between the boardwalk and my sundae.

"This lady has something to show you."

She pushed her way around the baby-faced officer. "You that private detective on the posters taped up around town?"

"Bad guys take 'em down as fast as I can put 'em up, but yeah."

Eneau mumbled something sounding like, "We do, too."

The woman spun, said, "Look at this," and pointed to her bare butt cheeks basking in the Ocean Mist moonlight.

I took a bite of my sundae. "Sorry I didn't take you to dinner, first."

"You need to help me." She pointed accusingly at Eneau. "This man wants to cite me for indecent exposure."

"Looks pretty decent to me," I said. "Otherwise, I'm not sure how I can help."

"My shorts weren't like this when I left my condo."

"So, you want me to find the rest of your outfit?"

She put her hands on her hips. "Someone has to do something. I'm a teacher. I can't get cited for indecent exposure."

My brownie sundae had melted into a brown sludge. I tossed it and my spoon into a garbage can, wiped my hands on my pants, and adjusted my tie. Seemed I'd be working the night shift.

Officer Seamus Eneau had just joined the force. Still wet behind the ears. Still too eager. I pulled him aside and spoke quietly. "Look, Seamus. Obviously, something is wrong here. This young lady didn't leave for her night out this way."

Some guy on the boardwalk yelled, "Get lost, you perverts!"

The three of us ran up the Jefferson Avenue ramp toward the voice.

A middle-aged couple, the target of many stares and looking confused, stood baring their posteriors to a large crowd. The couple must have felt the night's hot breeze kissing their assets and covered what they could with open hands. The crowd slinked away like someone had thrown a girly magazine into the middle of a Bible study.

I turned to my client. "Looks like you're not the only exhibitionist out tonight, doll."

A lady screamed farther down the boardwalk, and I sensed she suffered the same plight as my client and the couple.

"Seamus," I said, "you can spend the evening citing innocent tourists for indecent exposure, or you can start asking questions and help me get to the bottom— sorry— root of this problem."

"Delila," the teacher said.

"What?" I asked.

"My name is Delila."

I handed her my sport coat, which, given her height, would cover her goods.

She sniffed. "This smells like—." She sniffed again.

"Yeah, a hard-working man. Why don't you go home, change clothes, then come back to my office?" I handed her my card. "I'll need those shorts. Whatever you do, don't wash them."

A LIGHT KNOCK CAME FROM MY OFFICE door where the outline of a woman shuffled back and forth beyond the frosted glass.

"It's open."

The teacher entered and handed me my coat without looking at my face. "Thank you for seeing me, Mr. Grits." The adrenaline from her boardwalk incident must have worn off leaving only her embarrassment.

I motioned to a chair across from me. "Please, have a seat, doll."

She hesitated then sat. "My name is Delila."

"I called Officer Eneau a few minutes before you got here and wormed some information from him."

The Ocean Mist Police didn't usually share much. An ego thing. Afraid of me showing them up in the public eye. Fortunately, Eneau was still green and pliable.

"I bet you lost your phone," I continued. "Probably a wallet. Maybe keys?"

"Phone and wallet," she said.

"Same happened with the others on the boardwalk." I jotted on my steno pad her phone's model, number, and a description of her wallet and its contents. "Mind giving me your shorts?"

She squirmed a bit in her chair while handing me a plastic bag.

I laid the remnants on my desk, moved a floor lamp closer to us, and pulled a drinking glass from my desk drawer. Not every private investigator carried a magnifying glass like some Saturday cartoon, but moving the drinking glass up and down worked about the same way.

The edges look melted, I thought. *Certainly not cut.*

The tag in the waistband read *85% nylon 15% cotton.* I sniffed, felt a slight sting in my nose, lifted her shorts to my face, inhaled deeply, pulled the fabric back, and noted her expression—completely distraught over her phone and wallet.

"Don't worry, doll. We'll find your things." I tapped my pencil on the steno pad. "There's a chemical smell. You didn't use nail polish remover, recently, did you?"

She shook her head and rocked slightly in her chair like she had a thorn in her butt.

"You wouldn't happen to have a rash on your backside?"

She flushed.

I made a note of it. "Okay, that's helpful, too. I have some ideas and need to do a bit of research. Do you have another phone number I can use to reach you?"

"No, but the condo I'm renting is a short walk from here. Want me to come by tomorrow afternoon?"

"Can you give me another day? Say, swing by my office the day after tomorrow about 3:00?"

"Yes, how much do you charge?"

I handed her a contract laying out my rates. She read half of it and signed. Helping this poor woman could mean more than a few clams. If I found her belongings, I'm sure there would be others' phones, wallets, and finders' fees. Maybe even open some doors with the police department. Make the guys in blue— well, green for Ocean Mist— a bit more willing to work with me.

I NEEDED SOMEONE WITH EXPERTISE IN THE chemicals department, so I thought of my nephew and picked up the handset to the rotary on my desk. "Hey, sis, how are things in the South? Shame we don't get together as much, these days."

"Jimmy, we live in Bethany. Fifteen minutes from you."

"Yeah, well, there's that bridge and the way traffic is and all. Anyway, you think my favorite nephew would be interested in helping on a case?"

"On a case? Jimmy, he's twelve."

"I need him to look into a woman's shorts for me."

Silence.

"Hello? Sis?"

"You do realize, Jimmy—."

"Does your boy still have that chemistry set?"

"Why?"

"So, these folks were walking on the boardwalk when their shorts fell apart. Lost their keys, phones, wallets. I'd like to swing down tomorrow morning and have your son work some of his science magic. See if he can tell me what happened to the fabric. Give me an idea of what I'm dealing with."

"I can tell you what you're dealing with," she said. "You're dealing with—."

"Okay, I'll see you tomorrow at 8:00."

A BOY GENIUS. NO DOUBT ABOUT IT. Canisters of powdered chemicals, microscope, glassware full of bubbling liquids. All of this set up on his mother's back porch.

The short, skinny, freckled redhead with glasses thicker than the bottoms of coke bottles placed three little squares cut from the shorts in three separate test tubes suspended from a metal rack. He then lifted a beaker from above a Bunsen burner, poured a black liquid into a ceramic container with a handle, and handed it to me.

"What do you want me to do with this?" I asked.

"It's coffee."

"Oh, thanks."

He held an eye-dropper over the fabric sample in the first test tube. "This litmus solution is really sensitive. It'll turn red if there's any acid residue." Carefully, he added the solution to the test tube.

"That's redder than Rudolf's nose after a bender," I said.

"Huh?"

"Never mind, son."

"Someone used an acid, Uncle Jimmy. That's obvious. The real questions are what kind and how strong."

"So, you're saying we got someone spraying acid on unsuspecting tourists' shorts then scooping up whatever falls from their back pockets?"

He nodded. "I'll need time to figure out more. Can I keep the lady's shorts?"

I gave him a wink. "Just don't tell your mother."

My nephew seemed confused, but I couldn't blame him. This whole scheme became more complicated with each step I took to unravel it.

"Let's keep in touch," I said. "I got to get back to Ocean Mist to see the tinker."

"I DON'T KNOW, JIMMY. THIS IS WEDNESDAY, and it's one of my best nights."

The tinker and I stood next to his cart, which he had hauled up Adams

Avenue a few minutes earlier clanking and squeaking loud enough to announce he was open for business.

"Why is Wednesday better than any other night? What is it about Wednesday that makes people want to buy dented pans, old metal funnels, and mismatched cutlery more than other nights?"

The tinker shrugged. "Hard to explain the forces of micro economics, Jimmy. I just have to try and live by them."

"Okay, how about I pay you what you would make tonight plus ten percent?"

"Twenty."

"Fifteen," I countered.

"Twelve."

"Twelve? I just offered you, fifteen."

"Oh, yeah. Ten."

I straightened my jacket and tie. "You got a deal."

"What are we looking for?"

"Not what. Who. Someone's been spraying acid on backsides. Melts their pockets. Meet me at the corner of Jefferson and the boardwalk tonight about 8:00. I'll have more for you, then."

"Wow. Sounds pretty serious. What's this criminal's name?"

"I don't know who the person is, yet."

"I mean, every bad guy has to have a name, like The Butt Burglar?"

"There was no burglary," I said. "Nothing was broken into."

"Tushy Thief?"

"Just, be at the Jefferson ramp to the boardwalk at 8:00. Okay?"

I HAD TO GIVE THE TINKER AN ounce of credit for being on time, but I couldn't give him much more than that.

"What's with the trucker cap and camera?" I asked. "Are those yoga pants?"

"Well, you see—."

"What's on your t-shirt?"

He pulled aside a thick camera strap crossing his chest. "It's my tinkers' convention shirt."

"Tinkers have a convention?"

"This year's was in Atlanta."

I tipped back my hat and scratched my forehead. "So, why the crazy getup?"

"I'm undercover. A tourist, Jimmy. Get this, the camera is not just a part of my disguise. I can use it to take pictures of the Ass Snatcher."

"Not this again."

"Crack Crook?"

"Undercover?" I waved my hand at the families wandering the boardwalk. "Do you look like any of these people?"

He shrugged.

My phone dinged, and I reached for it to find a text from my nephew. *Tests done. Acid eats cheap stuff like nylon and polyester. Cotton takes time. Will make skin itch and burn a little but not dangerous in small amounts.*

"Alright," I said to the tinker, "you take from Washington Avenue north, and I'll take south. We're looking for anything suspicious. Anyone doing anything hinky around people's butts."

The tinker saluted me. "I'll keep my eyes glued to every—."

I raised my hand to stop his jabbering. "Just, use your cell phone and call if you see anything."

"Right."

With that, the tinker was on his way.

ANOTHER HOT NIGHT WORKING OCEAN MIST'S STREETS and boardwalk, the kind of night making you dream of a cool ocean breeze kissing your cheek. I took off my hat, loosened the band, and straightened the dampened brim. Hours of pounding asphalt and the boards, and I had nothing to show except for some real gum on this gumshoe's sole.

Nothing from the tinker, either.

Families started to thin. Small packs of preadolescents would soon rove the boards unsupervised. Explore their quasi-adulthoods. Then I saw her, a lady with a purse and cane walking behind and just a little too close to a bewildered and burned-out father. The modestly-dressed nondescript woman didn't seem to need the cane. I'd seen enough scammers in my time to tell she didn't put any weight on the aluminum stick.

I shoved the last bit of my funnel cake into my mouth, wiped my hands on my jacket, and rose to follow the woman, fixing my eyes on her like a two-bit reporter stalking a Hollywood starlet.

She used her cane-hand to toss wavy brown hair over her shoulder while taking three unaided steps.

Yeah, I'm not surprised, I thought.

She passed the ramp to Scoop and Shake, moved south past Happy Land, and stuck close to the father distracted by his whiny sticky-faced kids screaming something about hermit crabs. Her right hand clutched her purse, and she swung it awkwardly in front of her just a bit too close to the beleaguered dad's backside.

The man's pocket fell to pieces. His wallet dropped to the boardwalk.

Not much impressed me, but this woman had some moves. A small spike sprung from the end of her cane. She stabbed the leather billfold and picked it up like a jailbird piercing trash along the highway. The wallet sat on the ground less than half a second, maybe didn't even touch the boards at all, before finding its way into her purse. She turned naturally, gracefully, and walked down the Hamilton Street ramp.

I pulled out my cell phone and called the tinker. "I found a lady on the boardwalk. I'm following her down Hamilton toward town."

"You don't have time for that. What about our stake-out?"

"The lady is the one we're looking for."

"Oh, okay. I'm on the first block of Adams and heading your way."

"Stay on the line."

The lady walked with a purpose. Didn't check once for a tail before turning right onto First Street toward Washington Avenue.

I said to the tinker, "She's heading your way. Stay on the corner of Adams and First. She's wearing tan shorts, faded green sneakers, a black top, and carrying a purse and cane."

"Okay, what should I do?"

"Keep an eye on her. If she comes close, just look in her direction every once and a while, but not directly at her."

The woman crossed onto the town side of the street, and I stayed on the ocean side following about thirty yards behind her. Suddenly, she stopped and scanned the sidewalks.

I pulled my fedora low over my brow, flipped up my sport coat collar, faked interest in a store's window display of surfing teddy bears, and used the reflection from the glass to watch her resume her walk toward Washington Avenue.

I said into my phone, "She's still heading your way. Are you on the ocean or town side of First?"

"Ocean."

"Stay there. She'll be across the street from you, soon. Watch where she goes, but don't follow. If you can, try to take a picture of her without drawing any attention."

I allowed more distance between us and scolded myself for having gotten too close. The tinker came into view, and she continued right past him. I put away my phone.

"Did you get any photos?" I asked.

"Yep, lighting wasn't too good, and I can't speak for the composition in regard to the rule of thirds."

"Let's keep moving." I took the tinker's arm and pulled him along with me. "Do you remember seeing her on the boardwalk? She had to have come from your direction."

"No, I didn't see her."

The lady hooked a left passing the Pirate Cove Hotel and headed for the residential part of the street.

The tinker stopped.

"What's the matter?" I asked.

He reached to scratch his butt. His eyes grew wide.

"Turn around," I said.

The seat of his shorts was gone.

"So, you didn't see her, huh?"

The tinker scratched his butt, again. "She must have been behind me."

"Obviously."

He pointed up the street. "There. That house. She's going into that house."

"No, the garage next to it." I handed him my phone. "Find Officer Eneau in my contacts. Tell him what's going on and to come right away."

I jogged after her and stopped at the end of a short crushed-shell driveway to size-up a detached concrete block garage with folding overhead doors. A single standard door faced the street. A peek around the corner revealed the garage stretched all the way to the property's edge. Two sets of cars could be parked inside with a little room to spare.

Newspaper covered the standard door's windows. The property stood quiet. Just me and the crickets. I pressed my ear against an overhead door and heard nothing then tried the standard door, which was secured with a chintzy knob-lock meant to keep out honest people.

I didn't have a credit card, for reasons I won't get into, so I used my library card to release the lock pin between the door and its jam. The lock released with a click louder than what I would have liked followed by the creak of door hinges in bad need of grease, all of which brought a lump into my throat. Too late to turn back, so I walked into the darkness.

Racks of fluorescent bulbs buzzed to life above my head.

"Don't move." The woman leveled a pump-action pastel-colored squirt gun at me, the kind of gun kids pumped until reaching the pressure of the Alaskan Pipeline. Her particular model appeared to be made of metal and glass.

"Wouldn't think of moving, doll."

"I'm not a doll."

"As long as you're pointing that thing at me, you can be anything you want."

"You know, you're a real chauvinist."

"Hey, when a guy's got it, everything he does seems showy."

"And, you're an idiot." She waved the gun to motion me away from the open door.

Long tables filled with racks of chemicals, glassware, and burners surrounded us. Several plastic mannequins draped in bits of clothing stood at the end of a long open area in the back of the garage.

"You've got quite the shooting gallery over there," I said.

"Wondering how good of a shot I am?" She dropped her gaze and aimed the squirt gun a bit lower than my stomach.

"I don't have to wonder." I turned sideways. "I've seen your work on the boardwalk."

She smiled then doused me with a liquid smelling like my client's shorts. Only much stronger. More concentrated. Smoke rose from my clothes.

The lady laughed. "Just to make sure you stop following me."

My sport coat dropped from my shoulders and became a sizzling pile on the concrete floor. I felt a burning sensation on my thighs, looked down, and saw skin through disappearing pants. While yanking off my belt, I fell backwards into a metal shelf of beakers and flasks. I couldn't tear my clothes off fast enough to stop the acid's itching and burning.

The door to the garage slammed. She had fled into the night.

If I let her get away, I thought, *months might pass before she resurfaces in some other beach town. Even longer before reports of her victims reach me.*

I ran from the garage feeling like a boiling lobster and gritting my teeth. The acid's fumes burned my eyes, but I plunged headlong into the street knowing she would be out there, somewhere. That's when I found myself smack in the middle of what might have been the entire Ocean Mist Police Department.

High beams from cruisers parked in a semi-circle hit me like spotlights on a bigtime burlesque star. I never heard so many people groan, cough, and gag at the same time.

"I know," I called out to everyone, "this acid is pretty strong. Better not get too close." I tried to shield my eyes and scanned the light show. Our villain didn't make it very far. Officer Eneau had her cuffed and ducking into the back of a cruiser. I adjusted my hat and basked in the satisfaction of another closed case.

The tinker's voice came from beyond the bright lights, "Someone get Jimmy a blanket or something."

THE TEACHER KNOCKED ON MY OFFICE DOOR right on time.

"Nothing but good news," I said.

"That's great, because I can sure use some."

I slid a brown bag across my desk.

She opened it and beamed when she saw her phone and wallet. "Thank you, Mr. Grits." She turned the bag over in her hands. "Are these grease stains?"

"It's from my cheeseburger. Only bag I had."

"Oh." She placed it back on my desk.

"And," I leaned back in my creaky office chair, "the Ocean Mist Police Department is dropping the indecent exposure charge."

"Thank God!" She reached into her pocket and pulled out a wad of cash. "What do I owe you?"

I handed her my invoice. "It's all right here, doll."

She looked up at me. "You know, I'm really grateful, but I have to say you come across as a chauvinist."

I folded my hands on my desk and nodded with a smile. "Yeah, I get that a lot."

Reginald the Rocket

"**T**ake it easy," I said, "you'll wear a hole in my carpet." The pimply teenager wearing a *Flipping Phillip's Pizza* t-shirt, white sneakers, and pacing in the middle of my office hadn't come to deliver my lunch. He'd come to hire me.

"The guy just jumped from the doorway and grabbed the pizza out of my hands."

"Didn't take your money?"

"No, just the pizza. Second time in three days."

"Right in the middle of Washington Avenue's sidewalk? Right in front of everyone?"

The delivery boy ran his hand through a dark and curly mop of hair in bad need of a trim, at least from my perspective. "Yeah."

"There's police everywhere in the summer. Why didn't they stop him?"

"They tried, Mr. Grits, but he had a two-seater scooter running behind a dumpster, jumped in, and took off like a shot."

"One of those little tourist jobs? The bike cops can run one of them down."

"Not this one." The teen shook his mop. "It had an afterburner."

I leaned over my desk. "A what?"

"An afterburner."

"That's what I thought you said."

"You know, like on a fighter jet?"

"Yeah, I know." I took out a notepad and pen. "You sure you want to hire me? This sounds like a police thing. Or, maybe, the Phillips family would want to pick up the tab, if they're not happy with the police's work."

"I don't want to ask my boss."

"Afraid of losing your job?"

He nodded. "The first pizza they replaced, but they took the second one out of my pay."

"That ain't right."

The delivery boy reached deep into his pocket and pulled out a handful of crumpled bills and change, which he dumped onto my desk blotter. He reached into his other pocket, did the same, and said, "This is from everyone."

"Everyone?"

"This thief has been stealing from all the pizza guys and girls, the sandwich delivery people, and even Wu."

"Isn't Wu the delivery guy for the Chinese place on Jefferson?"

"No, that's Steve."

"Oh. So, all of you, Wu too, are hiring me?"

"I don't know his last name."

"Whose last name?"

"I don't think it's Wu Tu."

I rubbed my forehead. "Look, just—what did this guy look like?"

"Wu?"

"No, the guy who stole your pizza."

"Really short, like maybe four feet tall. Spikey gray hair and a beard braided with multi-colored beads. It hung all the way to his belt. Oh, and he wore goggles and a scarf."

I put down my pen. "Okay, who put you up to this?"

The delivery boy threw his hands in the air. "I'm not making this up."

"You're telling me, a little person with wild gray hair, goggles, and a scarf has been grabbing food from delivery people and escaping in a two-person scooter with a rocket on the back?"

"Don't forget the beard. He had a beard. A beaded beard."

I picked up my pencil. If I hadn't needed the money, I would have tossed this kid and his crumpled bills onto the street. "Was he wearing a helmet?"

"Yeah, neon green, and I think it had a light on the top like a yellow Christmas tree light."

"Did he say anything to anyone?"

"Not really. He, well, we've been calling it jibber jabber."

"Jibber jabber?"

"Yeah, he's not using words, like even from a different language. He just jibber jabbers. What he says doesn't make any sense, and he doesn't stop jibber jabbering."

"Why can't anyone see this guy coming? It's not like he would blend in with the crowd."

"That's why we need you. He just appears out of nowhere, and he's got all these places where he hides his scooter. No one sees the guy or his scooter until he jumps one of us and takes off."

"Okay, let me see what I can do."

No one knew Ocean Mist's nights better than me. I had staked out every alley, doorway, and shadowy grove. Had tailed pick pockets, cheating husbands and wives—every type of crook during every season. Patience and awareness. The keys to successful investigations. Easy access to milkshakes didn't hurt, either. Good places to take a load off the feet helped, too.

Despite my hawk-like senses, three nights walking Washington Avenue watching food delivery people buzz around like bees got me nowhere. I dreaded having to invest a fourth night into this case. Sweat from the summer heat and oil and vinegar drippings from boardwalk fries always did a number on my work clothes. Another night and I'd have to visit the dry cleaners.

Jefferson Avenue had a few restaurants and fast-food joints, so I left the main drag swinging east onto Second Street. The tinker's clanking and creaking cart greeted me at the ramp to the boardwalk.

"You're out pretty late," I said to him.

"Business has been good, and I didn't want to call it a night, yet. Sold a frying pan and a broken garlic press in just the last hour."

"Broken garlic press, huh?"

"Were you eating funnel cake?" The tinker pointed at my cheek. "You've got some powdered sugar right there."

"Oh, thanks."

"You know, Jimmy," he put his hands on his waist, and I think he puffed his chest, "you should really join the YMCA with me."

"I burn my calories on the chase."

"Then you have to find faster bad guys."

"You heard anything about someone getting the jump on food delivery kids? Snatching their food?"

"You mean other than you?"

"Yeah, okay, just keep your ear to the ground for me."

Then I noticed the trashcan behind him move; at least, I thought it moved. One of the blue metal barrels with the black vent-like tops lining the town's heavy foot-traffic streets. I blinked a few times and rubbed my eyes.

A couple of fellas walked by the can. One tossed a drink cup into the barrel's vent as they passed. The cup flew out the other side and into the street.

"There's something strange about that trashcan," I said to the tinker.

A boy wearing white shorts, a polo-shirt, and baseball cap stepped from a sandwich shop near the can. Two white canvas bags swung from his hands. He walked with the hurried purpose of a delivery boy wanting to get food to his customers quickly so he could get back and do it all over again for another tip.

A small hand from inside the can raised the lid. The blue barrel collapsed into a set of rings and painted fabric to reveal a strange little man. Spikey gray hair stuck out from his head like porcupine quills. Beads in his braided beard sparkled under the streetlamp. Swim goggles covered his eyes, and a checkered scarf hung from his neck.

Before I could tell my feet to move, the little man slung the collapsed fake trash can over his shoulder, tripped the delivery boy, and snatched one of the canvas bags from the sidewalk. This guy could move. He scrambled down the sidewalk like a monkey after a banana. I ran to the sidewalk trying to close the distance and rounded the corner just in time to see the little crook toss everything in his arms into a two-seater scooter, pull on a neon green helmet, and peel out onto Jefferson. He made a sharp u-turn then passed me belting a high-pitched "wee-hee." His scarf flapped behind him in the wind. A single yellow ornamental light bulb shown from the top of his helmet as he swung south onto First Street and disappeared into the night.

"Merry Christmas," I said.

"THAT WAS AN IMPRESSIVE MACHINE BUT NO match for a Mini-bullet 3000," the tinker said between draws on his Birch Beer.

It was two-for-one night at Down and Out Burger, a joint opened by an ex-major league pitcher known for his sinking slider.

"Mini-bullet 3000?" I placed my hat on our booth's table. "So, does one of those have a rocket, too?"

"No, and the rocket is just flash."

"Just flash, huh?" I tried flagging down our waitress.

"That scooter was souped up, but I could tell it wasn't a 3000 by the engine whine."

That got my attention. "You know about these things?"

"Yep, got one of my own."

"Really?"

He nodded and took a long hit from his soda.

I sat back and draped my arms across the top of the red vinyl bench. "Listen, I didn't get any action last night."

"What about that librarian?"

"That's not what I meant. The streets were quiet."

"Maybe we scared him off?"

"No, I'm pretty sure this guy will strike again tonight." The sandwich thief had headed south through the residential part of Ocean Mist, not exactly the kind of streets where I would want to tear after him in my Studebaker. "What are you doing, later?"

I MET THE TINKER ON HAMILTON STREET, where he had claimed a parking space for his scooter. He took a handkerchief from the back pocket of his sagging cargo shorts, polished a spot on the scooter's white hood above a stylized red *M*, put his handkerchief back into his pocket, and smiled like a proud father.

"What's the *M* for?" I asked.

"Are you serious?"

I stared at him.

"You remember that old cartoon Speed Racer?"

"No, should I?"

"The number five on the doors doesn't ring a bell?"

I shook my head.

"It's the Mach 5."

"As long as we catch the little creep, I don't care if it's the *Tinker Cart 2*. You have your phone?"

He held it up and waved it for dramatic emphasis.

"As soon as I see his trash can, I'll call you for a pick up. You gotta get that thing moving, because he's real slick. We won't have much time."

"I'm ready. You just tell me where to be."

SOME PRIVATE EYES RELIED ON FANCY EQUIPMENT like those thermal imaging and night-vision things I had read about in *Private Eye of Fortune* magazine, but I knew the simpler the tool, the more reliable the results. A ball-point pen was all I needed to test each of the blue trashcans I passed. Just a little tap, a resounding twang, and I moved to the next barrel while scanning for delivery persons.

The side streets seemed clear, but I couldn't imagine this thief would be on Washington Avenue with all of the people and bright lights. I swung down the avenue anyway, because I needed a burger.

I could tell right away the trash can in front of Down and Out wasn't quite right, mostly because I knew what to look for. This thief was bolder than hot peppers on cheese fries.

I pulled out my phone and dialed the tinker. "Swing around Washington Avenue and pick me up in front of Down and Out."

"I'll take a single and fries. No roll. I'm gluten free, you know."

"No, he's here. I'm about half a block from him."

"Oh."

The barrel collapsed just like the night before, and the little man grabbed a pizza box from a passing woman. She didn't give it up easily.

He yanked a couple of times while grunting something sounding like, "yubba-dubba, yubba-dubba."

She relented, and he ran toward the bandstand, tossed aside a tarp hiding his scooter between two life-guard jeeps, and peeled out onto Washington Avenue.

"That man can move," I said into the phone, "get here, now."

The thief sped by me with a "wee-hee!"

The tinker was no slouch, either. He handled his Mini-bullet 3000 like a pro weaving through cars and pedestrians, appearing and disappearing between SUV's and pick-up trucks, and leaving a trail of white exhaust puffs while his white helmet flashed under the street lights. He skidded to a halt in front of me.

"Get in." The tinker handed me a shiny yellow helmet.

Frowning at the molded plastic bubble, I asked, "Are those lady bugs?"

"It came with the scooter. Just put it on."

The snub-nosed vehicle leaned precariously when I stepped into the passenger side. Wedging myself next to the tinker wasn't easy.

"Move over," he said, "I can't breathe."

"Just drive! He's getting away!"

The tinker floored the accelerator. We sped after the food thief south on First Street, the same direction he had gone the previous night.

I pointed out over the hood. "There he is! Straight ahead. Do you see him?"

The tinker turned onto Paine Street.

"Where are you going?" I yelled while struggling to pull the helmet down over my head.

"He'll have to turn west because of Watchman's Pond. I'm going to cut him off."

The lady bug helmet passed down over my ears with a sucking sound, and I could finally see a full sweep of the road through the visor. A man, woman, and two little girls watched wide-eyed from the sidewalk.

One of the girls pointed in our direction, and I heard her over the engine's whine. "Can we ride in the funny car?"

The tinker said, "Lean toward me on the count of three."

"Why?"

"Three!"

The tinker's Mini-bullet spun around the corner onto divided Franklin Street nearly side-swiping a station wagon parked in the southbound lane. There couldn't have been much rubber on the scooter's small tires, and the long black streaks we left on the macadam made me wonder how long we had before a blow-out.

The thief turned onto Franklin ahead of us, and the tinker's daring driving had closed the distance at least a block.

We might just catch this guy, I thought.

The sandwich thief turned in his seat, gave a hand gesture unrelated to traffic signaling, let out another ear-splitting "wee-hee," and the back of his scooter became a Roman Candle of yellow, orange and purple. A blast of intense heat washed over us.

The tinker slammed on the breaks jamming my gut into the dashboard knocking the wind from me.

The rocket scooter tore off south toward Rehoboth Beach trailing a plume of fire. Another "wee-hee" reached our ears as a distant whisper.

I looked at the tinker, and he looked at me. Wisps of smoke rose from his clothes. Scorch marks streaked his helmet. The smell of smoldering polyester rose from my sport coat.

"That was some driving," I said.

"Thanks."

"No, I meant him."

"Thanks, anyway."

A strip of paper fluttered over the hood and landed in my lap. A glossy photo of a circus tent told me not all had been lost. Squiggly neon green letters read, *Jojo's Amazing Show of the Century. Now Appearing at the Bethany Fair Grounds.* I lifted the flier and looked at the dates. The next night would be the grand finale.

I asked the tinker, "Want to go to the circus?"

MY DAD TOOK ME TO THE CIRCUS when I was a kid. The main tent seemed like miles of canvas hanging over my head, and the tastes of caramel corn, cotton candy, hotdogs, and ice cream made my head spin. I loved it all until the clowns. The clowns scared the hell out of me. Never went back.

Jojo's Amazing Show of the Century's main performance would start at 7:00, and we rolled into the grassy parking lot around 6:00 giving us plenty of time to case the joint, or tent.

We found a roped area where the circus workers' trailers and recreational vehicles sat circled like wagons fearful of an attack. *Performers Only* signs proclaimed the obvious.

"We can't go in there," the tinker said.

"Why not?"

He pointed to one of the signs.

"Why don't you go get us a program?"

The tinker scampered toward the sideshows and main tent with his head bouncing atop his shoulders like an amazed child. I pushed down the rope and crossed into the performers' strange little village. Crossed into danger.

Tough to look like you belong backstage at a circus when wearing a coat, tie, and fedora, so I made my way around the outside of the circle pausing in the shadowy spaces between trailers to listen and steal glimpses of the activities happening in the center.

Acrobats walked through their routines on a roll-out mat, a magician inventoried his false-bottomed trunk and flimsy swords, and a woman wearing a skimpy red-sequined two-piece brushed a horse. My gaze lingered for a moment—I admired her technique—until the whine of a small engine drew me away from her. I rounded a camper following the smell of octane-rich exhaust but stopped short. My childhood trauma returned in a flash when I came nose to red rubber nose with a white-faced pink-haired clown.

"What are you doing back here?" The clown shoved me. "You have to leave."

"Sorry, I'm looking for a man about this tall." I held out my hand as high as my navel. "Gray hair and beard. Incredible scooter driver." I pulled a small steno pad and pen from my jacket pocket. "I'd like to get his autograph."

"I said, leave. Get your autograph after the show."

"When is it over?" I raised up on my toes and looked over his shoulder.

Some circus roadies stood around industrial-sized fans filling a large blue crash mat like the ones stuntmen used when filming action movies.

"If you don't leave this area now," the clown shoved me again, "I'll toss you out of the fairgrounds, myself."

"Alright," I put up my hands, "alright." I figured taking down someone dressed like a classless drag queen would be bad for business, so I backed away and stepped over the rope.

The tinker waited for me at the big top's entrance sporting a shiny red hat and a glowing neon purple necklace. He cradled in his arms a stuffed green dragon, bag of popcorn, and a sparkling blue wand.

"Having fun?" I asked.

He nodded. "They've got a strong man over there that can lift a wagon full of goats over his head."

"Goats, huh? Do you have the program?"

"Oh, the program. Sorry, I forgot."

A steady flow of people entered the tent, and I motioned to a lady selling programs as we made our way to our seats, which turned out to be spots on an aluminum bench bolted to risers. I stabbed my finger into a fold-out photo of the featured act. "This is him."

The tinker leaned over spilling popcorn into my lap. "Yep, Reginald the Rocket. Looks like he ends the show." The tinker brushed at the popcorn on my trousers.

"Hands to yourself, buddy." Rapping my knuckles on his forearm put him in his place. "Says here the show starts with Reginald's act and ends with him in the finale. The whole thing wraps up at 10:00. Reginald would have more than enough time to open with his friends, get to Ocean Mist with that scooter of his, stash it, mug a delivery person or two, and make it back for the send-off."

The lights dimmed. A single spotlight hit the center ring illuminating a man wearing a black waist coat, ribbon tie, red shirt, riding boots, and top hat. The crowd erupted into cheers and applause.

The tinker leaned toward me again. "That's the way to wear a coat and tie."

I closed the program and used it to point across the big top. "Want to bet that's part of Reginald's act?"

The tinker's head bobbled as his gaze followed a looping track. "This is going to be good!"

"You bet it is." I pulled out my phone and called the Ocean Mist Police Department filling them in on what I had found and suggested they get road blocks ready for Reginald and his rocket scooter. "No," I said into my phone. "Not since lunch and only two. Tell you what, have your beat officers ask a few delivery people. When you believe me, get those road blocks in place. I'll call after the opening act to confirm it's him."

A group of clowns, including the pink-haired bruiser, entered the tent and worked the crowd with slapstick. Roadies wheeled the rocket scooter onto the track.

"Look, Jimmy," the tinker tilted his popcorn box toward some clowns performing for the section of seats next to us, "isn't that the trash can the thief used?"

"Good eye." A clown put the can over a smaller clown, tossed in some crumpled paper, tipped it, rolled it, then collapsed it to free the trapped and trash-covered victim.

The clowns disappeared as quickly as they had appeared, and the tent went dark except for a spotlight shining on Reginald. He stood in his driver's seat and waved. The yellow bulb on his helmet blinked. "Wiggy wiggy doobly dee!"

Roadies pulled on a thick rope opening a panel in the top of the tent just above the track. A stream of sunlight revealed a steep ramp after the loop. Reginald sat, strapped himself into his rocket scooter, hit the afterburner, shot through the loop, let out his trademark "wee-hee," and launched himself out of the tent.

The crowd went bonkers.

I dialed the Ocean Mist Police Department. "It's him," I said to dispatch, "and he's coming."

The tinker stood and clapped wildly. "Wasn't that incredible?"

"Yeah, sure." I tugged on his arm. "We have to go."

THIS TIME, I CROSSED THE DIVIDING ROPE in plain view and led the tinker right into the center of the trailer and RV circle. I hooked my thumbs into my waist band and stuck out my chest defying anyone to try and remove me. "We're here to see the clowns!"

"You and a thousand other people, buddy!" A woman yelled.

The tinker adjusted the big stuffed dragon under his arm.

I glanced at him and asked under my breath. "Can you please get rid of that thing?"

"Sydney? You have any idea how hard it was to win him?"

"Alright, just stand there and don't say anything."

Enter the clowns. A small army painted in pastel war paint, Mylar sashes, rainbow wigs, and packing more than a few rubber chickens marched behind the tall pink-haired one.

Pink Hair said, "I told you to leave."

"Where's Reginald?"

"He's busy. Why do you want him?"

"I told you. I want his autograph."

"We deal with stalkers like you all the time, and it ain't pretty." The clowns all squeaked their rubber noses and stepped slowly toward us, a circus version of West Side Story. "This is your last warning. Leave."

I tossed one of my cards in his direction. "Jimmy Grits, Private Investigator. I can save Reginald a world of hurt if he just comes with us."

The clowns stopped.

Pink Hair asked, "Is he in some kind of trouble?"

"If you consider robbing delivery guys in Ocean Mist trouble."

"You can't be serious." The clown looked surprised. I thought he looked surprised, anyway. Hard to tell with all of the makeup.

"That's his thing, right? Steal from innocent hard-working Joes during the performance then use it as his alibi?"

A clown called from somewhere in the back, "Hey, Chuckles, is that where Reggie goes between acts?"

The pink-haired leader, presumably Chuckles, said, "Shut up," over his shoulder.

"How many of you are in on this?" I asked. "How many of you want to spend the night in a cell until we straighten this out?"

A lady clown, the queen of the village idiots, pushed her way to the front of the pack. "Mr. Grits, we're circus clowns. We live by a code, and I take exception to anyone accusing us of stealing." She lifted the bike horn hanging around her neck and honked it in my face.

"Look, lady, the guy you're stalling for has been stealing food from delivery people for at least two weeks. We have more than enough witnesses to prove it."

"He's not really a clown," she said. "He's a headliner. Frankly, he dresses like us, but he could never be one of us. Too much of an adrenaline junkie, if you know what I mean."

I tipped back my hat. "Not one of you, huh?"

Another clown from the back called out, "Reggie has been putting on some weight."

My phone vibrated, and I pulled it from my sport coat pocket without taking my eyes off of the clown posse. Three words had been texted to me by a friend in the Ocean Mist P.D. *We got him.*

"You're going to need a new headliner," I said and turned to the tinker. "Time to go."

On the way back to the car, the tinker asked me, "What about them?"

"What about them?"

"We saw the trash can in their act. They have to be accomplices."

"Accomplices? Listen to you. The kid tags along on a few cases with Jimmy Grits, and he thinks he's a detective." I unlocked the Studebaker's passenger door for him and Sydney the Dragon. "I'll give you this much, at least some of them are in on it, but we have our man, and I just don't have time for any more clowning around."

The Case of the
Missing Bandstand

"**Y**ou mean, the whole bandstand? That thing must be at least ten tons." I hung my sport coat and hat on the rack by my office door, crossed the room, and my desk chair squealed a welcome under me.

The mayor leaned against the door jam. Crossed his arms. "Everything above the masonry."

"What does the real mayor think?"

The mayor shrugged. "Does it matter?"

The mayor everyone knew, the one with the name plate in town hall, attended meetings and conducted ribbon-cuttings while the tall Abraham-Lincoln-looking guy darkening my door, the mayor with money and a book of favors, made the decisions. No elections. No term limits. The democratic process at its finest.

"The whole bandstand," he said. "There last night and gone this morning."

"Sounds like you need a contractor, not a private eye. Why are you telling me this?"

"Contractors mean time and money, neither of which Ocean Mist has right now."

"You mean, no money for the contractors in your pocket?" I opened my desk drawer. Pulled out a bottle of Jack and two coffee mugs. Just because I didn't like the guy didn't mean I couldn't drink with him. A finger's worth gurgled into each mug, and I slid the one with the rabbit and painted egg toward the mayor. "Happy Easter." I took my hit. "So, what can I do for the town of Ocean Mist?"

The mayor hung his baseball cap, which should have been a stove pipe hat, on the coat rack and took a seat across from me. "Find out who took the bandstand and get it back."

I poured another finger of Jack for myself and expected I'd do it again in a few seconds.

The mayor continued, "Someone who can tear the bandstand down and haul it away in the middle of the night with no one hearing or seeing anything can put it back, with a little persuasion."

"Persuasion, huh? Thanks for reminding me of who I'm talking to."

"Says the private eye on the mountain." The mayor picked up the *Jojo's Amazing Show of the Century* flier on the corner of my desk. "Been to the circus, Grits? They got this guy on a rocket-powered scooter that goes off a ramp—."

"Yeah, I know."

"Anyway, you've been working some miracles for us lately." The mayor lowered his head and rubbed his protruding brow. "I can't believe I'm saying this, but I'm not sure who else to turn to."

"Ocean Mist P.D.?"

"They're investigating, but my guys tell me they called in the State Police."

"And?"

"They're about to call the FBI. I mean, who steals a public building? City council is sitting around waiting for some kind of demand, and all the suits with badges are still trying to figure out if this is theft, vandalism, or some kind of ransom thing. We need someone doing some actual investigating."

"Someone not concerned with jurisdiction."

"Exactly. We don't have much time. There's a calendar full of booked events and rentals. Can you imagine if we had to cancel the performances, ask for reimbursements from entertainers, and return rental fees?"

"And, you lose your cuts. Maybe lose some hand-shake contracts and protection money?"

The mayor stood, looked down his nose at me, and scowled.

I smirked. "I'll come and take a look. About an hour from now work?"

Ocean Mist's less-than-honest Abe plucked his baseball cap from the coat rack and muttered, "I'll meet you there."

The office door shut behind him. I tipped the mayor's Easter mug over mine then added another finger from the bottle. With luck, I'd down a full hand before hitting the streets.

WORD OF A MISSING BANDSTAND PULLED A larger crowd than some of the concerts held there. Gawkers packed most of Washington Avenue's first block and fifty yards of the boardwalk in both directions from the big empty spot once home to an open stage covered by a shingled roof.

I made my way toward bright yellow police tape. The mayor stood within the cordoned area. Funny how the cops didn't mind having a crime boss hovering over their investigation.

I waved my fedora to a couple of Ocean Mist's finest. They discussed something intently. I waved my hat again. They stopped talking, looked in my direction, and restarted their conversation.

The mayor called to the two chatter boxes. "Someone let Grits into the scene."

The officers looked at me, each other, and threw two rounds of rock paper scissors. Even if I was a lip reader, I still couldn't have known the word the losing cop said. He lifted the police tape and walked me to the mayor.

No wonder the mayor needed me.

The bandstand's masonry platform and ring of brick pedestals remained, but all of the woodwork had disappeared: heavy wooden columns, thick laminated trusses, plywood sheathing, asphalt shingling, and windowed cupola all missing.

I said to the mayor, "You weren't kidding."

"The whole thing vanished into thin air."

I scanned the businesses lining the sidewalks. Mostly t-shirt shops, ice-cream joints, a few restaurants, and a bar with a large open counter facing the street. "Who've you talked to?"

"A couple shop owners and the cook at Tahmina's"

Truly a shame, I thought, *how the town made Tahmina's Indian Tandoori take down its sign. Those three neon capital letters really caught the eye.*

The mayor continued, "The cook told me the bandstand was here and everything seemed normal until at least 1:00 in the morning when he locked up and went home."

A familiar voice yelled, "So, what are you going to do about it?"

I turned to see the tinker having it out with a sour-looking Delaware Trooper on the edge of the crime scene.

"It's okay, blue. He's with me," I called.

The trooper lifted the tape.

The tinker stepped through, adjusted his cargo shorts, looked the trooper up and down, huffed, and walked over to me and the mayor.

"Making new friends?" I asked.

The tinker seemed really beside himself. "You got everyone here except Scooby Doo and the Mystery Machine. Why haven't you found the bandstand?"

"Easy," I said and held up a hand, "we're working on it."

The mayor did his best to read my face. "Does that mean you're in, Grits?"

"Of course, we're in," the tinker said.

I tipped back my fedora and folded my arms. "When did I add you to the payroll?"

"You don't have a payroll," he pointed at my gut, "but you could with the money you dump into Down and Out Burger. Anyway, you owe me."

The mayor walked away.

I lowered my voice, "Why are you so worked up about this?"

"Didn't you get my invitation?"

"What invitation?"

"Saturday is the Regional Amateur Electric Kazoo Band Competition. How are we going to hold it if the bandstand is gone?"

"Electric kazoo band?"

"I bet the person who did this didn't want our band to win again."

"You think someone did this to stop some kazoo contest?"

"The Regional Amateur Electric Kazoo Band Competition."

"Yeah, I know. How many people actually play electric—?"

"That's why it's regional."

"Oh."

"We're called the Ocean Mist Hummers."

"Okay," I scratched my head, "I was about to talk to the manager of that bar, over there." I pointed to the brightly painted facade with the fake thatched roof. The one with the counter facing the street. "They're probably open the latest on the block."

The tinker shook his head. "I already talked to her. She didn't see anything when they closed at 2:00."

I hid my disappointment. Really wanted to saddle up to the bar. "If the beach cleaners dragged the beach this morning, they were working by 5:30, that leaves about three and a half hours to pull off the heist."

"What about all of those windows?" The tinker pointed to the second and third stories above some businesses where landlords made extra cash by renting efficiencies. "Someone had to have seen or heard something."

I imagined a massive crane, flatbed, and maybe a couple of those mega pickup trucks owned by construction workers rolling down Washington Avenue. "I don't get it, either. Heavy equipment and a lot of guys with power tools not making any noise? No lights?"

I circled the crime scene looking for scuff marks, gouges in the street, even chips out of the curbs where there could have been large vehicles moving heavy loads. Nothing.

A high-noon sun broiled Ocean Mist. I took off my black sport coat, draped it over my arm, loosened my tie, walked across the boardwalk, and stood on one of the wooden benches overlooking the dune and ocean. Just looked out over the water for a long time.

I glanced down at the knee-high wood-slat fence holding back the dune from the boardwalk. Metal wire kept the slats more or less in place—leaning a bit to-and-fro from a long season of wind, rain, and playing children—but some seemed really crooked. I stepped off the bench and knelt.

"What are you doing, Jimmy?"

"The bad guys' equipment didn't come in from the street." Several fence sections had been broken, the slats cracked right in two, then repaired hastily with small bits of wire. "Go get me some napkins."

"What?"

"Napkins. Get me some napkins."

The tinker jogged across the boardwalk to Shuga's Sugar Shop while I collected stones from the sand. I placed a napkin weighted with a stone on the boardwalk where each broken fence section began and ended. When I stepped back from my work, napkin flags marked what appeared to be sets of tracks. Two large pieces of equipment had crossed the dunes, probably on steel plates, broken the fence, and crossed the boardwalk also on steel plates to reach the bandstand.

"If you wanted to get rid of any evidence, you'd have to clean up after yourself," I said. "Were the beach cleaners out this morning?"

The tinker shrugged.

Tractors dragging heavy metal rakes picked-up trash and smoothed the sand every few days and could have swept away any tracks between the water and the dune well before dawn, but something still didn't set right with me. The tall dune grass swaying in the breeze would have been crushed.

"What are you thinking, Jimmy?"

"I got some of the *how* worked out, but I'm still trying to wrap my brain around the *why* and the *who*."

"Those are the most obvious. It's one of our competitors."

"Really? Why on earth would anyone do this for a kazoo competition?"

"It's the Regional Amateur—."

"Yeah, I know. Back to my question, why?"

"To scare us, knock us off our game. To improve their chances of winning The Golden Kazoo."

"A kazoo? Made of gold?"

The tinker nodded.

"Okay, that's our only lead on the *why* and *who,* right now, so let's see where it takes us. Can you bring a list of bands to my office in an hour?"

"Sure. Should we tell the police what you found?"

I shook my head. "Just let the mayor know we might be on to something."

I TOOK A FUNNEL CAKE BACK TO the office. No matter how worked up the tinker had become, I refused to skip lunch. He charged through my office door exactly one hour after we had parted company. Sweat soaked his flowered shirt and cargo shorts.

"You've been busy," I said.

"And you have powdered sugar on your lips."

I wiped it away. "You bring the list of bands?"

The tinker dropped a program on my desk. "I highlighted our rivals."

"Okay, how about the ones that might have the means to pull off something like this?"

"You mean like a lot of money?"

"Well, yeah, but they don't have to be rich. Sometimes it's a matter of access to the right resources." I picked up the program, took a look at the bands, and flipped to the advertisements and sponsors listed on the back pages.

"I have some ideas." He reached into a cargo pocket and pulled out a folded spreadsheet. "This is a contact list for the band leaders. We'll call the ones we want to question, find out where they're staying, and I'll pay them each a visit while you..." The tinker rattled on with his junior detective nonsense.

I circled with a marker several advertisements and sponsors in the back of the program.

He propped his hands on his hips. "Are you listening to me?"

"Not really." I pushed the program across the desk. "Any of these businesses connected to the rival kazoo bands you highlighted?"

"Actually, the secretary of the Fenwick Island Doozies owns a big hardware store known for custom power tools."

"Fenwick Island Doozies?"

"They were furious with us last year."

"I don't need to know why."

"And," the tinker smacked the program with the back of his hand, "their treasurer has a water salvage operation."

I pointed to one of the circled sponsors. "Surf and Turf Salvage?"

"Yep."

"Now, we're onto something, but what about motive? I'm still not sold on the gold kazoo thing." I waved the marker for effect. "How would canceling the competition help the Dozers?"

"The Doozies."

"Right. Doozies."

"They'd get the home field advantage."

"What do you mean?"

"The competition would be rescheduled for the only other place we can hold it."

"Where would that be?"

"The pavilion behind the Fenwick Island Animal Shelter."

"Wouldn't that be animal cruelty?"

The tinker scratched his head, pursed his lips, and dove deep into thought. About what, I couldn't guess.

I took another look at the program and reconsidered the heist's time-line with an approach by water.

"I'm telling you, Jimmy, the Doozies are behind this! They'll do anything to get to nationals."

"There's a national competition?"

"Of course." The tinker walked circles in front of my desk. He hadn't deescalated since charging through my door. Still cocked and ready to fire. "So, we call the police now, right? Or, do we go to Surf and Turf Salvage and bust some heads?"

"Easy there, Knuckles. If this salvage guy has the bandstand, he probably didn't use any of his regular employees to take it. He'd need guys willing to keep their mouths shut."

"Like the band members? They'd jump at a chance for revenge. You should have heard their trash talk last year after the podium ceremony."

"I can only imagine."

"I'm sure their first chair kazooist was the one that vandalized my cart after the competition, too."

"How could you tell?"

"Oh, I knew it was him."

"No, I mean, how could you tell someone vandalized your cart?" I turned the marker over in my hand. "If the bandstand is out in the ocean, they're not going to bring it ashore. At least, not until it's torn apart so the pieces can't be identified."

The tinker's eyes widened. "So, you think it's still out there, somewhere?" He sounded hopeful.

"I'm sure it's not far. There might even be a plan to put the bandstand back together after the competition."

"We're going to sea, then." The tinker smacked my desk. "Meet me on the beach off Madison Street at 7:30."

"I didn't know you had a boat."

"Well, now you know."

THE MADISON STREET STRETCH OF SAND TENDED to be pretty quiet and sparsely populated at dusk even in the busy summer months. I walked the beach access ramp twisting through a dune and toward the water. A young couple played frisbee to my left. A mother and father and two kids built a sand castle by the water and near the tinker.

The tinker worked a bicycle pump inflating a black rubber raft, the kind used to carry people out to ships. I watched his ferocious up and down motions for a while then scanned the horizon. Nothing out there.

He stopped pumping and saw me standing on the beach. "I told you to wear your swimsuit."

I looked down at my blue trunks and flip flops. "Yeah, and I'm wearing it."

"Who wears a shirt and tie with blue sea horse swimming trunks?"

I tossed my sport coat and fedora into the raft. "We may be on the beach, but I'm still on the job."

The castle builders' mother ushered her family to their blankets, said something about having to leave, and they gathered their things quickly. Must have been their supper time.

The tinker held up the pump. "Can you take over for a while?"

I shook my head.

He resumed his frenzied motions.

"Where's your boat?" I asked.

"Right here," the tinker said. "She's the Tinker III."

"What happened to Tinker I and Tinker II?"

"Stories for another time. We need to get moving."

"Seriously, this is it?"

The tinker handed me a paddle and pulled the raft into the water. "Come on, Jimmy."

We towed the big black balloon into the breakers. I lost my footing twice before crawling over the raft's side, rolling onto the undulating floor, and clutching the paddle to my chest.

The tinker asked, "You ever watch those nature shows?"

I took a moment to catch my breath. "What, like on television?"

"Yeah, I saw one about walruses, and when they leave the water—."

"What's that got to do with anything?"

He bit his lip then crawled to the front.

"Where's your paddle?" I asked.

"I only got one. Besides, only one of us can paddle." The tinker attached a tube from a small hand-bellows pump to the raft's inflation nozzle and began to squeeze and release. "There's a small leak somewhere." Squeeze and release. "Haven't been able to find it, yet."

"This gets better by the moment."

The beach and boardwalk merged slowly into a hazy line behind us, and the sun hung over the town. We pushed eastward away from sunset's reds and oranges and into the dark blues of a coming night.

"Does this thing have any lights?"

"Oh, yeah." The tinker stopped squeezing the pump. "Just below deck, there's a switch next to the hatch to the galley. While you're down there, ask Cookie if our steaks are ready. I'm starved." He continued pumping.

The sun set.

We floated in the pitch black of a moonless ocean night.

I figured enough time had passed I could venture another question. "So, how are we going to see a salvage ship? Anything at all, for that matter, out here in the dark?"

"We don't need to see the ship. Just its lights."

I stopped paddling and took a look around. "I see something over there. Way over there."

"That's a cargo ship leaving the bay. I saw it before the sun went down."

"Want to switch?" I asked. "You paddle, and I'll pump?"

"Sorry, Jimmy. This takes a practiced touch."

An hour later, some bobbing lights turned out to be a fishing boat. Another hour passed, and we came upon a dinner cruise. Silverware clinking against plates and idle chatter drifted across the rolling water. I could hear full conversations before seeing anything. Strange how sounds carried across a dark ocean.

"Over there, Jimmy." The tinker pointed, but I couldn't see what he pointed at.

"Am I paddling in the right direction?"

"More strokes on the left."

"How many more?"

He cradled his chin while staring out into the black. "I'd say a two-to-one left-to-right ratio."

"Yeah, sure." I pulled the paddle through the water. "Now we're doing math problems."

About forty strokes later, I saw it, too. A set of lights way out there. Something big.

"Looks like two ships," the tinker said between labored breaths.

The next fifteen minutes of paddling felt like a week.

Definitely two ships floating side-by-side. One sat high above the water. Floodlights illuminated two massive winches, each the size of a small car, with short booms sticking through the back of the ship's side—called the bulwark, I thought. The other ship sat lower and turned out to be a barge. A few safety lights glowed dimly around its sides. Two pieces of construction equipment with large tires, much larger than I had ever seen around Ocean Mist, sat parked on the deck. I couldn't tell the type of equipment. Too dark and too far away.

"Paddle harder," the tinker said.

"Why? I don't hear any engines. Those ships aren't going anywhere."

"Yeah, but we're sinking."

I told my arms to dig more deeply into the water, and I thought they obeyed, but I couldn't feel them anymore, so I wasn't sure.

The tinker tried to speak through his heavy breathing. "Over there. Dingy."

"What did you call me?"

"No." The tinker grunted out a few more squeezes on the pump. "There-is-a-dingy-tied-to-the-barge. Go-there."

We pulled beside a rubber raft, bigger and more rigid than Tinker III, with a small outboard motor and tied to a ladder leading up the barge's side. The tinker tossed his hand pump overboard and leapt for the moored craft. The moment his weight left Tinker III, it folded in two, the bow and stern sandwiching me in the middle. Water washed over the sides to my right and left. The folded raft rose and sank each time I moved causing the bow to slap my face and stern to thump the back of my head.

"Jimmy, over here."

Caught between two giant clapping hands, I reached for the tinker. He took my arm, and I leaned toward the dingy falling with my chest against its firm inflated cylinder. I kicked against Tinker III, which helped propel me over the side and onto a wood-plank floor. Breathing heavily, I peered into a starless sky and promised myself this would be my last case involving boats.

"Here," the tinker dropped my water-logged sport coat and fedora onto my chest, "in case you get cold."

"Thanks." I sat up, shook my hat, smoothed its brim the best I could, and placed it on my head. The dingy felt sturdy under me. I patted its planked bottom thankful to be off the leaky balloon.

The tinker put his foot on the side and struck a *Washington Crossing the Delaware* pose. "I hereby christen this ship *Tinker IV*."

"Really?"

"The ways of the sea are steeped in tradition, Jimmy." He placed his hand on his heart and dropped his gaze toward the water where the *Tinker III* went slowly the way of her predecessors.

His mourning gave my heart a moment to slow, for the burning in my chest to subside, and a chance for the adrenaline of the chase to rebuild in my system. "Let's get moving," I said and reached for the barge's ladder.

I climbed cold steel rungs with the tinker at my heels and poked my head over the ship's side. Lights and sounds came from a raised wheel-house about forty feet away, but there didn't seem to be anyone on the deck. I couldn't tell for sure. Dim safety lights along the bulwark did little more than show where a metal handrail marked the ship's edges. Plenty of shadows for a man like me to use.

I ducked under the rail and whispered back down the ladder. "There's a crane and a flatbed truck up here. Both big enough to haul away the bandstand. I'm going to take a closer look."

The flatbed seemed the best place to start. I pulled my fedora down over my forehead and turned up my water-logged sport coat's collar.

Pitch-black night, crime all around, and me on the case— this is the world of Jimmy Grits.

Moving slowly from shadow to shadow pausing only to listen for conversations, footfalls, and any signs of bad guys, I made my way toward one of the vehicle's head-high tires. Sand packed its treads.

A marine salvage operation with a flatbed. These guys have to be our thieves.

I crept along the vehicle, slipping from one shadow to the next, until I found a set of crates fashioned as steps leading up to the bed. I looked around. Still no movement. No sounds. I climbed a few steps, reached upwards, and pressed my hand against the bed. Not wanting to become a silhouette against the glow of the safety lights, I slithered onto the bed like a snake.

"Oh, hey Jimmy."

I raised my fedora's brim. The tinker's white sneakers almost brushed my nose. "Get down," I hissed. "Someone is going to see you."

He put his hands on his hips and looked up at the wheelhouse. "I don't think so. The crew is having a pretty serious poker game."

"How do you know that?" I pulled the tinker down by his cargo shorts.

"Well, I walked over there under the steps, and I could hear them carry-ing on about someone getting a full house, and how that person was a—."

"Okay, I get it. Did you see anything belonging to the bandstand?"

"No."

Slender spikey shadows near the flatbed's cab caught my eye. I crawled closer with the tinker behind me. We only needed to cover a few yards to find wax-cardboard boxes filled with dune-grass plugs ready for planting.

I whispered, "This explains how they hid their tracks through the dunes. They probably hauled in planks or steel plates on this flatbed, used the crane truck to lay out a path, rolled over the planks, then replanted the crushed dune grass on their way back to the water."

"Wouldn't these big machines make dents in the dunes? Even with the planks?"

"Well, yes. They could have fluffed up the dunes before they left."

"You can fluff a dune?"

"Work with me," I said. "We have to go where the evidence takes us."

"Did they use a piece of equipment to do that?" He looked around. "What would a dune fluffer look like?"

"I tell you what, why don't you climb up the crane arm and try to get a look onto the other ship? I don't think anyone will be able to see you from the wheelhouse."

"Right." The tinker stood, straightened his shirt, and made his way to the crane as if strolling down the boardwalk to get french fries.

We're going to die here, I thought.

I climbed off the flatbed, stuck to the shadows, and circled to the front of the cab. A pile of sand filled the space between the flatbed and crane. The pile appeared to have been much larger at some point, since a huge bite had been taken out of the side nearest where I stood.

That's how they did it, I realized. *After pulling the big equipment out, they dumped sand onto the dune tracks then planted the grass plugs.*

"Hey, get down from there!" The shouting came from the other side of the ship near the crane. "What are you doing?"

I ran toward the voice expecting to see the tinker clinging to the boom with the crew below him wielding wrenches and fire axes but found only one monstrous guy with his arms folded, a torso like a bull, and a granite cube for a head. Something right from a Frankenstein movie.

I took off my fedora, creased its crown, and knew I'd have to keep the monster's attention long enough for the tinker to shimmy back to the deck. "Haven't you ever seen a tinker on a crane?"

The tinker, at least fifteen feet above us, swung from the crane arm, hit the flatbed bending his knees, and rebounded into a somersault off the truck's side landing on the deck with a shoulder roll.

The big guy and I stared.

The tinker hiked up his shorts. "Captain of my junior high gymnastics team."

Frankenstein turned toward me.

"Now, wait a second, buddy." I raised my hands and retreated toward the bulwark, the low side and thin metal bar being the only barriers between the deck's edge and the dark churning ocean. "We'll be happy to leave, if you just give us a minute."

His expression didn't communicate a willingness to discuss that option. He clenched his fists for a bit of the old rough and tumble.

I turned my dominant side toward him, opened my stance, and rolled my shoulders. "If you insist." In my line of work, sometimes you had to call upon all of your training, all of your experience, all of what you were as a private eye, and focus these into one pivotal moment.

An orange rescue float bounced from Frankenstein's head making the sound of a thumped milk jug. He spun, unfazed, and said to the tinker, "You two must be with those kazoo freaks."

The tinker retrieved the float by pulling its line. "You bet I am. First baritone kazoo of the Ocean Mist Hummers."

"Just for the record," I said, "I'm not one of the Hummers."

The tinker swung the orange float above him. A cowboy and his lasso. "I saw all of the wood and shingles in that ship. You're wrong if you think you can keep us from The Golden Kazoo just by taking our bandstand."

Frankenstein turned completely to the tinker giving me his back.

My heart pumped so hard I felt it beat against the base of my throat. I opened my arms, set my feet square against the deck, and drove forward launching into a full-body tackle. Frankenstein went down under me like a pot roast falling from a kitchen counter, and he didn't move.

"You sacked him." The tinker lifted Frankenstein's head by his hair. "Do you think his face was always this flat?"

"I don't know. I just met him."

"He landed pretty hard." The tinker released Frankenstein's hair, and his forehead clunked against the metal plating. "He'll be out for a while."

"You sure?"

"Pretty much. You can let go of him now, unless you want to go steady."

I wrenched my left arm out from under the guy, rolled onto my side, freed my other arm, and stared up into the starless sky for the second time that night. "Thank God for football camp."

"You played football?"

"I said, camp."

"Well, you certainly weren't a tight end."

Boots thunking on metal steps made us both look toward the wheel house.

Someone yelled, "What are you doing on our ship?" which was followed by, "What did they do to Clover?"

The tinker rubbed his chin. "You just tackled a guy named Clover."

"We need to go." I picked up my hat, got my feet under me, and made a full-out charge for the ladder we used to board the barge. "We're taking the dingy."

"Do you think its Clover's dingy?"

Grace had nothing to do with my descent, and it certainly had nothing to do with my attempts to get the outboard motor started.

"Here, let me." The tinker pushed me out of the way, had the motor going in seconds, and we pulled away from the barge just as a bunch of angry seamen leaned over its handrail and lobbed obscenities, several of which I noted for future use.

I reached inside my sport coat's lapel pocket on the off-chance my cell phone had survived. Saltwater dripped from the edges of a dark screen. "You have your cell?"

The tinker pulled his phone from his short's cargo pouch, unlocked it, and handed it to me. I dialed the Ocean Mist Police Station, and they assured me the Coast Guard would be on the way.

We beached the dingy near the end of Madison Street.

Ocean Mist's finest met us there a few minutes later.

I just wanted to get home, take a hot shower, and go to bed, but I knew better. Several hours of questioning and novel-length handwritten statements would come first.

I LEFT MY APARTMENT THE FOLLOWING AFTERNOON and pointed my loafers toward the boardwalk-end of Washington Avenue to find a good deal on a chilidog. Pick-up trucks and sport utility vehicles encircled the skeleton of a new bandstand.

About twenty guys wearing red t-shirts with the words *Ocean Mist Hummers* emblazoned in white across their chests played kazoos while carrying posts, planks, and all sorts of tools. I couldn't quite place the tune, at first, but recognized eventually an energetic buzzing version of "The Colonel Bogey March," which made me wonder what *The Bridge Over the River Kwai* would have been like with the Ocean Mist Hummers building the bridge.

The tinker saw me, put his kazoo in his pocket, dropped his board, and crossed the street. "What do you think, Jimmy?"

"Well, this is really something."

"You should hear us when the kazoos are wired to the amps."

"No, I mean the bandstand," I said. "You've really made progress. Have you even slept?"

"How could I sleep when The Golden Kazoo is in jeopardy?"

I nodded and scanned the construction site to find the most direct route to the hotdog cart.

The tinker placed his hand on my shoulder. "Jimmy, I really appreciate all you've done. You saved the competition and the bandstand."

"Any chance the town will pay me a finder's fee? I'm still waiting for the mayor to cough up what he owes me."

The tinker reached into his pocket. "Even better. Two tickets to the electric kazoo competition. These are hot. Completely sold out, but I pulled some strings."

"It's a public bandstand. How can you be sold— never mind."

National Institute of Dune Protection
8675 Three-O-Nine Drive
Harbordale, NC 15742

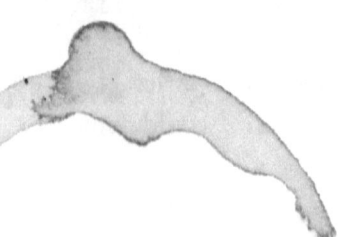

Dear Mr. Grits:

Your September press conference regarding the disappearance of the Ocean Mist Bandstand impacted significantly our institute's research into Mid Atlantic dune health and stabilization. Your responses to reporters' questions following the police chief's official statement were of particular help to us, and you might not realize the effect your investigatory process has had on our work.

Our primary focus has been on slowing dune erosion through the planting and cultivation of native vegetation. Your comments regarding the possible use of a "dune fluffer" to hide the tracks of large equipment crossing Ocean Mist's dunes inspired us to create a prototype "dune fluffer" to aerate packed sand, which, in theory, would allow oxygen to reach the roots of dune grasses.

Our prototype involves the use of a rake-like frame with perforated plastic tubing affixed to the frame's tongs. The rake is bolted to the front of an all-terrain vehicle. The ATV introduces the dune fluffer into the side of a dune. Pressurized air is passed through the rake's shaft then conveyed through the tubing; unfortunately, our field experiments have not been successful given our inability to find a compressor capable of producing the necessary pounds per square inch necessary to fluff a dune.

We realize you are a very busy private investigator; yet, if you find yourself available on any given weekend during the month of November, our team would appreciate your joining us on a field test of the dune fluffer. Your role in this experiment will be to blow into the end of our rake to provide the necessary force to test our equipment. We have every confidence in your ability to help us produce a successful outcome.

Sincerely,
Dr. Sandy Packer
National Institute of Dune Protection

The Mean Streets of Ocean Mist

"Couldn't tell you." I furled my brow to appear thoughtful and resisted the urge to tell the cologne-doused yuppie to go ask for himself. "Anyone here know if they'll take a coupon on half-price Tuesdays?"

The tourists paying attention to me shook their heads.

"Shouldn't you know?" The yuppie lifted his mirrored sunglasses and wedged them into his gelled hair. "You're the guide."

The aluminum pole and cardboard circle painted like a smiling pizza in my hand had grown heavy block after block, yet I figured I could still use it to club the man without too much of a problem. Couldn't risk losing the job, though, so I raised the sign above my head just like in the instructional video and led the restaurant tour group down Adams Avenue.

Ocean Mist buzzed with mid-summer activities. All crime-free thanks to my unwavering commitment to justice— put away a few miscreants, and word gets out. The rats scurry back into the sewers. I took the food tour gig to tide me over until the dry-spell ended, which I knew would happen soon.

Hungry vacationers wearing *Hello, My Name Is...* tags trudged behind me toward the intersection, where one of the strangest sites I've seen in Ocean Mist made me stop and stare.

Is that a mime?

Black and white striped shirt, black pants, matching smooth-bottom dancing shoes, black beret, white face make-up, and arms making locomotive motions all confirmed what my private eye instincts were telling me. He was, in fact, a mime.

A little boy wearing a Batman t-shirt pointed and laughed. A younger yet wiser kid hid behind his mom, and a gray-haired fellow lit a pipe and shook his head. The rest watched bewildered as the mime chugged his way across Adams Avenue toward us.

An older woman with an oversized pocketbook blinked at me through glasses with lenses from a NASA telescope. "Sir, is this part of the tour?"

I shook my head. "Only restaurants, ma'am."

The mime stopped, tipped his beret, and did a hoedown-like jig.

I wasn't quite sure what to do. Instinct told me to punch the guy, but I thought twice. Someone might take offense and withhold a tip.

After the jig, the mime removed his hat, waved it dramatically, and bowed. My tour group offered half-hearted applause, the kind when you can sense confusion between the claps. The reaction must have encouraged him, because he extended his arm and lunged forward as if an invisible dog got the better of him. The dog dragged him through his audience, its invisible leash tangling people, and the immersive act made them spin, bounce off each other, bump into the mime, and a few chuckled. A few. Only the children offered genuine laughter.

The lady with the thick glasses rolled her ankle. She fell on her backside. The group gasped. I reached to help her back to her feet, but she didn't take my hand.

She huffed and looked up at me. "When is this tour over?"

I took a few steps toward the mime. "Okay buddy, that's enough. You can take your show to the boardwalk. Chase some invisible gulls, or something."

The mime dropped his leash, put his hands on his hips, and tossed his head in indignation before stomping down Adams Avenue.

"Sorry about that, folks." I lifted the smiling pizza sign, turned, and started the group toward the next stop of our tour. "Things like that don't usually happen around here. Now, this is one of my favorites for a quick bite, Wing Dings and Things. Their chocolate dipped corndogs simply melt in your—."

"My wallet is gone." A guy wearing a salmon golf shirt with a tiny embroidered pony on his left breast felt his backside with both hands and spun in a circle as if he could see behind himself simply by turning. "It's gone."

"My cell phone!" An adolescent girl's face turned ghost white. "My phone! My phone is gone!" Her breathing quickened into a pained wheezing like an asthma attack.

Her mother pulled her close and cradled her head. "For the love of God, we have to find her phone! What kind of psychopath would take a teen's phone?"

I leaned my aluminum sign pole against a bench and put up both of my hands. "Let's all slow down. Please, everyone, check your pockets."

"I bet it was that mime," a lady said.

"Everyone, just stay calm. Let's not lose our heads." Sometimes, I forgot others didn't have my experience-honed deductive skills, so I softened my tone. "Think about it. What would a mime do with a phone?"

The group stopped rummaging in their purses and pockets and looked at me blankly until the clanking and creaking of the tinker's cart rounding a corner redirected their attentions.

"Hey, Jimmy."

Saved by the tinker, I thought.

He stopped pushing his cart and wiped his forehead with his sleeve. "What are you doing with that sign?"

"So, that about does it," I said to the group. "Thank you for your time, and please visit our website to rate your experience. If you do, you'll get a ten percent discount off your next tour with us."

Most of the tourists wandered off toward the boardwalk.

The man in the salmon shirt looked along the sidewalk for his wallet.

The mother sat her daughter on a bench and pressed a paper shopping bag against the teen's face. "Breathe into this, sweetheart."

The tinker asked me, "What's wrong with her? Should I call an ambulance?"

"Seems to have lost her phone. Don't bother."

"What's with the pizza sign? You leading some kind of tour?"

I nodded. "Something to do until something else comes along."

A voice came from down the block. "Someone stole my watch!"

"I think I've got to go," I said to the tinker. "If that mime really is a pick-pocket, I need to catch him before the police. If word gets out that he robbed members of my tour group right under my nose—."

"Yeah, you can't afford any more bad press."

"What are you talking about?"

"You're going to need some help. I was going to put my cart in the barn, anyway."

"You have a barn?"

"I rent space in one. Where do you think I keep the Mini-bullet 3000?" The tinker cocked his head to the side like a curious dog. "You don't know where I live, do you?"

I shrugged. "With other tinkers, in, like, a tinker commune or something?"

"I can't believe—. If you had taken the Ocean Mist Garden Tour, you'd certainly know where I live."

"Right, just give me a call when you're free." I gave my card to the man missing his wallet and one to the lady with the traumatized daughter. "I think I can get your wallet and your daughter's phone back. Swing by my office in about an hour." I hefted the sign pole onto my shoulder and tipped my hat to the mother. "Ma'am."

THE TINKER SAT IN THE CORNER OF my office with his legs crossed and a sketch pad resting on his knee. He worked a charcoal pencil across a page while I interviewed the mime's targets.

I finished quickly. They filed solemnly out the door, and the phone-deprived teenager still clutched the paper bag to her chest a moment away from her next fit of hyperventilation.

I sighed and rubbed my forehead. "What are you doing?"

The tinker held up the sketch pad to examine his work. "I'm using the witnesses' descriptions to make a composite sketch."

"You mean of the mime?"

"Of course."

"I saw him. He's a mime. I know what he looks like."

"You should know better than anyone, Jimmy. Recollections are very unreliable, especially those of victims in high stress situations."

"I wasn't stressed, and I'm not a victim. Let me see that." I snatched the notepad from his hands. "Why is his nose so big?"

"It's one of those big red rubber ones."

"He wasn't wearing a red nose."

The tinker raised the pencil to his lips and squinted into the distance. "No red nose, huh?"

"He's a mime. Not a clown."

"And a smart mime, at that. No red nose makes him less conspicuous."

I tossed the pad onto his lap. "I don't think we'll have any trouble finding him."

"So, when do we give him his criminal name?"

"The mime?"

"*The Mime.* I like it. Simple. Ominous."

I took my sport coat and fedora off the rack by the door. "This isn't helping. We need to get out there and look for him."

"Come on, Jimmy." The tinker ran a good half of a block ahead of me on the boardwalk, but he still trailed The Mime. Fortunately, the white make-up, black and white striped outfit, and beret made The Mime stick out from the vacationers like a zebra on a horse farm.

The Mime smacked the top of his head to hold down his beret, lifted his left foot, skipped on his right, and made a hard left entering Happy Land, which was packed shoulder-to-shoulder with sweaty adolescents, screaming kids, and adults dreaming of the closest bar— at least, I was.

The tinker stopped at the ring-toss game fronting the boardwalk, waited for me to catch-up, and said, "The YMCA is having a membership special, this month."

"What—does—that—have—to—do—with—anything?" I took off my fedora, leaned heavily on my knees, and scanned the thick crowd while my lungs and heart held a heated argument with my brain.

"Let's split up," the tinker said.

"Okay, I'll go in, circle around, and double-back flushing him toward the boardwalk."

"Right." He smacked me on the shoulder sending me stumbling forward. "Sorry."

I put my fedora back on my head, straightened my tie, and ran into the crowd. Screams from the kiddie rollercoaster and spinning swing ride mixed with the bells from the circling fire engines and lights from a hundred video games to create a sensory overload reminding me of the 1980's. I stopped in front of the fun house to get my bearings.

Didn't take me long to spot The Mime leaning on the arcade prize counter. He rested his head in his hand with his elbow propped on the glass and pretended to hold a conversation with a pretty Happy Land employee struggling to ignore him while still doing her job. This private eye knew a creeped-out woman when he saw one.

I managed just a few steps before The Mime spotted me, pushed away from the counter, and darted for the carousel. The crowd slowed him, so I managed to gain some ground until he shouldered a path through the carousel line raising protests from parents laden with stuffed animals and cotton candy. He hopped the gate and jumped onto the ride's moving platform.

A teenage boy in a red Happy Land shirt and tan shorts squeaked, "Hey, you need to give me your tickets!"

"Don't worry, I'll get him," I said following The Mime onto the carousel. I did my best to keep a steady jog while dodging oncoming horses and carriages.

A passing woman asked, "What are you doing?"

"Don't worry, ma'am. Just stay in your saddle."

My lungs ached, but I had to keep going. Had to push forward. Each passing second was another The Mime escaped justice.

A little girl with a pony tail pointed at me from her passing carriage, which I had just seen a few moments, ago. "Mommy, there's that funny man, again."

I glanced to my left. The pimply red-shirted teenager operating the ride stood with his arms across his chest and shaking his head. I kept dodging the stampede. My legs burned as I leaned forward into my zig-zagging run, yet I could still see the operator out of the corner of my eye. The teenager pointed just ahead and to my left into the walkway between the cattle-chute fencing for waiting riders and the turning platform.

The Mime had jumped from the carousel and was doing that

running-in-place thing mimes do. He looked over his shoulder. We made eye contact. I could see the panic in his eyes. He knew I was coming for him.

I weaved sideways and off the platform's edge.

The Mime bolted as much as one could while wearing black slippers. Small children and strollers became hurdles, yet he gained speed becoming a blurry checkered flag tearing off through Happy Land's side entrance and into the street. I followed, but dashing through the carousel's rainbow-colored herd had taken the best from me. I surrendered. A concrete and steel pylon helped to keep me on my feet for a few moments before I slid into a breathless squat.

"Someone call an ambulance," a tattooed guy with a flaming skull t-shirt said, "this man is having a heart attack!"

"I'm— not— having— a— heart— attack."

"Yes, you are."

"No— I'm— not."

A little girl with a soda and plastic purse in her hands ran over from the circling swing ride. "Don't die, mister."

My breath started to return. "I'm not going to—."

She splashed her soda in my face. "I saw that on TV. You throw a drink on someone having a heart attack."

I pushed myself to my feet, pulled a white handkerchief from my back pocket, wiped sticky cherry-smelling liquid from my cheeks, and took a few steps out onto the sidewalk. "Thanks, but I don't think that's what you do."

Without knowing which way to go, or which of the hundred shadows to check along the dark street, I decided to cut back through Happy Land to get the tinker. We'd have to try something else. Outsmart The Mime, since we couldn't outrun him.

"Hey, Jimmy!"

I heard the tinker's voice near the ticket booth, but I didn't see him.

"Over here."

Children and beleaguered parents surrounded me. No tinker.

"In here."

The tinker's head poked out from a pile of pastel stuffed animals inside a claw machine. "How did you get in there?"

"I hid behind the game to wait for The Mime. I was going to jump him when you flushed him out, but I started to worry I might miss him. The panel was off the back, so I just popped my head up and took a look around."

"Well, get out from there. I lost him."

"I can't."

"What do you mean, you can't?"

"I'm stuck."

I looked around to the back of the machine.

The tinker's mismatched sneakers slid against the concrete floor trying to gain traction, but he didn't have treads on his soles.

"Hold on. I'll rock the machine."

"Oww, Jimmy. No. Oww. Stop."

"Okay," I moved around to the front, "can't you just back out the way you got in."

The tinker shook his head causing a sad-looking elephant to lean awkwardly into his face.

A towheaded boy clutching a dollar bill glared at me. "Get out of the way!"

"I'm sorry, but you can't use this machine right now."

The boy shot a quick elbow into my man parts doubling me over enough to push me back. He slipped between me and the game's controls, fed his dollar into the machine with expert grace, and hit the blinking red button to engage an articulated arm from which a shiny metal claw dangled.

"Jimmy, the claw!" The tinker screamed.

The arm extended slowly from the side of the stuffed animal tank with a soft whir of gears and belts. There was nothing I could do but watch. The sharp-looking metal pincers opened over the tinker's head.

"For the love of God, Jimmy!"

I took off my hat and placed it over my heart.

"Stop moving," the boy said. "I want that unicorn."

The tinker closed his eyes and buried his face in the sad elephant's arms. "I'm sorry, Jimmy, for all of the times I called you fat."

The claw dropped right by the tinker's head, clinked shut, and retracted.

"You made me miss," said the kid. "I only have two more chances. Stay out of my way, this time."

Ideas can come to an experienced gumshoe like lightning bolts from the heavens, especially when the adrenaline is flowing and an innocent soul is in danger. I reached into my sport coat and pulled out my brass flask.

The claw machine's tank had to be made of plexiglass given all of the kids beating on it every day. Trying to shatter the side wouldn't work, so I banged my flask against the plexiglass right along the edge where a metal angle bracket held together the panels. I managed to pop out a panel enough to reach inside and snap the articulated arm controlling the claw.

The kid smacked his hand on the red blinking control button. "That's not fair! You can't do that!"

I put my hand on the top of the tinker's head.

"Jimmy, wait a minute—."

I shoved his head down through the hole in the machine, and he scrambled out the back coughing and rubbing his neck.

The little boy pressed his face against the plexiglass and looked longingly at the stuffed unicorn.

"I hate to be the one to tell you, kid," I said while unscrewing the top of my flask, "unicorns aren't real."

"WE NEED TO CORNER THIS GUY." I pounded on my office desk for emphasis. "Get him somewhere he can't run."

"You mean, set a trap?" the tinker asked.

"Yep, and I have an idea for bait. Lots of easy marks. Tourists taking in the sites and not watching their wallets, and we'll parade them right in front of The Mime."

"One of your restaurant-tour groups?"

I tapped the side of my nose and nodded.

"What's wrong with your nose?"

"Nothing. The problem is, he knows what I look like. You, too."

"So, we need someone else to lead the tour."

"We're talking the same language, today."

"Won't you lose your tour job if your boss finds out?"

"Sometimes, you need to put all of your chips on the table, my friend."

"This isn't the time to be thinking about food." The tinker snapped his fingers. "This is Edward's weekend off from Surf Services. He'd love to lead a restaurant group around Ocean Mist."

"What does Edward Pushwater know about restaurants? He lives underground."

"Well, he's not quite the expert you are," he motioned toward my gut, "but he's gotten around since we worked out his new schedule."

I leaned back in my chair, which screeched a protest. "I don't know."

"I got it, Jimmy. We get a bunch of old folks, put Edward in front of them, and The Mime won't be able to resist. Just think of all the oversized pocket books."

I STOOD OUTSIDE THE RESTROOMS NEAR THE bandstand and used a wet napkin to dab at the mustard stain on my new white shirt. *Why is it always a new shirt? Never an old one?*

A glance at the digital clock above the bank told me our tour group would arrive any minute, and still no—. There he was. Edward, his stringy gray mop surrounding a bald crown, strolled down the sunny side of Washington Avenue swinging abnormally long arms out of rhythm with his steps. He sported dress pants of the stretch-waistband variety, a white polo shirt, string tie, and red sneakers. He had certainly pulled out all of the stops for his first gig as a restaurant guide, and he greeted every-one he saw with an exuberant hello.

"Hey, Jimmy!"

I shook his hand. "It's been a while, Edward. How are things below the streets?"

"Oh, you know. Same old same old. Gotta keep the pumps going. The kids need their waves."

"Yeah, here. You'll need these." I handed him the long aluminum pole topped with the cardboard smiling pizza and a restaurant map.

Edward waved away the map. "I came up with my own route." He pulled from his pocket a scribble-covered envelope. "A culinary tour starting with a Scandinavian-leaning influence. The new place on Jefferson Avenue has a lovely Gravlax appetizer."

"Just, keep it simple, Edward."

"Gravlax is pretty basic when it comes to the Nordic regions. Raw salmon cured in salt and sugar."

I put up my hands. "Okay, okay. When The Mime sees you, don't let him get too close to your group."

Edward lifted his finger. "That's when I say we're going to In-A-Bind Bookshop for readings of local recipes."

I nodded. "The reading room is reserved. All you need to do is get everyone in there."

"Who's doing the readings?"

"There are no readings."

"No readings?"

I shook my head.

"Oh."

"Sorry to disappoint you."

A white bulbous passenger van covered in decals of open seashells lumbered down Washington Avenue. Vehicles caught in its wake honked and beeped. Late-morning sunlight made the van's open-shell decals iridescent in purples and blues.

"Mother of Pearl Retirement Community," Edward read from the van's side. "Shucking shut-ins for 20 years."

The van pulled to the curb at our feet. *They must have brought the whole Pinochle club.* "I shouldn't be seen with all of you, so I've got to go. It's show time, Edward."

"You got it, boss." Edward opened the van's sliding door and bowed with a dramatic sweep of his trollish arm. "Hello, ma'am. You're looking lovely today in that pink velour jogging suit."

I pulled my fedora down over my forehead, turned up my sport coat's collar, checked left then right to be sure I hadn't been made, and became one with the crowd.

THE SUN BEAT ON WASHINGTON AVENUE'S SOUTH sidewalk where I broiled in a shadeless spot across from In-A-Bind Bookshop. From there, I could see both corners of the block. Just as I stepped from the curb to get another frozen mocha from Java Bob's, Edward appeared with the Mother of Pearl Pinochle Club. The Mime followed making like he walked a tightrope with an imaginary umbrella.

I entered the book store, pulled a magazine from a rack, used it to conceal part of my face, and watched Edward lead the ladies into the reading room. Like a rat to cheese, The Mime tagged along.

Years of tailing had taught me how to move without a sound, and, with the magazine held in front of my face, the pick pocket had no chance of sensing my presence. I closed behind him, stood in the reading room's only doorway, and sprung the trap.

"Ladies," I said, "looks like you have a new friend."

The Mime's jaw dropped. The Pinochle club filed past me back into the store. A few took a moment to shake their fingers at the white-faced fiend, and one offered a reproach I would never repeat.

"We got him, Jimmy." My stooped frizzy-haired troll of a friend reached to take The Mime by the shirt and make the collar, but The Mime raised his hands between them.

Edward stopped.

The black and white-striped menace moved his palms left and right, outward from his sides, and behind him pushing on the air.

"Grab him, Edward."

"I can't. He's in a box."

I moved toward The Mime, took a deep breath, and puffed my chest. I don't like to intimidate, but sometimes letting someone see the tiger within can head-off trouble before it starts.

The Mime patted the air between us, shrugged, and smiled.

Reaching with my right hand, I turned an invisible knob, made a pulling motion, and swung a left haymaker catching The Mime square on the bridge of his nose. He flew backward over a folding chair knocking down a display of pens and pencils, bounced to his feet like a rubber ball, and wiped red splatter from under his nose.

Edward's jaw dropped.

"He should have locked his door."

I grabbed The Mime's shoulder, but he rolled his arm back then forward like a swimmer's stroke and broke my grip. The slimeball spun past me, lunged through the doorway, and zigzagged between the racks of best sellers toward the exit to the street.

"That mime has some moves," Edward said then fell in behind me as I made chase out of the reading room.

Somewhere ahead of us, still in the store, some lady said, "There he is, girls."

Edward and I rounded a table of James Patterson novels— as if his characters knew anything about real investigations— just in time to witness one of the most brutal attacks ever seen on the mean streets of Ocean Mist. The Mother-of-Pearl Pinochle Club had jumped The Mime between displays of calendars and hand-crafted soaps. A lady with a blue perm straddled his back and beat him over the head repeatedly with her handbag. Another tied his ankles with her beaded necklace, and a third kicked him in the ribs with her orthotics.

The color drained from Edward's face. "Jimmy, what are you going to do?"

I shrugged. "Wait for him to cry for help?"

PANTOMIME International
1563 Suite M Marceau Office Park
Walla Walla, WA 15555

Dear Mr. Grits:

I am writing on behalf of the twenty-three-member-strong Professional Association Nurturing Theatrically Organized Movements and Inspiring Mime Entrepreneurship to express our collective dismay regarding your treatment of one of our members. We will provide a comprehensive legal defense for this member, and we are confident he will be cleared of the terrible accusations lodged against him.

Furthermore, your disparagement of pantomime's practitioners is reprehensible. Mimes have dedicated their lives to the study and expression of deep emotion through movement. To have the likes of you suggest otherwise is an affront to culturally enlightened audiences around the world. You, sir, may consider this letter to be a squirt in the face from a trick corsage.

The acquittal of our valued member will vindicate not just him but mimes' contributions to the human condition in all corners of our globe.

Shirley U. Gest, President
PANTOMIME International

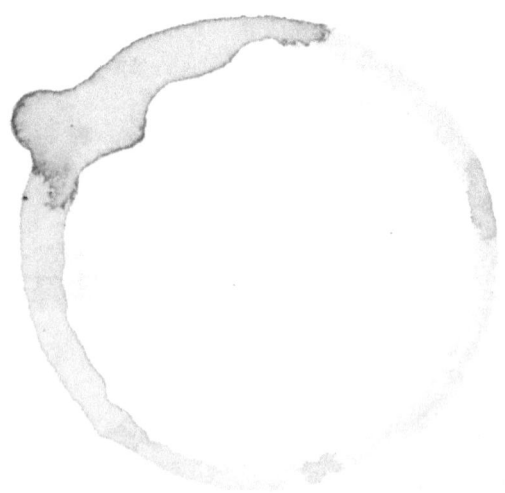

White Vinegar and Chow-chow

The news came to me like a slap on the face. Angela dropped *Private Eye of Fortune* magazine from the periodicals section. *How could she do this to me?* I considered canceling my library card, but I cooled off—cooled off enough to give her a bit of the old cold shoulder for the better part of a week. Then, she called.

She must've known I was sore.

When my phone rang, her voice came through real quiet. "Hello there, Jimmy."

"What's on your mind?"

She didn't answer right away, and I let the silence do its work.

"Haven't seen you in a while. I thought, maybe, you'd stop by to take a peek between some new covers."

I swallowed hard. *Tough to stay mad at Angela.* "You know I'm always up for leafing through your sheets."

She laughed. "Seriously, Jimmy. I've got a problem."

"I thought we were being serious."

"Can you help me?"

"Sure, doll."

"Can you come to the library?"

Like my mother always told me, once you butter your grits, it's time for breakfast. "See you in about twenty minutes?"

"I'm wearing black."

"Ten minutes?"

She hung up.

I grabbed my fedora and coat from the rack.

THE BELL HANGING ABOVE THE LIBRARY'S OLD wood door announced my arrival, but all I got was a glance from Angela. She stood behind the circulation desk and faced a middle-aged man sporting a checkered sweater vest and tweed smoking jacket. He leaned forward pressing his leather elbow patches against the century-old oak. I didn't need to be a career private eye to know he tested my girl's patience.

"You know what I mean, lady. The books in the special room."

Angela pulled back from the desk. Her forced smile didn't falter in the least. She reached slowly into her black dress and retrieved reading glasses on the end of a pearl chain. She placed the glasses across the bridge of her nose, touched one of the temples with the gentlest of moves, cleared her throat, and wrinkled her button nose in one of those *okay, you got me* kinds of ways. "Now I understand."

Angela bent slightly at her waist, reached under the circulation desk, pulled out a 44-caliber magnum revolver, used both thumbs to cock the hammer, and pointed it center mass. Her voice dropped four octaves. "You must not have heard me. I don't know what you're talking about!"

"Wo there, Angela." I stepped forward. "Let's just take a breath."

Elbow Patches raised both hands and backed toward the door. "Okay, I'm sorry. I'm just going to leave, now. I'm sorry."

The door banged shut behind him.

Angela lowered the magnum, released the hammer, shook her head, and laid the gun on the desk.

"What happened, doll?"

"That guy was here yesterday, and he gave me this." She handed me a slip of paper. "I saw him pass our windows this morning. That's why I called you. Then, he came in again."

I eyed the gleaming canon while unfolding the note. *The Pennsylvania German Recipes of Edna Mae Stoltzfuss, Circa 1791.* "Okay," I said, "what happened next?"

"What do you mean, what happened next? You saw what happened next."

I pushed back my fedora, scratched my head, and reread the slip of paper.

Angela sighed. "Jimmy, that's one of the books in the basement. You know, the archives."

"How would he know about the archives?"

Angela shrugged. "That's the bigger problem."

"It's a recipe book. Can't you just bring it up after hours and let him look at it tomorrow?"

Angela slid a book from the top of a pile on the desk, placed it between us, and opened it to the inside of the front cover. "I can't believe you just asked me that, James." She lifted the revolver by the barrel, turned its cylinder a few clicks, then smacked the butt against the cover, which left a return date in red numbers.

My heart slowed. "That's some date stamp."

"What, Joey?" She lifted the stamper and shook it at me. "Old Joey here has cut our overdue list in half."

"I bet he has."

"Now do you see why I need your help?"

"This guy looks harmless, but give me some time. Let me ask around and do some surveillance. Meanwhile," I took the stamper from her and looked into the cylinders just to be sure, "try to relax."

THE SOUND OF A MATCH SCRATCHING AGAINST brick and the glow of a small flame behind a cupped hand stopped me in my tracks. Elbow Patches took a drag from his pipe and stepped out of a dark doorstep. "Why are you following me, Grits?"

I owned Ocean Mist's nights. Its streets. Its sidewalks. Always one with the shadows. Someone must have warned this guy. No other explanation for him making me.

"Why are you so interested in that book?" I asked.

"It's not a book. It's more of a scrapbook. Recipes and notes. Someone's personal collection." The man took another step forward closing the already short distance between us. He wore the same sweater vest under his tweed jacket he had worn in the library. "I just want to sign it out for a few days. What's the harm in that?"

I heard the tobacco leaves burning in his pipe bowl, and the smoke smelled pretty good. If it wasn't for those addiction and cancer things, I might have taken up the pipe at some point in my life, but I chose other vices. "Why do you want it? There are a million recipe books out there."

"You know what, Grits. Maybe you can explain to me why it's so much trouble to sign-out a book from this town's library?"

"No one has ever complained, before. Maybe it has something to do with you."

"Touché, my friend." He took another drag. "Since the library is a publicly funded institution, I cannot be denied access to any of its holdings. Any of its holdings." He took the pipe from his mouth and jabbed its mouthpiece in my direction. "I would hate to have to go public with any complaints, especially ones that might bring light to any rats, or special books, in the library's basement."

I bore my stare into his steel gray eyes. "I don't usually ask the same question twice, but you caught me on a good day. Why this book?"

"Scrapbook."

"Okay, scrapbook."

"It's not for me. It's for my," he paused, "partner. A very silent partner."

"I don't care who it's for. The question is the same. Why?"

Elbow Patches shrugged, took another drag on his pipe, and exhaled a billowing cloud of sweet-smelling smoke in my direction.

The next thing I knew, I looked into the face of some young guy kneeling over me as I lay on the sidewalk.

"You alright, sir?"

"What?"

"You don't look so good."

He helped me to my feet.

"I'm fine." I looked around me. The street spun.

The guy steadied me. "Easy there, sir."

"What time is it?"

"Dude, it's like two thirty in the morning. I just happened to see your loafers sticking out over the doorstep."

Two thirty? I've been out for almost five hours.

My phone rang. Angela. "Everything alright, doll?"

"No, Jimmy. You need to get to the library. We've been robbed."

"On my way."

ANGELA STOOD AT THE LIBRARY'S DOOR AND unlocked it when I approached. Red teary eyes and a slight wobble as she backed away from the door told me more happened than a simple robbery.

"Was it the guy in the tweed jacket?"

She nodded.

"What did he do to you?" I scanned her face and reached to run my hand over her head for signs of injuries, but she pushed it away.

"I'm okay, Jimmy." She tucked some long red locks behind her ears and kept her eyes on the floor. "I was working late—."

"Working late? You didn't want to leave the library, did you?"

"Would you just listen, Jimmy?"

"Okay, take a breath and tell me what happened."

"He waited outside. Waited for me to lock up then blew smoke in my face. Next thing I knew—."

"You woke up on the floor with a headache."

"Yeah, how did you know?"

"He did the same to me. What did he take? That recipe book?"

"He knew where to go. My office. Behind the filing cabinet. He even knew the combination to the door at the end of the tunnel."

"This guy take anything else?"

Angela shook her head.

"I'm going to walk you home."

"IT'S ACTUALLY PRETTY SIMPLE, UNCLE JIMMY." My red-headed and freckled nephew leaned back in his lawn chair at the picnic table on my sister's screened-porch, kind of a three-season laboratory for the little genius. "He probably smokes this stuff in low doses mixed with regular pipe tobacco to build up a tolerance. When he needs to put someone to sleep, he leaves out the tobacco. If he's built up enough of a tolerance, the smoke probably doesn't bother him much while anyone else blacks out on the spot."

"Can you make some kind of antidote? In case this guy tries again?"

"You don't need an antidote. Just don't inhale."

"I've heard that somewhere, before."

"Wait until the smoke clears or step away."

"Seems too simple."

"I have another idea." My sister's boy got up from his lawn chair and went to a small wood chest in the porch's corner. "You can always snuff the pipe."

"You thinking of some kind of fire-suppressant? Maybe a compressed carbon dioxide delivery system? It would need to be small enough for me to strap to the inside of my wrist and cover with my sleeve."

"Not exactly." He brought a small book bag back to the table, rummaged through it for a moment, and withdrew a lemon-yellow plastic squirt gun.

"Do I need a permit for one of those?"

He shook his head, went inside the house, came back a minute later wiping his hand on his shorts, and handed me the gun. "I loaded it for you."

"Thanks." I put it in my coat pocket.

I EXPLAINED THE CASE TO THE TINKER leaving out the part about the book coming from a secret room in the library's archive. He paced my office with his hands clenched at his hips. The robbery really got him going. Revealing the existence of a secret archive would have made his head explode.

"How could someone do this?" he asked.

"This really bothers you, doesn't it?"

"Well, doesn't it bother you, Jimmy? The public library is sacred, a democratic institution dating back to Benjamin Franklin. Ocean Mist's library belongs to all of us. It's a public suppository of information."

"You mean, depos—."

"We need to find this guy and return the book."

"That's why I need your help. Hear anything on the streets?"

"Not about a recipe book." He scratched his chin. "Why would someone want a recipe book that badly?"

"The restaurant game is pretty fierce here in town," I said.

"That's it, Jimmy. The owner of the Pink Flamingo wants to open a restaurant across from the bookstore."

"The Pink Flamingo? Isn't that a strip club off of Route One?"

"A male review. A lady named Bumper owns it."

"Bumper, huh?"

The tinker nodded and got a faraway look in his eye.

"So," I said, "what else do you know about this proposed restaurant?"

"It's going to be a themed restaurant. Pennsylvania Dutch cooking."

"The owner of a strip club—."

"Male review."

"The owner of a male review wants to open a Pennsylvania Dutch restaurant featuring Amish cooking?"

"Don't forget Mennonite. Both Anabaptist groups originated in Europe's Pfalz region before persecution led them to seek refuge in Central Pennsylvania."

I tipped back my hat and rubbed my forehead. "Why do you know all of this?"

"Genealogy. My maternal grandmother's family—."

"Were Amish tinkers from the Pfalz region?"

"Mennonite tinkers."

"Okay," I pulled down my fedora, "the club owner could be a suspect, but I'm not convinced of motive. Why Pennsylvania Dutch in this town?"

The tinker leaned on my desk. He needed a shower, probably since the previous Wednesday. "Know of anywhere you can get a shoo-fly pie or pickled pigs' feet in Ocean Mist?"

I shook my head. "Maybe we should take a closer look at this Bumper."

The tinker got that far away look in his eyes, again.

After a moment, he said, "We have some history."

"Why does that not surprise me?" I pulled out my desk drawer and got the keys to my old black Studebaker.

THE PINK FLAMINGO SAT BACK FROM THE highway far enough not to attract the attention of family vacationers but accessible enough for those desiring the distractions of dancing men. The parking lot seemed pretty full for late on a Tuesday night.

The tinker reached into the back seat for his bag and pulled out sunglasses and a familiar-looking trucker hat.

"What are you doing with those?"

"We don't want to be recognized. This is a stake out, right?"

"No, we have to go inside and ask questions."

"How about I stay here and watch the entrance?"

"What is it with you and this Bumper lady, anyway?"

"You want me to go in there, don't you?"

"Of course. Especially if you have connections."

The tinker opened his door.

"And leave the hat and glasses in the car."

We crossed the parking lot to a scene reminding me of a gangster's speak easy in an old black and white movie. No windows in the cinder-block wall except small frosted rectangles of thick glass near the roof line. A single bulb in a wire mesh cage lighted a heavy steel door, and a big guy with a flat nose sat on a stool underneath the light.

"Hey, buddy," the big guy said, "haven't seen you in a while."

The tinker didn't look up from his feet. "How you doing, Al?"

"Not too bad. It's Tuesday, you know?"

"Yeah, I know."

The tinker cocked his head at me. "It's a five-dollar cover, Jimmy." He banged on the door, it opened, and he slipped through with his chin tucked against his chest.

The big guy stopped me with a light backhand against my gut. "You heard him. That's ten bucks."

"A math teacher, huh?" I handed him two Lincolns.

A blast of hot sweat-heavy air hit me when I entered a dim-lit room packed with people. Red and pink tinted lights and loud throbbing music made my brain go numb. A throng of people packed the dance floor whooping and hollering at a half-naked man bathed in spotlights on a small elevated stage. He wore a cape, wooden platform shoes, and clogged to electronic drums and a chest-thumping base coming from speakers taller than me. A mirror ball the size of my Studebaker spun above the dance floor casting starlight throughout the room. Beyond the crowd, the tinker bellied-up to the bar, which I found to be made of painted plywood and two-by-fours.

"Can I get you a drink, Jimmy?"

I shook my head.

The tinker nodded a thank you at the bartender and lifted his glass. "What, exactly, are we looking for?"

"I thought I knew, but I'm having a hard time thinking." I tried not to look at the stage, but it was like trying to pass a traffic accident without turning your head. "Anything that might point the finger at this Bumper."

"Give me another," the tinker said to the barkeep.

"You need to slow down. I need you sharp."

The bartender presented another glass of gold-colored liquid to the tinker, and he downed it in five gulps I could hear above the music. He turned the glass upside down, smacked it onto the bar, and wiped his mouth with the back of his hand. "Best apple juice this side of Highway One."

"What did the bouncer mean by *it's Tuesday?*"

"We won't find anything out here." The tinker rose from his stool. "Come on. I have an idea."

We skirted the crowd and made our way along the wall and through the shadows to an unmarked swinging door painted flat black. The tinker took a quick look around then pulled me by the arm through the door into a long hallway of water-stained avocado wallpaper. Bare bulbs dangling from the ceiling cast dim pools of light on cracked and curling linoleum.

"If there is any evidence," the tinker said, "it'll be in the heart of Bumper's operation."

By that, I guessed he meant the kitchen, which was to our left. Even the smell of cooking grease couldn't quite mask the smell of sweat still hanging in the air. This little peek behind the scenes convinced me not to patronize any of Bumper's present or future restaurants.

"Do you know where you're going?" I asked.

"Let's see what's in here." He opened a door and stepped through before I could stop him.

Shelf upon shelf of pickled vegetables, cans of sauerkraut, canisters of Saffron, and more varieties of vinegar than could be found in all of Ocean Mist's grocery stores filled a room almost as large as the Pink Flamingo's dance floor.

"Look at all of the chow-chow," the Tinker said.

"Huh?"

"Chow-chow. It's a pickled bean salad."

"Oh."

The pantry's contents confirmed the town's gossip about the new restaurant, but nothing I saw connected Bumper to the book heist. I pulled out my phone and snapped photos until I felt a meaty hand clamp onto my shoulder.

"You two aren't supposed to be here."

I realized something about male reviews. The staff tended to be large insistent men hard to ignore.

The tinker said, "We're inspectors."

Not bad, I thought. I pulled out my private investigator identification, flashed it faster than the big guy could read it, and said, "Some of your vinegar is out of date. Expired."

The big guy didn't take his hand from my shoulder. "I think we need to see Bumper."

The tinker might have sworn under his breath, but I couldn't tell for sure.

I turned my shoulder away from the guy making him lose his grip on my sport coat. "We'd have to see her about these code violations, eventually."

The big guy gestured toward the hallway. "After you, gentlemen."

We twisted and turned through hallways connecting what appeared to be a jumble of mobile homes and trailers all joined to the cinderblock building we first entered.

"Door to the right," the big guy barked from behind us. "Knock first."

The tinker did as commanded.

A hoarse and gritty female voice said to enter.

I followed close behind the tinker and scoped-out the office over his shoulder. Dingey gray walls, overhead pipes, and no windows made me wonder what the lowly employees' breakroom looked like.

The tinker gave a slight nod to a woman sitting behind a paper-cluttered desk. "Bumper."

Bumper took a long drag on a cigarette. Placing her age would have taken some work. Her gravelly voice and leathered skin made her look sixties, but the smoking meant she could have been fifties, maybe even forties judging from the tar-browned walls. Above all else, my instincts told me this bleach-blonde beehived chimney was in bed with Elbow Patches. Maybe literally. My skin crawled.

She squinted at the tinker through a fresh cloud of smoke. "You not working, tonight?"

I turned to the tinker. "Working?"

The tinker glanced at me. "Side job."

I wasn't sure if he meant that for me or Bumper. "How many side jobs do you have?"

"The secrets we keep," said Bumper. "Oh, the drama." She reached for a planner, flipped some pages, sighed, and slapped it closed, which revealed the well-worn cover of a stitch-bound antique-looking book underneath it. She pointed her cigarette at me. "I always wanted to meet one of the Blues Brothers. You Belushi or Akroyd?" She croaked-out a chuckle, coughed, and patted the old book sprinkling ash over its leather. "I'm guessing this is what you're after."

The tinker spun toward the big guy and punted. The cretin's grandchildren would one day feel the impact.

I lunged for the desk and used both hands to scatter Bumper's stacks of papers into a cloud fluttering around her head.

The tinker snatched the recipe book. "Run!"

The big guy tried to stand. A tough task with knees locked together. I covered his face with my open hand and shoved. He crumpled against the wall and made a noise like a cartoon mouse. We bolted down another dim avocado-papered and linoleum corridor, hung a left, and found a dead end.

"I thought you knew your way around this place?"

The tinker shrugged. "I usually work the front."

We doubled-back past the office, where I glimpsed Bumper helping the big guy to his feet. "They're coming after us."

We checked a few open doors looking for an exit but found only dressing rooms harboring oiled men in various stages of primping; fortunately, they showed little interest in two panicked guys running through their place of business.

"This way, Jimmy."

The tinker took me into a hallway with no doors and only a set of steps leading to a wing of the stage. A rough-looking woman holding a clipboard stood just inside the curtain. She chewed on a pencil and rolled her head cracking her neck.

"Looks like the end of the line," I said. That's when I saw Elbow Patches standing in the opposite wing. He tapped the bowl of his pipe against the palm of his hand emptying ash and bits of his wacky tobaccy around his feet. I spun on my heel to check the hallway behind us.

The big guy, now with a crowbar, pointed at me and said, "There you are."

"We're trapped," I said to the tinker, but he had already climbed the steps and spoke with the lady holding the clipboard.

She nodded, wrote something, and motioned for me to join them.

Not eager to reacquaint myself with the big guy or to meet his new crowbar friend, I climbed into the wing and poked my head beyond the red-velvet curtain's thick folds looking for some type of aisle through the shoulder-to-shoulder crowd, some way we could slink from the stage and make a break for the door.

The tinker took my arm and pulled me out from behind the curtain. The floor lights fired to life, and I found myself center stage with hundreds of eyes fixed upon me. Having worked a lot of adultery cases, I knew cougars and bears when I faced them.

"What are you doing?" I asked the tinker.

Two spot lights bathed us in changing colors as filter wheels spun slowly through the beams. I felt hot, and not in a good way.

The lady with the clipboard spoke into a microphone. "Ladies and gentlemen, the Pink Flamingo welcomes, all the way from the town of Ocean Mist, White Vinegar and Chow-chow!"

"What?" I asked the tinker out of the corner of my mouth while keeping my gaze on the audience.

"Just dance, Jimmy." The tinker dropped the recipe book onto the stage, swayed his hips, and slowly unbuttoned his faded red-and-yellow-flowered Hawaiian shirt.

"No way!" I turned toward Elbow Patches whom I knew I could take with a jab-cross combination, but I second-guessed myself seeing him press his thumb into his pipe bowl.

"Jimmy, you have to do something. Just move." The tinker circled behind me, pulled my sport coat off of my shoulders, and, before I could snatch it from him, he tossed it into the crowd.

"That's my coat!"

"You have others."

"No, I don't!"

The audience erupted into a frenzy of catcalls. The music seemed to grow louder, if one could call the pulsating base and synthetic sci-fi sounds music.

Some guy yelled, "Take it off, fat boy!"

I would've punched him had I been close enough.

The tinker tried to restore my dignity. "Hey, that's take it off Chow-chow!"

Despite the confusion and my disgust, I recognized the smell of Elbow Patches' wacky tobacco smoke drifting onto the stage. The guy with the crowbar stood laughing in the wing to my right. He and the audience were as good as brick walls, so our only option was through Patches and his growing cloud.

My nephew's squirt gun. The gun was in my sport coat pocket, which now floated through the crowd and landed on a tall cocktail table well out of my reach.

"I need my gun," I said to the tinker while he taunted the audience with the zipper of his cargo shorts.

"You have a gun?" He didn't take his eyes off of the crowd. "Since when did you start carrying a gun?"

"I guess we both have secrets, don't we?"

"Why didn't you use it, before?"

"It's in the pocket of my sport coat. We have to get it."

"No problem." The tinker sauntered his way to the edge of the stage, turned his back to the crowd, and raised his arms over his head.

Those not already on their feet stood. The room pressed toward the stage raising their arms the same as the tinker. He fell backwards onto a sea of hands, and his smile told me he enjoyed every moment of being carried back and forth above the crowd as they chanted, "White Vinegar, White Vinegar, White Vinegar!"

On his third pass near the cocktail table, he snatched up my coat and swung it in circles over his head. The crowd loved it and tossed him upwards then caught him over and over like riding a bucking bronco. Somehow, he managed to ride his way back to the stage and resume his dancing like he had never left.

"You've done that before, haven't you?" I asked.

"You have to try it, Jimmy." The tinker went through his gyrations and rid himself of his cargo shorts while watching me fish in my coat. The gun had nestled itself way down in the pocket.

"You got it?" he asked.

I drew the small hunk of plastic, held it up to the spot lights, and felt a renewed confidence, a kind of warmth in its yellow glow.

The tinker stopped, put his hands on his hips just above the elastic waistband of his boxers, and said, "Are you kidding me?"

The crowd booed.

I faced Elbow Patches, took a deep breath, and charged while unleashing a barrage of squirts aimed for the pipe in his mouth. He cried out and covered his eyes exposing his glowing pipe bowl. Within seconds, my expert marksmanship followed by an overhand right put out more than his wacky tobaccy.

I waved for the tinker to follow me.

He scooped up the recipe book, and we rushed down the steps from the wing toward a red exit sign.

THE TINKER SAT IN THE STUDEBAKER'S PASSENGER seat shivering in his boxers and staring at the brake lights in front of us. We drove half way to Ocean Mist in silence getting a few awkward glances from neighboring cars at stop lights.

"So," I said letting the o-sound trail off a bit too long, "you've danced at the Pink Flamingo, before?"

"Yep."

"That what you meant by working in the front?"

"Yep."

"And, you never told me?"

"Nope."

More silence.

"I don't tell you everything," the tinker snapped.

"Obviously."

More silence.

"I needed the money."

"Okay."

The tinker folded his arms and turned toward the passenger door.

I pulled up to his house. "Call you tomorrow?"

"Alright."

I drove back to my office and circled the block slowly checking the shadows before parking and going inside. Even with the door locked behind me, I didn't feel safe until I pulled the shades and reloaded the squirt gun. I moved my chair tight against my desk where I watched the hallway through the frosted glass of my door. Still another couple of hours before the sun would rise over the Atlantic, and I didn't want to endanger my bombshell librarian by calling and returning the recipe book before daylight.

I opened the old book. Flipped from one brown, crinkly, handwritten note to the next perusing ingredients lists and hints on how to properly brown pie crusts in a brick oven. Maybe the adrenaline still drifting around in my bloodstream caused my agitated thinking, but waves of anger rose and fell within me knowing Bumper and her no-good-nicks still conspired to create an underworld empire based upon pork and sauerkraut.

"What's next," I asked my drooping fern, "an illegal saffron trade?"

I TIPPED MY FEDORA BACK FROM MY brow. "How appreciative are you?"

Angela leaned way over the circulation desk.

Look at her eyes, I thought. *Look at her eyes.*

She placed her hand on my cheek, planted a soft kiss very close to my lips, and hugged the recipe book in a way making me jealous. "I can't thank you, enough."

"I'm just getting started, doll."

"What do you mean?"

"That guy with the pipe and his boss Bumper are still out there, and I don't have anything to make a collar. Anything that will stick. Maybe some drug charges for Elbow Patches, if we can nab him with his pipe, but Bumper will just find someone else to take his place. I have to find a way to take her down with him."

"I'm sure you'll think of something." Angela took the recipe book back into her office. "I changed the combination to the archives."

"That won't be enough." The library wouldn't open for another hour, but the previous night and a lack of sleep made me jumpy. I looked around just to be sure no one lurked between the shelves. "Bumper and Patches know about the room. Its secrecy had always been its best security. Buildings can be broken into and locks can be picked."

She grunted, and the scratching sound of her cabinet sliding back from the office wall to expose the access tunnel followed. "I'm sure you'll think of something. We got the book, and now we know we have to move the archives. Can we just call this a victory?"

I walked to the large picture window looking out on Washington Avenue, folded my arms, and watched early risers haul their chairs and coolers toward the beach. My sense of justice just wouldn't allow me to think of this as a win without someone behind bars.

A pink Cadillac with chrome wheels slowed to a crawl in front of the library. Smoke seeped from the edges of its windows and doors. I reached into my pocket for the squirt gun, flung wide the library's old wooden door, and stepped into the sun. The Cadillac sped off leaving a trail of tire rubber.

Something told me I hadn't seen the last of Elbow Patches or Bumper.

Skee-Ball Granny

Ocean Mist's streets and boardwalk released a day's worth of stored heat adding to an already sweltering night. I took off my fedora, loosened its damp band, and straightened the brim. Moving from bench to bench, french fry stand to funnel cake joint, I had nothing to show for my sweat and aching feet.

Just as families took young ones back to cramped motel rooms and packs of adolescents began their nightly roving of the boards, an unhappy looking tinker emerged from Zoiker's Arcade. He clenched a circular bag with stiff leather handles. A couple of guys followed close behind, none too happy either. All wore the same style orange and brown bowling shirts. The guys looked familiar, but I couldn't place them. They headed in my direction.

The tinker gave me a curt nod. "Jimmy." His voice had none of its usual *hey there, hi there,* and *ho there* cheer.

"What's eating you?" I asked.

One of the guys said, "Good question. You got an hour?"

The tinker put his free hand on his hip and half turned toward the arcade looking like he wanted to bum-rush the place. That's when I saw the big sequined *OMB* on the back of his bowling shirt.

"The old lady took us again," he said.

"Took you in what?"

"Skee-Ball. What else?"

"You mean, the game where you roll balls up a ramp—."

The tinker kept his glare on Zoiker's door as he finished my question. "And sink them in the holes of a bull's-eye." He sighed then motioned at his friends. "You remember..." and he rattled off a few names, which didn't help me place the guys.

I shook hands all around. The others had the same *OMB* on their backs. "Are you some kind of team?"

The tinker whipped his head around and scowled at me. "You're looking at the Ocean Mist Ballers Skee-Ball Team, which also happens to be the Ocean Mist Hummer's baritone section."

The electric kazoo band, I realized. More than a year had passed since that whole bandstand fiasco.

"Sorry, guys," the tinker said. "My friend Jimmy is one heck of a private eye, but he doesn't get out much."

I frowned and rubbed my neck. "What's with the purse?"

"This isn't a purse. These are my balls." The tinker lifted his bag, which, with a second glance, looked more like a small bowling ball bag than something to be carried about town. "My grandfather taught me everything he knew, gave me his bag and balls, and made me promise I'd take care of them."

"Did he?"

The tinker nodded. "They're worn really smooth, but they just don't make balls like these, anymore."

"Yeah, okay," I said and raised my hands to cut him off and save him from himself.

"No, really Jimmy. His balls are family heirlooms and take a lot of care."

"He's right," said one of the Hummers. "If he doesn't oil and rub his grandfather's balls regularly, well, you don't want to see what happens when one dries out and cracks."

Another Hummer put his hand on the tinker's shoulder and pointed at the arcade. "Hey, there she is."

A helpful little boy held the door for an old lady using a walker. She wore high-riding polyester pants and an open sweater featuring kittens. She struggled to get through the door because of an oversized purse hanging from one walker handle and a canvas shopping bag hanging from the other. Long strands of tickets looped and curled from the bag. She handed the boy some tickets and patted him on the head.

"Is that the lady who took you at Skee-Ball?" I asked the tinker.

He scowled at her. "She's the one."

The lady shivered and pulled the sweater tightly around her despite the 95-degree heat. I'd seen a lot of scammers in my time, and old blue hair didn't come across as a fake when she put her weight on the walker and shuffled forward, yet she seemed a little too—something.

I scratched my cheek. "Huh."

"Huh, what?" The tinker turned to me and folded his arms.

"Nothing. How do you think she took you?"

One of the Hummers said, "We have no idea, but she's mopped the floor with us the last three tournaments. We're not talking about beating us within a few points. She averages at least thirty more than our high-est-scoring team member every game."

"Is that a lot?"

The tinker answered, "Of course it's a lot." He dropped his arms and took a few steps in the old lady's direction.

I grabbed him by the back of his shirt. "Hold on there, Skee-Ball Wizard. She's still an old lady, even if she is a con."

"See," the tinker redirected his anger toward me, "you did see some-thing, didn't you?"

"Maybe, but it's just a game, guys. Why don't we get some ice cream and call it a night?" I didn't need to be a career private eye to read the looks they gave me and realize the peril I faced. Without another word, I backed away slowly.

THE TINKER STOOD AT MY OFFICE DOOR with his hands on his hips, "So, Skee-Ball is just a game?"

"Good morning to you, too." I closed the folder in front of me, tapped its edge on the desk to seat some loose pages, and added it to a considerable pile. "Come on in. I need a break."

"I didn't come here to give you a break, Jimmy. You've been summoned."

"Summoned?"

"The council wants to see you."

"Council? What council?"

"You better come with me."

"Really? I need to finish these case files."

"This is big, Jimmy."

"Okay," I took my coat and hat from the rack by the door, "after you." We made our ways south on the boardwalk toward Watchman's Pond. "Where are we going?"

The tinker stopped at the end of the boardwalk. One of the Ocean Mist Ballers I met the previous night approached from the street.

"You're going to have to take off your hat, Jimmy." The tinker nodded to his teammate.

"Why?"

"Secrecy, Jimmy."

"Is that a hood?"

"You need to trust me, Jimmy."

The Baller placed the sack over my head, took me by the elbow, and we walked what seemed like two blocks in silence. I made mental notes of the changes in the ground: boardwalk to sidewalk to street and back to sidewalk. Variations in heat on my shoulders, walking in and out of heavy shade cast by the big trees near the cottages on Knox Street, helped me keep tabs on our locations.

We stopped walking.

"Hey," some guy said, "can you tell me how to get to Down and Out Burger?"

"Sure." The tinker gave him directions.

We started walking again with the Ocean Mist Baller still guiding me by the arm. The sounds of traffic grew louder, which I thought placed us near Franklin Street.

"Mommy, why does that big man have a bag over his head?"

"Shush," a lady said. "It's not polite to point, honey."

"Even if he can't see me?"

We must have followed Franklin Street over the Watchman's Pond Bridge then headed toward the big homes along the water between Ocean Mist and Rehoboth Beach.

The ground changed from asphalt to unevenly set stones, probably a slate walk. A door opened. Air-conditioned air struck my face. We went inside, the door clicked shut behind me, and the Baller led me deeper into the house and down a staircase.

A basement? How can there be a basement this close to the beach?

The tinker removed the bag over my head. We stood in a room with no windows. A large flat screen hung from the wall. A leather couch worth more than my Studebaker faced the television, and a fully appointed bar filled the corner; all one would expect from a rich person's recreation room, except for two heavy oak doors better suited for an 18th century English manor.

The Baller knocked once on the doors, paused, then twice, paused, once more, and called out, "We're here."

The doors swung into a long stone chamber lit by gas-fueled wall sconces. Four women and three men wearing crimson robes sat around a massive mahogany table, and a particularly serious-looking lady sat at its head facing me.

She said, "Welcome to The Skee-Ball Council, Mr. Grits."

"Should I kneel?"

The tinker didn't raise his gaze from the floor. "That won't be necessary, Jimmy."

A man at the table pointed at us. "Silence!"

The tinker genuflected and took a step backwards.

"Mr. Grits," the serious-looking lady continued, "you're here because of a great evil befalling Ocean Mist."

"Great evil?" I turned slowly moving my gaze around the room from face to face. "Somehow, the words 'great evil' and 'Skee-Ball' don't seem to go together."

"See, I told you," a councilman said, "we can't expect him to help us."

I agreed. "From the looks of things, you need Sir Lancelot. Not me."

"Jimmy," the tinker whispered, "just listen."

The woman cleared her throat. "Skee-Ball Granny has been cleaning out prize booths up and down the boardwalk."

"Skee-Ball Granny?" I folded my arms. "Your kingdom is surely doomed."

The tinker leaned toward my ear and whispered, "There are powers at work here you don't understand."

"Obviously," I said.

"Give it to him," the woman said.

Another robed man slid an envelope across the table toward me.

The woman continued, "This might change your mood."

I stepped forward, took the envelope, and thumbed through a wad of cash.

"Consider it a retainer," she said.

"You have my attention."

The man who gave me the envelope rose from his chair and leaned on the table. "Find out how Skee-Ball Granny is beating the games, and do it before the Skee-Ball Quarterfinals."

"Skee-Ball Quarterfinals? When are they?"

The tinker covered his face with his hands. "Seriously, Jimmy? Three days. They're in three days."

"Any longer than that," the woman continued, "and two of the three arcades will enter bankruptcy proceedings. The other will fold within the month."

I tucked the envelope inside my sport coat. "Bankruptcy?"

"The fates of our boardwalks' arcades are in your hands, Mr. Grits." The woman nodded at the tinker.

"Take off your hat, Jimmy."

"Do we really have to do the hood?"

The tinker held open the sack. The weight of the money in my pocket squelched the argument rising in my throat.

NOTHING RUINS THE FIRST BITE OF A cheesesteak like shattering window glass and the jangle and slap of an aluminum shade against a window frame. I jumped from my desk chair, knees bent, hands raised in fists of steel, and my senses knife-sharp. I slid to the left of the window and lifted a bent slat of the shade just enough to get a good look at the small yard and trash corrals between my building and the beach-themed knickknacks shop behind it. No one there.

A ball rolled across the floor and came to rest in the corner. "A Skee-Ball," I said to myself. The miscreant breaking my window had wrapped the wood ball in a note constructed from carefully glued words cut from a magazine:

Dear Mr. Grits,
We know for whom you are working. Reconsider your involvement. Poking your nose into this will bring more than a broken window.
Yours truly,
Skee-Ball Granny

Once my temper cooled from the broken window, I took a closer look at the note. The word *whom* reminded me of my grandmother's frustrated attempts to teach me the word's correct use. *Whom* also pointed to the note's authenticity as having been written by an elderly lady. Skee-Ball Granny gave up another important point of information with the word we. She worked with at least one accomplice.

I dialed the tinker on my cell. "You ever see someone with the granny like a son or daughter?"

"Not that I can remember." I heard a ball roll down a wood ramp, the *whup* of it launching from a ball hop, and the *thunk* of it hitting a backstop. "Hard to know for sure, though. When I'm competing, Skee-Ball is on, and I'm in the zone. Just me, the ball, the ramp, and the holes, you know?"

"No, I don't." I heard cheesy beeping music. "Are you in an arcade?" I expected the tinker to be peddling mismatched metal utensils and trinkets from his cart. "Where are you?"

"My living room."

"You're playing Skee-Ball in your living room?"

"Every day."

"When do you work?"

"Why? You got a job for me?"

"Actually, I do. Surveillance."

"When?"

"Now."

"Okay, give me ten minutes. Your office?"

"No. Boardwalk. At the bandstand."

I WATCHED THE EBB AND FLOW OF people cramming the boardwalk. Tough to see where one family ended and the next began, but easy to find the tinker in his brown and orange Ocean Mist Ballers shirt.

"Hey, Jimmy."

"Hey, yourself." I used my handkerchief to wipe sweat from my neck. "Every July 4th weekend you need a shoehorn to get onto the board-walk." I handed him the note tossed through my window. "A message from granny."

"People think this crowd is for the 4th, but it's not." He read granny's cut and glued text. "This certainly fits her modus operandi."

"Wait a minute," I tilted back my fedora and scratched my scalp. "What do you mean these people aren't here for the 4th?"

"Some are, but most came for the Skee-Ball Quarterfinals tomorrow night."

"You're telling me, these people are here for a Skee-Ball game?"

He nodded still staring at the note. "Quarterfinals."

"Is that why you keep wearing that God-awful shirt?" Every time he turned his back into the sun, rays reflecting from his sequined OMB destroyed an orbiting satellite. I pulled down my hat to try and protect my eyes. "What were you saying about her M.O.? Have you seen other notes?"

"No, but this fits the council's profile. Meticulous and polite with psychopathic tendencies."

"Slow down. We suspect her of cheating at Skee-Ball. Not being a serial killer."

He waved the note in front of me. "How much more do you think it would take to push her over the edge?"

A crowd gathering outside the door to Zoiker's arcade stole my attention from the tinker's rambling. "Anything Skee-Ball related going on at Zoiker's, this afternoon?"

"No, why?" He followed my gaze up the boardwalk. "Nothing sanctioned, anyway. Think we should check it out?"

I answered with my feet, but couldn't get within fifty yards of the door. A crowd tried to squeeze its way into an arcade capable of holding less than a fifth of those trying to enter.

The tinker caught up to me, patted my back, and slipped past me. "Just stay close, Jimmy."

Those in front of us shimmied to one side or the other when they saw the tinker's shirt. He worked its magic, moving into and through Zoiker's like a Jet from Westside Story, until we reached the back wall lined with Skee-Ball games. There, with her blue perm, propped by her walker, and dressed in muumuued glory, stood Skee-Ball Granny. No one in the arcade played a game, spoke a word, or seemed capable of breaking his or her stare from this master working her machine. Even the video games surrounding her fell silent.

Granny peered at the scoreboard flashing "500," licked her lips, and squared herself for another roll. A substantial backside wiggled beneath a billowy pink muumuu printed with gingerbread men and rolling pins. "Granny needs a centennial."

The ball left her hand, bounced from the side of the lane, launched from the ramp, flew over the scoring bull's-eye in the backstop's center, and thunked into a tiny 100-point hole in the upper corner. She lifted her hands above her head revealing ankle stockings and white sneakers, made a whoop-whoop sound, and turned to bask in the crowd's cheers.

The tinker leaned toward me and said from the side of his mouth, "That was nothing, just a two-thirds bank-shot roll with a backspin to the opposite corner."

The spectators watched granny pluck another ball from the return chute, but not this detective. I observed the crowd. Looked for the person not as impressed as the others. The only person appearing to have seen it all before. The one concentrating on something other than granny. Didn't take me long to find a guy watching the Skee-Ball machine and not her. Watching so closely he didn't appear to blink.

I measured him up pretty quickly. He sported a black mullet and the kind of long greasy hair reminding me I needed to change the oil in my Studebaker. A wire snaked from his t-shirt's collar up into his mane. I tried to inch a little closer without much luck, so I simply stood and watched. When he turned his head slightly to the left, I could see the wire ended in a small loop. His hand moved in his pocket.

I took out my phone and snapped photos of granny—just one more admiring fan—but turned every so often to capture the guy with the antenna. Meanwhile, granny lit the scoreboard sinking balls into the hundred and fifty holes in rapid succession.

I tapped the tinker's arm. "You always bring your own balls to the arcade?"

"Of course."

"Granny do the same?"

"No professional would use someone else's balls."

Granny saw me. Her adulation-fueled smile faded for a moment. She wagged a finger, said something to a little boy standing next to her, turned her attention back to the game, and massaged a wood ball like a major league pitcher looking for the perfect grip.

"Hey, mister." The little boy had somehow crawled through the crowd and tugged at my coat. "The Skee-Ball lady wanted me to give you these." He handed me a wad of Zoiker's prize tickets. "She said you should get yourself something nice."

I couldn't help but glance at the glass prize case filled with plastic spider rings, glow sticks, and stuffed bears. "Tell you what, kid. You can have these tickets if you do something for me."

"Yeah, what?"

"See that guy with his hands in his pockets? Go over there, wait for my signal, and then bump into him."

"Why?"

"Just make it look like an accident." I peeled some tickets from the wad. "Half now and half when the job is done."

He dove back into the crowd and surfaced right where I had wanted him. Granny's arm began its downward swing toward her release point. I gave my little arcade urchin a nod. He threw his body chest-first into the mullet-headed man's thigh—overdoing it a little, in my opinion—knocking him off balance. Granny's Skee-Ball went wild bouncing from the top of the cage at the end of the ramp then disappearing into the big ten-point hole at the bottom of the board.

Breathless silence.

No one moved.

Women and men began to weep.

A priest recited the Rosary.

You would've thought the Hindenburg went down over town hall.

"Good work," I said to the boy. He took the rest of the tickets and looked up at me with red eyes and a tear on his cheek. "What just happened? What did you make me do?"

"Nothing, son. Everyone has a bad toss now and again." I took the tinker's arm. "Let's get out of here."

"No way, Jimmy. This is just getting good."

"It's not going to happen again. We need to leave."

The tinker pushed past me working his shirt and opening a path back onto the boardwalk.

"You were right," I said to him, "something isn't right with her."

"It's about time you came to your senses. I'm telling you, she's a free game away from baking our tongues into a pie."

"That's not what I meant." I showed the tinker the photos on my phone. "Have you ever seen this guy before?"

"Looks familiar. I think he's one of her groupies."

"He's not a groupie, and she isn't working alone." I dialed a number.

"Who are you calling?"

"My nephew."

Red-headed, bespectacled, freckled, thirteen, and a genius, my nephew sat on the chair in the corner of my office. A large gym bag full of gizmos and gadgets lay open at his feet. The tinker stood in the doorway rocking on his heels with his arms folded.

"Can't you just stand still?" I asked the tinker.

"The quarterfinals are in a few hours, Jimmy. What are you going to do? The Skee-Ball Council is counting on you. I'm counting on you."

I took off my hat and smoothed its brim. "So," I said to my nephew, "what do you think?"

"It sounded possible when you described it over the phone, but I don't know, Uncle Jimmy." He swung his feet kicking at his bag of gadgets. "By the way, my mom is picking me up at ten."

"Yeah, okay."

"She said no later than that. I have a recorder lesson at 8:00 tomorrow morning, and she said no junk food. Last time I came home with hives."

"On my honor." I crossed my heart. "Now, back to granny. Is it at all possible? A radio-controlled Skee-Ball?"

"You're talking some serious tech, Uncle Jimmy. An outer shell with an interior sphere separated by precisely-machined steel bearings in an oil-bath. Inside the sphere would be a gyroscope, short-range receiver, servomechanism, small but powerful magnets to move a weight changing the ball's center of gravity, and you'd need a very strong battery. Lithium-ion, at least."

The tinker dropped his arms. "That has to be it. Magnets inside the balls move liquid mercury around, and they use gravity to guide the balls toward the high-point holes."

My nephew shook his head. "Liquid mercury isn't very magnetic. It would have to be metal shavings of some sort. The weight wouldn't be enough to change the ball's course dramatically, but it could be enough to give someone with a true talent for the sport an edge over the competition."

"Did you say, *for the sport?*" I put my feet on my desk, my chair squealed a complaint, and I pointed at the tinker. "Have you been talking to him?"

The tinker stepped up to my desk and leaned on his fists. "Always with the condescension. I'll ask again, what are you going to do about that woman?"

I slid open a drawer, reached for my bottle of Jack Daniels, glanced at my nephew sitting in the corner, and slid the drawer shut with a sigh. "The moment the guy with the hidden antenna got bumped, granny's throw went wild. No matter how they're doing this, we need to cut the connection between them."

"That's where I come in. Right, Uncle Jimmy?" My nephew pulled from his bag an old transistor radio wired to a lantern battery.

The gadget drew the tinker's attention away from me. "What have you got there?"

"I put this together on the way over. It should interrupt transmissions to a crystal-controlled superheterodyne receiver like the ones used to control old model boats and planes. I also added a broad-spectrum jammer in case they're using a more modern 2.4 gigahertz system."

"You built that on the way over?" I asked. "You live fifteen minutes away."

"It's the best I could do on short notice."

I stood, picked up my hat, and said to the tinker, "Call your Skee-Ball Council. They're going to want to be at the quarterfinals, tonight."

Spectators packed Zoiker's. The tinker's team shirt and leather handbag of family balls got the three of us inside and right up to the stanchions and red velvet ropes dividing the audience from the Skee-Ball machines. My private eye senses registered and measured every glance and twitch of every person we passed.

"Granny isn't here, yet," I said. "That guy helping her isn't around, either."

The tinker stepped over the rope, turned, and placed his hand on my chest. "I'm afraid I can't get you any closer."

"This will do." I hiked up my pants and scoped-out the best spot to watch the audience. "Good luck!"

"Luck has nothing to do with this, Jimmy. Just give me an equal playing field, and I'll bring granny to her artificial knees." The tinker strutted to the other Ocean Mist Ballers and joined in a testosterone-laced round of high-fives.

"Where do you want me, Uncle Jimmy?" My nephew's voice cracked, and he adjusted his glasses. He didn't seem to like the press of people, the air you could cut with a knife, or maybe knowing granny and her sidekick would soon commit a crime, or something close to it.

"Come over here." I led him to the prize case managed by a young lady wearing a red apron. "Miss, what do you say you let my nephew sit back there in that corner?" I slipped her a Lincoln. "He doesn't like crowds."

"What, you want some game tokens for this?"

She wasn't a sap. "Alright," I gave her another Lincoln, "but that's all you're getting." I turned to my nephew and pointed to a spot about ten feet away. "I'll be watching over there. When I give you the signal," I tapped the side of my nose, "that's when you jam the transmission."

"Sure, Uncle Jimmy. What's the signal?"

"When I tap my nose."

"Oh."

The arcade's lights went low and a hush fell over the room. Fog spewed from machines tucked in corners. The public address system blasted a melody taking me back to Sunday nights laying in front of my grandparents' television. My grandmother would proclaim, "Bubbles in the Wine," when the theme music for Lawrence Welk's weekly hour of jazz began.

Granny entered. The crowd cheered and parted before her. An over-sized purse hung from a walker handle, and a ball bag strikingly similar to the tinker's hung from the other. Her accomplice, the man with the wire, sported a fresh t-shirt and followed at a comfortable, inculpable, distance. His black mullet glistened. Tension lines across his forehead and around his eyes betrayed his nonchalant stride, a stressed conman trying to look natural on his way to the big score. His free hand fidgeted with something in his pocket. Probably some type of controller.

Granny didn't compete in the first two rounds, but the tinker did, and he owned his Skee-Ball machine, dropping ball after ball in the fifty-hole and even sinking a nearly impossible hundred-pointer in the upper left corner. One of Zoiker's managers wrote the tinker's name and his score on a dry-erase board resting on an easel—the highest number of the night, so far.

An hour's worth of triumphs and heartbreaks played out in front of me before granny hobbled up to her machine. The wire antenna rose from the back of her accomplice's shirt and into his hair.

I glanced at my nephew. He sat on a milk crate behind the girl at the counter, his eyes fixed on her backside, and probably didn't even know the competition had begun. Deep in my sport coat pocket I found a stray honey-roasted peanut, which I bounced off of his forehead. He looked in my direction then at granny and gave me a thumbs-up.

I didn't want to play our card too soon, so I let granny have her first roll. She sank a hundred-pointer. The tinker scowled at me. Granny drew back for her second roll. I tapped my nose giving my nephew the signal. Her ball jumped from the ball hop, smacked against the backstop missing the bullseye target, and rolled into the gutter.

The crowd gasped.

I gave her the next roll, which she sank into a fifty. She drew back for her fourth roll, and I tapped my nose again. This time, she scored an amateurish twenty-pointer.

A sharp crack came from behind the prize counter, the sound you hear when a squirrel crawls into a transformer atop a telephone pole. My nephew's red, usually curly, hair stood upright. Eyes as big as saucers. The girl at the counter used her apron to snuff small flames dancing on the makeshift jamming machine.

I turned back to the Skee-Ball competition.

The tinker read my face. Tears welled in his eyes.

A whiff of something acrid hit my nostrils like the smell of lightening lingering after a thunderstorm. My nephew had emerged from behind the prize case and stood at my side. Little puffs of smoke rose from his clothes and hair.

"What a rush, Uncle Jimmy."

Granny finished her game with a few more fifties and a forty, nowhere near enough to put her name on the board, but she still had another full game to play. Her balls rolled down the return chute smacking together like a wooden Newton's Cradle. She massaged the first ball.

I turned my head. I couldn't watch.

Granny dropped the ball into a hundred-point hole. The crowd went wild. Her gyrating victory dance, the way her muumuu swirled about her octogenarian curves, made me sick.

Is there no justice in this world?

The man next to me gulped a gallon-sized soda with reckless abandon. My highly-tuned mind connected his drink with my pursuit of the pick pocket mime through Happy Land, the little girl clutching her plastic purse, her concern for my heart, and what I needed to do.

"Hey, buddy," I said, "I'll give you a buck for the rest of your soda."

"Are you serious?"

"Alright, two bucks." I pulled my National Organization of Investigators and Researchers identification card from my pocket. "Official business."

The guy handed me his soda, and I gave him the Washingtons.

No one moved aside with my polite "excuse me's," so I muscled open a path. Granny's accomplice saw me coming, eyed the soda in my hand, covered his face with his arms, and screamed like a little girl. I doused him with orange-smelling sugar-water. Sparks, pops and crackles from his pocket, and more than a few insults from surrounding spectators, halted the competition.

"Sorry, there pal," I said while trying to wipe soda from his shirt. "So many people here, I think I tripped over someone."

The soggy man smelling of burnt plastic with a hint of orange looked at granny. "Nanna, my balls. What do I do?"

"That's Grits!" she yelled. "I told you to watch out for him!"

"You're her grandson?" I tilted the empty mega-cup in granny's direction. "Must be something to have a star athlete in the family."

"Ladies and gentlemen," Zoiker's manager said into a microphone, "the previous ball will be removed from the scoreboard, and the house will grant a reroll. When you are ready, madam."

With the poisonous influences of machines stripped away, we arrived at the human essence of it all, the tinker's raw nerve and Skee-Ball skills pitted against an elderly woman wearing a muumuu.

Granny's next roll landed a fifty, as did her next. Two balls to go. She trailed the tinker by eighty. The crowd hushed. Held their breaths. The old woman stared into the ball in her hand, glanced at the backboard, shook her head, and took a step back from the machine. The crowd exhaled as one. Some nervous chatter spread through the arcade but stopped suddenly when granny approached the ramp, swung her arm, and rolled up the middle. Her ball bounced off the fifty's rubber ring, swung along the forty hole's lip, and landed in the thirty.

One ball left. Fifty points to tie, which might have meant a sudden death roll-off, but I really didn't know. Her only path to certain victory was a Hail Mary hundred pointer in an upper corner. Someone from far behind me began a slow clap. Others joined. The room filled with a beat growing in volume and tempo soon shaking the floor.

The moment the ball left her fingertips the clapping stopped, time itself slowed, and the sound of wood traversing wood filled the room. Granny went for the big one. All or nothing. The purest of silences befell Ocean Mist when the ball took flight from the ball hop making its way toward the corner hundred-point hole. The ball bounced from its rubber ring into the net above the sideboard and rolled to the bottom for ten.

The Ocean Mist Ballers went nuts. The tinker jumped so high I thought he'd hit his head on the ceiling tiles. Zoiker's manager placed a ring of petunias around the tinker's neck, and his teammates hoisted him onto their shoulders. I wished I could have celebrated with him, but I had to finish the job.

Granny scanned the arcade looking confused, not quite registering her defeat, and only regained her wits when she saw me. She scowled and scooped her balls from the return chute. With ball bag on one wrist and purse on the other, she grabbed her walker's handles and made a shuffling dash for the door passing her still bewildered grandson.

"This isn't over, Grits," she hissed at me.

"Right you are, granny." I gave her some space then exited to the board-walk where I found her standing alone in the center of a wide circle formed by robed and hooded figures carrying torches—The Skee-Ball Council.

One of them extended her hand from deep within a crimson sleeve and pointed. "Skee-Ball Granny, turn over your grandson's balls."

Granny pivoted trying to find an opening in the ring of council members. "Police," she cried, "help me! Police!" Even if there had been a gap between the staff-wielding council members, she would never have made it through the hundreds of gawkers behind the circle.

"The police have no jurisdiction here," the council lady said. "Not over Skee-Ball."

I stepped up behind granny. "It's over. Just give them what they want."

She tossed her Skee-Ball bag at the speaker's feet.

The council lady picked up the bag. "You have proven yourself unworthy of the game. Depart this boardwalk and never return."

Each robed figure threw down a small canister of flash powder. I averted my eyes, but not fast enough. The flashes burned white spots onto my retinas. When my sight returned and the smoke from the powder cleared, someone from the crowd said, "Um, we can still see all of you."

The council members looked at one another, raised their torches, formed a line, and processed down the boardwalk.

I adjusted my hat. "Well, granny, now it's over."

The Lighthouse Keeper's Ghost

Part 1: Quest to the Tower

"I've been waiting seven months for this." Waves of heat washed over me from a row of steam pots hanging over a steel fire ring in a ramshackle pavilion behind an even more ramshackle seafood joint, Chicken Neck Nellie's Crab Shack.

"First of the season, and always for you, Jimmy." Nellie's nickname Chicken Neck had nothing to do with her appearance and everything to do with her crabbing obsession, chicken necks being the favored bait with locals. Ironically, Nellie didn't have a neck because of her previous vocation, professional body building.

The distinctive salt and curry-like smell of Old Bay seasoning made my mouth water. "Seems the season starts later every year."

"Maybe if you went neckin' with me, you wouldn't have to wait so long."

"I'm not that kind of guy, Nellie."

"You know what I mean." Nellie slid her hands into yellow oven mitts. "You still sweet on that girl?"

"What girl?"

"That librarian, Angela. Always dresses so fancy."

Angela's skirts and shoes probably seemed fancy compared to Nellie's collection of frayed jean cut-offs and muck boots.

"All of Ocean Mist knows it, Jimmy. Why can't you just admit it?"

"How are the crabs looking?"

She lifted a lid, fanned away steam, added water from an old tin cup, stirred the crabs, and replaced the lid. "Another few minutes."

Nellie's Crab Shack lived up to its name. A roof missing most of its shingles protected picnic tables covered in brown-paper, folding chairs, and a cash register on a card table—a place mostly for locals who didn't care about atmosphere. Locals with connections knew the real action took place out back at the grills and fire rings.

The tinker rounded the shack at a full run and skidded to a halt. "I've been looking all over for you."

"Here I am. Some of my detective skills finally rubbing off on you?"

He said something involving the word *missing,* but I really didn't care.

Nellie hoisted a pot onto a crumbling brick knee wall encircling the fires. Her arms bulged with all manner of stone-like muscles under well-browned skin. She tipped the pot onto a metal grate draining briny water from a healthy pile of jumbo males. Fat crustaceans gleamed red in the afternoon sun. Nellie had really outdone herself.

"Are you listening?" The tinker took me by the arm and seemed as steamed as the crabs. "Angela is missing."

"Okay, take it easy." I reached for my cell phone and dialed Angela's number. "She's probably reading one of her books and forgot we live in the real world."

"Well, she isn't reading at the library. It's closed."

My call went to voicemail. I dialed again, and my heart rate increased with each ring. Her recorded greeting played. Concern overpowered the usual magic I felt when hearing her sultry voice. "Hey, doll, call me as soon as you get this."

"Well?" asked the tinker.

I locked eyes with him for a moment then turned to Nellie. "As much as I'm itching for your crabs, duty calls."

I SHOOK THE LOCKED LIBRARY DOOR BY its doorknob then looked in through the big picture window. No lights. No bookish visitors. Angela didn't take vacation days. I couldn't think of a time I saw her ill. She never closed the library without some kind of sign or note on the door. My heart turned to lead.

"Do you have a key?" the tinker asked.

"A key? Why would I have a key to a place like this?"

"Well, you know. You and Angela."

"What about me and Angela?" I stepped back from the door, looked around the old brick library's front, peered through its window again, and peeked around the building's side. "Follow me." I plowed a path between chest-high shrubbery and the library's wall toward the back then tapped a window pane above my head. "Help me up."

"What do you mean?"

"Give me a boost to that window."

Angela had complained about its busted latch for months.

"Are you serious?"

"Cup your hands, and I'll—."

"No way. I told you to join the YMCA with me."

"Don't you think your fat jokes are getting old?"

The tinker stepped back, looked me up and down, and started to speak, but something behind me caught his eye. He retrieved a metal wheelbarrow propped against a nearby shed and flipped it over under the window. I stepped on the barrow, tried lifting the window, and banged on its frame with my palm, which persuaded the lower sash to give enough for me to pry my fingers underneath and shove it open.

With both hands gripping the sill, I pulled upward and pressed my penny loafers against the bricks. Must have been my worn soles, because no matter how quickly I moved my feet I couldn't gain enough traction to scale the wall.

"You keep that up and you won't need to join the YMCA."

"Push."

"Push what?"

"Just help me up."

The tinker drove his shoulder into my backside raising me enough to reach through the window, grab the side of a bookcase, and drag myself inside and over the back of an upholstered reading chair. I took off my hat and sat on the chair to catch my breath.

"You okay, Jimmy?"

"Yeah, I'm fine. Meet me around front. I'll get the door." The library was dark, especially the back part where book shelves obscured some of the old windows. I pulled out my cell phone and tapped on the little flashlight picture. The phone cast just enough light to show dust dancing in the gloom. "Angela?"

Black shadowy corners everywhere. Any perp could be lying in wait. Ready to pounce. I would have to rely on my keen senses. Listen for breathing. Be aware of any air moving across my skin alerting me to movement. "You in here, doll?"

Having watched Angela close before walking her home, I knew where to find the first floor's light switches behind the circulation desk and headed there. I stopped at her office door and shined my light through the window. Several open books lay strewn across her desk, a definite sign our fussy librarian had met foul play. She never left a book laying open anywhere. Ever.

"Hey—." The voice came sharp and quick and out of nowhere.

My whole body lurched, I fell against the office door, and my heart kicked into overdrive like tramping the accelerator on a sportscar. Sometimes, every life experience, every ounce of a person's being, can be gathered into a single moment of action, and this detective focused all of it into a raised left fist, a boxer's stance, and an aggressive sweep of the lobby with my single diode's light.

The tinker stood in front of me with his hands in his cargo short's pockets. "Did you find her?"

"Don't do that."

"Do what?"

"How did you get in here?" I felt like a helium balloon until my body burned away the unneeded adrenaline.

"Found a key. I tripped over one of those hollow rock things on my way back through the bushes. Looks a lot like the one I use to hide a spare key to my house." The tinker flipped on the lights. "You don't look so good."

"Just one switch. Turn off the others. Did you lock the door behind you?"

"Why?"

"Go lock it. We don't need anyone coming in here asking questions about books."

I made a quick sweep of the lobby. Nothing seemed out of place, no evidence of a struggle, but the previous day's headlines graced the newspaper rack.

The tinker reached into the circulation desk's book return slot and pulled out a paperback. "What do you think of Hitchcock?"

"Never heard of him." I made my way back to Angela's office and tried the knob. Locked. "Any chance you found a key for this, too?"

"Nope."

The jam gave under my shoulder. Splinters of pine showered the floor.

"Jimmy, take it easy." The tinker followed me into the small windowless room.

I glanced at the filing cabinet hiding the tunnel leading to the archives. Didn't look like anyone had messed with it. The thought of Bumper and Elbow Patches having kidnapped Angela crossed my mind, and I cursed myself for not having figured out how to put away those two for good.

The tinker turned on a desk lamp. "Is Angela's desk always this messy?"

"No." Books of stitched fabric and leather covers opened to thinned and browned pages lay on her desk.

"Either someone else used her desk," said the tinker, "or something spooked her to leave it this way."

"No one else is allowed in here, and Angela doesn't get spooked." I lifted one of the books and turned it over in my hands.

"You know how to use that?"

"Funny." I sat in her chair and sifted through the tools of the librarian trade organized neatly inside the desk.

"Do you think she would want you going through her drawers?"

"I'm a private eye. I go through a lot of people's drawers."

"Take a look at this." The tinker held up a small notepad of scribbled sketches and numbers. "This drawing looks like a room here in the library. See all of the shelves?"

I cocked my head to look at the sketch from a different angle and could tell easily which room Angela had sketched, the one under our feet, but I couldn't tell the tinker. "What are those numbers?"

"It's a pattern." He bit his lip, flipped the pad around, and smacked it with the back of his hand. "Volume numbers and page numbers. This one is underlined."

The entry matched what appeared to be the oldest book on the desk. When I opened the leather cover, its pages folded out making it more of a folio than an actual book. "These are an architect's drawings. Hand-drawn." I flipped through a couple. All drawings of the archives.

The tinker pointed at a page. "You see that cross section?"

"I'm not blind. It's right under my nose."

"It's a basement, so it isn't a building around here."

He tried to take the folio, but I yanked it from his hand. "Why not?"

"Can't build underground in Ocean Mist, Jimmy. Too close to the water. Sea level and everything."

"Tell that to Edward."

"Surf Services is way up Washington Avenue. We're talking at least forty feet above the water table. Maybe that's why it's underground?"

"Maybe." I put down the folio and leaned forward. "Are all these books about architecture?"

The tinker picked up a book, looked at its spine, picked up another, and opened to the first page. "No, this is about lighthouses."

"Lighthouses?"

"Yeah, you know, the towers with the lights to keep ships—."

"I know what a lighthouse is."

The tinker pointed to the footer of a drawing in the folio. "Can you read that writing? I think it's a name."

"Fred Ferdinand."

He used the numbers on the notepad to check some pages in the books. "All of these references are about this Ferdinand guy." He stabbed his finger at a photo of the Ocean Mist Lighthouse taken long before it started falling into the marsh north of town. "Looks like he designed and built ours."

Why would Angela be interested in the Lighthouse? I folded my arms, leaned back in the chair, and scanned the room to be sure my attention on the books didn't keep me from noticing other clues. Nothing caught my eye. "Seems it's our only lead."

"What do you mean?" Even in the desk lamp's yellow light, I could tell the tinker went pale.

"We need to check out the lighthouse."

"I'm not going out there."

"Why not?"

"It's haunted. Didn't you see that episode of Delaware Ghost Snatchers?"

"How do you snatch a ghost?" I got up from the chair. "Not like you can slap cuffs on one and toss him into a holding cell."

"They don't snatch ghosts. It's more of a history-type show. They—."

I waved-off his answer. "Don't have time for history shows. I live in the here and now."

"Well, you should've found time for this one. The Ocean Mist Lighthouse guided ships toward the Delaware Bay for almost two hundred years, and it kept a lot of ships from running aground on the sand bars between us and Lewes."

"So, what makes you think its haunted?" Ghost stories were as plentiful as sand fleas around town, but I pretended interest to keep the tinker occupied while I tried to think.

"It's like all haunted lighthouses. For every soul signaled away and kept safe, a darkened lighthouse claims a soul until its keeper returns to restore its light."

"How poetic."

"Besides, the swamp swallowed the road leading to the lighthouse years ago. There's no way to get out there."

"How sure are you of that?"

"Positive."

I couldn't dismiss the possibility someone dragged Angela out there. Elbow Patches. Bumper. My heart started to race, again. *We're going to need waders,* I thought while folding and stuffing some of the lighthouse drawings into my pocket. I checked my watch. *We'll need flashlights. Maybe even a rope or two.* "Can we get there by water? What about the *Tinker IV*?"

He shook his head. "Parasailing accident."

"What is it with you and boats?"

"I live hard, Jimmy."

WE TOOK THE STUDEBAKER NORTH ON FIRST Street toward the marsh and swung through a development of swanky houses, much like the ones on the south end of town where the tinker took me to see The Skee-Ball Council. Something in my brain clicked so loud I could hear it, or maybe it was the Studebaker's carburetor. "What can you tell me about the house where The Skee-Ball Council meets?"

"What are you talking about?"

"The cult with the robes, torches, and secret club house. Where you took me when granny scammed all the arcades."

The tinker sighed, folded his arms, and leaned toward me while keeping his gaze through the windshield. "It's best we never speak of The Skee-Ball Council, Jimmy."

My detective brain made a connection the average Joe would never make. The council met in an underground room made of stone, a lot like the library's archive, and it's pretty close to the water. I couldn't let go of the idea.

"The houses on the south end of town are all new houses," I said.

"What?"

"All new construction."

"So?"

"Any mention in those history-type shows about old buildings on the south edge of town?" *No one would build a room like that these days, but a person might build a house over one.* "Maybe near The Skee-Ball Council's secret clubhouse?"

"It's not a clubhouse, and I told you—."

"Just, answer this one question, and I'll forget all about The Skee-Ball Council."

"Promise?"

"Absolutely."

"No."

"No what?"

"No mention of an old building near The Skee-Ball Council in any shows I've seen."

The Studebaker hugged a lazy curve pointing us toward a thick green tree-line marking the edge of the marsh. "What else do you know about this lighthouse? From your television show?"

"You've grown up in Ocean Mist, Jimmy. You should know this history."

"Don't have much use for history. The past is the past."

"You haven't had much use for salads, either, and look where that's gotten you."

"Just tell me what you know."

The tinker sighed. "The ghost of an old lighthouse keeper haunts it."

"Why is that?"

"One of the last keepers—I forget his name—had a problem with the bottle. Sometimes, he got so drunk he couldn't keep the lighthouse's oil lamp lit. One night, a ship ran aground on a sandbar throwing some fishermen overboard. One got tangled in the lines and drowned. The dead fisherman turned out to be the keeper's son."

"This history or legend?"

"A little bit of both, I guess. Sailors and fishermen sometimes report seeing a light come from the top of the lighthouse on real dark nights. The light lasts a minute or so then goes out, but no one on shore ever says they can see it."

"That's all you got?"

"I've also heard stories about a figure with a lantern walking between the run-down keeper's house and the lighthouse."

"That could be anyone."

"No way, Jimmy. The only way to get out to the light and keeper's houses—the ruins, anyway—is with a small boat or at low tide by foot, and that's foolish. The marsh is nothing but thick grass and mud."

"We're going to have to find a way."

"And, it's protected land."

"Protected for what?"

"Water snake nesting area."

"You're making that up."

The tinker shook his head.

"Why is Angela so interested in the lighthouse?"

"We don't know that she is, Jimmy. It's just your hunch."

"It's where the evidence is leading us."

Roadside gravel and bits of shells crunched under the Studebaker's smooth tires as I eased us to a halt. Air smelling of plant rot and dead fish poured through my open window. I got out, hiked up my pants, and took in the scenery. Lewes' distant wind turbine stood motionless in thick air hanging above brackish water. Swamp grass had overcome a shed-sized *Dead End* sign like everything else left unattended on this end of town.

The lighthouse stood much farther from the road than I had expected.

I propped my elbows on the car's hot metal roof. "Why do you think the lighthouse is set back so far into the marsh?"

"It didn't use to be. The marsh just keeps growing."

"What do you mean, keeps growing?"

"It's alive, Jimmy." He stared off over the brush. "It's alive."

I followed his stare, which went nowhere.

"Okay," I said, "let's get this show on the road." I loosened my tie, slipped out of my sport coat, and kicked off my shoes to wrestle my legs into heavy green-rubber waders borrowed from Nellie. The tinker lifted the suspenders over my shoulders so I could snap each to the bib, and I returned the favor before putting my shoes in my pack and slipping back into my sport coat.

My patience ran thin watching the tinker fuss with his rope, hiking poles, water bottle, and flashlights, and I scowled at the sun for moving so quickly down the western sky. I imagined Angela bound at the top of the lighthouse, her cries for help swept away by the ocean's winds. *She could be out there all alone—or worse. Elbow Patches and Bumper could be grilling her about old recipe books.*

"We're burning daylight," I said. "Lead the way."

The tinker parted face-high grass tanned with road dust and picked his way down an embankment of blue-gray granite boulders quarried from somewhere inland. I followed him to ground covered by a thatch of dead grass and sticks held together by the gnarled roots of stunted pine and sumac. The tinker probed the tight weave with his rubber boot.

"What's wrong?"

"I told you, this is a water snake nesting area."

"I thought you made that up."

He pointed to a Delaware Natural Resources sign to our right.

DANGER!
WATER SNAKE NESTING AREA
ENTRY PROHIBITED

"Oh." I looked around my feet and felt my heart skip a beat when I wondered if fangs could pierce our waders. "You see any snakes?"

"All of these sticks and roots—everything looks like snakes, and why do I have to go first?"

"You know more about the marsh than I do."

"Just because I watched an episode of Ghost Snatchers doesn't make me a herpetologist."

What a strange time to bring up something so awkward. "I know a good doctor—."

"No, Jimmy, a herpetologist. Someone who studies amphibians and snakes."

"Yeah, okay. Just watch your step."

We pushed through the chin-high trees. The first thirty to forty yards into the marsh felt like walking on the bottom of a dried-out basket, and over the next twenty yards the basket became spongey with black water gurgling up around my feet. Ground vines with yellow and white flowers twisted through the thatch. Patches of cabbage-like plants with waxy leaves appeared here and there in the swampy spots.

The ground dropped a few inches more onto a mudflat, probably covered at high tide, where we stopped to decide our next move. Cattails and brown reeds sprouted in clumps dotting an expanse of dark still pools and soggy earth. Water lilies by the thousands created floating green paths winding to nowhere.

The light and keeper's houses stood upon a raised bump of land at the marsh's heart and at a distance farther than I would want to walk even if not slogging through a snake nesting ground. If the tinker was right about the marsh being alive and growing, it certainly kept its distance from the crumbling and leaning ruins.

The tinker pointed at a more or less straight ridge of mud and grass leading toward the lighthouse. "We should try over there. I think that was where they tried to build a road a few decades, ago."

"The whole thing sank, huh?"

"Road didn't last a year. Used all kinds of fill, pylons of all sizes, but the marsh swallowed whatever they dumped or drilled into the bottom."

A Cadillac-sized mosquito dove for my cheek. The constant buzzing around us made thinking next to impossible, and the sun striking my waders cooked my legs, which soaked my dress pants in sweat.

The tinker looked over his shoulder. "Do you think we should turn around? This is really slow going."

"Angela is out there."

"You think."

"I know."

The tinker plodded ahead sticking to the ridge of grasses growing from sand darkened by years of decayed plants. He stopped from time-to-time to poke around his feet with his hiking pole and consider options before hopping to the next perch of dirt.

We made some progress for about an hour until the tinker's foot slid from a crown of earth. He wobbled and flapped his arms like a wounded pelican. A face-plant to end all face-plants brought about a dramatic explosion of murky water, and the tinker disappeared.

I dropped to my knees. Plunged my hand into the mire searching for anything to grab. "Can you hear me?" I leaned farther over the water. No sign of him. "Swim for my voice!"

His head popped up between some lily pads, and he spewed a brew of decaying plants and insects back into the marsh. His coughing made every waterfowl within earshot quack, honk, and squawk and spurred them into flight across the Delaware Bay to the safety of New Jersey.

"Are you okay?"

The tinker nodded yet coughed up more bits of rotting leaves and bugs.

"Give me your hand."

He wiped a soggy weed from his forehead then reached awkwardly for me.

I pulled.

He didn't budge.

"Give me both hands."

Pulled again but no use.

"I can't move, Jimmy."

Water sloshed over the waistband of his filled waders. The water and his body weight rooted him into the bottom deeper than any of the salt-stunted trees ringing the marsh.

I tipped back my fedora and scratched my head. "Why didn't you watch where you were going?"

"I did. The ground just gave way." He smacked both fists into the water. "That's why they call this a marsh."

I knelt, worked my way to a seated position swinging my feet into the water, and pressed both palms into the dirt next to my thighs. Seemed pretty solid. "Can you reach a little farther?"

With firm grasps on the tinker's forearms, I leaned way back and pulled. My wader-covered butt cheeks gripped what might have been the only solid piece of dirt between the Studebaker and the lighthouse.

The tinker shot free of his waders and landed on my chest. A frightened cat couldn't have climbed my body faster to escape the water, and I could tell from the multi-colored dinosaurs passing my face he had left his cargo shorts in the waders.

I lay on my back for a moment, eyes closed, listening to the hum of insects. *I'm a private eye. A life-long detective. Why am I here dressed like the Gorton's Fisherman and crawling through snake-infested mud? Angela. That's right. Angela.*

I rolled onto my knees and found the tinker standing in his dino-boxers, fists on his hips, bathed in the light from a falling sun. His soaked Hawaiian shirt stuck fast to his scrawny torso. *Our newest superhero— Pathetic Man.*

"Can you reach my waders?" he asked.

"No, they're gone."

"How are we going to get my shorts?"

"We're not."

"I need my shorts, Jimmy."

I stood sounding like a rubbed balloon. "Come on, let's keep moving."

"It'll be dark, soon."

"Yeah, that's why we need to get to the lighthouse."

"No, Jimmy. We have to turn back. We can't be over there when it's dark."

"We have to be sure Angela isn't there." I handed him his pack.

He took out his sneakers. "After all of this, you really think she's out here?"

I grabbed the tinker's hiking pole from the goo, poked a clump of weeds, and took a leap of faith, the next of a couple hundred more in our path. "We're closer to the lighthouse than the road. I'm not going back."

The Lighthouse Keeper's Ghost

Part 2: A Tomb for Jimmy

We picked our way across the marsh gambling with each step, choosing each shock of grass and lump of bare earth more slowly and carefully than before the tinker's swim, until we reached a narrow stony beach encircling the lighthouse island.

Brush and scraggly trees held together a chest-high bank of sandy earth. Roots stuck from the bank, crooked arthritic fingers pointing back in the direction we had come. I grabbed and pulled some of those fingers to help me scale the dirt wall then crawled my way through thick weeds.

The tinker scrambled behind me rustling every branch, twig, and leaf in his path.

"Can you keep it down? People way over in Lewes can hear you."

"Look at my legs."

"Do I have to?"

"Didn't you see those thorns and burn hazel?" He rummaged through his backpack, retrieved a bottle, and poured water down his red and scraped bird legs.

I peeled off my rubber outerwear, fixed my dress pants, readjusted my belt, and slipped on my loafers. Professional look, professional performance. I held up the limp waders. "Want these?"

"Are you kidding? I could camp in those. A few tent poles and a little stove—."

"Yeah, okay. Why don't you go back and look for yours?"

"You said they were gone. Besides, I'm not going back into the marsh by myself."

Time wasn't our friend, so I didn't argue and made a quick visual sweep. Sized-up our options. The keeper's house didn't look to be more than a pile of old boards and loose stones. "We'll start with the lighthouse."

The tinker exchanged his water bottle for a flashlight from his backpack. "Lead the way."

We headed east, and I saw how the marsh had surrounded the island leaving only a few distant dunes to stand as the last barrier between marsh and ocean. I circled the lighthouse, reduced by the ravages of time to a leaning concrete tower, and found a gaping black rectangle where, judging by rusty hinges still bolted to a concrete frame, a heavy door once stood.

A persistent breeze complained in my ears, and I tried to ignore it while listening for other sounds from within the lighthouse. Didn't hear any cries for help, which relieved me a little. A little. I pulled a flashlight from my pack and reached into my sport coat pocket for the drawings I took from the library.

The tinker pointed his light into the doorway. "Well, are you going inside?"

"Give me a minute."

"It's cold out here. Loan me your pants for a while?"

"That's not going to happen." I added my light to the doorway and stepped into the damp concrete cylinder to find the ground floor empty except for a family of rats. They shrieked and scurried across some exposed joists then up through a hole in the wood plank ceiling. A drawing showed weights on ropes hanging from the lantern room at the top of the lighthouse through the floors' centers to where we stood. I shined my light up after the rats. The beam passed through at least one more floor but diffused too much after that for me to see anything.

The tinker scratched his head. "Are you really sure we need to—?"

"Yep."

He took a deep breath and let it out slowly making a blowing sound. "In for a penny, I guess." He went straight for a spiral iron staircase, took the railing in both hands, and tried to shake it. "Seems sturdy. You see anything up there?"

"Nothing." I cupped a hand around my mouth. "Angela?" Only the wind answered.

The tinker stepped back from the staircase and motioned with his hand. "After you."

I started to climb with the tinker trailing me. The first landing brought us to a doorway without a door. I stepped inside a semi-circular room and washed it with my flashlight. The drawings showed barrels stacked floor to ceiling, and I imagined each filled with whale oil. Nothing there, anymore.

We found the same with the bunk room off of the next landing, except a good portion of the room's ceiling had collapsed. More climbing took us past another empty room then to an opening in the staircase rail where the next landing should have been. Across the gap stood a shut door.

"That's strange."

"What do you see, Jimmy?"

"A door. The drawing shows this was the watch room, something like a study for the keeper."

"Want me to knock?"

"No, I don't want you to knock." I pointed my flashlight into the void beyond my toes knowing the long drop ended at a stone floor. "We can't get to it."

The sound of the tinker rummaging in his pack made me turn around.

"I have an idea." He pulled out a rope with a three-pronged hook tied to its end. "Stand back."

I shook my head and watched him throw his grapple, again and again, to try and hook the next twist of staircase above our heads. "For crying out loud, give me that." I climbed the stairs, hooked the grapple into the railing above the tinker, tied off the rope for good measure, and lowered the end to him. "Now what are you going to do?"

"Watch and learn, Jimmy." He wrapped the rope around his waist and tied some kind of knot no self-respecting Boy Scout would consider. "One, two, three!" He leapt across the void and slammed into the door with his shoulder. His breath escaped from both ends, and the impact bounced him into a slow spin.

"You okay?"

He moaned, and it sort of sounded like a *yeah*.

"Pretty sturdy door, huh?"

A few boards lay stacked next to my feet. I eyed the gap from above and thought maybe someone had cut the wood to fit between the staircase and the ends of some exposed joists under the door. When I lifted the boards, patterns in the dust told me someone had moved the pile within the last couple of days. I descended the stairs, dropped the wood, held the stair railing, reached for the band of the tinker's dinosaur boxers, and pulled him to safety.

"I felt the door give a little." He coughed. "I think I can get it open this time."

"Well, if you think so."

The tinker counted to three, swung, hit the door hard, and got the same painful result.

"I got a better idea." I retrieved the tinker again then fit the boards into the gap.

"You could've told me you found those?"

"Didn't want to discourage you."

A tentative step onto my bridge, a little bouncing motion, and I figured it would hold me. The door's iron latch gave freely, and its hinges groaned. I swept my light around the room without stepping across the threshold. The lower levels' collapsed ceilings didn't inspire trust.

An old roll-top desk sat next to a window-hole facing a quickly-darkening ocean. A few empty shelves. Bits of rags, a broken chair, and lots of foot prints in the thick dust around the desk. I back-tracked the prints with my flashlight's beam to a spot in front of my loafers. *Small shoes. Small feet. Definitely not Elbow Patches. Maybe Bumper?*

I shined my light on the desk again and noticed a chunk had been taken out of its side. The damaged wood appeared much lighter than the wood around it, like a fresh wound, and in the center of the wound a small dark rectangle. An empty compartment of some kind.

"Someone has been here," I said to the tinker.

"Aren't you going inside?"

"No, whatever was here is gone."

The next floor housed the service room— empty— leaving the

lantern room at the top. End of the line. Glass ground by decades of wind and rain crunched under my shoes. Just enough metal framing remained to show the dimensions of the once fish-tank-like chamber in the center. A sewer-grate-sized hole in the floor ringed by rusted iron bands marked where the large whale-oil lamp once warned-off sailors from sandbars and marked the approach to the Delaware Bay.

I stepped onto the widow's walk encircling the lighthouse and leaned on a wrought-iron rail to catch my breath from the long climb, which, with our slog through the marsh, had almost beaten me. Almost. I looked out over the island. Faint orange glows from the west horizon revealed a square of land resisting the marsh like the tinker had said.

"Hey," I turned to a shivering tinker squatting in the exposed lantern room, "you said the marsh spread out and around the lighthouse, right?"

"It grew, Jimmy. It's alive."

"Yeah, okay. So, why around the lighthouse? Why didn't the marsh just swallow it like it did the road and everything else?"

"This place is cursed."

"I thought you said it was haunted?"

The tinker shrugged. "Both."

"You see any ghosts around here?" I looked back out over the railing and traced the island with my gaze. *Definitely a square.* "We haven't seen any snakes, either."

"Just because you didn't see any, doesn't mean they're not there."

"Ghosts or snakes?"

"Both."

"You're not being much help." I watched the last of the sunset die. Pale light from a three-quarter moon turned the marsh into a maze of silver-gray grasses and black still pools.

"I'm cold," the tinker said.

"Of course, you are. You're in your underwear."

"I'm going down."

"There's nothing more for us up here, anyway."

We stepped out of the lighthouse into a concert of frogs, crickets, and squawking herons. A newly-risen moon and cloudless sky gave us just enough light to make out the silhouettes of brush and a few short and sickly trees marking the island's boundaries.

The tinker asked, "Are you going to tell me what's going on in that head of yours?"

"Just following the clues. Where my instincts tell us to go."

"Well, there is nowhere else to go."

"The keeper's house."

He threw a thumb toward the ruins. "That pile of sticks?"

"Yep."

"Angela isn't here, Jimmy. She's probably back at the library now dusting books and alphabetizing magazines." He grabbed my shoulder, yanked me around, and pointed. "What's that?"

Something dark moved along the island's edge about thirty yards from us. A figure. I swore it wasn't there a moment ago. My keen private eye senses would have never missed movement so close. The figure paused, turned, and walked slowly toward us.

"Angela?" I called.

"Quiet, Jimmy. That's not Angela."

A light winked on near the figure's waist. Not a focused light, like a flashlight, but more like a lantern.

The tinker's hand trembled on my shoulder. "That's the lighthouse keeper's ghost."

"Of course, it is." I waved. "Hey, buddy."

The figure stopped.

The tinker ducked back into the lighthouse. "What are you doing?"

I folded my arms and squared my chest, "If it's the ghost, he probably wants into the lighthouse."

The tinker jumped from the doorway and spun—a groundhog caught in the open and without a hole. "We have to get out of here!"

The figure lifted its lantern revealing a black oil-skin coat like fishermen wore a hundred years ago. The light hung for a moment near the hood's opening where there should have been a face.

I dropped my arms. "You might be right about this guy." A chill spread from my spine to my fingers and toes. "Are you the lighthouse keeper's ghost?"

"What's it to you?"

"He's not in a good mood, Jimmy."

I stepped to the side and pulled the tinker out from behind me. "If he's a ghost, do you think he's ever in a good mood?"

The tinker must have dug pretty deep to find some courage. "Are you the drunk keeper whose son fell off a fishing boat?" Misdirected courage, but courage nonetheless.

"I wasn't drunk, kid."

The ghost extended his lantern toward the tinker. The hood tilted downward. "What's with the big lizard?"

The tinker looked toward his feet.

"He's talking about your boxers."

The tinker put his hands on his hips and stuck out his chin. "I like dinosaurs."

The figure grunted, lowered its lantern, and resumed his slow approach.

"He's still coming toward us." The tinker slipped behind me, again. "What do we do?"

"The keeper's house. Fast!"

We ploughed through knee-high weeds. Tripped over unseen rocks and sticks until we reached the ruins.

The tinker cast his flashlight beam back toward the lighthouse. "Did he follow us?"

"I don't think so," I managed between wheezes.

"You okay, Jimmy?"

"Pollen is killing me."

"You picked up hay fever in the lighthouse?"

"Just give me a minute."

The keeper's house, abandoned in the middle of a swamp for a century, had turned into a heap of field stones, rotting beams, and clapboards. I traced the surviving foundation with my flashlight then stepped through what might have once been the front doorway. The tinker didn't follow me. "Are you coming?"

He whipped his head back and forth between the keeper's house and lighthouse so quickly I swore I heard a rattle. "Where do you think he's going?"

"That old guy?"

"Yeah, the ghost."

"I don't know, to do ghost things? Who cares? Are you going to help me, or do you want to go back and ask about his to-do list?"

"Okay," the tinker ran both hands into his hair and held on for dear life, "but I still don't know what you think we're going to find."

Professionals like me looked for patterns, anything a bit more than the random, even when searching through a collapsed building, and I found one of those patterns. Boards had been tossed aside to make a path. I pointed with my flashlight's beam. "You see this?"

The tinker peered around me. "Someone stacked those."

"Sure didn't collapse that way."

"The piles are even arranged by size. Someone really uptight. Maybe Angela was here?"

"What, exactly, do you mean by that?"

"Easy, Jimmy." The tinker swallowed hard. "Just that she's a librarian, and all. They have to be super organized."

"Uh-huh."

The path led us to a cleared spot of sturdy oak floor, which surprised me given the decay around us. The floor must have been well-covered until recently, but that couldn't have been enough to keep the wood from rotting. I tapped my loafer against it then stomped. *An airspace below us? Something keeping the damp ground from the wood?* A glint stopped the sweep of my light. A small square of mortared bricks, an iron plate, and a key hole with a key protruding from it.

"Take a look at this." I pulled out the key and raised it for the tinker to see. Wrought iron and its head stamped with a symbol resembling a lighthouse.

"That's like the one for Surf Services."

"Sure is." I put the key in the hole and turned it. Sounds of chains tightening, misaligned gears grinding, and pulleys squealing for oil made me step back.

"What's happening, Jimmy?"

"We're about to find out."

A section of the floor under the tinker's feet began to fall away like a slow-moving elevator. The tinker's knees buckled, but he recovered and scrambled up out of the growing opening.

I jumped down and waved for him. "Get down here."

The tinker shrugged, tossed his pack to me, and jumped.

We descended a shaft made of stones fitted so tightly I couldn't see any mortar in the joints. Moonlight gave way to black. I twisted the end of my flashlight adjusting the lens to give me a wide beam.

Chains attached to each of the platform's corner's fed into some hidden mechanism above our heads. Two more chains passed through holes in the platform and into the darkness below us. More grinding and squealing until we bumped to a stop at the mouth of a tunnel barely wide enough for a man of my stature.

"Follow me," I said. Our weight leaving the platform triggered a release sounding like the catch of a Saturday Night Special. The elevator flew topside and slammed back into place. "Well, that was dramatic."

The tinker tugged on my arm. "Look at this." He pointed his beam to an iron plate embedded in the wall. An empty key hole. "Did you bring the key?"

"No."

"Now what, Mr. Follow Me?"

"We go the only way we can." I started down the tunnel, which led about twenty feet to a door.

"Is it locked?"

"Doesn't look like it." I lifted the latch, pushed, and put out my arm to stop the tinker from passing me. "Wait a minute."

My light cut through the black illuminating a wedge of what appeared to be a large, empty stone room. I took a step. A sharp pain above my ear and the sound of a melon getting whacked with a hammer made the darkness around me go even darker.

SOMETHING WARM BRUSHED MY CHEEK WAKING ME enough for the pain above my ear to finish the job.

"Jimmy, I'm so sorry." A glow bathed Angela's face. An angel hanging in the darkness.

I sat up and waited for my vision to clear and the world to stop spinning. "Who clubbed me?"

"I didn't see it was you," she said.

The tinker's face appeared cheek-to-cheek with Angela within the light of the flashlight in her hand. "He's kind of hard to miss."

Why couldn't she have clobbered the tinker?

She handed me the flashlight. "My batteries died hours ago. I could only see shapes from your lights."

"Don't worry about it, doll." The bump above my ear stung and felt hot to the touch but no blood. "What did you hit me with?"

Angela held up an open hand and pressed her fingers together. "My Tae Kwon Do instructor calls it a sudo."

"Felt real to me."

"No, Jimmy," said the tinker, "the word sudo in Korean means knife hand."

I had expected a wrench or baseball bat. "A karate chop?"

The tinker patted me on the shoulder. "There is no such thing as a karate chop."

"Thank you, Jackie Chan."

Angela stroked my cheek, again. "Jackie Chan studies Kung Fu, Jimmy. That's Chinese."

"Okay, okay. Enough with the class on Asian Studies. Can either of you tell me where we are?"

"Well," the tinker flashed his beam spastically while walking a circle around a large, mostly empty, stone room, "this place has to be at least half the size of the island."

Angela leaned in close and whispered, "Room look familiar?" She then said to both of us, "From what I read, smugglers used this place during Prohibition."

The tinker kicked something, and it made a tinkling sound. "Explains the broken bottles."

"All of them broken?" I stood with a groan, more from disappointment than pain.

Angela brushed off my jacket and held out my fedora.

I wondered if the woman standing in front of me wearing khaki cargo pants, hiking boots, and an olive drab shirt was a dream. Her outfit got the adventurer in me going, whether real or not. "You seem pretty calm for being trapped down here for two days."

"Actually, I've only been here since yesterday afternoon." Her voice came across confident. Steady. "It took me a while to find the key in the lighthouse and to clear out the trap door."

"You shouldn't have gone off on your own like that."

"Didn't you get the note I put in your office mail slot?"

The tinker stopped his rummaging and shined his light in my face. "Jimmy? A note?"

Angela moved out of my light, but I didn't need to see her to know her body language. Rigid back. Stone-cold expression. A clenched fist or two. "Jimmy, do you think I would have come out here by myself without telling someone?"

"I should have checked my mail, I guess."

"How did you find me, since you didn't get my note?"

"We used all those books on your desk in the library. The bigger question is, how did you find this place and why?"

The tinker resumed his rummaging. "Those are two questions, Jimmy."

"You're not helping." I used my flashlight to find Angela. "Question number one, then. How did you find this place?"

"I learned my detective skills from the best."

My cheeks warmed. "Well—."

"Read every Sherlock Holmes in the library. At least twice."

"Sherlock Holmes, huh? Any of your detective skills tell us how to get out of this museum?"

"The way you came in."

The tinker shot a question across the room. "You think she'd still be here if she knew how to get out?"

"When I saw your desk, doll, I knew something was wrong. I've never seen a book out of place in the whole library."

The tinker said, "You've never been in the whole library."

She uncrossed her arms. A bit of a thaw. "I've been researching for months and got really excited when I found what I needed. I thought I could get out here and back in a few hours."

"A few hours?" I touched the sore spot on my head and winced. "It took us a few hours just to get to this island."

She turned away from me. "This is so embarrassing. I didn't think anyone would see my desk."

"Nothing to be embarrassed about, doll."

She sighed. "Either of you bring anything to eat?"

The tinker opened his pack and pulled out what looked like a bag of potato chips. "Yeah, here."

Angela swooped upon him like a starved vulture, tore open the crinkling plastic, and crunched. She handed me a flakey chip, stopped after a few chews, and held the bag up in the light. "Vegetarian Pork Rinds?"

"They're organic, too," said the tinker.

Angela gave me what amounted to a pork-flavored wood shaving and used another to point at a wall. "There's a key hole over there near your head. I found it just before my batteries died."

I asked, "Maybe another way out of here?"

"I don't think so." Angela crunched again. "It should be what I'm looking for."

"Which goes to my second question. What are you looking for?"

"A journal."

"All of this for a book?"

The tinker blinded me with his flashlight. "Journals are interactive guidebooks to the soul. I've been journaling for years. It helps me sort through the messy inner workings of my subconscious."

"Why doesn't that surprise me?"

Angela swallowed a mouthful of fake fried pork skin. "Have you tried therapeutic coloring? I find mandalas to be—."

"Like I said, all of this for a book?"

"An important book, Jimmy." Angela's mashed-plant and pork breath hit me almost as hard as her karate chop. "A journal belonging to the architect and mason who built this room."

More pieces fell into place. "I bet this architect built more than this room." I tapped the side of my nose in the light of my flashlight for Angela to see.

"What's wrong with your nose?" they asked in harmony.

"Nothing. This architect wouldn't happen to have been Fred Ferdinand?"

Angela stopped mid-bite. "How did you—?"

I pulled the folded papers from my pocket and waved the pages above my head. "I'm a detective, remember?"

The tinker abandoned the refuse he poked through in the corner, walked over to me, and put his hand on my shoulder. "You seem stressed, Jimmy."

SLEEP CAME AND WENT ABOUT EVERY FIFTEEN minutes. My exhausted body wanted rest from a trek across a swamp and up a lighthouse, but my mind worked on overdrive trying to get us out of our mess. Laying on cold stone with a folded sport coat under my head didn't help with the shuteye.

I shivered, rolled onto my side, and realized the shaking wasn't me. The vibrations came through the floor. I bound to my feet, heard the sounds of chains, pulleys, and gears, and darted for the elevator shaft with the tinker behind me and Angela at his heels.

An expanding square of morning light made me shield my eyes. My pupils adjusted slowly from our nine hours of darkness. I quieted my mind, stilled my body, and called upon my sharpened private eye senses ready to face whatever new danger descended from the surface.

"Is it the ghost?" asked the tinker.

Bigger square. Brighter light.

"Not unless he likes daylight." I pushed Angela back from the shaft, pulled my hat brim down making it tight against my forehead, raised my fists, and assumed an aggressive fighting stance. "This could get ugly doll."

My eyes hurt from the many hours of darkness, but I didn't turn away and willed myself to stand firm. Two boots and the frayed edges of jean cut-offs appeared above the platform's edge.

The tinker threw his hands into the air and cried, "Nellie," like this was her surprise party.

Chicken Neck Nellie finished her descent bathed in a pillar of light. Gloves, pliers, varying spools of cordage, and long metal tongs dangled from carabiners hooked to a thick leather carpenter's belt. Muscles of a former body builder bulged, and my hope returned.

Angela shouldered her way around me. "Did you take the key out of the lock?"

Nellie stepped into the tunnel.

"Wait!" The tinker threw himself onto the elevator.

The scrawny little guy moved like a cat when he wanted to but not fast enough to beat the release of the unseen catch. The platform and tinker hurtled toward the world above us. Given the velocity and sudden stop at the surface, the platform probably catapulted him a good fifteen feet into the air. I wished I could have seen it.

Nellie reached into a pouch on her belt, pulled out a flashlight, and held up the small iron symbol of our freedom. "Why did he do that, and why is he wearing dinosaur boxers?"

I rubbed my jaw. "Hard to say why the tinker does anything."

Angela spun me by the arm. "You really need to be nicer to him. Give him some credit. He did that in case she didn't have the key."

Heat rose into my cheeks. "If you say so."

You were the one that cold-cocked him in the library. I kept that thought to myself, turned back to the dark room, and considered lowering the elevator with the key and calling it a day, but Angela went to all of this bother for a reason, even if it was for some book.

"Come on, doll. Let's see if we can open that lock on the back wall, get what you came for, and all go grab a burger."

Flashlight beams bounced from floor-to-ceiling and wall-to-wall as we walked.

Angela asked Nellie the now-tired question, "How did you find us?"

"I was on my way to check my crab pots, and I saw Jimmy's car."

"You always crab so early?" asked our librarian known to alphabetize encyclopedias well-before breakfast.

"I pull my first pots at dawn. It's the only way I can check 'em all, clean my catch, and start steaming the first batch by 10:30."

I pointed my flashlight at the iron plate and keyhole in the wall. "Talking like that when I'm this hungry just isn't right."

Nellie continued, "Some old guy waved me over to the island. I thought something might have happened to Jimmy." She held the key out for me.

I left it hang there. "Old guy? What did he look like?"

"He wore one of those old-time rain coats. I didn't get a good look at his face, now that you mention it. It was still pretty dark, and his hood covered everything. I guess he was old. He moved really slow."

"Did he say anything to you?" I fought back a chill creeping through my body.

Nellie shook her head. "Not a word. He waved me over, and I followed him here. All he did was point to that key in the lock."

Angela shouldered her way between Nellie and me, snatched the key from Nellie's hand, put it in the lock, and turned it.

More grinding gears, clanging chains, and metallic squealing. A few stones receded from the wall creating an alcove and a wood shelf descended into the space. Angela reached for two leather-bound books.

"Can we go now?" My question came off more impatient than I would have liked, but Down and Out Burger had a half-pounder or two with my name on them, and I had had enough of lighthouses, underground rooms, books, and old kooks wandering around in the dark.

The key called the elevator, and we all climbed on, but it stopped with a lurch halfway between Hades and the ground floor.

The tinker, high above us, peered over the edge. "What happened?"

Angela called up to him. "The elevator is stuck." She looked at me then back to the tinker. "Might be too much weight."

Nellie tugged each of the chains suspending us. "These two go through the platform. Probably connected to the drive shaft." She heaved on one. Her muscles became rocks, and she grunted like a moose in heat. The platform inched downward. She heaved on the other chain. The platform inched upward. "This is the one." She pulled again, and the platform moved another foot or two, but her next tug only lifted her body.

"Now it's the opposite problem," the tinker said, "you need more weight. Jimmy, grab her legs."

"Hey, why do you think—."

Angela folded her arms and glared at me. "Yeah, Jimmy. Grab her legs."

I knew a lose-lose proposition when I saw it, so I took one on the chin to work the problem and wrapped my arms around Nellie's tree trunks. She grunted and pulled, reached, grunted and pulled, reached, lost her grip, and sat on my head.

"Sorry, Jimmy."

"Oh, he doesn't mind." Angela's words bit hard. "Do you, Jimmy?"

Nellie stood, wiped her hands on her cut-offs, and went back to work.

We stepped into the ruins of the keeper's house and made our ways out of the rotting timbers and clapboards. I never thought the smell of swamp gas and feel of hot summer sun on my black sport coat would be so welcome.

Angela didn't look at me once.

"Nellie, can you fit all of us on your crab boat?" I asked.

"Sorry, but it's not much of a boat. Only big enough for me and a few crab pots."

"Thank you, Nellie," Angela said, "but you've already helped us enough." She lifted a tarp revealing an ultralight.

"Wow," the tinker swung under a wing and ran his fingers along some metal wires holding fabric tight to a frame, "we ran right past this in the dark. Is it yours?"

"You bet." Angela patted the engine compartment. "Want a ride back to town?"

The tinker climbed into one of the two seats.

I tried to will Angela to look at me. "How long until you'll be back?"

"What do you mean, Jimmy?"

"To get me."

"Jimmy, this is an ultralight."

I didn't like the way she emphasized *light*.

"You mean—."

The tinker buckled his seat harness. "The hike will do you good."

"Back across the marsh?"

Angela fussed with some hoses in the engine. Still didn't look at me. "Meet in your office after I close the library?"

I tipped back my hat, glanced at the sun, and wiped my forehead. "I guess."

The tinker sat his pack on his lap. "Remember, Jimmy, just because you don't see the snakes doesn't mean they're not there."

Angela grabbed and spun the propeller. The engine whined to life. With a few bounces and a little dip when the craft passed over the island's edge, Angela and the tinker took to the sky.

"Well, Nellie, it looks like—." I turned to find Nellie puttering through a sea of lily pads. "Alright, then. See you around."

My office door opened stirring me from a Down and Out Burger induced nap. I dropped my feet from the desk, sat upright, and made another mental note to oil the chair's swivel and springs. In sauntered Angela. High heels. Black dress. Not a hair out of place. A guy would have never guessed she had spent the last two days trapped on an island dressed like Safari Barbie, but this private eye knew better than to take her sparkling peepers, deep lean over my desk, and pouty lips to mean all was right in our world.

"Hey there, doll."

"Hey there, yourself, Jimmy."

"Liking your new books?" I scratched a mosquito bite on my arm. One of about a thousand pockmarking my body.

"You bet. I'll be studying those for a while."

Awkward silence.

"Was it all worth it?"

"Jimmy, I wasn't out there on some fool's errand." She stepped back from my desk, went to the window, and turned the blind's rod to let more light into the room. "I thought you trusted me more than that."

"Oh, I trust you, doll. I trust you enough to know when you're in trouble and need me."

"That doesn't make any sense."

I shrugged, opened a drawer, and pulled out my bottle of Jack Daniels. "Face it, doll, you need me."

She sighed and lifted an aluminum slat to get a better view. "We have to move the archives. That's why I went out there."

"Old news. I figured that out the moment I stepped into the room under the keeper's house. But, way out there in the marsh?"

"No, Jimmy. Not there. That's why I need the books."

"This Fred Ferdinand guy. He built the archives?"

"Yes, and maybe other rooms like it around Ocean Mist."

How many points would I score telling her I've been to two others, one the size of an underground stadium housing Surf Services and the other a secret meeting room for The Skee-Ball Council? More than a few points. Probably enough to get me out of the dog house, but what good is a private eye without discretion.

"What's next?" I asked.

"We find one of Ferdinand's rooms we can use or a mason that can work from his notes. A mason we can trust."

I drank in her profile along with another hit of Jack.

She turned back to the desk and folded her arms. "You think this Nellie can keep her mouth shut?"

"Chicken Neck? Yeah, she's a good kid."

"Really? How well do you know her, exactly?"

I rose from my chair, moved around the desk, and took Angela's arms. "Nellie and I have history, but only you give me everything a guy could need."

"Oh," Angela relaxed a bit and inched closer. "Everything?"

"Yeah, doll. Well, except one thing."

"Is that so?" She moved in real close. "What would that be?"

"Nellie gives me crabs."

Jimmy Grits
the Hodad

A pimply teenager presented me with a cup of golden-fried-potato-stick heaven through the Down and Out Burger take-out window, but the unmistakable clicking of a Geiger counter broke my concentration.

"Mr. Grits, your fries."

"Right, sorry kid." I paid and tipped my fedora. "See you around."

The clicks came again, and I followed the woodpecker-like sounds to a narrow service alley behind Shuga's Sugar Shop on Washington Avenue only a few yards from the boardwalk. The back door leading to the kitchen stood open, which seemed to me like an invitation.

"Hey, Shuga?" I entered and came face to face-shield with a two-legged marshmallow, a person in a full hazmat suit who waved a Geiger counter over my fries. The letters NRC ran down the suit's sleeves.

A woman's voice came from deep within the billowy Tyvek. "You must be Jimmy Grits."

"Your Geiger counter tell you that?"

"Let's just say you match your profile."

"Don't believe everything you read on the internet." *I had told the tinker to take that down.* "I'm not desperate and single."

"Not that type of profile." The lady's face shield tilted downward for another look at the radiation detector. She removed her hood and extended her hand. "Gloria Radnor, Nuclear Regulatory Commission, but you can call me Glo."

I shook her gloved hand and pointed to her Geiger counter with a fry. "What are you looking for?"

She wiped her glove on her Tyvek. "You were going to be my next phone call, Mr. Grits."

"Call me Jimmy."

"My source says your services are discreet."

I popped another stick of golden deliciousness into my mouth. "Your source, huh?"

"Jimmy, we're facing a big problem. One we need to solve quickly to avoid public panic."

An experienced private eye like me didn't need someone from the NRC to tell me hazmat suit plus Geiger counter equalled trouble. "What are you looking for?" I asked again.

Another marshmallow with legs approached the kitchen from the sales-room on the boardwalk side of Shuga's. The human confection wore a harness supporting a small terminal, video monitor, and an array of antennae and tubes leading to some sort of air sniffer making faint shushing sounds. The combination suit and portable laboratory made the marshmallow need to shimmy sideways through the door.

"You people mean business." I frowned into my empty fry cup.

"Hey, Jimmy."

No, it couldn't be, I thought. I stepped forward to get a better look through the face mask. The tinker. "What are you doing in that get-up?"

Glo plucked a device from the tinker's harness. "We're short-handed."

"You must be." Glo seemed more interested in the device from the tinker's harness than anything I could say hinting at Ocean Mist's secret wave-making machinery, so I asked the tinker, "Isn't this your weekend to work for Edward?"

"This is more important. Edward was very understanding."

"More important?" I didn't like where any of this was going. "Neither of you have told me what the problem is."

The tinker took off his hood and exchanged concerned looks with Glo.

Glo shuffled to the corner of Shuga's kitchen where discolorations and scratches in the tile floor showed where a sizeable piece of equipment had sat. "Someone stole the nuclear-powered taffy puller."

I really wished I had more fries. "Wait a minute. You mean to tell me Shuga has a taffy machine powered by—."

The tinker completed my sentence. "Nuclear fission." His fingers clicked and clacked over the terminal suspended chest-high in front of him. "Can you imagine the panic if word of this got out to the public?"

"Of course." I chucked my cup into a trash can. "A nuclear device in the hands of a thief out there in Ocean Mist—."

Glo touched my shoulder and looked me right in the eyes. "That's only one of our problems. Shuga's Sugar Shop only has a few days-worth of taffy in its inventory."

Feeling left my fingers and toes.

The horror. The horror.

I put my hands on my hips and scanned the pristine kitchen. "Can't Shuga make some the old-fashioned way until we find the puller?"

The tinker looked up from his monitor. "That's the thing. Shuga's taffy isn't the best because of his secret recipe, but it's the taffy puller, too. The puller stretches every strand of taffy 42.3 million times before it's cut into pieces and wrapped." He leaned in close, put up his hand to hide the side of his mouth, and lowered his voice to a whisper. "Some say the puller came right out of the Manhattan Project."

"Oppenheimer and everything, huh?"

Screams.

Lots of screams outside and from the direction of the boardwalk.

I spun and barreled out to the service alley then onto Washington Avenue only to be halted by a flood of terrified swim-suited vacationers running from the beach and heading inland. The largest wave I had ever seen rose in the distance, crested in a white maelstrom of froth and spray, and crashed onto the beach with a deafening explosion, its waters halted only by the dunes and boardwalk. I stood dumbfounded.

The tinker waddled up beside me still cocooned within his Hazmat suit and portable laboratory. "What's going on?"

"It's the waves."

"Not again."

"Yep, only this time we've got the opposite problem."

Another huge swell rose chasing sun-and-fun-goers deeper into town.

The tinker pointed. "Up there. Is that a surfer?"

A tall scrawny guy stood on the front edge of a large wood board, rode the monster over what used to be the beach, and kicked-out back over the crest to disappear on its backside.

Impressive.

"Maybe you should've worked this weekend. What do you think has gotten into Edward?"

The tinker stumbled backwards when the crashing wave's vibrations passed through our feet. "I have no idea."

"We better get to him fast. The dunes won't hold up for long."

"This and Shuga's taffy puller on the same day?"

"One crisis at a time, my friend. There's only so much Grits to go around."

"Actually, there's quite a bit."

I looked at him sideways.

The tinker turned and waddled as quickly as he could down Washington Avenue toward the drawbridge and secret access tunnel to the town's Surf Services more than a half-mile inland. The gear harnessed around him clanked and smacked and swayed with his shortened and encumbered stride.

A brisk walk brought me beside him. "Why don't I get the Studebaker while you take off that silly suit?"

"There's no time, Jimmy." A half block later, he stopped, doubled over, and tried to catch his breath. All of the gear hanging from his harness and the billowy Tyvek must have really weighed him down.

"Are you sure? I parked the car right over there."

He reached up, put his hand on my shoulder, and pulled himself upright. "Okay, I should give this stuff back to Glo, anyway."

"Tell her I'll get on the taffy puller case as soon as I can."

The tinker and I slipped down the canal bank and under the drawbridge's east tower. After checking to be sure nobody could see us, he unlocked the door to the Surf Services tunnel. I hadn't been back under the streets since we had convinced Edward to return to work. Imagine my surprise when I entered the cavernous room of coal bins, furnaces, pumps, and giant gears and also found floor lamps, a leather easy chair, an end table with a small diffuser spewing puffs of Lavender mist, and a velour couch accented with flowered throw pillows.

"I like what the two of you have done with the place."

"Thanks, but we don't have time to talk decorating, Jimmy." The tinker threw his key on Edward's desk and disappeared into an aisle of pistons chugging at an incredible rate.

"Are those supposed to be going that fast?" I took a few steps closer to the machinery then thought better of it and backed away.

"No," the tinker yelled from somewhere among the shadows and clouds of smoke. "Edward? Hey, Edward, where are you?"

I went down another aisle calling for the trollish little man and found him tied to a chair and gagged with an oily rag. "Over here!" I pulled the rag from his mouth. Whoever bound Edward meant business. The rope's knots didn't release easily. "You okay?"

Edward gulped some air. "Jimmy, he did something to the main drive shaft."

"Who? What did he do?"

Edward coughed and pointed. "Take me over there."

I threw Edward's arm across my shoulders and lifted him from the chair to his feet. The tinker joined us as we made our ways toward a piece of machinery I could only describe as the Industrial Revolution's wicked stepmother.

"What did this guy look like?" I asked.

"Really tall, skinny, and he had long blonde hair covering his face. I caught him messing with the main drive shaft."

The tinker rushed ahead of us apparently knowing where to find the shaft.

This guy had really gotten the better of Edward. The little toad could barely stay on his feet. I felt bad for him and stopped so he could rest. "How did he get in? How did he even know about this place?"

Edward put his hand on a railing to steady himself. "I have no idea."

"Jimmy, you're going to need to see this," called the tinker.

I left Edward and followed the tinker's voice around a dark corner.

He sat on his haunches and rested his chin in his hand. "So much for one crisis at a time. We found Shuga's taffy puller."

Two opposing L-shaped mechanical arms stuck out of the top of a stove-sized machine. The arms, apparently between which gobs of taffy would be stretched, remained motionless, while the rest of the machine rumbled and rocked violently. A chain ran from a hole cut in the side of the puller out into the cacophony of Ocean Mist's giant wave machine then came back to form a loop.

I took off my fedora and wiped sweat from my forehead. "Can you disconnect this thing?"

"I wouldn't know where to begin."

"We need to get Edward." I led the tinker back to where I had left the Surf Services expert, who had sunk to the floor in a ball. "You don't look so good, Edward. How about a drink?" I reached inside my sport coat for my flask.

"Yeah, I could really use a Shirley Temple."

I left the flask in my pocket. "The guy that jumped you hooked-up a nuclear-powered taffy puller to the wave machine."

Edward blinked at me a few times. "I think you're the one needing a drink, Jimmy."

I reached again for my flask. "We've got waves that'll turn the board-walk into a pile of tooth picks within the hour."

The tinker knelt and placed his hands on Edward's shoulders. "We need you to take a look. Do you feel up to it?"

"Do I have a choice?"

"We're running out of time." I took a hard pull of Jack. "The dunes must be beaten to nothing, by now."

We walked Edward to the taffy puller. He inspected the machine being careful not to touch it, traced the chain into the darkness, and shook his head. "I have no idea."

I turned to the tinker. "You looked pretty comfortable with all of that Nuclear Regulatory Commission gear. Are you sure you can't do anything?"

"How many times are you going to ask me? I just follow YouTube videos whenever Glo wants me to do something."

Edward rubbed his chin. "How did they make a reactor that small?"

"What about Glo?" I asked. "You think she can help?"

The tinker shrugged, pulled out his phone, and tapped it a few times. "Hi, Glo. What's going on?"

Pause.

"Oh, you know. Hey, listen, what if we find the taffy puller and need to take it apart?"

Pause.

"Yeah, seriously."

Pause.

"Can you do it?" The tinker examined his fingernails. "How long would it be to bring in your team?" The tinker looked at Edward. "Two days?"

Edward shook his head.

"No sooner than that, huh?" The tinker started to gnaw on his cuticle. "Uh-huh." He checked his fingernail. "I think it's playing at the Rehoboth Theater. Want to go?"

I snatched the phone from his hand and hung up on Glo.

Edward limped to an old-school control panel of lighted indicators and gauges with needles showing pressures and speeds. "I don't want suits poking around down here. They'll just ask a bunch of questions and create a lot of paperwork. Our best bet is for you to catch the guy and make him undo all of this." He pulled a lever resulting in the sound of a teen driver grinding the gears of a bus. A turned dial made something bang then whir like an empty blender the size of the Empire State Building. "I just disconnected the drive shaft from the flywheel to stop the waves, altogether. This will buy us some time."

"How much?" I asked.

Edward shrugged. "However long we have before that nuclear thing overheats."

"You mean," the tinker stepped back from the rocking taffy puller, "before it melts down?"

"You got it."

I motioned for the tinker to follow me and asked Edward, "You okay if we leave you here?"

"With a melting down nuclear reactor? Sure. I'll be fine, Jimmy."

I headed for the tunnel.

"If you think of it, could you bring back some iodine tablets?"

I CLIMBED INTO THE STUDEBAKER AND REACHED across to open the door for the tinker.

"Passenger door still broken?"

"Don't use it that often."

"What's next?"

"We need to pay the mayor a visit." I swung the old girl onto a vacated Washington Avenue, and we headed toward emergency vehicle lights near the beach.

"The key, right?"

"The mayor copied the key to Surf Services when the three of you worked out your contracts, and I'm willing to bet he made more than one. A guy like him doesn't collect power by turning down a chance for access."

"I have a contract?"

I looked him in the eye. "You're telling me you don't?"

He shook his head.

"At any rate, all this business with the waves will get his attention. He'll probably be on the beach when we get there."

I was right.

Less-than-honest Abe stood on the beach next to a still ocean. "What's going on this time, Grits?"

"We're here to ask you the same question. Seems someone else has a key to Surf Services and used it to get the better of Edward."

The mayor tried to read our faces. "Can't the part-timer take over?"

"Edward will be fine. I'll be sure to pass on your concern." I removed my fedora and wiped my brow with a handkerchief. "You might want to know we have a bigger problem than the waves. We're hours away from Ocean Mist becoming another Chernobyl, unless you're straight with us."

"Chernobyl? What are you taking about?"

"How many copies of the Surf Services key did you make?"

The mayor furled his protruding brow and crossed his arms over a puffed chest. "What are you saying?"

His posture combined with his height must have intimidated the denizens of his shady world, but not me. "I didn't hear your answer."

"Hey, unc!" Three surfers with sizeable old-style wood surfboards strode up to us. The one who spoke did so from behind a curtain of stringy blonde hair encircling his head.

The mayor threw a thumb in the surfer dude's direction. "My nephew."

The tinker seemed to admire the boards. "Those are some pretty heavy guns."

I raised my fists, bent my knees, and stepped to take a shoulder-on stance with the surfers, but none made any kind of move to draw. They gave me some looks— probably thought twice seeing I was ready for trouble— then shifted their attentions back on the tinker.

"You had some akaw moves on those bombs," the tinker said. "That hang ten into the kick out, really aggro, dude."

The nephew flashed the tinker one of those extended pinky and thumb gestures. "Dude, you surf?"

"Junkyard dog, at best."

"Your friend?"

The tinker looked at me and shook his head. "Hodad."

The nephew stroked back some of his soggy blonde locks giving us a momentary glimpse of his beady eyes, "We were all amped, but, like, the waves went ankle busters. You can go grab your gun while I bring back the bombs."

The mayor dropped his arms and turned away from me, but not fast enough to hide his look of realization. "It's time for us to go."

"Hold it." I opened my sport coat wide and worked my thumbs into the elastic waistband of my pants. "How are you going to bring back the waves?" I tilted my head toward the tinker. "That is what the kid meant, right?"

The tinker nodded.

The mayor took his nephew by the shoulder. "We're leaving, Grits."

I stepped forward. "You're into this up to your Neanderthal fore-head, mayor."

The nephew's friends wedged themselves and their boards between me, the mayor, and his nephew.

"Back off, quimby," said one.

Followed by, "Yeah, back off, quimby," from the other.

"It's Grits. Jimmy Grits." I pushed them aside and called after the mayor. "You know who's responsible for this, and you're going to come crawling back to us to fix things. Just make sure it isn't too late."

The surfer dudes followed the mayor and his nephew down the boardwalk.

The tinker peered out onto a quiet ocean. "The nephew fits Edward's description."

"Sure does."

"Did you see his t-shirt?"

I watched the mayor and surfer gang become small dots down the boardwalk. "All I saw was red."

"Yeah, I could see the steam coming out of your ears."

"Whose t-shirt? What about it?"

"The nephew. *Stanford* was printed across the back."

"So?"

"Stanford has one of the best nuclear programs in the country."

MY COFFEE FROM JAVA BOB'S DIDN'T LAST long, and I considered my options for my next caffeine fix. "We need your friend Glo."

"You heard Edward." The tinker sipped his tea. "We don't have two days to wait for her team to get here."

"We don't need her team, just her help to get enough evidence to put the screws to the mayor, and there's no reason for her to know about Edward or what happened to the taffy puller."

"What do you mean, Jimmy? This kid stole a nuclear device. The NRC isn't going to just look the other way."

"That's why we need to keep this small. Quiet. Just us and your friend."

"But, Glo is in the NRC."

I drained my cup and tossed it in a trash can. The tinker had a point. We can't get her involved without bringing in the whole federal government. Too many people poking around. Too much paperwork. Too much time. It would all get in the way of my Grits magic. "We don't need her, just that suit you were wearing."

"You want me to *borrow* a multi-million-dollar personal radioactivity safeguards system with synergistic nuclear detection and remediation functionalities?"

"Is that the suit with all of the gizmos?"

The tinker nodded. "What do I tell her?"

"Tell her we're chasing down some leads, and we can't afford someone from outside Ocean Mist, especially a fed, spooking our informants."

"If that doesn't work?"

"Tell her you'll take her to a movie."

The tinker got a dreamy look in his eyes. "Glo is radiant, isn't she?"

An hour later, the tinker and I stood outside a two-story Victorian home repurposed into an office building where the mayor did all of his underhanded mayor things. The place saw as much traffic as the actual town hall, just not through the front door.

I knew enough about backdoors to know when and where to use the quiet approach. Visiting the mayor about his nephew wasn't one of those times. We needed to make some noise and draw some attention, both of which the mayor avoided. Bad for his type of business.

I double-checked the tinker in his giant robot-marshmallow looking outfit. "You ready?"

The large hood with plastic visor bobbed up and down.

We squeezed into the vestibule. Two potted ficuses flanked a glass door with a push-bar. A poster-sized reprint of an early 20th Century Ocean Mist aerial photo faced a set of buzzers and mailboxes. Small name tags identified the businesses connected to each buzzer, mostly lawyers and accountants connected to the mayor's operations, except for one marked simply "Suite D." I pressed its worn brass button.

A woman's voice crackled through an old speaker. "Can I help you?"

"Jimmy Grits to see the mayor."

"I'm sorry, but he is not in at the moment."

"Tell him he can either talk to us or the NRC and its big brother the FBI."

"One moment."

A loud click came from the glass door. She didn't offer an invitation to enter, but I didn't need one, nor did I need directions to the mayor's office. We stepped into a vacant reception area at the foot of a polished oak staircase. Narrow halls flanking the staircase led deeper into the converted home's ground floor, and the stairs rose to a landing illuminated in reds, oranges, and greens from light entering a large stained glass window of tangled vines and flowers.

Suite D, the mayor's office, took up a majority of the second floor, and my knees ached as I began to climb the stairs. The throbbing reminded me of the recliner I wanted to get for my office.

"Jimmy?" The tinker stood at the bottom of the steps.

"What's the problem?"

"I need some help." Clutching the banister with both hands, he lifted his leg and tried to fit his boot on the first step, but it kept sliding to the landing.

"Can you even see out of that thing?"

"You need to give me a hand."

I went back down then helped him climb making sure both of his feet rested surely on each step. The equipment's weight must have tired him quickly. His heavy breathing inside the hood sounded like a carpenter sawing a two-by-four.

"Ever the gentleman, aren't you Grits?" The mayor stood on the landing.

I knew better than to look up at him and instead checked behind us. Two ham-fisted brutes in slacks and open-collared shirts appeared from the side hallway. They planted themselves at the base of the stairs.

"Nice of you to leave your ivory tower, mayor." I squared my body, hands on my hips, to challenge the bean-pole of a man standing in front of the large stained glass window. He had the dramatic lighting, but I had the bulk.

"No, Jimmy! Don't let go!"

I spun.

The tinker's glove reached for my arm but only brushed it.

His call for help came too late, and I grabbed nothing but air. The tinker banged, clanged, and bounced backwards toward the reception area umphing and humphing between words muffled by his hood. Words I'm sure unfit for most ears. He stopped at the goons' feet.

"Sorry, kid." I turned back to the mayor.

"What's with all the performance art, Grits?"

"We're here for your nephew."

An urgent beeping came from one of the tinker's gadgets.

I couldn't hear myself think and needed to be sharp to face-down Ocean Mist's godfather. "Can you quiet that thing?" I loosened my tie.

"Jimmy," the tinker pushed himself to his feet creating far more racket than the beeping, "it's a radioactivity alarm." He fussed at his belt, raised to his face shield a metal box connected to a nozzle, and flipped open a small monitor. "I'm detecting gamma rays." He turned pointing the nozzle at one goon then the other, each stepping back, in turn, with their hands raised.

The mayor looked to his left and right.

"Listen, mayor." I jabbed a finger in his direction for emphasis. "Your nephew stole Shuga's nuclear-powered taffy puller and hooked it up to Edward's wave machine so he and his surfer gang could hang their tens."

The tinker lowered the box gizmo. "You mean hang ten, Jimmy."

"Quiet, I'm talking up here." I took a few more steps toward the mayor for added intimidation. "Like I said to your secretary, you can help us or the full force of the U.S. Government will be at your door."

The mayor pulled a pack of gum from his pocket and peeled the wrapper from a stick. "Easy, Grits. What's a nuclear-powered—."

"Taffy puller." I pinched the brim of my hat and pulled it down tight over my forehead. "It pulls taffy."

The mayor peered around me at the tinker. "Where's the— ahh— radiation coming from?"

"Somewhere upstairs."

"From me?"

"No, it can't come from you."

"How much radiation?"

"Have you noticed any fatigue? Minor swelling or aches in your joints?"

"No."

"Sterility?"

The goons dropped their hands to their groins.

The tinker continued, "Bleeding from your rectum?"

"My God, no," said the mayor.

The goons retreated farther from the tinker like he was the source of the radioactivity.

"Well, the readings are much too low for any of that."

The mayor put the gum in his mouth. "Then, why did you ask?"

One of the goons let out a long and slow breath.

"Just curious. Help me up the steps, and I'll find where it's coming from."

"Okay boys," the mayor sighed, "help him."

The goons took the tinker by the arms, lifted him from the floor, and carried him past me to the second-floor offices. The suit's gadgets sucked air, beeped, whirred, and led us to a cubby the mayor had loaned to his nephew.

The tinker wrestled-off his hood. "The levels are really low, so I think it's just some residual uranium. Your nephew must have brought parts of the machine here, at some point."

"Why would he do that?"

"That's a good question," I said. "Where is he?"

"What does it matter?"

"Look, mayor," I picked up a file folder from a desk, turned it over, and tossed it back where I had found it, "your cooperation includes making your nephew unhook the taffy puller from the wave machine and return the puller to Shuga's Sugar Shop before the suits reach Ocean Mist."

"How much time do we have?"

"I don't hear the helicopters circling, yet."

The mayor pulled a cell phone from his pocket.

I FOLDED MY ARMS AND LEANED AGAINST one of a thousand pipes in Surf Services while watching the mayor supervise his nephew.

Stanford's miscreant surfer-dude crawled out from behind a gear assembly the size of a Volkswagen Beetle and wiped his hands on a rag. "Am I, like, going to jail, unc? I'm doing everything you asked."

Edward started up the wave machine and scampered from one cluster of pulleys, pistons, and shafts to another in his hunched knuckle-dragging way. He stopped and looked around. "Is something burning?"

The tinker yanked me away from the pipe. "Jimmy, your jacket."

I used my fedora to pat-out the flame then moved in front of the nephew. "We should put you behind bars and throw away the key, but I think we can arrange something."

The mayor glanced at me.

If I give the feds the nephew, they will need to do their own investigation, conduct interviews, gather evidence for a trial, and our sleepy little all-American Ocean Mist will become a three-ring circus. I pointed my hat at the taffy puller. "How fast can you get that thing back to the candy store and running again?"

The nephew rubbed his jaw. "Before slack tide brings the foot slappers."

"When is that in normal-person time?"

"About 9:00 tomorrow morning."

I wrapped my hand around the nephew's upper arm and squeezed vice-like to make sure I had his full attention. "How much do you like California?"

"What are you doing with your hand?"

I squeezed harder. "How much do you like California?"

"Dude, waves are gnarly in Cali, not like these ankle busters. Barrels I can stand in and ride all the way home, and when the—."

"Yeah, okay. Make sure you're on a plane there by noon, tomorrow.

You ever show your face again in Ocean Mist, you'll wish you were nice and safe in a federal pen."

The nephew yanked free of my hold. "Plane by noon? Who does this hodad named after a breakfast side dish think he is?"

The mayor didn't take his eyes off of Edward doing his Edward things. "You'll be taking the bus."

Professional Association of Taffy Stretchers and Yankers
1275 Copper Kettle Road, Suite E
Glucose, California 01010

Dear Mr. Grits:

You may be surprised to know, Ocean Mist confectioner Shuga Johnson's use of a nuclear-powered taffy puller is an insult to the Professional Association of Taffy Stretchers and Yankers' dedication to satisfying our nation's desire for desserts and a happy ending to every meal. Our efforts to persuade Mr. Johnson to abandon his dangerous machine and return to tactile techniques have been fruitless.

Our slogan, "Pull until the job is done," reflects our core belief hands-on pulling is not only gratifying but the only method for yielding a high-quality product. We know you have experienced firsthand the benefits of our organization's work, and we hope you will use your influence with Mr. Johnson to further our cause. I ask you to please reflect long and hard on my request and to provide us with a hand in this matter.

Mr. William "Tug" Hardy, President
PATSY

The Case of Bumper's Car

Part 1: The Chase Is On

Danger wished me a *good morning* even before I could unlock my office door. A silhouette on the wrong side of the frosted glass. Some Joe sat at my desk. Every muscle and nerve came alive for whatever dance this guy wanted to start. I pivoted into the alcove between door jam and wall becoming one with the plaster.

He couldn't have seen me.

My advantage.

My move.

I knew the play. Turn the knob, jump through the doorway with a loud yell, catch him off guard, and dive over the desk pinning him to the wall. Simple. Nothing fancy. The kind of tactic featured in *Private Eye of Fortune* magazine.

I drew a deep breath then burst into the room with a roar.

The tinker looked up from my desk. He or my chair squealed.

Fortunately for him, my well-honed body control and willingness to sacrifice for the innocent saved him from a world of hurt. I collapsed my knee and tumbled letting each of several bounces absorb some of the force of my lunge until slamming shoulder-first into my desk.

"I've tripped over that threshold, too," he said. "You really need to screw that down."

I took a moment on the floor to let my adrenaline run its course, scooped my fedora, grabbed the edge of my desk, and pulled myself to my feet. "How did you get in here?"

The tinker turned a page of a spiral-bound book. "I used my key."

"You don't have a key."

"What do you mean?"

"What do you mean, *what do you mean?*"

The tinker reached into his pocket, pulled out a key clipped to a rabbit's foot, and placed it on my desk.

"Where did you get that?"

"From you, remember?"

"No, I don't remember."

The tinker dabbed at his book with a small white brush. "You gave it to me when I fixed the window Skee-Ball Granny broke."

"And, you gave it back."

"Not my copy."

"Okay, forget the key. Do you know how dangerous that is?"

The tinker eyed the small white brush. "Correction fluid? As long as I don't inhale—."

"Don't come in here without telling me." I stretched my back hoping the pain would go away with just the right lean. "Is that a new calendar?"

"Of course. It's January."

I leaned closer. "That's last year's calendar."

He pointed his little brush at me. "That's why you're a detective." He dabbed another number on the calendar page. "Buying last year's is cheaper."

"And you change all of the dates?"

"I couldn't use it unless I did."

"At my desk with my correction fluid?"

"By the way," the tinker pointed his brush at the black rotary on my desk, "your phone rang a few minutes ago."

"Who was it?"

"I didn't answer."

"Why not?" I hung my hat and coat on the rack by the door and realized this would be a busy day, because the phone rang again. I pointed at it. "Aren't you going to get that?"

"I'm not answering your phone, Jimmy. Where's your sense of boundaries?"

"Okay, just get out of my chair." I shouldered my way behind the desk and lifted the receiver. "Grits Detective Service."

"Yeah, hey there Jimmy, it's Rocco."

"You got something for me, Rocco?" Informants didn't come any better than Rocco. He had good eyes, ran a tight crew, and knew the streets. His thick New York accent was the only tell he didn't grow up in Ocean Mist.

"Me and the boys saw the Cadillac you told us about."

The tinker leaned over my shoulder. "Ask Rocco how his aromatherapy shop is doing."

"I heard him, Jimmy. Tell him were runnin' a special on our new hyacinth-lavender infusion."

"Okay, I'll do that. When did you see the car?"

"About fifteen minutes ago."

"Where?"

"Just down the block from the museum."

"Pink?"

"No, the museum is white. Nice shutters."

"Not the museum."

"Oh, yeah. The Cadillac. I saw it up the road and took a little walk. When I got close, I could smell cigarette smoke, too. Just like you said."

I scribbled date and time on my steno pad. "You said a block from the museum, huh?"

"Yeah, they just opened a new exhibit on the old Ocean Mist Cannery, and—."

"Thanks, Rocco. If this lead pans out, you want me to drop payment in the usual spot?"

The tinker hadn't moved out from behind me, and he needed a bath. "Tell Rocco my new diffuser works great."

"You know, Jimmy," Rocco said, "you should think about getting a diffuser for your office. A high stress job like yours? I can get you one, cheap."

I handed the receiver to the tinker. "Here, Rocco wants to talk to you." I pushed up from my chair, grabbed my jacket and fedora, and closed the office door behind me.

I CIRCLED THE MUSEUM'S BLOCK IN THE Studebaker, a black cat prowling the neighborhood. No sign of Bumper's pink Cadillac, but, if Rocco said he saw her car, he saw her car. I pulled into a spot near the door to the old beach-cottage-turned-museum, rolled down my window, and sucked in the crisp January air half expecting to catch a whiff of Elbow Patches' wacky tobaccy. Wherever Bumper was, Elbow Patches would be nearby.

I didn't want to rush into anything, so I sat and scoped-out the neighborhood. A weekday in January. No out-of-towners heading for the beach or boardwalk. Most of the little bungalows up and down the museum's street had their shades pulled and windows tight, all winterized and abandoned until the spring. No one in or out of the museum, which didn't surprise me. Twenty minutes could hardly be called a stake-out. Sometimes, I'd park in front of a mark's place for hours. I'm a man of patience, but I saw no need to burn more time watching this dead zone.

I stepped from the Studebaker, leaned on the roof, and took another look around. A few squirrels argued over some frozen acorns, an old lady walked a dog smaller than the squirrels, and I could barely hear myself think over the ruckus the rats with bushy tails made wrestling in the dead leaves. I rolled my aching shoulder and reached across to rub the spot where I had hit my desk.

"Hey, Jimmy!" The tinker jogged toward me from down the block. His puffy ski jacket swished with each stride. "Rocco said the cannery exhibit is Smithsonian quality, but I didn't expect you to be interested in it."

"I'm not. Rocco saw Bumper's car near here."

"Is that what you guys were talking about?"

"You were there."

"Yeah, but I could only hear one side of the call. Why didn't you tell me he saw the Cadillac?"

"You were busy. Something about lavender." I pulled my fedora down over my brow. "Think of anyone else who might like to join us?"

"Well, I could call some of the guys on the Ocean Mist Ballers, they—."

"Just, come on."

I led the tinker up a broken shell walk to the museum's entrance. The old cottage's aluminum-framed screen door hung awkwardly from mismatched hinges. I swung it open carefully, pushed through the unlatched front door, and a muscle-bound man more suited for a gym than a ramshackle museum sat in the entryway behind a card table and plastic cash register repurposed from some kid's playroom.

"You work here, buddy?"

Before the big ox could get a word out, the tinker chirped from behind me. "He's a docent, Jimmy."

"I'm sure he's a decent fellow." I tossed a thumb over my shoulder. "You'll have to excuse my junior detective friend back there. He thinks he's got to size up every Joe we meet."

The guy behind the table tried to talk again, but the tinker cut him off. "No, Jimmy. He's the museum's docent. He gives tours." The tinker hung his coat on a peg by the door.

I guessed he meant to stay awhile.

"Actually, I'm also the director, curator, archivist, and head custodian. My aunt helps out sometimes. She's the assistant custodian."

"Uh, yeah. My mistake. So, anyway, we're here for the nickel tour."

The docent rose from his chair banging the table's edge with his thighs causing the whole set up to rock forward almost dumping the register on the floor. "I keep doing that." He moved the table's items into their original positions and looked me in the eyes. "You gentlemen want to see our new exhibit on the cannery?"

I had come for Bumper, but I played along. "Sure. I like to see old cans."

The docent reached into a box for a couple of tickets.

I turned to the tinker and whispered, "You've been to these types of places. Do we take notes or something?"

The tinker shook his head. "Not on your first visit. Just take it all in. Appreciate the breadth of the exhibit, the variety of mediums used to create the immersive historical experience. On my second trip to an exhibit, I usually free-write impressions—."

"Yeah, okay. I get it."

Beeps from the child's register brought my attention back to the table. The big guy struggled, his fingers too big for the buttons, and he cursed each time he cleared his entries to start over again.

"Can I just give you a Lincoln, and we call it even?"

He looked up and smiled a bit sheepishly. "Admission is actually six."

I shook my head and handed him the Lincoln and a Washington.

"Sir, that's six apiece."

The tinker patted me on the shoulder. "You can't put a price on our history, Jimmy."

I paid. "Let's get this show on the road."

We walked from the entryway into what must have once been the cottage's living room. The docent made a motion with his hand like he revealed the grand prize on a game show. "This is our permanent exhibit. You'll find everything from the oldest beach umbrella excavated from the end of Washington Avenue to horse shoes found under the floorboards of the old stable."

I rubbed my cheek. "Ocean Mist had a stable?" Pretending interest always helped with my deep cover assignments.

"Yeah, over where Down and Out Burger is, now."

The tinker pointed to a yellowed and grainy photo framed behind a thick glass. "That was the stable, which was also the original Ocean Mist Fire Department. They had a wagon with a water pump and everything."

The docent smiled and nodded. "You know your history."

"Well," the tinker straightened his Hawaiian shirt— I think the same shirt he got when we had tracked down Edward in Bermuda— and lifted his chin a bit, "I just completed a history minor from Refton College of Pennsylvania— online."

I moved to a plexiglass case holding some rusty nails and bits of rotted boards. "What are these?"

The docent reached behind the case and flipped a switch. Small lights within the display flickered to life. "Those are rusty nails and bits of rotted boards."

I tilted back my fedora. "You don't say?"

He nodded. "From the original boardwalk."

"Oh." I realized I had found the tinker's long-lost brother.

The docent pointed to one of the nails. "Notice the texture of the rust and the flat surfaces. Those were hand forged."

I stepped toward a doorway. "What's in there?"

"That's our traveling exhibit on local amusements." The docent led us into what might have once been a small dining room given its connection to a gutted kitchen.

The tinker pushed ahead, turned, and put his hands on my chest. "Wait, Jimmy." He looked as giddy as a school girl. "You've got to see this. This is my favorite piece in the whole Ocean Mist collection."

He moved aside and pointed to a battered Skee-Ball machine. A broken leg made the game list like a boat taking on water. The light board at the top must have been hit with a kid's baseball, and the wood ramp's dry-dullness told me no one had played the game for decades.

The tinker folded his arms and smiled. "I've put together a fundraiser to get it restored."

"Let me know where I should send the check." Something looking like a bobsled caught my eye. "And that?"

The docent straightened his back. "That is our pride and joy. An original bumper car from Happy Land."

A bumper car? Coincidence? "You said this was a traveling exhibit."

"That's right. We loan it to other museums a lot. In fact, it's only here a couple months each year."

"Really?"

"The exhibit just came back from The Fenwick Island Historical Society."

I stepped closer to the car. "So, what's so special about it?"

"This is the oldest surviving car from Happy Land's bumper car ride, which was installed in 1928. See the pole in the back?"

"Yeah."

"There's a metal brush that attaches to the top. The brush scraped against a ceiling grate with current running through it, and that was how the car got its power."

"Okay, what's so special about it?"

"Well," the docent paused and glanced at the tinker, "it's really old, one-of-a-kind, and part of Ocean Mist's past."

"So is my sofa, but you don't see me parading people through my living room."

The tinker moved up beside me. "There's also a mystery connected to Happy Land. You know about the family that opened the park?"

"I heard of them. The Gleesons."

"Great-great-granddaddy Gleeson struck it big in the Klondike Gold Rush— 1887 or 1888, I think. The family used part of his fortune to open the amusement park, but no one knows where the rest of the money went."

"Maybe he bought a whole lot of bumper cars." The here and now gave me more than enough mysteries to handle. I didn't need history-teacher drama.

The docent pointed over my shoulder. "That's a photo of Great-great-granddaddy Gleeson in his workshop."

Just what I was looking for, another blurry and yellowed photo.

This one featured a smiling old guy standing behind a craftsman's table strewn with tools and a crooked calendar tacked to the wall behind him. For the life of me, I couldn't see anything worth Patches' and Bumper's time in this place. "What else do you got around here, Mr. Docent?"

We covered the rest of the museum in about 20 minutes, including the new cannery exhibit. Exactly 18 minutes more than I thought it should take. As far as I was concerned, we came up empty.

I stepped outside. Sunlight and fresh air helped me shake off museum drowsiness.

Bumper must have her eye on something else around here. Maybe something in one of the houses on the block.

The tinker closed the screen door behind us. "Wasn't that a great representation of the cannery industry? Imagine, 10,000 cans of bunker oil leaving Ocean Mist every month."

"Bunker what?"

"You know, bunker oil, from the boney and oily bunker fish? A substitute for whale oil?" He must have misinterpreted my look of complete disinterest as confusion, because he kept going. "Bunker chum, too. For commercial fertilizer producers?" The tinker huffed and shook his head. "Weren't you paying attention?"

Something tickled my highly tuned nose, and it wasn't fish, bunker or otherwise. "Do you smell that?"

"Sorry, Jimmy, last night was Taco Tuesday with the Ballers."

"No, not that smell." Elbow Patches appeared from behind the museum strolling along a hedgerow less than ten feet from me. We locked eyes. "I smell smoke."

Patches cupped a hand under his tweed jacket's leather elbow, propped his pipe arm, took a few puffs, and looked up into the sky. "Nice day, isn't it Grits?"

"Strange place to take a walk."

He shrugged and took a step in our direction.

My heart skipped a beat when I realized my nephew's squirt gun was in my desk drawer. "That's close enough."

"I'm looking at buying around here. What do you think of the neighborhood?"

The tinker pointed across the street. "I hear the Jacksons might sell. Property values have increased in this part of town about 7% over the past couple of years."

I turned and scowled.

"Sorry, Jimmy."

I shrugged off my jacket, unbuttoned my shirt's cuffs, and rolled my sleeves. "Something tells me you're looking for more than just real estate."

"Oh, like what?"

"You tell me."

Elbow Patches chuckled and puffed on his pipe. "I'm not interested in fighting, Mr. Grits. I leave that to the less evolved."

"Who said I was looking for a fight?"

"No one said that, Jimmy, but he inferred it from your posture. He then implied you're less evolved. Based on what you took away from the museum, I'd say—."

Elbow Patches pointed his pipe stem at me. "You're either itching for a fight or going to do some yard work."

"Why don't we cut a deal? Take your pipe and head back to the rock you crawled out from under, forever, and I won't take you and your girlfriend downtown."

The tinker tapped me on the shoulder. "Technically, we are downtown."

"Take a step back, would you?"

Elbow Patches chuckled again, turned from us, and took to the sidewalk. "I'll see you around, Grits. Who knows? Maybe we'll be neighbors." Puffs of gray smoke trailed him. "By the way, I hope your shoulder feels better."

He's been watching me. Knew I was here the whole time.

I went the opposite direction, opened the door to the Studebaker, and said to the tinker, "Well, are you getting in?"

"That depends, are you going to slug me?"

"Why would I slug you?"

"Looks like you want to slug somebody. Bumper and this Patches guy really get you worked up, don't they?"

"Just get in the car."

"You really need to be more aware of your body language."

THE TINKER STOPPED SHORT AT MY OFFICE door, and I just about rear-ended him. He kicked at the threshold. "Yep, you should really screw this thing down before someone else takes a nose-dive."

I tossed my hat onto the desk. Hung my coat on the rack. "You knew Bumper pretty well, back in your dancing days, didn't you?"

"Kind of," the tinker looked at me real hard, "but, not in that way. Our relationship was purely professional. I wasn't one of those kinds of dancers."

I sighed. "Did she strike you as—."

"She never hit any of us."

"No," I shook my head, "that's not what I meant. Do you think she would have any interest in that old bumper car?"

"I don't think so. She's a business woman and master choreographer."

"A master choreographer?" I tried to picture the bleach-blonde dried apricot of a woman moving on a dance floor but thought better of it before too many images came to mind. "Bumper, a master choreographer?"

"That's where she got her nickname. She invented *The Bump.*" The tinker spread his legs, squatted, and pulled back his hips.

"Please stop. I'll take your word for it." I turned on the small space heater next to my desk, put my feet up, crossed my arms, and tested the limits of my reclining office chair. "They're up to something, though. What did the docent say about Grandpa Gleeson?"

"You mean Great-great-granddaddy Gleeson?"

"Yeah, him."

"He made a fortune in the Klondike. A huge strike. Just about froze to death rafting back down the Yukon River to cash in his gold."

"You know anything more about this guy?"

The tinker shook his head. "The historical society or library would have something more about him."

"We can't let Bumper and Elbow Patches take over Ocean Mist while we're sitting around reading books."

"What if we find you some with pictures?"

"Not even then."

"Well, why don't you just call Angela?"

I sat up. My office chair squealed. "Now you're talking." I lifted the rotary phone's receiver and dialed.

"Why don't you get rid of that thing?"

"My phone? Why would I—."

"You have a cell. Do you keep that one for show?" He looked around the room. "Like, all this other stuff, to create an old-timey private-eye atmosphere?"

"Atmos— what are you talking about?" Angela's breathy voice came on the line. "Hey doll, can I ask you a favor?"

"Well, that depends. What's in it for me?"

I loosened my tie. "Well, what would you like me to do for you?"

The tinker leaned over the desk and spoke at the phone. "We can help you spruce up the reference section, like donate a new volume of—."

"You tell whoever that is I don't need to spruce up my references!"

I covered the mouthpiece. "Why don't you wait outside?"

"It's cold out there."

"You're making it really cold in here."

"Who is that, Jimmy?"

I removed my hand. "Sorry about that, doll. It's just a new client."

"New client? Who is he?"

"Uh, I'm helping him find his family's antique marbles. Seems he's lost a few."

"You bring him down here, and I'll show him where his marbles are!"

"Don't tell her it's me. I can hear her. She's mad about something."

I put my hand back over the mouthpiece. "What makes you think that?" I took a breath, removed my hand, and said, "Look, doll, I'm sorry about all of this. I just need you to do some research for me."

"Not for whoever that is."

"No, not for him. A completely different case."

"Okay Jimmy, I need to get my notepad." Some shuffling. The click of a pen. "Go ahead."

"Could you look into the story of Granddad Gleeson?" I imagined Angela scribbling away with her reading glasses perched on the tip of her button nose.

"Do you mean Great-great-granddaddy Gleeson and his gold strike?"

"Heard of it?"

"As much as you did in local history class."

"Right. So, anything you can find about his missing gold would be helpful."

"Well, Jimmy, if I could have found anything about his missing gold, I'd be running a much bigger library."

"I'm not looking for the gold. Just want to see if any information about it relates to my case."

"Just for you, Jimmy."

I hung up the phone and pointed at the tinker. "You have to stop doing that."

"Doing what?"

"Talking when I'm on the phone."

The tinker looked puzzled.

I changed the subject. "Have you been back to Bumper's place lately?"

"Not since our big number. You know, the night we found the recipe book? Ocean Mist's dance community is still talking about it."

"I'm sure they are." I reached into my desk drawer, moved aside my bottle of Jack Daniels, pulled out my nephew's squirt gun, and held it up to the light. Still loaded.

The tinker pointed his chin at the translucent bit of plastic. "What do you need that for?"

"We're taking a ride out to Bumper's place."

"The Pink Flamingo?"

"She got another club?"

"No, but do you really need to bring the piece?"

"Just hand me my coat."

I DIDN'T EXPECT A CROWDED CLUB ON a wintry Tuesday afternoon, but I didn't expect an empty parking lot, a sign with peeling paint, and broken windows. No one seemed to have been around for months.

I positioned the Studebaker near the front door, reached across the tinker's lap, opened the glove compartment, and gave him my binoculars. "What do you make of this?"

"Really nice. You get these at the camera shop on Third Street?"

"No, I mean this." I motioned to the Pink Flamingo's run-down façade.

"Sad. Soul-crushing sad. Another small-town cultural institution lost to the pressures of corporate America and its cheap and shallow digital entertainment."

I stared at him for a moment.

"Why are you looking at me like that?"

"You do realize the Pink Flamingo was a dive-bar strip club run by criminals?"

"Don't belittle what you don't understand." The tinker's face softened. His chin even trembled. "It wasn't like that at all." He turned his body toward me. The seat's black leather made a groan-like rubbing sound. "The Pink Flamingo opened doors for many dance artists and gave them their big breaks. The club served an important role in Ocean Mist's arts community. I mean, think of all the lost pageantry."

"Pageantry? You gave us the stage names White Vinegar and Chow-chow."

The tinker peered out the windshield, got a far-away look in his eyes, and whispered, "Our day of glory, Jimmy. Our day of glory."

The club turned out not to be abandoned. The Pink Cadillac eased to a stop in the street across from the parking lot's entrance. I took back and looked through my binoculars. Smoke seeped from door edges and cracked windows. Tinting kept me from seeing much more. Bumper— or, whoever sat in the driver's seat—just idled the boat of a car, its rumbling engine begging for a tune-up.

I put the Studebaker in gear, closed our distance, and stopped. "Slide over and take the wheel. I'm getting out."

"Why? What are you going to do?"

"I don't know, yet." I checked my squirt gun and tucked it into my coat pocket. "Just be ready to roll."

A frigid January wind slapped my face. I kept my gaze on the Cadillac and walked with purpose getting to within a few yards then made a rolling motion with my hand.

Nothing.

I moved closer, leaned down to the passenger window, and rapped the glass with my knuckle. "Hey, I want to talk to you."

The Cadillac's wheels squealed, and I jumped back before getting clipped by the rear fender. A cloud of burnt-tire smoke poured over me, filled my nose and mouth, and made me cough.

I pivoted on my heel and made for the Studebaker's passenger door. The moment my butt hit the seat the tinker tramped the gas. The old girl showed us she still had it in her. We leapt to the lot entrance, and I could see the Pink Cadillac making for Highway One.

The tinker slammed on the brakes.

I brought my arm up to keep my forehead from bashing the

dashboard, my private eye reflexes saving me from what could have been a concussion. "What are you doing?"

"I have to signal, Jimmy." He clicked on the blinker.

"Just go! They're getting away."

We peeled out, again. Ramshackle buildings, rusted chain-link fences, all manner of industrial decay lining the road flashed by us in brown and gray blurs.

"There!" I pointed through the windshield. "The on-ramp to the highway."

The tinker wove through sparse midwinter traffic. "I've been driving the Mini-bullet a lot, lately. Do you think I should get my license renewed?"

"When did you last drive a car?"

"Prom night. Didn't turn out very well."

"How long ago—. Tell you what, if you catch the Cadillac, I'll take you to the driver's test myself."

We inched closer to the Cadillac on a straight stretch of highway between Ocean Mist and Rehoboth, close enough I swore I could smell Bumper's cigarette smoke.

We approached the intersection with Route Nine, a confluence of traffic from Lewes, Ocean Mist, and Highway One. Always a hairy crossover regardless of the time of year, but the Cadillac showed no signs of slowing and passed into the intersection as the light switched from yellow to red.

"Hold on, Jimmy!"

We blew through the crossroads seconds behind the pink menace. Tires screamed. A chorus of car horns. A siren.

The tinker white-knuckled the steering wheel. "What do we do?"

"It's the Highway Patrol." I had some mutual understandings with the local LEO's, but not much sway with the state officers. "We're going to have to pull over."

The tinker eased us onto the berm, cut the engine, and glanced nervously into the rearview mirror. Alternating red and blue lights reflected onto his face. He turned toward me and brought his knees up to his chest. "Okay, let's switch."

"What are you doing?"

"I don't have a license. We have to switch!"

"I can't—."

The tinker managed to slip his leg over my thighs and sit on my knees facing me with his body wedged between my chest and the dashboard. I tried to slide under him, but we both froze with a knock on the driver side window.

The tinker called over his shoulder, "Just a minute," and said to me, "can you reach the window crank?"

"Gentlemen, I need to see your hands."

"Show him your hands, Jimmy."

I lifted my right over the tinker. "You're kneeling on my other hand."

"Gentlemen, you need to stop what you're doing and show me your hands."

The tinker tried to push against the steering wheel. "Sorry, officer, we just need another second."

I had trouble taking a breath. "You can't sit like that. Get off of me."

"I'm trying. I'm stuck."

"Okay, you two, out of the car."

The tinker motioned for the officer to come around to the passenger side. "We're going to need some help, officer."

"You're telling me."

"No, really," the tinker said, "do you have a jaws-of-life?"

I grabbed the tinker by the shoulders, tossed him toward the driver's seat, opened my door, and rolled out onto the oily gravel along the highway. By the time I stood and brushed off my coat, I could see the patrolman's back-up roaring toward us.

The Case of Bumper's Car

Part 2: Night Ops

"**Y**ou have one phone call, Mr. Grits." The trooper led me from my holding cell to what might have been the last pay phone in southern Delaware. She handed me a quarter, which I fed into the slot.

I needed someone I could trust with deep pockets, the kind of guy who worked like a dog and didn't have time to spend a dime—Edward Pushwater. "Hey, it's Jimmy. I'm in a bit of a fix."

"What happened?"

"I need bail and a ride back to town."

"Bail? Where are you?"

"Rehoboth State Police Barracks." Surf Services chugged in the background, and I pictured Edward standing between pipes and pumps the sizes of small houses. "You know I'm good for the bail money, right?"

"Sure, Jimmy. I just need to call—."

"He's here, too. We'll explain everything when you get here."

"I guess I can leave for a little while." There was a pause, and I imagined Edward looking around measuring up his machinery. "I'll get there as soon as I can."

"Thanks, Edward." I hung up the phone. The trooper motioned for me to head down the bright white-tiled hallway back to my cell. A door opened along the way, and the tinker popped out with his own escort. I stopped. "You use your phone call, yet?"

"Yeah." His escort gave him a nudge to keep him moving. "Didn't you get it?"

"What do you mean?" The lady trooper behind me gave me more than a nudge. "Easy, doll. I'm on your side."

"Do I look like a doll, to you?"

I spoke over my shoulder to the tinker. "What do you mean, *didn't I get it?*"

"My voicemail. I called you."

EDWARD LED US DOWN THE BARRACKS' STEPS. I guess he felt bailing us out of the pokey required formal attire, because he wore a tie matching his coveralls. He might have even trimmed his crown of stringy hair and polished the top of his head.

The tinker looked into the sky and took a long breath like he had been held in a sweat box for a month. "We really appreciate this."

"Don't mention it. I just can't believe you guys got into a high-speed chase down Route One."

I took my phone out of a plastic personal belongings bag. "Danger is my partner, Edward."

Besides the tinker's plea for me to spring him, Angela left a long message about Great-great-granddaddy Gleeson. Nothing new there, but I listened a second time just to hear her voice. I liked to do that with her messages.

Edward pulled car keys from his coveralls' pocket. "Where's your Studebaker?"

"Impounded."

The tinker walked to the far side of Edward's 1971 sky-blue Gremlin parked on the street in front of the barracks, folded the passenger seat forward, and wedged his way into the back. "Was that Angela?" he asked me.

"Yeah, but she didn't find anything new."

Edward's stubby bubble-looking car needed some serious suspension work. It creaked and sank when I sat in the front passenger seat, not to mention the interior smelled of coal smoke. He got the engine turned over on his third attempt. "So, what's next, Jimmy?"

"You know where the Pink Flamingo used to be?"

"Yep."

"Can you take us there?"

"You got it."

The tinker unzipped his ski jacket, pulled his Hawaiian shirt to his nose, and took a big whiff. "I need to go home, first. Clean up and change."

I looked back at him. "You needed to do that last Tuesday. How long is that going to take you?"

"About three hours. I have other stuff to do, too."

"Our trooper friends just gave Bumper and Patches a huge head-start. Can't it wait?"

"No, why do you want to go back to the Flamingo, anyway? We still have no idea what they're up to, and, frankly, I haven't seen any proof they're up to anything at all." The tinker seemed really irritated. "I can't keep putting my life on hold for your cases, Jimmy."

"What do you have to do?"

"Take a shower."

"For three hours?"

The car's engine knocked and whined.

"I have a class to get to."

"Oh, on what?"

"What's it matter? You're just going to tell me to skip it."

"How do you know? What's your class?"

"Celtic Dance."

"You're right. Skip it."

The tinker mumbled something. Probably uncomplimentary. "You still haven't told us why you want to go back to the Pink Flamingo."

"That's where we last saw Bumper's Cadillac."

"No, the last time we saw the Cadillac, it was flying through a busy intersection on Highway One."

Edward interrupted us. "How about I take the two of you to the Flamingo, tonight?" He tried to find common ground, mend the fence, but it didn't help the case. "You both could use the rest and a chance to decompress."

"Sitting on our hands will only widen Bumper's head start."

Edward looked into his rearview mirror. "Will 10:00 give you the time you need?"

The tinker grunted.

Our driver-turned-mediator drummed his fingers on the steering wheel. "10:00 it is."

"What about Surf Services?" I asked.

"I've been experimenting with a new automation system. Tonight seems a good time to test it. Better than the middle of the summer."

The Gremlin rumbled to a stop in front of the tinker's house, which still boasted Christmas lights and plastic reindeer grazing on his frosted lawn. One deer leaned to the right and looked as if it had found the bottle in my desk. I got out and folded the seat forward to release the tinker. He went right to his front door without so much as a *see you later*.

"That man ain't happy," Edward said from inside the car.

I plunked onto the passenger seat and closed the door. "He'll get over it."

Edward pulled away and headed for my office.

I climbed the stairs moments later having to pause halfway feeling weak in the knees from twenty-four hours of getting nowhere. *Maybe 10:00 wasn't such a bad idea.*

SALT-HEAVY MIST ROLLED DOWN WASHINGTON AVENUE freezing on anything it touched, including my trench coat and the heavy duffle bag of tools resting at my feet. Blowing into my hands thawed my skin just long enough to experience the sting of refreeze. A cold night had its upside, though. Mental clarity.

Too many coincidences. Bumper's Pink Cadillac returns after no sightings for months. Elbow Patches appears and comments about my shoulder, which means he saw me get out of my car in front of the museum. The Pink Flamingo goes belly-up, but Bumper and Patches draw us away from there.

I knew enough about the minds of criminals not to ignore these closely-occurring coincidences, and I needed to know why they didn't want me around the abandoned dance club.

I turned up my trench coat's collar against a gust having traveled from way down by the water's edge. I listened to the wind while mulling over my suspicions until the Gremlin, its windows thick with fog, slid to a stop at the curb.

A blast of heat struck me when the tinker opened the passenger door. He stepped onto the sidewalk sporting a long dark coat, black knit hat, black gloves, and black leather pants.

"Well," I said, "if it isn't the Man In Black himself. What's with the getup?"

"You know better than anyone, Jimmy. There's no room for mistakes in night ops."

"Night ops, huh?" I leaned into the car and looked across the empty seat at a similarly monochrome figure hunched over the wheel. Edward's stringy gray hair snaked out from beneath a black hat and over a black peacoat's collar. He revved the Gremlin's 120 horsepower engine and smiled at me.

The tinker pulled a small tube of grease paint from his pocket and smeared some along his jawbone. "We were prepping for this the last hour. What about you?"

"You're still sore with me, then, huh?"

The tinker pocketed his grease paint and folded forward the passenger seat. "Not at all."

We stood looking at each other.

"Well," I motioned toward the back, "go ahead."

He shook his head. "Nope, shotgun."

"What are you, twelve?" I pulled my coat around my waist and measured the V-shaped gap between folded passenger seat and door frame. "Seriously?"

"Come on, guys," Edward said, "the moon is rising at 11:30, and there isn't any cloud cover. We're wasting the darkest part of the night." He spurred the Gremlin's 120 horses.

I tossed my bag onto the floor behind Edward, stepped into the back, and swung my butt toward the bench seat, but I got hung-up on the door latch and had to retreat back to the sidewalk. Stepping inside then ducking didn't work either. I bent forward on my third attempt, reached inside with both hands, and propped my upper body on the seat, but my hips got wedged firmly between the passenger seat back and door frame. No amount of wiggling freed me from the Gremlin's vice grip.

The tinker shoved against my backside.

"Hey, watch it. Just give me some space."

"You need a lot of space, but don't worry. Edward, can you come around here and give me a hand?"

The two of them shoved me into the back, where I knelt dog-like across the bench seat. I scooped my hat from the floor and started to turn into a seated position, but the passenger seatback thumped into place and both car doors slammed.

"One of you needs to put your seat forward so I can turn around back here."

Edward looked at me in the rearview mirror. "No time for that, Jimmy." He gunned the engine, and we rumbled down Washington Avenue to the next intersection where a squealing U-turn pointed us toward Route One.

"Come on, guys, just pull over a second."

Edward spoke into the rearview mirror. "We don't want to call any more attention to ourselves, and we'll be at the Pink Flamingo in fifteen minutes."

I managed to turn onto my side and lay across the bench in the fetal position. "Don't pull into the parking lot. Do a pass first to see if anyone is there then park in that old machine shop's lot around the corner."

They'll be watching for the Studebaker. Not Edward's car.

I felt the Gremlin slow, and I lifted my head to see through Edward's window. No cars in the Pink Flamingo's lot. No light coming through the grimy newspaper-covered windows. A couple of turns, and we stopped. The tinker got out and pulled his seat forward freeing me to crawl backwards toward the door then shimmy out by dropping my legs and rolling onto the ice-cold asphalt. I stood, brushed grit from my dress pants, adjusted my coat, and reached back into the Gremlin for my duffle bag and hat.

The tinker put his hand on my shoulder. "See, it wasn't that bad."

I shrugged off his hand and watched Edward dodge back and forth from fence post to telephone pole to dumpster in his hunched knuckle-dragging way trying to hide his approach to the Pink Flamingo.

"You don't have to do that." My voice echoed between the squat brick and concrete buildings surrounding us.

Edward, crouched behind a street sign, looked back at the tinker and me, waved us forward, then continued his ambling back and forth from cover to cover down the shadowy street.

The tinker and I followed using the sidewalk.

Our approach from the back of the once flamboyant and bustling club enabled us to check for vehicles parked near the service entrances. No one in sight. An empty main parking lot. I felt confident the coast was clear. Mostly confident.

I called to Edward belly-crawling through crunching winter-browned weeds along the building, "Hey, we're going in over here."

The stage doors the tinker and I had escaped through during our brief appearance at the Pink Flamingo lay just around the corner from the street, beyond the sight of anyone driving by and beyond notice from the other entrances and windows.

The tinker shook a chain threaded through the doors' two steel handles and a hefty padlock. "Got anything for these?"

I unzipped my duffle bag. A medium-sized bolt cutter made short work of the chain. Fortunately, the chain served as the only lock for the doors, which I closed behind the three of us. The tinker and I switched on flashlights.

Edward squeezed a red-filtered lamp over his knit hat. "Can you guys dim those flashlights? We'll be seen."

"By who, the rats?" I walked a few yards to a small set of stairs.

A moment later, I stood center stage and the events of my last and only night at the club came rushing back. Bright lights, the press of the audience, the tang of old sweat in the air, the heat, and the throbbing music. The memories hit me like a slice of pizza having spent too many days on my end table. I shook off the images and reminded myself to focus on putting away Bumper and Elbow Patches, the criminals responsible for that night and much more.

Broken drop ceiling tiles and bent aluminum tracks hung from wires screwed to wood joists. Stacked tables and chairs lined the walls. Finding a light switch would have done no good. Most of the fluorescent bulbs had dropped from their fixtures and become impossible puzzles scattered across the floor.

Taut strings tied to stanchions formed a grid in the large open space in front of the stage. I traced a string with my flashlight beam and came upon a cardboard box with an upright broom handle taped to its end. Then I found another. And another. Six boxes total.

"Hey," I called to the tinker, "you see these?"

The tinker scratched his head. "Yeah, I don't get it."

I shrugged. "I don't either, but I'm sure this is what Bumper and Patches didn't want us to see."

Edward stood at the bar moving something around, but I couldn't tell what because of his dim red light.

I made my way to him. "What did you find?"

"Drawings." Our paramilitary troll lifted papers. "Not very good ones, but I think these are cars."

A crash came from deep within the building.

"We're not alone," I whispered. "Use your phones. Take as many pictures as you can. Fast!"

Tiny LEDs struggled to cast aside the dark and dust.

Edward shoved the drawings into his pockets.

"Jimmy," the tinker clicked off his flashlight, "I hear footsteps."

I switched off my light and grabbed Edward by his peacoat's collar. "We have to go. You lead. We'll use your headlamp."

Moments later, we piled into the Gremlin with me riding shotgun, and I didn't let out my breath until we reached the highway.

"What a rush!" Edward banged on his steering wheel. "You two do this all of the time?"

The tinker poked his head between the bucket seats. "Seems like it."

"Take us back to my office, Edward. We need to look at our photos."

"You must live for this stuff." Edward banged again on his steering wheel. "Why don't we go to my office? I just put a fresh ink cartridge in my color printer. I think I have some photo paper, too."

I pulled my fedora down low and closed my eyes. "Sounds good to me."

THIRTY-THREE EIGHT-BY-TEN GLOSSIES COVERED the floor in front of Edward's desk, and I still couldn't make heads or tails out of the strings and boxes. The drawings of cars confused me further. The three of us stood staring at our night's work surrounded by hyperactive machines.

"I guess you couldn't turn off those pumps for a while, could you?" The constant churning and chugging didn't help with my concentration.

Edward put his hands on his hips and scanned the machinery-filled chamber. "Surf Services can't stop for anyone, Jimmy. You of all people know what happens when we mess with this beauty."

I wish I didn't.

The tinker moved a photo toward me with his toe and pointed to a broom stick taped to the back of a box. "What's this?"

"A broom stick," I said.

"I know that, but why does every box have one?"

I moved across the room and turned my head to get a new perspective. "Edward, can you hand me one of those drawings?" I held up a simple line figure scratched on tablet paper. "This really does look like a car. If someone made that box from this drawing, and it's supposed to be a car, what kind of a car has a pole sticking out of it?"

The tinker squatted and pointed to another photo of a box and stick. "What about a bumper car?"

THE SUN ROSE ABOVE THE BOARDWALK AT the end of Washington Avenue. I could only guess how many townspeople woke to the growling of Edward's Gremlin as we raced through Ocean Mist's residential streets.

"Hey, Angela," I said into my cell, "when you get this, I need you to try and get ahold of someone to let us into the historical society's museum. I'm about to break this case wide open, but I need to get inside as soon possible. Thanks, doll." I disconnected and twisted my neck to speak into the back seat. "Any luck?"

"No one is picking up." The tinker leaned forward between the front seats with his phone to his ear. "There's usually someone at the society by 10:00, but that's three hours from now."

I kept flipping through the Pink Flamingo photos. "We can't wait that long."

Edward asked, "What about your friend from the library?"

I shook my head. "There's always a way inside a joint."

The Gremlin rumbled to a stop outside the museum. I started up the crushed shell walk with the tinker and Edward in tow. My skin crawled like whenever approaching the scene of foul play, and this private eye's sixth sense never failed him.

The front door stood ajar.

I held up my hand and drew my nephew's squirt gun. Its yellow plastic glinted in the January sun. "Hold on a minute."

"Boy," Edward said, "you mean business."

"Wait here." I stepped off the walk, crept through the frosted grass, and stood to the right of the door. The screen squealed on its hinges even though I opened it slowly, which stole the element of surprise. *No choice, now,* I thought. I kicked open the door aiming my squirt gun dead center down the narrow hallway.

The big docent lay across the card table half risen from his chair like he had tried to get up fast but got stuck before passing out. The little plastic register lay burst open on the floor with its bills and change scattered across the hardwood. A familiar heavy herb smell lingered.

Elbow Patches' wacky tobaccy.

I ducked into each room clearing the small museum in a matter of seconds then waved the tinker and Edward inside from the entrance.

The tinker eased the docent back into his chair. "What happened to him?"

"Elbow Patches happened to him." I nudged the register with the tip of my penny loafer. "They weren't here for the cash."

The tinker tapped the guy on the cheeks. "Buddy, wake up. Can you hear me?"

The docent stirred.

I put the squirt gun in my pocket making a mental note to get a shoulder holster. "Edward, watch the door."

"You got it, Jimmy."

"Hey," I snapped my fingers at the tinker, "your docent friend will be okay. You need to come and see this." I led the tinker into the exhibit with the bumper car, which lay overturned and disemboweled. The electric motor had been torn free of the chassis and the seat tossed into the middle of the room.

The tinker covered his mouth and spoke through his fingers. "Why would they do such a horrible thing?"

Bumper and Elbow Patches seemed three-steps ahead of me since Rocco had provided our first lead, but shrewd detective work kept me right on their heels, and every case had a moment when a private eye's experience, intellect, and instinct came together with a divine spark of realization, when all of the clues and beat-work finally mattered, when the puzzle started to show its picture, and it all made sense.

I pointed to the yellowed and grainy photo of Great-great-granddaddy Gleeson standing at his workbench with the cockeyed calendar tacked to the wall behind him. "That ain't a calendar." Pushing my fedora back and putting my nose to the glass gave me the details I needed to confirm my deduction. "That's a grid."

I took a picture of it with my phone.

The tinker folded his arms and looked really hard at the photo. "I don't get it."

"The strings at the Flamingo made a grid, too. We just need a set of coordinates." I lifted the broken bumper car seat, turned it over, and did the same with another part I couldn't identify. Nothing.

"Coordinates? You mean for like a treasure map?"

"Yep." A glint caught my eye. I knelt next to the chassis and tapped a little bronze plate screwed to the inside of the motor compartment. I pulled a notepad from my trench coat and jotted down the twelve letters and numbers separated by a bunch of dashes. "I'm willing to bet a year's worth of funnel cakes this is what Bumper and Elbow Patches came here to get. How many boxes with broom sticks did we find on the floor of the Flamingo?"

"Six, I think."

I tapped my notepad. "And we have six sets of coordinates right here."

"So, all we need is the map."

"No, not a map." Great-great-granddaddy Gleeson stared stone-faced at me from his photo, and I stared back at him. "Find a couple of aspirin for the big docent guy then meet Edward and me at the car. We need to take a ride."

I dialed my genius nephew and headed for the front door. "Hey kid, you at home? Good. I'm sending a guy to get you. Name's Edward. He'll be there in about forty-five minutes. Pack a pair of rubber gloves with your gizmos. Right, we'll be working with electricity. No, don't tell your mom."

We piled into the Gremlin, Edward just as bouncy and upbeat as the day began. I could have used some of what he had.

"Your new surf automation system is going to get the full test today. I need you to take us to Happy Land then go to Bethany to pick up my Nephew." I scratched out an address on my small note pad, tore off the sheet, and passed it across the seat. "Bring him back to Happy Land as fast as you can."

Edward took the address and stuffed it into his ashtray. "What's at Happy Land?"

"What half of Ocean Mist has been looking for the past hundred years. More importantly, something I've been looking for the past nine months."

The tinker poked his head up between the seats. "The Jenkins' cat? I'm surprised it hasn't—."

"No, not the cat. Bumper and Elbow Patches."

The Case of Bumper's Car

Part 3: The Ride Downtown

Edward eased the Gremlin past Bumper's Pink Cadillac sitting alone and still near the back of Happy Land. "You sure about this, Jimmy?"

"You bet I am."

He stopped just long enough to dump the tinker and me then tore off toward Bethany.

Waves pounded the sand just beyond the dunes. Clouds rolled in from the southwest. The air had become damp and tasted like snow.

Nothing seemed amiss on Happy Land's street side. Orange overhead doors rested flush against the ground, and I tugged each padlock securing the doors to U-bolts set in the concrete sidewalk.

Nothing peculiar.

Nothing quieter than a locked-up Mid-Atlantic beach amusement park in January.

The doors on the boardwalk side seemed just as secure until I got to the last padlock. It lay open next to its U-bolt.

Someone had a key.

I put my finger to my lips, pointed to the lock, and took off my hat so I could press my ear against the ice-cold rolling door. Silence. I hiked up my pants, crouched, grabbed the door's handle with my left, and whispered to the tinker, "You ready?"

He nodded.

I used my right hand to count down from five then took the handle with both hands and stood. The door turned out to be heavier than I expected and squealed and clanked with each retracting panel. Holding the monstrosity at my waist, I tossed my chin toward the opening, but the tinker just looked at me. My legs shook. The dull ache in my shoulder turned into a sharp sting.

"Now," I said.

"Now what, Jimmy?"

"Go."

"Go where?"

"What do you think? Go inside and hold it open for me."

"Oh." The tinker ducked through. His fingers grabbed the bottom of the door. "You really need to work on your communication. I'm not a mind reader."

We got inside, eased the door back into place, and double-timed it into an alcove between arcade machines. I rolled my shoulder, grimaced, and hoped Bumper and Patches didn't hear us.

"Are you okay? How's your shoulder?"

"It's fine." I poked my head out from the alcove and peered into what looked like a playroom for a giant's child. Rides of fire engines, racing-striped sports cars, airplanes suspended at the ends of mechanical arms, and oversized fiberglass flowers, their colors dulled by shadows, all frozen in time and waiting for riders that wouldn't come until the first warm days of spring.

"You hear that?" I asked.

"Yeah, sounds like talking."

A narrow space between arcade machines formed a path with great cover leading deep into the amusement park and toward the voices.

"Follow me." I took a few steps then realized the tinker hadn't moved. "What's the matter?"

"I can't go that way." His eyes looked like golf balls.

"Why not?"

He pointed to the claw machine.

I rubbed my face with both hands. "For crying out loud, that was over a year ago. Just close your eyes and walk past it."

"Jimmy, I can't. I still have nightmares."

I went back and grabbed his ski jacket's lapels.

"Jimmy, I said I can't."

"Stop whining." I dragged him past the claw machine. "See? No problem."

"My therapist would not have approved."

"Please extend my apologies."

We weaved our ways through the rest of the machines and came to the arcade's end. Only the carousel lay between us, the bumper car ride, and some poor guy tied to a wood chair slid against a steel and cement pylon. The tinker craned his head to the side and looked really hard in the tied-up guy's direction.

"You know him?" I asked.

"Of course. That's One-handed Harry. He's a Happy Land celebrity."

"Celebrity, huh?" *Explains where they got the key to the lock.*

"The newspaper did a human-interest story on him last summer. He started as a game barker, worked his way up through the kiddy rides, and made it to the top in less than three years."

"The top?"

"Yep, the Hurricane Train operator. All of that came crashing down, though, after the fishing accident."

"Is that how he lost his hand?"

"He lost his hand?"

"You said he's One-handed Harry."

"Yeah, but he didn't lose a hand. One-handed Harry is his amusement park name. A carny name. It must mean something in their culture, like David in Hebrew means beloved. Anyway, Harry got a hook in his good eye."

"He only had one good eye, but his name is one-handed Harry?"

The tinker nodded. "Completely blind, now. He can't operate anything above bumper cars."

"A blind bumper cars operator?"

"You say that like it's a problem."

I realized why I had worked solo for so many years.

I pulled out my phone to call in Ocean Mist's finest. Time to make a couple of collars. Bumper and Patches had given me everything I needed to take them down: assaulting the docent, vandalizing the museum, kidnapping the Harry guy, and dragging him to Happy Land. I just needed to put a net over these two before they could give me the slip.

A lady dispatcher came on the line. "This is 9-1-1. Ocean Mist's City Council reminds you to recycle your Christmas Tree by contacting Owl Scout Troop 13. You can find their contact information and availability on the council's website. What is the nature of your emergency?"

"This is Jimmy Grits. I'm down at Happy Land. I've cornered two kidnappers, and they have Harry Hands."

The tinker pulled the cell from my ear. "No, Jimmy, it's One-handed Harry."

"I told you not to talk over me while I'm on the phone."

"Look buddy," the lady said, "this number is for emergencies only. Call someone else about your hairy hands."

I jerked my phone back from the tinker. "No, doll. Just one hairy hand."

"Sir, I am not your doll, and I am not comfortable with this conversation."

"Listen, just send a couple boys with cuffs down here right away."

"You should know this conversation is being recorded."

The tinker rose onto his toes and leaned into my phone. "Tell her about Patches and his pipe."

"You want the police, Mr. Grits? I'm sending them!"

"Hello?" My connection seemed to drop. "Hello, doll, can you hear me?"

"Do you think she got the message, Jimmy?"

I glanced at the tinker and wished I had the time to give him a message of my own, but justice waited for no one. "I'm going to get closer."

Shadows and I always got along, whether in an alley or the parking lot of some seedy bar, and Happy Land's shadows were no exception. I edged my way around the last game machine, eyed the distance to the carousel, and made my move ending up behind a pink giraffe.

From there, I could see all three actors in this dirty little play: Bumper,

Patches, and the back of the summer-ride-operator's head. Zip ties bound Harry's hands to the arms of the rickety chair, and some kind of straps looped around his chest and legs.

Bumper eased a car down the ride's oval track keeping her gaze on the metal floor. Her bleach-blonde beehive drooped making her head a sad question mark. She stopped, hopped out, and moved another car in the same way. "What about now?"

Patches stood at the ride operator's podium with a large sheet of paper in his hand. "I think that one over there needs to be moved back about two feet." He looked over his shoulder at poor Harry. "What do you think, blind man?"

A muffled sound came from the chair.

Some movement and swishing sounds to my right made me lower my head behind the carousel's giraffe. I pivoted, staying within the creature's shadow, and saw the tinker duckwalking low behind the fence along the ride's perimeter. His ski jacket sounded like a dishwasher's brush on a crusty pan.

"Hey," Bumper's distressed-frog voice made the tinker freeze, "who's there?"

No telling how long until the police arrived, so I made my move and stepped out from behind the giraffe. "The gig is up, Bumper. You and Patches are going down and going down hard."

"Grits!" she croaked.

Patches folded up his paper, stuffed it into his smoking jacket's pocket, took out his pipe, thumbed the bowl, and struck a match. Bumper hopped from her bumper car onto the track and looked around, presumably for the quickest escape route.

I ran for Patches, but, before I could get to him, he climbed into a car and tramped the accelerator. His head snapped back against the padded headrest, and his tires squealed leading into the track's first turn. Water droplets ran down my wrist when I pulled my nephew's yellow beauty from my coat pocket. *Leaking. How many squirts do I have left?*

Patches puffed like a steam engine on a midnight run, and I noticed he must have packed his bowl with a different blend. Smelled stronger, made me woozy even at that distance, and the smoke came out thick and fast. His plan became clear— create a wacky tobaccy smoke screen to try and hide their escape.

I propped my gun arm on the ride's fencing, braced my wrist, and looked down the yellow barrel. The trigger felt cold and wet against my finger. I lined-up the plastic nub with Patches' approaching car, took a deep breath, let it out slowly, and laid down three quick bursts. Nowhere near hitting the target. Not because of my marksmanship, but the gun just didn't have the pressure to reach far enough.

Heavy smoke hit my nostrils, made my head swim, and drove me back from the track's edge. Patches smoked a year of his life away with each lap.

If I can't get to Patches, maybe I can nab Bumper.

I turned to find the tinker toe-to-toe with Bumper by the Giant Toad Ride. A stand-off. The looks in their eyes told me everything I needed to know about their history, and it wasn't good.

The tinker lunged, but instead of grabbing her shoulders, he made two circular motions with his arms, kicked up one of his heels, and clapped dramatically above his head. Bumper responded with a box step combined with a sultry hip sway then some move related to disco. What I thought would be a simple restraint for the tinker turned into a full-blown dance-off in front of a fiberglass amphibian.

Meanwhile, Patches had completed enough loops around the track to create a storm cloud of smoke. I couldn't get close enough to see the track let alone all of the exits from the ride, exactly what he wanted, but I could still hear his engine whine. I had to act fast before he escaped from behind his smoke screen.

A bunch of grunts and banging of wood against the concrete floor brought my eyes to Harry. He yelled incoherently through the rag tied across his mouth and rocked in his chair to get someone's attention, but I couldn't help him.

I went to the ride-operator's podium and found a big red button among the controls. I slammed it with my palm.

Patches' motor stopped.

The cloud of wacky tobacco smoke began to dissipate, and I made a best guess about which side of the track he would choose for his escape. I took several strides to my left, but stopped and made an about face when I heard a ruckus.

The big docent stood at the right-side exit shaking his hand like he had just hit something hard. Patches lay motionless at his feet. "You and the lady owe me twelve dollars."

"How'd you know we were here?" I asked.

"Your friend told me before he left the museum."

Now that you mention him—.

I ran for the Giant Toad Ride and found the tinker stripped of his ski jacket and engaged with Bumper in some kind of grinding motion making me sick and confused at the same time. Bumper's knees buckled, and she collapsed panting on the floor, the victim of the tinker's gyrations and a four-pack-a-day habit.

"It's all over, Bumper," I said. "There's nowhere for you to go, and I got enough evidence to put you and your boyfriend where you belong."

The tinker put his fists on his hips, did a dramatic pelvic thrust, and held his head high.

I untied Harry and asked the docent, "How did you get in here?"

"The loading dock's overhead door is open."

"Open?"

"Near that Pink Cadillac."

The tinker saddled-up next to us, did some deep knee bends, side stretches, and pulled his left knee to his chest. "That was intense."

"I'm sure it was," I said.

Distant sirens announced more visitors on the way, and, a few minutes later, some battering noises followed by the sheering of metal told me the police didn't see the open loading dock, either.

The lead officer, wearing a tactical belt better suited for a pack animal, made his way to the middle of us and folded his arms. "We're here for the pervert making the phone calls."

The tinker pointed at me. "You're looking for Jimmy."

"Now, wait a minute," I pulled Harry up from his chair, "you need to talk to this guy."

Harry told his story to the arresting officers, and the cuffs came out for Bumper and Patches.

I reached inside Patches' smoking jacket, pulled out his pipe, and handed it to the officer. "Make sure he doesn't light up in your cruiser." I also retrieved the folded paper and put it in my pocket.

"Harry," I said to the ride operator, "do you think you can convince the police to let us stay and help you secure the building?"

"I guess, why?"

"If my hunch is right, we're about to make the biggest discovery in Ocean Mist's history, right here on your ride."

Harry didn't need to identify himself or his position— being a local celebrity, and all— so the police let us alone with promises of coming to the station first thing the next day to make our statements.

We caught our breaths while watching Patches' cloud disperse. My shoulder really hurt, my back ached, and having only had a nap over the past thirty-six hours started to catch up with me. My red-headed nephew and Edward came in through the door the police had busted open.

Edward looked around the empty amusement park. "We passed the police. What happened?"

I straightened my hat. "Bumper and Patches finally got what they deserved."

Edward punched at the air and stomped his foot. "I miss everything!"

"What's on Patches' paper?" the tinker asked.

I unfolded a diagram of the ride with a bunch of "x's" placed on a grid. Letters went down one side and numbers along the other, but I couldn't tell how to hold the drawing. I called up the photo I had snapped of Great-great-granddaddy Gleeson, zoomed into the calendar-looking grid behind him, held up my tiny screen, and compared it to the bumper car ride's metal track.

My nephew dropped a large duffle bag and slinked out of an over-stuffed backpack. "I wasn't sure what we would need, Uncle Jimmy, so I just brought everything."

"That's great, kid. Edward, can you go back to the car and get my folder with the photos?"

"Sure thing."

I picked up my nephew's duffle bag and led him to the bumper cars. "What did Edward tell you?"

"He didn't stop talking the whole way here. Something about him saving your life when you were jumped at a strip club."

"Okay, we'll sort that out later. Right now, I need your help to figure out the combination to a lock."

"What kind of lock?"

"A pretty complicated one, it turns out. You see how these bumper cars are all spread out on the track?"

My nephew nodded and pushed his glasses up to the bridge of his nose.

"Well," I took off my fedora and used it to point while I spoke, "each of the cars has this pole sticking up out of the back to make a connection with the metal grate up there."

"That's how bumper cars work, Uncle Jimmy."

"Right. So, if we place the cars at just the right spots on the track and turn on the juice, it should be like finding the right set of numbers on a combination lock."

"That sort of makes sense."

"What do you mean, sort of?"

"Well," he adjusted his glasses again, "the grate above the floor has a negative charge, and the metal track has a positive charge. Someone pushing on a car's pedal allows electricity to flow through the motor. It completes the circuit."

"Right." I scratched my chin. "So, what's the problem?"

"We need a person in each car to push the pedals down at the same time. If it's not at the same time, one or more of the motors will engage and move the cars out of place before the combination is completed. Timing is everything." My nephew stepped onto the track, walked behind a car, looked up, looked down, and said, "Or, we can run wires from the poles to the metal brushes under each car then just turn on the electricity without engaging the motors."

Bumper and Patches could never have beaten us. They didn't have a boy genius.

"Just tell us what to do, kid."

My nephew called to Harry. "Sir, could you please cut the power to the bumper cars?"

I opened the duffle bag full of gizmos and gadgets to look for something resembling an ordinary tool box. "Never mind, Harry. I already killed it with that big red button over there."

My nephew wiped his glasses on his t-shirt and looked at me with an expression conveying a seriousness beyond his years. "Never work on anything electric without turning off the power at the supply. We need to trip the breakers."

Harry stood from his chair and leaned on a concrete and steel pylon to steady himself. "Hold your horses. I'll get 'em before you all barbecue yourselves." His hands shook and legs wobbled from his ordeal.

The docent took Harry by the elbow. "Let me help you."

Harry led him toward one of Happy Land's back rooms.

"What's next?" I asked my nephew.

"Can you give me a flathead screwdriver?" He turned it over in his hand and inspected the back of a bumper car until Harry called an all-clear. "This panel has to come off so I can disconnect the hot wire from the terminal block."

"The terminal block, right." I watched him remove some screws. He handed me the panel. "So, uh, how's school?"

"Fine." His fingers separated a multicolored spaghetti of wires held together by a bunch of clamps fastened to a ceramic square.

The tinker walked onto the track. "The terminal block. Good place to start."

I mussed my nephew's hair. "That's what I thought, too."

"I'm concentrating, Uncle Jimmy." He patted down his orange puff, pursed his lips, and made a couple of turns on a clamp's retaining screw to free a thick black-rubber-sheathed copper wire.

I cradled the small of my back. Lifting the overhead door really did a number on me. "There are a bunch of black ones. How do you know which to disconnect?"

He ran his finger along a wire snaking into the pole leading to the ceiling grate. "I just traced the one going into here."

The docent walked Harry back to his chair at the building pylon, and I called to the lug, "We can use another couple of hands."

The docent joined our electrician's tutorial on the track, and we split up to disconnect the power feeds to the remaining five cars we needed for the combination.

One by one, my nephew went to each car and used little plastic caps to twist together new pieces of wire to the ends of the hot wires, which he then joined to the metal brushes under the chassis. The dust must have aggravated his allergies. He sneezed and wiped his nose on his sleeve. "How do you know where to move the cars to make the connections?"

Edward bounced up to the ride's fence and waved the folder full of photos. "We have these." He helped me spread the prints on the concrete next to the ride.

I laid Patches' diagram among the prints and flashed to my nephew the notepad where I had jotted the museum car's serial number. "These are the coordinates for the grid. How's that for first-class detective work?"

He pushed up his glasses.

I loosened my tie. "Let's set up a grid and move these cars into place. Harry, you got any string and spray paint around here? We need to mark the floor."

"Wait a minute, Uncle Jimmy. There can't be a grid on the floor. The brushes under the cars are too big, so you can't get a precise or reliable set of points. The grid and points for your combination have to be up there." He pointed to the metal grate. "The contacts at the ends of the poles are much smaller."

The tinker leaned toward my nephew's ear. "I tried to tell him that."

"I heard you, and no, you didn't."

"I did. You just don't listen."

Harry lifted his hands in the air. "Can you just get on with whatever it is you're doing? I have a headache!"

My nephew walked to the other side of the track without looking down from the grate. "Our next problem is to figure out which side of this metal rectangle is the y-axis and which is the x-axis."

I moved some of the photos around the floor with the tip of my penny loafer. "X- axis, right. I see."

My nephew turned to Harry who sat with his arms folded and his face sour-looking. "Sir, do you have a ladder that reaches the ceiling?"

Harry huffed, held out his arm like a wing for someone to take, and disappeared with the docent in the direction they had gone to cut the power. A minute later, they reappeared with the muscle-bound docent carrying an old wooden step ladder.

I took my nephew's arm before he could climb. "You stay down here. Tell me what to look for." The ladder creaked and wobbled until I made it to the last two steps putting me at eye-level with one of the rails.

"Do you see any letters or numbers, Uncle Jimmy? Probably at the welds?"

The amusement park's dark interior and the grate's black metal made seeing anything more than general shapes difficult even with the help of my phone's LED. I ran my finger across the rail. A thick layer of grease, sand, and grime made me wonder how electricity could even pass into the cars. I pulled out my handkerchief and wiped off a section. Our freckled wonder deserved another *that-a-boy*. The letters "F" through "J" stamped at regular intervals appeared right at the welds.

"There are letters along this side. Harry, you got any rags and degreaser?"

"In the machine shop." The blind bumper cars operator pushed up from his chair, held out his arm for an escort, and the docent took it.

I wiped away more grime with my handkerchief. "And another ladder, too."

"You think I'm running a hardware store?" Harry and the docent headed toward the back of Happy Land. "I just want to go home and listen to the news."

"Hey Jimmy," Edward tugged on the hem of my pants, "I'm going to get us a pizza."

"Good idea. I'll take a pizza, too."

By the time lunch arrived, we had set up the second ladder and cleaned the rails well enough for me to read the letters and the docent to read the numbers. The tinker and my nephew pushed the cars around until their contacts touched the overhead grid at the coordinates scribbled on my notepad.

I used my sport coat sleeve to wipe sweat from my brow. "Alright, I think that's it. Everyone off the track. Let's turn on the juice."

The docent climbed down from his ladder. "I got it, Harry. Don't get up." He made his way to the breakers, and his voice echoed through the cavernous Happy Land. "Everyone clear?"

Edward bounced on the balls of his feet and alternated his gaze between the back of the building and the bumper cars. His bald crown and swishing stringy hair reminded me of a spinning car wash brush. "Go for it!"

Pops and showers of sparks came from all but one car. Nothing else happened.

"Cut the power!" Acrid burned-rubber smells from century-old electrical insulation filled my nostrils. I tried to fan away the fumes with my hat.

"Power's off." The docent's voice bounced around the building's girders and from the ceiling at my head.

"Don't worry, Uncle Jimmy." My nephew jumped onto the track with screw drivers and pliers sticking from his pockets. "It's probably just a bad connection." He fussed with the uncooperative car's wiring and hopped back off the track. "Try again."

All of the cars spat sparks and crackled with electricity. A loud screech of metal-on-metal—some unlubricated mechanism moving after a long time of not moving—drew my attention to the steel and cement pylon next to Harry's chair. A plate released and swung out and downward on two hinges. No one saw it soon enough to give the blind bumper cars operator a warning. The plate banged him square on the forehead, and he hit the floor like a sack of potatoes.

The tinker ran to Harry's aid. "Harry, can you hear me?" He dragged him out from under the plate. "Harry? Hey, Harry?" The tinker tapped his cheeks lightly. "Wake up, pal."

The fireworks stopped, but the grate and track still hummed with current, something I could hear and feel in my bones. "You can kill the power."

"We done?" the docent called back.

"Yeah, that did it. You can come back."

I crossed the ride to the pillar, pulled out my cell phone, and used its light to look inside an alcove about the size of an apple crate. No gold, but I pulled out a stack of yellowed and brittle papers tied with a piece of faded red ribbon. I blew across the bundle's top. A cloud of one-hundred-year-old dust made my nephew sneeze. "Sorry about that."

"That's okay." He wiped his nose on his sleeve.

The docent looked over my shoulder. "Those are stock certificates."

Harry moaned and pressed his hand against his forehead.

Dim gray spilling from a skylight helped me read the large faded cursive text across the top of the first sheet. "The Ocean Mist and Georgetown Canal Company."

The tinker just about knocked me over trying to get in close enough to see the certificates. "There's no canal to Georgetown."

"Could someone help me up?" Harry asked.

"I can't believe it." The docent shook his head and smiled. "There's an old wives' tale about a bunch of venture capitalists funding a study just before the Great Depression to see if a canal could be built between here and Georgetown, but historians never found any proof."

"Well, I'm holding your proof."

My nephew adjusted his glasses. "That doesn't make sense. There isn't a large enough body of water near Georgetown to connect to. It would be like a canal to nowhere."

"Actually," the tinker pulled my arm down and just about poked the certificates with his nose, "there was a bunker boom right around that time. They might have thought Georgetown could provide workers and cheap land for new canneries." The tinker looked at the docent. "Wasn't there a railroad passing through Georgetown?"

The docent nodded. "The Baltimore and Eastern Railroad."

"Now I get it!" The tinker threw his hands into the air. "Bunker trawlers could steam up the canal to Georgetown, sell their catches to the canneries, and the canneries would process the bunker for oil and chum then use the railroad to ship their products all over."

I sighed. "Ship bunker chum, huh?"

The tinker smacked my shoulder. "Brilliant, isn't it?"

Harry staggered to his feet. "Can I go home, now?"

I tilted the papers to make better use of the gray coming through the skylight. "Looks like old Gleeson sank his gold into a washout company. So much for the treasure at the end of the rainbow." I stepped to a trashcan with a big duck's head and tossed the papers into the dustbin of history.

The tinker and docent dove into the duck's mouth almost cracking heads.

Mr. I've Got a Minor in History came up first with a fistful of the certificates. "This discovery rewrites Ocean Mist's past, Jimmy. These are better than gold."

"Wish I could agree with you. I don't think Great-great-granddaddy Gleeson would've agreed with you, either."

Some gold would have been nice, especially with the traffic fines waiting for me at the Rehoboth barracks, but putting Bumper and Patches behind bars on kidnapping, aggravated assault, destruction of public property, and a bunch of other charges seemed a pretty good consolation prize.

The Case of the Diamond Putter

Part 1: Teed Off

"Grits Detective Service."

"Hallo, I'd like to spek with someone bout yur agency's services."

"Well, you got someone." I squeezed the receiver between my cheek and shoulder, slid aside my desk planner, and unwrapped a Down and Out Burger double-patty masterpiece.

"Aye, well, me name is Gilmer Aitken."

"What's your trouble?"

"It sems someone chore a family heirloom."

"I'm sorry, I think we have a bad connection." I took a bite of my burger and splashed vinegar on my fries. "You're breaking up."

"It sems someone chore—nae, stole—stole me family heirloom."

"It sems? Oh, seems." I took another bight. "Does that mean you're not sure?"

"Nae, sir, I'm sure."

"You sound English. You English?"

"Nae, Scottish."

"Scottish, huh? Ain't that the same?" I decided my fries needed more vinegar. "Hello? You still there?"

"Cun I spek with Mr. Grits, or should I just leave a message?"

"You're talking to him. What did the Ocean Mist police say about your robbery?"

"Polis are draggin their fet. I need *mae* attention to this."

"Who's May?" I checked the bottom of my bag for runaway fries.

"Mae attention. I need mae attention."

"I know what that's like." I took another bite of my burger. "What can you tell me about your heirloom?"

"It's very valuable."

"How valuable are we talking?"

"Me surance adjuster says it's worth ninety thousand."

I choked on a fried onion. "You mean dollars?"

"I'm nae talkin pounds."

"Of course, you're not. That would be a heavy heirloom."

"I think it's a wee mae than ninety."

"Well, Mr. Aitken, you certainly have my attention." I picked up my pen and smoothed a corner of my burger wrapper. "Give me your address, and I'll be right over."

"I cunna meet ya now. I'm readyin for the match."

"Match?" Silence. "Hello?" I pressed the receiver tight against my ear. "You there?"

"The match, Mr. Grits. I'm Gilmer Aitken."

"Yeah, I got that already. What match are you talking about?"

"I'm defendin me title at Peter Putter's Miniature Golf Course at noon."

"Title?"

"Aye. Delmarva Platinum Ball Champion."

"Huh. That's a new one. Just so I understand, this miniature golf title is more important than a hundred-thousand-dollar heirloom?"

"I need to win as mae as I cun." He sighed. "The purses sem to get smaller every year."

"If you say so. I'm not the guy to help you with a purse, unless it's stolen, but I can help you find your heirloom." I glanced at my wall clock. *Eleven fifteen. Plenty of time to finish my burger and to get to the boardwalk.* "How about I meet you after your match? We can talk particulars and grab some lunch."

A SPRING SUN HANGING IN A CLOUDLESS sky warmed my shoulders.

I unbuttoned my sport coat and loosened my tie before turning east on Washington Avenue toward the beach. I could have taken the Studebaker, but the beautiful weather convinced me to walk the three blocks to the boardwalk.

Sneakers slapped the concrete heavy and quick behind me. The tinker stopped, put his hands on his knees, and sucked wind.

"Why are you in such a hurry?"

"I'm going to be late for the match."

"The miniature golf thing over at Peter's?"

"What else?" He tugged on my arm. "Come on."

"Easy there, Flash. I don't have to be there until after that Gilmer guy finishes."

"Why would you wait?"

"I can't talk to him while he's playing."

"You're going to talk to Gilmer? Gilmer Aitken?"

"He's a client."

"You're kidding?"

I shook my head. "Tell you what, why don't you run ahead and save me a spot?"

"You got it, Jimmy. You think you can get me his autograph?"

"No promises. We got serious business."

The tinker sped off toward the boardwalk.

The warming trend brought weekenders from Washington, D.C. and Baltimore. Hints of summer's sights, sounds, and smells surrounded me: t-shirts and shorts, screeching gulls competing for french fries, and whiffs of coconut sunscreen from passing women. I smiled. Not just because of the dames but also the inevitable uptick in crime. My bread and butter.

The scene up the boardwalk stopped me in my tracks. Spectators swarmed aluminum risers near Peter Putter's Miniature Golf Course. They packed narrow benches butt cheek to butt cheek and peered through the chain-link fence bordering the course. The closer I got to Peter's, the quieter the boardwalk became. No crying babies. No radios blaring. No one said a word. Quiet as Angela's library.

I climbed to the third row and took a seat next to the tinker.

He pointed and whispered, "That's Gilmer Aitken over there."

"You mean the guy wearing the blue golf shirt and green dress?"

"Keep your voice down, Jimmy. It's a kilt, not a dress."

Gilmer reached into a purse-looking bag slung over his shoulder, maybe the one he told me about, and pulled out a white handkerchief. He wiped his brow then adjusted a golf cap resting like a floppy pancake on his bushy red hair. A strong breeze rustled his kilt, which I could hear from the bleachers given the crowd's silence. His knee-high green and brown wool socks seemed a bit much for the warm day.

"So, where's the bagpipes?"

A no-necked guy near the fence wearing a *Peter's Primo Miniature Golf Course Staff* t-shirt pointed at me. "No talking in the stands."

I tipped my fedora to him.

Gilmer stepped up to hole nine, the one just past a fiberglass volcano puffing vapor clouds. He looked down at a little rubber pad to consider the three dents serving as possible tees then lifted his putter's handle to his face as if sighting some target much farther than the plastic cup five yards from his feet.

I looked at my watch.

Gilmer leaned to the left, leaned to the right, stared intently at the oversized bowling balls in the near green, and stepped to the side moving his gaze to a set of giant pins encircling the hole.

"Okay Gilmer," I said, "you want a hole-in-one or a strike?"

Five spectators turned in unison and shushed me.

I raised both hands in apology then checked my cell phone for messages.

Gilmer stepped back from the tee-pad, turned from the fairway, squatted, and stared at the boards beneath him. His kilt rode up revealing more of his pale bird legs than I wanted to see.

The crowd released a collective breath.

"What's the matter? What happened?"

A woman in front of me stood, turned, and gave me an eyeful of *Gilmer Girl* emblazoned in glittered letters across her bust-filled t-shirt. "Look buddy, you blow this for him, and I'll beat you all the way back to whatever sorry excuse for a forties jazz club you crawled from."

The tinker lifted a hand between the woman and me. "I'm sorry, ma'am. This is his first time at a competition. He has a lot of questions. It won't happen again."

The sun struck her *Gilmer Girl* lettering, and I shielded my eyes. "Mind switching off your high beams, there lady?"

She huffed. "Misogynist!"

The tinker patted my shoulder. "No, Jimmy's a detective. The Ocean Mist Spa has a great misogynist, though. I go to her every four weeks for my neck."

The lady shook her head and sat.

Gilmer stood from his squat, lifted his putter over his head, and did a straddle stretch.

"So, why doesn't he just hit the ball, already?"

"Patience, Jimmy."

Something I saw made me lean forward, tilt back my fedora, and squint. I thought maybe looking through the chain links played with my vision, but no. A tuft of orange chest hair billowed from Gilmer's powder blue golf shirt's unbuttoned V-neck.

Gilmer returned to the tee-pad, repeated his pre-putting ritual, and committed to a swing, which seemed to work since his ball passed between the oversized bowling balls, bounced through the forest of pins, and dropped into the hole. The crowd went nuts. Everyone jumped to their feet, stomped, cheered, and screamed in adoration. I thought the whole set of risers would overturn. Gilmer plucked his ball from the plastic cup and scrubbed it against the tuft of chest hair sticking from his V-neck.

"Is that some kind of good luck thing?" I asked the tinker.

"What?"

I shouted into his ear so he could hear me above the celebration. "Why did he rub his ball in his chest hair?"

"He's cleaning away grains of sand that could interfere with its roll. He's also scuffing the gloss on the ball for better contact with the club's head."

"You're kidding me?"

"Peel back the layers, Jimmy. Miniature golf is just as much a science as an art."

A scrawny-looking man wearing a bleach-white visor, stiff button down, and well-pressed khakis took Gilmer's putter, put it in a golf bag, and gave him another.

"This guy has a caddy?"

"Of course, Jimmy, but he's not called a caddy. Gilmer is stepping up to the tenth hole, so you need to be quiet."

"Are there really eighteen of these?"

The tinker nodded without looking away from the next fairway.

The match droned onward, and it seemed forever until Gilmer finished the last hole. I made for the attendant's shack at the course's roped-off entrance; unfortunately, so did most of the spectators. People pressed into the narrow space between risers and golf course with raised cell phones yelling praise for Gilmer and pleading for autographs. Gilmer reached a hand out to his caddy who handed him a pair of sunglasses before proceeding to the rope, where he signed golf magazines, big glossies, posters, and even a few body parts while smiling for photos.

His caddy moved to the fence near me and the tinker. "You Jimmy Grits?"

"Yeah, how'd you know?"

The caddy looked me up and down. "A lucky guess." He stuck two fingers in his mouth and whistled. "Bert, these two."

The no-neck guy with the *Peter's Primo Miniature Golf Staff* shirt locked eyes with the caddy then called to us above the cries of adoration. "Follow me, I'll get you inside." He pushed his way through the fans making a hole.

Gilmer nodded when we neared the rope and raised his hands like making a benediction. "See ya at the wards podium." He gave one final wave then retreated into the golf course. After a few strides, he said over his shoulder, "We cun get some privacy in the clubhouse."

Gilmer led us to a matte-green corrugated aluminum shed pockmarked with rust patches and speckled in bird droppings. The door stuck in its track, but Gilmer kept at it until the flimsy sheet-metal panel relented with a screech. He pulled a chain turning on a hanging lightbulb and slid shut the door behind us with the same struggle he had opening it. He offered seats on stacked boxes marked *Golf Balls* and *Putter Grips*.

I shifted my weight on the boxes under me. The pile seemed unsteady. We huddled together like school children hiding from parents. "I thought you meant clubhouse, as in a golf course clubhouse?"

Gilmer leaned back, looked to the ceiling, and cried, "Aye," while clapping his hands above his head. "I needed that win!"

The tinker stared at Gilmer without blinking. "That was an incredible game."

I stared at Gilmer, too, because I just couldn't take my eyes off of the orange bird nest of hair just under his throat.

Gilmer gestured toward his caddy. "This is me lad, Paddy."

The box under me sank on the right side. "How long have you been Gilmer's caddy, Patty?"

"No, it's Paddy for Paddington." Paddy rearranged the putters in Gilmer's golf bag. "I'm not a caddy. I have a BS in MGS."

"I'm up for Chinese." My stomach growled at the thought. "All that talk about MSG is a lot about nothing. Never did me any harm."

"No, Mr. Grits. I have a BS in M—G—S, Miniature Golf Science."

"Well, I certainly get the BS part."

The caddy scowled at me. "A person needs a degree in MGS to become a stroke specialist."

"Is that what you are?" I hoped I had misheard him. "A stroke specialist?"

The tinker bobbed his head. "I remember reading about Paddy's signature stroke, the *Long and Slow with a Twist*."

I covered my face with my hands.

The tinker kept talking. "His stroke revolutionized the short game."

Paddy fussed with the clubs in Gilmer's bag and didn't look at me. "So, what's your claim to fame, Mr. Grits?"

Gilmer took a golf pencil from behind his ear and pointed it at the tinker. "Yur a miniature golf man. Want us to give you un autograph?"

The tinker pulled an old Peter's Primo Miniature Golf score card from the pouch of his cargo shorts. "Please! I kept this card from when I was a teenager." He handed the card to Gilmer. "Three holes-in-one that day."

Gilmer signed the card. "The wards ceremuny starts soon. We shud get to business. What's yur first step, Detective Grits?"

"Well, tell me more about your heirloom."

"It's a putter. Ben in me family for generations."

"A putter?" The boxes under me sank to the left, which evened things out, but my knees now came to my chest. "A golf club worth a hundred thousand dollars?"

The caddy's eyes sparkled. "The grip is set with diamonds, Mr. Grits. Lots of diamonds."

"I need to study the crime scene as soon as possible. The longer we wait, the more chance it becomes contaminated."

"Well, it was stolen from me house. Paddy and me are the only ones livin there."

The boxes under me made a sound I didn't like. I stood banging my head on the corrugated roof. Crushed my fedora's crown. "When can we see your house?"

"There's a news conference after the wards ceremuny. I'll need a couple of hours." Gilmer pulled a business card from his pocket, scribbled his address on the back, and handed it to me.

"You got it." I slid open the metal door, stepped into the sunlight, and looked back at the tinker. "You coming?"

We made our ways out of the miniature golf course, through the groupies still packed at the entrance, and stopped at a burger stand on the boardwalk where I ordered a double with bacon to go.

The tinker got an ice cream cone and licked at a mint chocolate chip scoop half the size of his head. "I was on track to become a world-class miniature golfer, you know. Practiced three to four hours six days a week. Sometimes seven."

"You don't say?"

"I was good, too. Under par on every boardwalk miniature golf course in Delaware, Maryland, and New Jersey."

"I thought Skee-Ball was your thing."

"Not at first."

"What happened?"

"Well, two problems derailed me." The tinker took a few more licks. "First, there was an incident with a golf obstacle, a mechanical alligator."

"How could that—?"

"Second, there was my mother."

"You're confusing me."

"She thought I spent too much time alone with my putter and stopped taking me to courses."

"Do you ever think about what you are going to say before you say it?"

The tinker lowered his cone and cocked his head to the side. "This is a strange time to get philosophical, Jimmy." He put his hand on his hip. "If my brain controls my mouth to form words, wouldn't I have had to think about what I am going to say before I say it?" He shrugged. "Anyway, I know a lot about the miniature golf scene."

"Okay, what's the deal with the caddy? Why's he living with Gilmer?"

"That's how they did it in miniature golf's golden age. Stroke specialists never left their golfers' sides." He tongued a trail of melted mint running down his wrist. "You don't like Paddy, do you?"

"No."

"Why not?"

"The man didn't want us there. I could sense it."

"You just met him. Give him a chance."

"I give everyone a chance, unless I don't like them."

The tinker's ice cream flipped off the cone and plopped on the boardwalk. He stomped his feet. "That always happens!"

"What are you, nine?"

The tinker tossed the cone into a trashcan. "You headed for Gilmer's house?"

"I need to stop at the office. Eat my burger and make a call." Since the tinker kept a foot in the miniature golf world, I decided to bring him on the case. "Why don't you meet me there in an hour?"

OCEAN MIST HAD ENJOYED SOME RECENT PEACE and quiet, mostly because of me. Shorts Lady, Reginald the Rocket, Skee-Ball Granny, The Mime, Bumper, Patches—all in the pokey—and Surfer Dude banished to the West Coast. Even the mayor and his network had been quiet, which meant Ocean Mist's underworld had coughed up a new threat.

I wedged my rotary's receiver under my chin, dialed with one hand, and fished in my desk drawer with the other for a bottle of Jack. "Yeah, Rocco, I got a job for you and your boys."

"Sure thing, Jimmy. You think any more about a diffuser for your office?"

"A what? What are you talking about?" I found the Jack tucked behind some old *Private Eye of Fortune* magazines.

"A diffuser, you know, for essential oils. They're good for stress reduction, like we talked about when we found that smokin' lady's pink Cadillac."

"She was anything but smokin', Rocco." I looked for my mug but couldn't find it, so I took a belt right from the bottle.

"I mean like cigarette smokin', but short older women with beehives can get me going."

The mental image made me take another belt. "I need you and your boys to keep your eyes peeled for a golf club with diamonds studding the shaft. Check out all the pawn shops, public and private, if you know what I mean."

"What about jewelry stores?"

"I wouldn't bother. This is a high-profile piece needing some special care to fence."

"You got it, Jimmy."

The tinker stepped into my office. "Who's that?"

"It's Rocco, if you must know."

"Tell Rocco—."

"Gotta run, Rocco. Keep in touch." I hung up the receiver.

The tinker leaned on the door jam. "You getting a diffuser?"

"No, I'm not getting a diffuser." I motioned to the chair across from my desk. "I need to pick your brain. What do you know about this Paddy the stroke specialist?"

The tinker reached into his cargo shorts and pulled out a flier. It featured a glossy of Gilmer standing with Paddy. The two held a large gold cup between them. "Paddy is exactly what he says he is, a professional. He's been with Gilmer for the past decade. Since they partnered, Gilmer hasn't lost a match."

"You say ten years?"

"Yeah, why?"

"That's a long time to be second fiddle."

"I see where you're going with this, Jimmy, but Paddy is a dead end."

"Oh?"

"Paddy is a local. Born and raised in Ocean Mist. He's one of the good guys."

"You sure about that?"

"Paddy's family built and ran the old Conch Shell Miniature Golf Course."

"The abandoned one way out by the sewage treatment plant?"

The tinker nodded.

"Isn't that what closed it down? The plant?"

The tinker shook his head. "Most people think that, with the smell and all, but it actually had to do with a problem in the course."

"What kind of problem?"

"Someone messed up when they poured the cement for the 18th hole. When the green was layered over the contoured base, the fairway sloped right into the hole."

"So?"

"Jimmy, what do you know about the 18th hole of any miniature golf course?"

"It's usually the last one."

"And?"

"It comes after the 17th hole?"

The tinker stared at me for a moment. "If you get a hole-in-one on the last hole, you get a free game. Paddy's family had to give away so many free games, they went bankrupt in a little over a season."

"Are you telling me, the 18th hole put them in the hole?"

"Yeah, I guess." The tinker refolded the flier and put it back into his pocket. "All of this happened before the city built the new treatment plant."

"That's some story, but it doesn't remove this Paddy guy from the suspect list." I looked at my clock then pulled Gilmer's address from my pocket. "We need to go. Gilmer's news conference should be over. He'll be headed back to his house."

WE TOOK THE STUDEBAKER TO OCEAN MIST'S south side where the rich folk lived in their eight and ten-bedroom homes. The same part of town where The Skee-Ball Council held their meetings. My cell rang a couple of blocks before Gilmer's house.

"Hey, Rocco. That was fast."

The tinker leaned from the passenger seat to say something into my phone, but I pressed it to my chest. "Put a sock in it."

"You were right, Jimmy. That putter is raising eyebrows."

"You found it?"

"No, but one of my boys said someone tried to fence the putter over on Hamilton Street."

I knew the joint. Dark and dirty. Along an alley with little foot traffic on or off-season. Certainly not open to the general public. It belonged to the mayor. "I'm guessing this person got the cold shoulder."

"My guy said there was something not right about the piece."

"You mean, something not right about a putter covered in diamonds?"

"That might be it."

"Did your guy get a description?" I pulled the Studebaker to the curb and let her idle.

"Someone dressed for the middle of January— scarf over the face, wool cap, big coat. Could have been anyone."

"Thanks, Rocco. That helps a lot." I ended the call, pulled a steno pad from the glove box, and jotted some notes. "The putter is still in Ocean Mist. Someone tried to sell it."

"Great! We still have a chance of getting it back. That should put Gilmer's mind at ease." The tinker nodded in apparent agreement with himself.

"You need to keep this quiet. Don't say nothing about this to Gilmer."

"Wait, do you want me to say something or not?"

"I just told you, don't say nothing."

"But, if I don't say nothing, doesn't that mean I should say something?"

"Like I said before, put a sock in it."

I pulled away from the curb, and we found Gilmer's place in a little under a minute. Every house on Ocean Mist's south side had white siding, a gabled roof with lots of dormers, and more bedrooms and bathrooms than any lone furniture store could furnish. Vacationers biked and walked through the neighborhood to gawk at all the big houses, but I always thought the developer lacked creativity. Each house looked like the one three doors down, which looked like the one three doors farther along the street. The whole community had only three or four home designs scattered around to give the illusion of variety.

A skilled detective like me picked up on those kinds of patterns, this particular pattern broken only by Gilmer's house, which looked to be made of honest-to-God stone, and I'm not talking the thin façade-type glued to backing board. A four-story tower stood at each corner. Flags of white "x's" over blue fields flew from each tower, and I eyed the home's battlements just in case guys with bows and arrows guarded the frontyard.

The Studebaker crunched up a circular drive of marble pebbles. I parked her next to a Rolls Royce. Summer rays bouncing from polished chrome left starbursts in my eyes even from a glance. We approached an oak front door with a wrought iron handle in place of a knob. I didn't see a knocker. No button for a doorbell.

The tinker reached for a rope. "I think we pull this." A church-like bell rang from inside and somewhere above us. "This is cool." The tinker pulled again. "Sanctuary!" And, again. "Sanctuary!"

I yanked the rope from his hand. "Would you knock that off?"

Paddy opened the door and stepped back to let us into a tall foyer made of dark wood paneling. A bronze bell hung from a heavy timber frame in a belfry, and I got a little dizzy gazing upward at it.

"They're here," Paddy shouted over his shoulder, "if you couldn't tell."

We followed him down a short hallway, passed Gilmer's golf bag propped against the wall, and entered a cavernous room with a stone hearth filled with blazing logs. Leather couches and armchairs formed a semi-circle facing the fire. Each seat had an end table next to it with a lamp covered by a red and green plaid shade. Several large stained glass windows featuring castles and sheep—a lot of sheep—let some light into the room. Despite the light from the windows, the lamps' red-green glows, and the firelight, the room remained dark, cursed by the same wood paneling as the foyer and hallway.

One of the leather armchairs called to me, so I settled into it.

Paddy walked by me. "Please, have a seat."

"I already did." I placed my fedora on an end table.

The tinker plopped onto a neighboring couch. "I'll take this one, thank you."

I pointed at the fire. "A little warm outside for that, don't you think?"

Gilmer entered from a side door. He had traded his kilt for a pair of pantaloons puffed at the ankles and tucked into suede boots. A dark green golf shirt had replaced his powder blue one, which, with his tuft of orange chest hair, complemented the lamps.

Gilmer carried a cup and saucer to the fireplace where he rested his elbow on the mantel. "There's somethin bout a wood fire. Reminds me of Scotland. Cun we get ya some tea?"

"Tea? You mean from little bags?"

Paddy lifted a saucer and cup from an end table and claimed a spot against the mantle opposite Gilmer. "We never use bags." He sipped.

"Neither did my Nanna." The offer of tea didn't bring my departed grandmother to mind so much as the empty shadow box above Gilmer's hearth. The box looked like the one Nanna used to display my grandfather's burial flag.

Gilmer followed my gaze to the wood and glass case. "That's where I kep it. Me diamond putter. Ya see, Mr. Grits, the name Gilmer means sword bearer in Scottish. That putter is like me family's sword."

"You don't say? Does the frame lock?"

"Aye." He ran his finger over a keyhole on the side.

"So, the person who stole it had a key?" *Or, took the time to pick the lock rather than smash the glass or pry the case from the wall. Someone who didn't want to cause a lot of mess or damage.*

Gilmer nodded. "Paddy, mind handin Mr. Grits the papers?"

Paddy took a blue folio from his end table and slapped it down on mine.

I opened the folio and spread several legal-looking forms under the lamp's yellow pool of light. "What are these?"

The tinker swung his feet up onto the couch, laid back, and put his hands behind his head. "Those look like papers, Jimmy."

"Always the helpful one, aren't you?" I shifted my gaze to Gilmer. "Papers for what?"

"Surance adjuster wants you to sign. Proof yur investigatin."

I closed the folio and tapped its cover. "I'll take these back to my office."

Gilmer looked like he wanted to say something but didn't and added another log onto the fire.

Time for me to stoke a fire of my own. "A caddy for miniature golf? There's only one club, right? A putter?" I glanced at the tinker. Tapped the side of my nose.

"Sometin wrong with yur nose, Mr. Grits?"

The tinker shook his head. "He just does that sometimes."

Paddy looked me over, pursed his lips, and made a raspberry sound. "Being a stroke specialist may seem simple to someone like you, but putters come in different sizes, weights, and metallurgical compositions for the heads and shafts."

"You're right. It does seem simple." I turned up the heat on him. "Must be tough always being the side kick."

"What do you mean?" He sipped from his tea cup.

"You know, standing in Gilmer's shadow. Being the other guy in all the photo ops."

"I'm doing just fine, thank you."

I nestled into the warm, soft chair, took my hat from the end table, and placed it on my knee. "Of course, you are. I mean, look around. You're living in this place."

"Paddy is part of me team. I cunna do without him." Gilmer raised his cup toward Paddy, and Paddy did the same back at Gilmer.

"That's my point. At one time, I'm sure Paddy dreamed of becoming a big miniature golf hero."

Gilmer shook a finger at me like my fourth-grade teacher used to do. "Paddy is a hero to stroke specialists around the country."

"Around the world." Paddy sipped.

Gilmer lifted his tea cup again. "Around the world."

I leaned way back in the armchair and shifted my weight back and forth looking for the sweet spot in the leather. "Yeah, right, but does Paddy ever think about striking out on his own? Making something more of his life?"

Gilmer's back straightened. "Mr. Grits, I take good care of me own. Paddy is family. Cun we ples get back to me missin putter?"

Paddy put down his saucer. "What do you mean, you take care of your own? If anyone needs taken care of, it's you. Especially now."

Here we go. A crack in the veneer.

Gilmer stepped away from the mantel. Extended his hands. "Why ya so angry, me lad?"

"What do you think it feels like standing in your shadow? Being just your stroke specialist in all the articles and television pieces? Good enough to polish your putter, but never—."

The tinker crossed his feet on the couch. "You know, Paddy has a point. That's a real difficult space to live in day-to-day."

I ran my fingers along my fedora's brim. "Must be hard to accept you've given all of your dreams to someone else. Makes me wonder how you feel knowing you can't make up for all of those lost years."

Paddy took two steps toward me and pointed to his chest. "Oh, I've more than made up for it, Grits, and I've more than made up for my family!"

"That's funny," I leaned way over and tapped the tinker's leg, "I didn't say anything about his family, did I?"

Gilmer took Paddy by the arm. "Paddy, what's all this bout?"

Then came the final tell. Paddy glanced at the empty glass case above the fireplace.

"Paddy," Gilmer released his stroke specialist's arm, "not ya?"

I put my hat on and pushed myself out of the armchair.

Paddy shifted his weight onto his back leg and raised his fists between us. "Back off, fatso!"

I pulled my hat down over my brow and rolled my shoulders.

The tinker swung his legs off the couch and popped to his feet putting him right at my side.

Paddy pushed between us and leapt onto the leather arm chair planting one foot on the seat and his other on the back. Momentum knocked over the chair, which he rode with his hands firmly on his hips. He then dove into a forward roll and slid his arm through the leather strap of Gilmer's golf bag propped against the wall. Somehow, by the time Paddy rose to his feet with the bag slung over his shoulder, he had two clubs in his hands, which he swung windmill-like in front of him while making a high-pitched martial arts scream.

"Gentlemen, please. This is me home."

I hiked up my pants. "It's all over, Paddy. We're on to you."

"Be careful, Jimmy." The tinker retreated behind a couch. "Stroke specialists are certified in putter defense."

"Putter what?" A flash of light from polished metal, and my world went black.

The Case of the Diamond Putter

Part 2: In the Bag

A little orange cat. Cute little Persian kitten. I blinked to try and clear the colors splashing and floating in front of my eyes. The colors expanded and disappeared but the orange kitten didn't move. I reached and pet the little fella crouching there in front of my face. "Good little kitty."

My vision cleared.

The Scotsman leaned over me holding a wet washcloth to my forehead. His ginger man-wool puffed from the unbuttoned V of his golf shirt two feet from my nose. Bile rose into my throat. A full-body shudder brought me to my senses. I started to sit, but a hand on my shoulder eased me back to the floor.

"Stay still, Mr. Grits. Ya took a wallop from Paddy's club."

The tinker's voice came from somewhere near my head. "Yeah, take it easy, Jimmy. You may want to keep your hands to yourself, too."

"Let me up!" I shook off Gilmer's washcloth, stood, wobbled, and caught myself on an end table. "Where's my hat?"

The tinker handed me my fedora, and I made my way down the slanting and rocking hallway toward the front door.

"Mr. Grits," Gilmer sounded concerned, but I knew exactly what I was doing, "are ya sure you cun drive?"

I grunted something close to a yes.

"It's okay. I can drive Jimmy home."

"No, you can't." I turned to scowl at the tinker but fell against the wall. "Not after last time."

Gilmer caught up to us and held out the blue folio of insurance papers. "Don't forget this."

I snatched it from his hand. "Can't forget those, can we, Gilmer?"

The tinker draped my arm across his shoulder. "Let me help you."

By the time we got to the Studebaker, the world, for the most part, had righted itself. I turned the old girl over and listened to her purr.

"Jimmy, you have any idea where we can find Paddy?"

"There's more to all of this than just finding Paddy."

"Well, obviously. Like, why would he do this to Gilmer?"

That wasn't what I meant, but I decided not to burst the tinker's hero bubble. Not just yet. "Don't worry, this case is practically solved."

"Don't say that."

"Why not?"

"Whenever you think the case is practically solved, bad stuff happens."

"No, it doesn't."

"Yes, it does. What do you call getting beaten up by clowns? Jumping from a sinking raft in the middle of the ocean? Getting locked in a stone room?"

"Those clowns didn't beat up anyone, and that was your raft. Besides, I've got a lead."

"What is it?"

"We need a few things. A couple of flashlights." I looked west and squinted into a brilliant sunset. The bright light reminded me of the clubbing I had taken to my head. "Some aspirin wouldn't hurt, either."

"Where are we going?"

"To play a round of miniature golf."

I PARKED THE STUDEBAKER ALONG A ROAD well beyond the interests of any townies or tourists. Head-high weeds thicker than a sleeve of Down and Out Burger fries lined the berm. The whole twisted mess formed a green wall. We swept our flashlights back and forth looking for some way through, some path made by man or beast, but no luck. If the tinker really did know his history, whatever survived of Paddy's family's miniature golf course lay right off the road in a weed-infested lot near the sewage plant.

I sniffed the air, and the smell of the chase wasn't the only odor filling my nostrils. "You sure it's back there?"

The tinker stood on the tips of his toes and held his light high trying to look over the weeds. "I'm sure of it. The Conch Shell course closed long before I started playing, but I've seen plenty of old photos."

"Grainy yellow ones in that historical society of yours?"

"Yeah, and the society belongs to all of us, Jimmy. It's our heritage."

"Right." I pushed aside some grasses and pulled apart vines to make an opening. "Let's make like Jonah and part the sea."

"Moses. His name was Moses."

"You talking about Bathtub Gin Moses?" I plowed a path. Shined my light downward to make sure I didn't lead us into a marsh. "I could use some of his swill right about now. My head is killing me."

"No, Jimmy. The Bible's Moses. Moses parted the Red Sea. Not Jonah."

I stopped, removed my sport coat, and slung it over my shoulder. Sweat glued my dress shirt to my chest and stomach. The plastic buttons rubbing against my skin annoyed me. "How far do you think we've gone?" I pointed my flashlight behind us.

"I'd say about ten yards or so."

"That's it?"

"Yeah, there's the car." The tinker's beam reflected off a chrome bumper.

I slogged onward crunching a mat of grass, vines, and twigs under my feet. The moon rose above some trees just to our south, and the pale light revealed what I thought was a sewage tank. When I got closer, it looked more like one of those large satellite-type dishes scientists pointed into the sky to try to talk to Martians.

"That's it, Jimmy."

"That's what?"

"The course. Conch Shell Miniature Golf."

A few more steps brought me to ground more gravel than dead plants—an old parking lot. I pointed my light toward the big white dish-looking thing. "What is that, exactly?"

"Hole number seven. It had a giant cement conch shell obstacle no one could ever get through on a single stroke."

"That must be two-stories high."

"When miniature golf was king, Jimmy, courses were its palaces."

"Well then," I kicked a bicycle, a shiny new model propped against a post, "this must be one of its royal carriages." A trail led from behind it back into the woods. "Someone else is here."

"What do we do if it's Paddy? He's a miniature golf ninja."

"I told you not to worry."

"Are you sure?"

I patted my sport coat's pocket. "Oh, I'm more than sure."

A concrete path starting near a dilapidated shack led us around rotting boards once edging fairways and a graveyard of broken and maimed ocean-themed obstacles: a giant starfish with a dangling arm, an octopus short a few tentacles, and a headless mermaid.

The tinker stopped every now and again to take in the remains like some awestruck pilgrim. He pulled out his phone and took a photo. His flash lit what might have been the third hole.

"You want me to come back and get you when the case is closed?"

"Sorry, Jimmy. What are we looking for, anyway?"

A private eye's hunch couldn't always be put into words, but I knew something waited for us in Paddy's ancestral haunt. "We'll know when we see it."

Hole number seven's two-story cement conch shell sat near the back of the ruined course. The small whorls way above our heads twisted downward expanding into a gaping mouth on the ground. I could have parked three Studebaker's inside and still had room for a snack bar. "All of this for one hole?"

"Isn't it wonderful?" The tinker pointed his flashlight into some weeds. "Those boards must be what's left of the steps going up to the platform where the hole began. You had to hit your ball down a long fairway and into the narrow end of the shell. Your ball would twist and spiral around before dropping onto a green."

"What, a green in there?"

"Yep."

I waved my flashlight around the conch shell's opening. No loose sand, dead leaves, or pieces of old boards. Someone had cleared the entrance. "Stay close."

"We're not going inside, are we?"

"We go where the evidence leads us." Thick plastic strips hung from a frame of new wood just a few paces inside the entrance. I parted the barrier and listened. Nothing. "Keep your eyes peeled."

We went deeper into the shell where the hole's green must have been. A work bench lined a wall with boxes of hardware and tools scattered over it, mostly lengths of pipes, valves, gaskets, and fittings suited for a plumber's workshop. Two gas tanks, the kinds used to fill balloons, stood in the corner. I just didn't get it. Rummaging through the parts and tools didn't offer any clues until I found what looked like some sort of trigger mechanism. *Is Paddy making a bomb?*

A clank of metal came from behind us. I spun on the balls of my feet. Cat-like. Always ready. The caddy stood in the concrete tunnel with his putters drawn and crossed in front of him blocking the only way out.

"Thank you, Grits, for coming here. You saved me the trouble of hunting you." He swung the clubs in interlocking figure-eight patterns. The metal flashed in our beams. "Hunting you like prey."

I took the tinker's arm and moved him behind me. "It doesn't have to go down this way."

"It's never too late, Paddy," said the tinker. "Tell your story to the police. Deals can be made. I understand what it's like for you. The world will understand."

I whispered over my shoulder. "You're laying it on pretty thick, don't you think?"

Paddy took a step toward us. His clubs sliced the air. Hummed. The figure eights filled the entrance. No way around him.

"Last chance." I squared myself in a boxer's stance. "You don't want to do this."

Paddy stopped his twirling, changed the grip on his right club, and led with his left foot.

His decision made my night.

I pulled from my coat pocket my nephew's little yellow beauty filled with the vinegar from the bottle I used on my morning's Down and Out Burger fries and gave Paddy what he deserved—three streams dead in the eyes.

The concrete conch shell acted like an amphitheater amplifying and projecting his screams, which must have awakened everyone from the towns of Rehoboth to Lewes. He dropped his clubs and pressed his palms into his face. For good measure, I unleashed a right uppercut under his chin snapping his head back and bouncing his brain around his cranium. He dropped like a bag of golf balls.

The tinker pushed around me. "Vinegar. That's what I smelled. I thought it was just you."

I pointed to the work bench. "Use those zip ties on his hands before he wakes up."

My hand hurt, but the rest of me felt more satisfied than I had been for weeks. I stepped over Paddy and headed toward the shell's entrance to get some air. A slim black leather bag leaned against the wall just inside the dangling plastic strip barrier. *That wasn't there a few minutes ago.* The bag's cinch came undone when I lifted it. Out fell another golf club.

The tinker pointed his light at my feet, and a galaxy of stars encircled us. "What a way to close the case, huh, Jimmy?"

"The case isn't closed, yet, and the night's not over. Let's get Paddy and this club back to the car."

I put the bejeweled putter and its bag in the Studebaker's trunk, and we shoved Paddy into the backseat. Sitting felt good, and a post-adrenaline crash hit me hard. I paused and took a deep breath before turning over the engine. *Maybe it's time to give up the all-nighters?*

The tinker sat watching me. Didn't seem phased by our scrape with death. "Are we taking the putter to Gilmer?"

"You could say that." I pulled out my phone, dialed 9-1-1, and heard the lady night dispatcher's familiar voice. "Yeah, this is Jimmy Grits. I need a couple of units out at Gilmer Aitken's place." I pulled off the berm and pointed the old girl back into town. "Of course, this is the same Grits. How many Grits do we have in Ocean Mist? Uh-huh. No, not those kinds of units. Cop cars with cops inside. Yeah, I know. Uh-huh. Look, I'm sorry about all of that the last time I called you, but something big is about to—. Uh-huh. Okay, I'll do that. Is someone coming?" I braked for an intersection. "No, that's not what I meant. I don't want to go down—. Look, can you just tell me if a unit, cop car, is on its way? Thanks." I put my phone back into my pocket.

"You really need to patch things up with that lady." The tinker looked into the back seat. "Why don't we just take Paddy to the police department first then return the putter?"

Paddy groaned.

A strong vinegar smell filled the car.

"I hate to tell you, but there's more to this story, and you're not going to like it." I cracked a window.

STROBING RED AND BLUE LIGHTS GREETED US in Gilmer's driveway, and his front door stood open. "Grab Gilmer's insurance papers from the glove compartment." The tinker handed me the blue folio, and I took the putter case from the trunk.

We marched Paddy through the door and into the big room with the stained glass windows and fireplace. A fire crackled and popped despite the late, or early, hour. The Scotsman stood behind a couch in a bath robe and slippers. His orange chest hair pushed its way between his robe's lapels. An Ocean Mist policeman and a policewoman flanked him.

"Mr. Grits, ya found me Paddy!"

"You didn't think I would?" I gave Paddy a little shove toward the policewoman. "You'll want to hold onto him, doll."

She scowled. "I've heard about you and your sexist comments."

"For the record, I don't try to sound sexist." I touched the brim of my hat and pointed at her. "Some of us just got it."

"She said, sexist, Jimmy." The tinker shook his head. "Sexist."

Gilmer stepped toward me and reached for the leather putter case. "Is that me putter?"

"Oh, this." I pulled the case away from him, opened it, and took out the club. "No, it's not." I tossed the putter into the fire.

The tinker lunged for the hearth and grabbed a pair of fire tongs. "What are you doing, Jimmy!"

"Well," I said to Gilmer, "are you going to help him save your priceless family heirloom?" I held up the folder of insurance papers. "Or, would you like us to finish the insurance claim forms, first?"

The tinker used the tongs to retrieve the putter. Flames danced along the rubber grip. He tried to put out the club by waving it around the room but only created trails of smoke and noxious fumes.

Paddy's mind must have started to clear. "Let it burn. The only thing more important to that man is his golf game."

I slapped the blue folder onto an end table like Paddy had done about ten hours earlier. "The problem is, that isn't his club, is it Gilmer?"

"What are ya sayin, Mr. Grits?"

I took off my fedora and used it to point at the club. "That's a fake." I walked over to the empty glass and wood case above the mantel. "Somehow, you knew Paddy had his eye on your club, so you took out an insurance policy, made a fake, put the fake in the case, hid the real one, and waited for Paddy to steal it. You get to keep your family heirloom, collect the insurance money, and dump your whiny, sanctimonious stroke specialist all in one— stroke."

Gilmer scratched his orange tuft, looked at each of the officers, and laughed. "Well, Mr. Grits, ya tell a good story."

"I ain't into stories."

"Jimmy is right." The tinker dropped the club and tried putting it out by stomping on the shaft. "He only reads if there's pictures."

Gilmer's smile vanished. "Yur no better than day-old hagas, Grits. All of ya want me real putter? It's right here in me bag."

The Scotsman reached behind the couch and lifted a golf bag to his shoulder, but he didn't pull out a club. He swung the bag downward, pointed its mouth at me, and squeezed it under his armpit like a set of bagpipes. A loud *thrump* came from inside the bag, which fired a golf ball across the room striking my gut, stealing my wind, and sending me to my knees.

Gilmer pulled two balls from a pouch on the bag's side, scrubbed them against his chest hair, and fed each into some type of receiver. "Git out of me house!"

The officers drew their guns, but Gilmer shot both from their hands in rapid succession.

Still gasping, I crawled behind an end table. *Paddy must have made the golf ball cannon in his conch shell workshop—all of the valves, pipes, air tanks, and the trigger. We didn't face two separate criminals, a thief and a fraudster. They were partners in this together from the start.*

"Go, me lad! Run while ya cun!"

Paddy took off for the door with his hands still zip-tied behind his back, but the tinker leapt over a couch and tackled him.

Another golf ball shattered a lamp near my head sending the shade into the air and its wire harp falling to the floor next to my knee. I bent the harp straight, stuck my fedora on its end, and raised it above the end table.

Gilmer yelled, "Fore," and shot my hat from the wire prop.

A pause in the barrage. Hissing. The slap of leather and jingling of buckles.

"Nae! I need mae balls!"

I stood with my vinegar-filled squirt gun drawn. Ready for action.

The policewoman moved for the golfer.

Gilmer held the bag between them and thrust it trying to fend her off, but she swatted it from his hands. Clubs clattered around Gilmer's feet distracting him long enough for her to take him to the ground with an armbar.

"Help me, Jimmy." The tinker struggled to stay on top of Paddy who flopped like a fish out of water.

We wrestled Paddy flat and held him there until the policeman replaced Paddy's zip ties with cuffs. Our helpful LEO's hoisted both washed-up golfers onto the couch and propped them to face justice square in the eyes.

The policeman took a moment to catch his breath, reached into a pocket of his tactical pants, pulled out a small spiral-bound activity log, and detached a pencil from a rubber band holding it together. "Alright, all of you, I have a lot of questions. First," he pointed his pencil at Paddy, "why does this man smell like pickles?"

THE TINKER AND I LEFT GILMER'S PLACE just as the sun rose over Ocean Mist. I needed sleep, more aspirin, and hoped the tinker would keep his mouth shut until I dropped him off at his house. That didn't happen.

"Remember back at Gilmer's place, before Paddy smacked you across the head with the golf club, and I said he had a point?"

I didn't need him to remind me about my head, which still ached worse than the morning after a night out with my friend Jack. "What are you talking about?"

"You know, always the side kick and never the hero."

"You talking about you?"

"Yeah, I mean, who's the first person you call when you need help?"

"Okay, I see your angle. You want in?"

"Just a little appreciation every now and then."

"Appreciation, huh. How about I double your salary? Will that make you feel better?"

"I didn't know I got a salary."

"Well, that's why I want to double it for you."

St. Puddermoore College of Leisure
8761 Fair Way
Wedge Iron, Wisconsin 98732

Dear Mr. Grits:

The arrests of Gilmer Aitken and his stroke specialist Paddington Kaik have rocked our college and the very foundations of the miniature golf world. Few will take up a putter in good conscience unless upstanding people like you speak to the physical, emotional, and spiritual benefits of this great pastime.

Our Department of Miniature Golf Sciences invites you to be the kick-off speaker for an upcoming symposium. We aim to restore honor to this discipline and increase enrollment in our programs. St. Puddermoore College of Leisure is the only self-accredited institution to offer full bachelor and master degrees in Miniature Golf Sciences.

In my humble opinion, this event could make you the face of a miniature golf revival. Please know, if you accept our offer, you will not incur travel, lodging, or any incidental costs. The symposium, like all of our programs and course offerings, is conducted online.

Sincerely,
Aloysius Well, Provost
St. Puddermoore College of Leisure

Up in Flames

I rode the old grinding elevator to the surface, sucked in some fresh air, clicked off my headlamp, and followed the path through the ruined lighthouse keeper's house toward our make-shift landing strip. The sun had not even cleared the horizon, and I knew we were in for a hot day.

My favorite red-headed librarian lifted a gas can to refill her ultra-light's tank. "Last flight until tonight."

I retrieved a crate of books from the passenger seat. "Figured as much. Was this number ten?" Hours ferrying books, document tubes, and artifacts from the library made all of the trips run together.

"Eleven, I think."

Thanks to Bumper and Elbow Patches' Pennsylvania Dutch cookbook heist, the last two weeks of my life had been spent relocating Ocean Mist's secret archives—two weeks of nights, anyway. I despised those two crooks more and more each day.

Angela shook the gas can next to her ear. "What's it like down there?"

"Damp and dark."

"Edward?"

"Still banging around. You still think it was a good idea to trust him? Loose lips and all."

She sighed. "How many times have we been over this? Edward is the only one that can climate control that space. We need it fast, by the way."

"Yeah, I know. I'll check on him."

I lugged the night's last crate onto the elevator platform and rode it, clanking and rocking, into the ground. Battery powered lanterns cast small pools of light along the passage leading to the big stone room where I had rescued Angela and found Fred Ferdinand's journals. My back cracked when bending to place my load in the room's corner with the other crates.

"Boo!" Edward jumped from behind a shelf and shined a flashlight under his chin making him look more trollish than usual. "Did I scare you this time? Did you think I was the lighthouse keeper's ghost?"

"You scared me as much this time as the other five times. Are the solar panels going to work? We need the dehumidifiers running before all of this old paper gets ruined."

"We should know when the sun comes up."

"It's already up, and that's what you said yesterday."

"Well, dehumidifiers pull a lot of juice. I'm hoping for at least two during the day and enough battery power for one overnight."

"I guess that will have to do, for now."

"A vapor barrier on the floor and maybe up the walls could help."

"Yeah, vapor barriers. That's what I said to Angela. Vapor barriers."

Ocean Mist's only private eye, the only person fighting criminals be-yond the law's reach, spending his nights lugging books no one reads and talking about plastic-wrapping a dirt floor.

The old elevator's chains rattled and clanked through rusty pulleys announcing Angela's descent. "Jimmy, you have to come out and see this."

"What's going on?"

"I don't know, but it doesn't look good."

The three of us took the elevator to the surface, and Angela pointed over the marsh toward town. Puffs of black smoke, like those from a se-ries of explosions, rose into the sky near the boardwalk. Our little island lay too far away to hear any sirens, or blasts for that matter.

"Doll, I need to get back to my car and fast. I don't have enough time for the raft. Can you give me a lift over the marsh?"

Angela stepped back and looked me up and down. "I guess we'll have to try sometime. May as well be now."

Given the number of cattails and tops of red-green sumacs chopped in the propellor and blown back into our faces, I knew this would be my last ultra-light flight with Angela. Simply too much man for the little aircraft. We landed just feet from my Studebaker on the dead-end road poking out over the marsh. I thanked my girl, and she headed back to pick up Edward.

A steady pillar of smoke fed a black mushroom cloud growing in a crystalline blue oceanside morning. Traffic cops and fire vehicles kept me from parking any closer than a couple of blocks from the boardwalk. I couldn't tell what had exploded and burned so fiercely, even when I took to the sidewalk and reached the closest fire engine about a half block from the source of smoke. Every firehose in Ocean Mist doused the inferno.

"Jimmy!" The tinker waved frantically for me to join him across the street. He stood surrounded by three Ocean Mist police officers. His cargo shorts' edges looked charred. His Hawaiian shirt smoldered.

I left the sidewalk, stepped over rivulets, and navigated around puddles. Something caught my eye under a pickup truck's back bumper. *A frying pan?* Then, a few feet away from that, a badly bent carpenter's saw next to an old hand-crank-eggbeater.

Then it all came together. Someone blew up the tinker's cart.

I SHOULDERED BETWEEN THE OCEAN MIST OFFICERS and tinker knowing he needed my help. A crime of this magnitude required the quick thinking and experience of a professional. "You should have called me right away."

An officer looked up from his small spiral activity log. His stubby pencil hovered over a clean page ready to record what I'm sure he thought would be a key piece of investigative information. His baby face told me everything I needed to know about him, and his question confirmed my conclusions.

"And, you are?"

"Who do you think I am?"

Another officer answered the rookie's question. "That's Jimmy Grits."

I unbuttoned my sport coat and hooked my thumbs in my belt. "Why don't you write that in your log?"

The rookie slid the spiral-bound pad into his breast pocket. "Is this part of my initiation?"

The other two officers shook their heads.

"Okay," the rookie pulled the activity log back out from his pocket and licked the tip of his pencil, "let's start again."

I took the tinker's arm. "We're wasting time, here."

"But, Jimmy, I need to file a report. We need the police to collect evidence. Chase down leads."

I tapped my hat brim with a finger and pointed to the rookie. "We'll call it in when we've solved the case." Still holding the tinker above the elbow, I dragged him off the curb. "The only thing they'll be chasing are their tails." Gray wisps rose from his salt and pepper mange, and I patted the top of his head until I felt sure nothing would take flame. "Let's get you some clean clothes and try to pick up the trail before it grows cold."

We walked the few blocks to the tinker's house. He took a shower, changed, and sat on his couch in the living room kneading his hands. I claimed an armchair, which still smelled of the mold-ridden vacant house he had rescued it from.

He hung his head and moaned. "Why would anyone do this, Jimmy? How am I going to make a living? Do you have any idea how many generations of my family built their lives from that cart?"

"I don't know, two?"

"That sounds about right."

I set my fedora on the coffee table and scratched my forehead. "Let's stick to your first question. Consider motive. Any other tinkers looking to muscle in on your turf?"

"No, the Tinkers' Guild wouldn't allow that."

"There's a guild for tinkers?"

"Jimmy, let's stick to my first question. Why?" He got off the couch and plugged in his Skee-Ball machine. It started blinking and beeping.

"Do you have to do that, now?"

"It helps me think." He sank a ball in the forty-point hole. His second bounced off a rubber bumper and plunked into the twenty-point hole.

"Boy, you sure are a mess, aren't you?"

"My whole world just went up in flames. What do you expect?" His next ball bounced around the backboard finally settling in the ten-point hole.

The Skee-Ball game got me thinking. "Have you run into that old lady and her grandson? The ones that tried to cheat you out of the championship?"

"No, they've been banned from every self-respecting arcade on the East Coast."

"What about The Skee-Ball Council? Have they heard anything from those two?"

"I don't know what you're talking about." The tinker released his next ball too early, and it banged into the edge of the ramp then rolled across the floor to my feet.

"I'll take that as a no." I picked up the wood ball and turned it over in my hand. "Still, granny would have motive."

The tinker threw his hands into the air, yelled at the machine, and yanked its cord from the wall receptacle.

"We need some eyes on the street." I pulled out my phone and dialed my New York-transplant informant Rocco.

"Yeah, Jimmy. What can I do for you, there?"

"You notice the activity on the boardwalk this morning?"

"How could I miss it? It was bigger than a Bronx dumpster fire."

"Well, we could use you and your boys."

"Just tell me what you need."

"We're looking for an old lady with a walker. She wears muumuus and usually has her grandson nearby. He has long black hair that looks like he hasn't washed it since he was a teenager."

"Uh, hold on there a second, Jimmy." Rocco yelled something to someone near him. Actually, Rocco might not have been yelling, since most conversations with him, even of the *yeah, how you doin'* variety seemed like yelling. "Tell you what there, Jimmy, can you video call me? I may have something."

"Call you right back?"

"Yeah, just give me a minute."

I cut the connection.

"What's going on?" The tinker shuffled from one foot to the other then walked to the kitchen without waiting for a response.

"Rocco wants to show me something."

Kitchen drawers opened and closed. Utensils and pots clanged. "What does he want you to see?"

"Don't know." I made the video call to Rocco, and he answered while walking along the boardwalk.

"Jimmy, take a look at this." He pointed his phone at a fold of light blue fabric printed with tiny kitten faces. Whatever the material covered, it bounced up and down— the right side rose as the left fell and vice versa.

"What am I looking at?"

"Oh, wait a second. I gotta zoom out." A muumuu-covered gravity-challenged backside framed by a walker's aluminum legs filled my screen. "This who you're looking for?"

Someone from off-camera yelled, "Get away from that old lady, you creep!"

Rocco spun the camera to face a burly guy wearing a Best Dad Ever t-shirt. "Mind your own business, buddy. Can't you see I'm investigatin', here?" Rocco walked around the old lady to give me a front view. "This better, Jimmy?"

The old lady stared intently at the boardwalk, breathed heavily, and clutched her walker's handles making like she hurried along yet covered only a few inches at a time with each extension of her arms. The past couple of years hadn't been kind to her, but no doubt about it. Skee-Ball Granny herself.

"That's her, Rocco."

"Get out of my way, you hooligan!"

"Does granny know it's me, Rocco?"

"Nah, Jimmy. I don't think so."

"Good. Let's keep it that way."

The tinker called from the kitchen, "Did Rocco find her?"

"He did," I said back toward the kitchen. "Rocco, it sounds like she's saying something. Can you hear her?"

"I can do better than that." His video-feed swept around the busy boardwalk for a moment then gave me a close-up of granny's whiskered chin.

"Can you pull out a little more, Rocco?"

Sweat dripped from her cheek. She seemed really intent on getting somewhere fast despite her actual progress.

"Get that thing out of my face!"

"Take it easy, there, granny. This is official business."

"Who're you talking to?"

"Detective Jimmy Grits."

"I told you not to tell her."

Granny stopped and shook a fist at the phone. "His hobo friend stole my title, and he's getting what's coming to him."

The image changed back to Rocco's mug. "You getting this, Jimmy?"

"Yeah, she ain't too happy, but she needs to say something incriminating."

The tinker returned from the kitchen smacking a rolling pin in the palm of his hand. "I know how to make her talk."

"What, you going to bake her a pie?" I shook my head. "No, not you Rocco. Let me listen some more."

"Eat my stockings, you fat forties-detective-want-to-be—."

An authoritative off-camera voice interrupted the audio. "Sir, please step away from her."

"Uh-oh, Jimmy. It's the man."

"What man?"

"You know, the man. Five-O. The police. I gotta go. We'll work out payment later." Rocco ended the call.

The tinker kept smacking his palm with the rolling pin. "Well, where is she?"

"Put that away."

He waved the pin in my direction. "We don't have time to fool around. She's been on the run for over two hours."

"I said, put that thing away."

The tinker went into the kitchen, opened and closed a drawer, and returned empty handed, but a meat tenderizer hung from his belt. "You going to tell me where she is, or not?"

I sighed. "She's on the boardwalk. I heard Happy Land's rides when we were talking."

"That's only a block and a half from my cart. See, arsonists do like to hang around and see their work."

"We need more than a piece of crime television trivia to make a case against her. Besides, from the way she was moving, she made a break for it long before the explosion."

The tinker bit his lip and flopped onto his couch. "We both know she did it."

Private eyes worth their dimes followed evidence to conclusions, not the other way around, but explaining procedure to the tinker wouldn't have worked. "Show me where you keep your cart."

WE WALKED FROM THE TINKER'S HOUSE TO a row of nineteen-thir-ties-era postcard beach homes tucked into a heavily-treed part of old Ocean Mist. A gravel drive led between two cottages to a fieldstone build-ing with a timber roof. Sagging leaf-heavy tree limbs and ivy-draped walls hid the barn from the street.

"I never knew this was here."

The tinker opened a padlock holding together two large sliding wood doors. "Not many do. It's the last of its kind in Ocean Mist. Someday, it will be turned over to the historical society."

The doors' rollers squealed in overhead tracks. Sunlight revealed a storage space crammed with old wagons, car parts, and agricultural equipment not having seen any oil or grease in at least a century.

The dust made me sneeze. "All of this yours?"

"No, it belongs to an antiques collector. Along with the barn. He rents space to me for my cart."

We weaved through the relics to the back and a metal cage elevator big enough to park a car. He lifted the cage's front, motioned for me to enter, and closed it behind us.

"Excuse me." The tinker reached for a lever sticking from a housing on the floor. "The ride is a little bumpy."

"Is this thing safe?"

"Absolutely."

"Where does it go?"

The tinker pulled the lever. The cage rocked and rumbled for a moment then stopped. He reset the lever and lifted the metal door for me to exit.

"What are you doing?"

"We're here. Second floor."

"We didn't go anywhere."

"Technically, no, but the rent is cheaper for a second-floor space."

"Are you serious?" I stepped out of the cage and scratched my head. "Just show me where you keep your cart."

"Right over here, Jimmy." The tinker led me to an empty space the size of his cart in the barn's back corner. "This is the spot."

I pointed to a sliding door much like the one at the barn's front. "You move your cart in and out through there?"

"Well, yes, on the first floor."

I stared at him.

"What?"

"Never mind." I pulled a penlight out of my sport coat and walked a basic search grid. Grease spots on the concrete slab. Bits of metal. Random screws and nuts. Bins stacked in tidy rows filled with all sorts of odds and ends lined the empty space.

"Notice anything out of place, lately? Anything odd?"

"No, today was just like any other day."

I kept working my grid.

"Who else knows about your rental?"

"Just me, you, and the landlord."

"We can probably rule out your landlord, because blowing up your cart would have risked blowing up his barn and everything in it."

"I'm telling you, Jimmy. It was granny and that scum of a grandson."

I pointed my penlight at a box of circuit boards, loose transistors, diodes, and bits of wire, which stood apart from the rest of the tinker's wares. "What's that?"

"Extra parts from my new microwave."

"Microwaves don't come with extra parts."

"I had to make some modifications so it would work with my cart's battery."

"You installed a microwave on your cart, and your cart has a battery?"

"Actually, several batteries connected in a series circuit." The tinker rummaged through some bins. "Here, this is about the microwave." He handed me a letter.

Congratulations,

Eat-n-Run Incorporated is pleased to provide you with a free Zap and Go microwave to promote our newest line of superior quality appliances designed especially for caterers, food-truck operators, and street-cart industry professionals. We hope you take advantage of this promotion and join our Eat-n-Run family. Please visit your local Eat-n-Run retailer indicated below at the date and time listed to receive your free microwave. Don't forget our corporate motto, "Eat-n-Run with us, but never run with scissors!"

"You don't own a food truck."

"Of course not."

"Then, why does your cart need a microwave?"

"Jimmy, a guy has to eat. There's nothing like a hot burrito when I'm on."

"On what?"

"You know, when I'm wheeling and dealing to make the green."

"Okay, more to the point, why were you selected to receive a microwave? Why you?"

"That, I'm not so sure about."

"Did you enter a contest?"

"No."

"Could it have had something to do with that tinker guild you mentioned?"

"I don't think so."

"I hate to be the one to tell you this, but nothing in life is free." I lifted a piece of circuit board, turned it over, tossed it aside, and poked around the other *extra* parts. "How did you know how to modify the microwave for your cart?"

"The dealer helped. He gave me a set of directions specifically for a tinker's cart."

"For a tinker's cart, huh? That didn't strike you as odd?"

"Why should it?"

I clicked off my penlight, slid it back into my sport coat pocket, and adjusted my hat. "That's our first real lead."

THE TINKER POINTED THE WAY TO THE Eat-n-Run dealer; or, more accurately, a beach cottage's carport he visited three days earlier. I eased the Studebaker to the curb and took in a gingerbread-looking single story surrounded by a flawless lawn. Scalloped wood trim painted glossy white finished every edge of the cottage, and its bright pink paint reminded me of the stomach-ache remedy I drank after chili dog night at the Down and Out Burger.

No sign of any kind of business.

"You sure this was the place?"

The tinker jumped from the car and ran up the driveway. "There was a store, right here. In the car port. The guy had a sign in the front yard, tables full of appliances right over there, and even a work space with tools and a computer right back there."

"You do realize this is someone's driveway?"

"It was right here. I'm not crazy, Jimmy."

I could have argued his last point, but I left him pacing and knocked on the front door. Nothing. Frilly window curtains kept me from seeing into the cottage, even when I peered between my cupped hands held against the window. The pane seemed to vibrate under my fingers, so I pressed my ear against the glass. A heavy bassline tickled my cheek.

I pulled away from the window and motioned for the tinker. "Follow me." We walked along Hansel and Gretel's house checking windows as we went. No luck with the windows, so I banged on the back door with the side of my fist.

A man easily my size opened the door. Frantic drumming, loud growling, and a throbbing bass, which I had felt against my cheek at the front window, hit the tinker and me like punches to the face. The man's long black beard hung in two braids over a faded black t-shirt with *The Undead Gerbils* emblazoned in lightning-like letters over an illustration of rodent skeletons playing instruments. His frayed and ripped jeans appeared stained with tomato sauce—I hoped.

"How can I help you?" The guy lifted a square of fabric, which he proceeded to stitch with a needle and thread.

"My friend came here to pick up a microwave a couple days ago—."

"Three days, Jimmy."

"Right, three days ago. He says you were selling appliances out of your car port."

The man stopped mid stitch and looked up from his fabric square. "I beg your pardon."

I felt a tug at my sleeve. "This isn't the guy."

"Do you have a partner? Someone working for you?" I asked.

"Sir, I don't know what you're talking about."

I looked back at the tinker.

"It was here."

The guy stood back from the doorway. A half-finished quilt lay draped across a kitchen table. "You want to come in? Let me get the music." He disappeared down a hallway.

Smells of bleach and pine met us inside the door. The kitchen appeared spotless, except for pieces of fabric and sewing tools covering the counter. The tinker reached for the quilt on the table and felt its edge. "This is some fine work."

I smacked his fingers. "Don't touch that. It doesn't belong to you."

The growling and throbbing stopped. The guy returned. "I apologize for the mess."

"You should see Jimmy's place."

I rubbed my chin. "Like I was saying, my friend here picked up a microwave from a guy in your car port a few days ago. You know anything about the Eat-n-Run Appliance Company?"

"Never heard of it. Can you hand me that thimble? It's right there on the end of the counter."

"Anyone else here we can talk to?"

"Nope."

A shelf of porcelain gnomes stared at me from above the refrigerator. They judged me silently. Gave me the creeps. "Who owns the house?"

"It's mine."

"This is yours?"

The guy looked up at me, unclipped a shiny metal chain from his belt, pulled from his pocket a long black leather sheath, placed it on the table, coiled the chain, and resumed his stitching. "Just had the house painted. I'm particularly pleased with the white trim. What do you think?"

The tinker put his hands on his hips and scrunched his forehead. "Where were you three days ago?"

The man reached slowly for the sheath.

The muscles across my shoulders and neck tensed. My mind ran through all of the possible scenarios—strike, block and counter, step back to open the space between us to increase response time, step forward to jam up his weapon arm—every tip from every issue of *Private Eye of Fortune* magazine ran through my mind in less than a second. I balled up my right hand and chose a spot just behind the man's right temple where I would strike, but I eased when a pair of silver scissors slid slowly from the black leather sheath.

He snipped a thread from the cloth in front of him. "I just got back from the Wilmington Quilting Convention last night. Been there since last Thursday."

Something told me I could believe this guy. Maybe it was his quilter's running stitch. "Anyone ask to use your house or driveway?"

"No, could you hand me that light blue square?"

The tinker turned around, picked through a pile of fabric scraps next to the sink, and lifted a square. "This one?"

"Wait a minute," I reached for the scrap, "let me see that." A pattern of little kitten faces dotted a light blue field. "Where do you get your quilting fabric?"

"Usually, it's just left over from other projects."

"You wouldn't happen to make muumuus, would you?"

"They're my bread and butter."

I held up the fabric square and locked eyes with the tinker.

The tinker nodded. "I think you should get one."

"No, this is the same fabric granny wore." I leaned on the table and placed the square in front of the guy. "You sell a muumuu made of this fabric to an old lady, recently?"

"Just a couple of weeks ago. She's my best customer." The guy didn't miss a stitch.

"I'm afraid I'm going to have to keep this." I put the square in my pocket. "Evidence."

He shrugged.

"Did this lady know you would be out of town?"

"Yeah, I asked her grandson to water my flowers."

"Where do they live?"

I PARKED TWO BLOCKS FROM GRANNY'S HOUSE.

"Why are we stopping here?" The tinker leaned forward like he could will us closer to the house.

"I need you to listen to me."

"Okay."

"No, I mean really listen. Are you listening?"

"Yes, I'm listening."

"Granny and her grandson know us, and we need to collect as much evidence as possible, so no drama. Do I make myself clear?"

"Drama?"

"No charging up to the front door, no accusations, and no Skee-Ball trash talk."

"You don't give me enough credit, Jimmy."

"You've been talking to Angela, haven't you?" I got out of the car, straightened my tie, and spoke over the hood. "Let's approach through the backyard. If there's some cover, we can stake out the house for a while."

We crouched behind a chain-link fence and some scraggly bushes along granny's rear property line. The spot gave us a good view of the house. I didn't see any movement through the windows. No one seemed to be home, but most stake outs involved long periods of watching nothing happen. Part of the game. Besides, I needed some time to think, so we settled into the shrubbery.

The tinker might have been right. Granny and her grandson are plausible bombing suspects. They know enough about the tinker to create an opportunity with the free microwave, have history with him, and a motive— vengeance always being a strong one. If the grandson can make remote controlled Skee-Balls, he can make a bomb, hide it in plain sight, and detonate it remotely.

I pointed to the house's corner. "Look over there."

"The trash cans?"

I pulled out my phone, clicked on the camera, zoomed on the cans, snapped a couple of images, and held it up to the tinker. "See that cardboard poking out between the cans? Doesn't that look like one of those yard signs with the metal pins?"

"Let's get it."

"No, we get closer to see what it is, snap some photos, and leave it there for the police to find, if we call them."

"What do you mean, if?"

"We still don't have enough to prove anything."

I scanned the neighbors' homes. Middle of the day. Working family neighborhood. All quiet, but that didn't mean there was no one around. *This will have to be fast. Cat-like.*

A pat on the tinker's shoulder gave me his ear. "You stay here."

I moved to the end of the bushes, grabbed the fence's top rail, stuck the tip of my penny loafer between metal links, and pulled myself up to leap into the yard. The fence must have been old. The corner post bent like a plastic straw sending me and several fence sections collapsing onto some purple hydrangea. I somersaulted over the fence and rolled to a stop with my chin grinding into the grass.

The tinker used the fallen fence to walk over the hydrangea and into the yard. "Good thinking, Jimmy."

"Stop," I half yelled and half whispered. "Get down."

He pulled out his phone, ran to the trash cans, and snapped away.

Not wanting to increase our chances of being seen, I crawled through the open lawn to the tinker. "What are you doing?"

"This is it, Jimmy." He pulled the yard sign out from between the cans. *Eat-n-Run Appliances.* "You believe me, now?"

"Okay, put that back."

He shoved the sign between the cans, lifted a lid, and shooed some flies.

"We can't stay here." I grabbed his arm and pulled him toward the driveway, our fastest route off the property. A tarp-covered car stopped me in my tracks.

"I thought you said we can't stay here."

The shape looked familiar, and a peek under the heavy gray plastic at the vehicle's grill sent a chill down my spine. "No, this can't be—." I took a corner of the tarp and yanked. A pristine 1965 Shelby GT350R Ford Mustang glistened in the sun.

The tinker pointed to the rearview mirror. "A handicapped tag. Must be granny's car."

Skee-Ball must have been really good to the old woman.

I moved around to the driver's side to drool over the instrument cluster, but something else caught my eye. "Take a look behind the driver's seat." I pulled out my phone and video recorded a box full of electronic parts and a partially disassembled microwave. "I'd bet you a hundred bucks that's not what a microwave is supposed to look like on the inside."

"Do we have enough now? Can we call the police?"

I glanced at the house. *Still no sign of anyone. The grandson may still not be wise to us.* "Let's see if we can get something more on granny."

I PUSHED THE STUDEBAKER TO HER LIMIT making a beeline for the boardwalk. Not a parking space within sight, so I pulled up onto the sidewalk near an access ramp about three blocks south of Happy Land. The old girl hopping the curb scattered some jumpy end-of-season tourists. I rounded the car, tipped my hat, and nodded to a young lady. "Sorry, ma'am. This is a matter of public safety."

The tinker pulled up his cargo shorts and followed me, his sneakers slapping the boardwalk at my heels. "You still haven't told me where we're going."

Two Ocean Mist officers ran up to join us.

"Detective Grits, what do you think you're doing? You can't park on the sidewalk."

"News to me." I scanned the late afternoon crowd. "Get your cuffs out, because I'm going to help you make a collar."

"A what?" asked one officer.

The other responded, "He means make an arrest."

"Why didn't he just say that?"

"Pay attention, boys." I ran the numbers in my head. Roughly two and a half hours to get to Happy Land, a block and a half from the cart explosion. Almost five hours since then. "We should be right on top of—."

A family sharing a tub of french fries parted revealing granny hunched over her walker. Her muumuu covered backside pumped away propelling her down the boardwalk. The day's humidity had done a number on her silver-blue perm, which lay wilted down over her forehead. She couldn't see much giving me the edge to circle wide and confront her head-on.

"Well, granny," I put my foot in front of her walker's leg stopping her cold, "it's time you and your grandson faced the music."

"I'd know that penny loafer, anywhere. Out of my way, Grits."

"In a hurry, granny?"

"I have a roast in the oven."

"Where's your grandson?"

"How should I know?"

One of the officers stepped between me and granny. "Mr. Grits, you need to leave this poor woman alone and go move your car."

"Officer, you're not only looking at the notorious Skee-Ball Granny, but, as of this morning, the Tinker Cart Bomber."

"Prove it, Poppin' Fresh!" Granny poked me in the stomach. "Hoo-hoo!"

"Really, Detective Grits?" The officer placed his hand gently on granny's shoulder. "Ma'am, I'm so sorry about this. Is there someone I can call for you? Maybe get you to a bus?"

"Thank you, dear, but I'm doing just fine. Isn't that right, Grits?" She lifted her walker and jammed its rubber-foot onto the top of my loafer.

I swallowed a yell, stumbled backwards, saw stars, and picked up my foot holding it in both hands.

The tinker turned his head and winced. "Jimmy, that must hurt."

I hopped a few times, lost my balance, and fell onto my ass. "Don't let her fool you. Check the handbag hanging from her walker."

The second officer, to this point watching with his arms folded, asked, "What, exactly, do you expect us to find in her bag, detective?"

"Give me a minute to lay-out our evidence. You'll have reasonable suspicion."

The tinker wedged himself between the bleeding-heart officers and granny. "Tinkers don't need reasonable suspicion." He reached into her bag and yanked out a handful of its contents, which scattered onto the boardwalk: a pack of chewing gum, knitted change purse, a bingo card, an upper denture plate, and a remote detonator.

"You really shouldn't have done that." I finished my last note for the case file, closed the folder, reached into my desk drawer, and pulled out a bottle of Jack. "The judge will probably throw-out the detonator."

"The way I see it, grabbing the detonator from granny's bag gave the police a reason to hold her. They were about to send her home on a bus, remember?"

"Point taken." I blew the dust out of a mug and hoped the alcohol would kill whatever grew on the bottom.

"When do we start looking for the grandson?"

"We don't. He'd never let go of her apron strings, so I'm sure he'll turn up sooner or later."

"Any word on what was in the house?"

"My contact in the department said they found more than enough bomb-making materials to put granny away for a long time. They also found a draft of the phony Eat-n-Run letter."

"Can they connect the bomb materials to my cart?"

I motioned with my mug to the phone on my desk. "Waiting for a return call from the fire marshal."

We sat in silence for a few moments. I enjoyed the chance to rest before having to go back to the lighthouse island.

"Can you help me with the insurance company? I might need some of your notes."

"It's all here." I patted the folder. "This isn't my first rodeo." I drained my mug and poured another finger. "What are you going to do, anyway?"

"You mean with my business?"

"If you want to call it that."

"Well, I'll have to build a new cart and restock my merchandise."

"Where does a tinker get new merchandise? Is there some kind of tinker warehouse, somewhere?"

"No, yard sales, mostly. You'd be surprised what people keep in their garages and closets."

I lifted my mug and toasted my filing cabinet. "Actually, I wouldn't be surprised in the least."

Eat-n-Run Incorporated
1993 Fast and Ready Industrial Park
Gasington, Illinois 77345

Dear Mr. Grits:

Our company is committed to manufacturing safe high-quality cooking appliances. We are aware of last month's explosion in Ocean Mist and the suspected involvement of one of our Zap and Go microwave models. Please know, any similarities to past explosions are completely coincidental, and claims of our microwave causing or contributing to any such explosions are half-baked.

We understand a non-qualified technician installed a Zap and Go on the tinker cart lost in this unfortunate incident. A close reading of our installation instructions, specifically page thirty-five, clearly states not to install this model on a tinker cart. Additionally, article two, section three, paragraph five, line seven of our warranty invalidates any claims for replacement or reimbursement should any such installation be attempted on a tinker cart. Despite Eat-n-Run's clear lack of involvement with this incident, we are not without sympathy for the tinker cart owner.

We have not been able to locate said owner and are asking for your help to convey to him a gift of condolence. Please expect a shipment to your office of five thousand Eat-n-Run microwaveable Afterburner Bean Burritos known by our product slogan, "Afterburner Burritos— rocket like a jet fighter!" We believe this letter and gift discharges us from any and all perceived liabilities for any past, current, or future injuries.

Sincerely,
Mr. Chip Frier, President
Eat-n-Run Incorporated

Prison Break

Part 1: Life Ain't a Picnic

For a guy making a living facing down criminals and gangsters, I never expected a filing cabinet to test my will of steel. Emptying the cabinet's four drawers took less than ten minutes, but rearranging the hundreds of folders stuffed with notes, photos, negatives, affidavits, and a million other records took hours. None of it fit my idea of public service. I sat on the corner of my desk, folded my arms, and glared at the open drawers gaping like four drunken loudmouths at a bar.

Maybe donuts will help? No. Just prolong the inevitable.

I scooped some folders from the desk and knelt by the bottom drawer.

"Hey, Jimmy, did you see this?"

Always ready for danger, I sprung to my feet but the top drawer got the better of me. I banged my head and kicked over a pile of papers adding at least another hour to my already tedious day. "See what you made me do? Why didn't you tell me you were coming?"

"Sorry, Jimmy. Why don't you get someone to help you with those?"

"Not these files." I rubbed the back of my head with one hand and patted a stack on my desk with the other. "This is a thousand hours' worth of Ocean Mist's secrets all right here. For my eyes, only."

The tinker handed me a newspaper. "Here's something else for your eyes."

Half-Baked Escape Attempt From Ocean Mist Prison!

I folded the paper and held it out to him. "Those guards over there are top of the line."

"No, Jimmy. You need to read it."

"I don't have time—."

"It's The Mime. He tried to get out."

"Why should a criminal wanting to escape from prison surprise anyone?"

"Just read it."

"Tell you what, why don't you give me the highlights?"

The tinker plopped into a chair. "Inmates working in the kitchen got to talking and figured, if a person on the outside could bake a file or hacksaw into a cake and pass it to someone on the inside, why couldn't they just reverse the whole thing?"

"You lost me. Why would inmates want to pass a hacksaw to someone outside the prison?"

"Not a hacksaw."

"Wait a minute," I unfolded the paper, "you've got to be kidding me."

"I'm not. One of the inmates on kitchen detail was taking a personal improvement course on marine biology. That was how they got their hands on a wetsuit and scuba tank."

Right there, in black and white, I found the worst idea to ever cross my desk:

Inmates working for Ocean Mist Prison's catering service attempted to bake one of their own into a cake Sunday morning. The plan called for the convict to emerge upon the cake's delivery to Chicken Neck Nellie's Crab Shack for a retirement party scheduled that afternoon. Prison guards discovered and rescued the inmate, identified as The Mime, upon detecting the smell of burning rubber coming from his wetsuit stolen from a marine biology program. Prison medical staff provided first aid until paramedics arrived to transport The Mime to Ocean Mist Medical Center. The inmate suffered second and third degree burns over seventy-five percent of his body.

I glanced over the top of the newspaper. "Seventy-five percent? Why didn't anyone hear his screams?"

"Jimmy, he's a mime." The tinker leaned forward and grabbed the paper from my hands. "There's something not right about the whole thing. I just can't put my finger on it."

"I can tell you what's not right. These guys are fools." I looked back at the paper in his hands and fixed on a big black and white photo of paramedics wheeling The Mime into an ambulance. "Wait. Give me that." I stabbed the image with my finger. "The guy climbing into the ambulance next to the gurney, does he look familiar to you?"

The tinker took back the paper and looked at the photo so hard I thought he might hurt himself. "Hard to tell with the surgical mask and scrubs, but, now that you mention it," he rose from the chair and slapped the paper with the back of his hand, "that looks like Patches!"

"Yeah, a lot like him. I'll bet you, Patches convinced The Mime to get baked into the cake. The whole time, Patches planned to escape in the responding ambulance dressed like a prison nurse."

"What are we going to do?"

Only a bottom feeder like Patches would sacrifice a fellow inmate so cruelly. There's no honor with that thief, and I can't let him roam Ocean Mist's streets. "We start at the beginning. The very beginning."

"There's no one here." The tinker sank deeper into the Studebaker's passenger seat, folded his arms, and closed his eyes. "There was no one here yesterday, and there was no one here the day before yesterday. How much longer do you want to sit around counting rats?"

"Stake-outs can go on for days." The former Pink Flamingo, which had become a hollow shell of cinderblocks and strung-together trailers, seemed our best starting point. Our only starting point. "Patches has to come up for air some time. He always comes back here. This place is an idiot magnet."

"I worked here."

"Yes, you did."

"I'm telling you, Patches is on some Pacific island drinking from a coconut. That's what I'd be doing." The tinker shuffled his duct-taped sneakers over the mail covering my floor. "Shouldn't you read some of this?"

"It can wait."

"You're not doing anything better, right now." He picked up a hand-written envelope and slid his finger under the flap. "This is from the Ocean Mist Prison. Don't you think you should open this one?"

"Looks like you already are."

"It's an invitation, Jimmy."

"From the prison?"

"Yeah," he cleared his throat, "you are cordially invited to the First Annual Ocean Mist Prison Inmates' Law Enforcement Appreciation Picnic to be held in our yard on the afternoon of June 15th." He held up the invitation. "That's two days from now. Want to go?"

"Who's holding the picnic?"

The tinker's mouth moved as he reread silently. "The inmates."

"Why would inmates host a picnic for law enforcement?"

"Bad decisions don't make bad people, Jimmy."

"Jimmy Grits doesn't picnic when a criminal is on the loose."

The tinker gestured toward the empty building. "How is this helping? The trail is cold. We didn't even have a trail to start with." He put the invitation in the glove compartment. "Don't think of this as a picnic. Think of it as a fact-finding mission."

"What are you talking about?"

"Maybe someone at the prison knows Patches' plan."

"Why would they tell me?"

"You're the detective. Do some snooping around. We certainly aren't getting anywhere here."

THE TINKER NAGGED ME RIGHT UP TO the morning of the picnic. I relented, and we climbed into the Studebaker. The day's humidity could've steamed dumplings on the dashboard adding to my list of gripes about spending a day at a prison picnic.

At least we'll get a couple burgers and maybe some macaroni salad out of this.

We cruised with open windows down Washington Avenue, crossed the canal drawbridge, and slid onto Highway One. The first exit after Ocean Mist took us inland about a mile past a chicken processing plant then to the first of three fence and razor-wire checkpoints.

Glitter-paint signs reading *Welcome Ocean Mist's Finest* and balloons decorated each gate, and all of the guards wore shorts, t-shirts, and pointy party hats along with their usual tactical belts.

"Boy," the tinker leaned out the window to get a better look at a poster, "the inmates really went all-out for this."

"You could say that."

"Why are you always so pessimistic? You need to have a more positive outlook on life, Jimmy. You need to trust in the good living inside each of us."

"Who made you Ocean Mist's Dalai Lamea?"

"Dalai Lama, Jimmy. It's the Dalai Lama."

"No, I meant Dalai Lamea."

There may have only been two or three open parking spaces in the visitor lot, which held more marked cars than a policemen's convention. I stepped out into the day's full heat, grabbed my sport coat from the back, and checked my tie in the side view mirror.

The tinker tossed my fedora over the hood. "Don't forget this."

"Never." I swept my gaze across a sea of interceptors, paddy wagons, SWAT vehicles, and even a bomb-disposal unit. "Perfect day for someone to hold up the Ocean Mist Bank."

"Positivity, Jimmy. Positivity."

"Yeah, yeah."

We buzzed in through the visitors' entrance and worked our way through guard stations, turn-styles, and metal detectors before reaching the prison yard. Two large tents, picnic tables, columns of smoke rising from a line of grills, and an inflated pastel-colored castle filled the sprawling area of concrete and gravel. The canvas tents looked like army surplus, each one large enough to drive a tank through.

"Hey," the tinker tugged on my sleeve and pointed, "they have a bouncy house."

"Why don't you go check it out, and I'll grab a hot dog?"

The tinker scampered toward the billowy castle, and I loaded down a dog with as many condiments as I could find— breakfast seemed a distant dream.

"Hey there, Grits." A lady wearing an orange jumpsuit, lace-less shoes, and a balloon animal on her head stepped up next to me at the hot dog table.

"I remember you. You're the boardwalk pick pocket."

"No hard feelings." She constructed a loaded hotdog in a little paper boat. "Glad you could make the picnic." Her gaze rose slowly from my feet to my face, probably reminiscing about the night she doused me with her clothes-eating acid and got the full Grits experience. "Your friend here, too?"

"Right over there." I used the remainder of my bun to point at the tinker whooping and leaping around inside the bouncy house.

"Good. I hope you both enjoy this. You certainly deserve it."

"Yeah, thanks."

She walked away with her head hung low.

I'd be embarrassed, too, with her reputation.

Almost three decades working Ocean Mist's streets made most of the faces around me familiar. Inmates and law enforcement, alike. Even if I couldn't recall all of the names, I knew them, and they knew me, and every last one of the boys and girls in uniform deserved appreciation. I reminded myself, though, I didn't come for the picnic. Or praise. I came for the case. The serious business of crime-fighting.

I had a hard time imagining an inmate dropping a dime on Patches, especially since aiding an escape meant adding time to a sentence and probably a stint in solitary. With my senses heightened, I weaved my way between tables then entered a tent filled with games.

Sometimes, simple awareness provided this private eye with important information, a lead, but if being present to the moment didn't work, I figured eaves-dropping on a motor-mouth inmate's blabbing, striking up a conversation with a lonely-looking outsider sitting in a corner, or exchanging war stories with some guards to loosen a tongue or two might.

None of it worked.

Nothing.

Nothing but ring tosses, water balloons, eggs on spoons, cops, criminals, and stuffed animals.

I made my way to the next tent. It covered a large dance floor made of interlocking wood panels surrounded by folding chairs. A small stage, podium with a microphone, arena-sized speakers, and a DJ console lined the far end.

No one there.

I lingered appreciating a few moments alone in a quiet oasis where I could collect my thoughts. My peace didn't last long, though. Something metal clanked followed by a babbled curse and angry garbled words. I assumed my fighting stance knowing I couldn't let my guard down, even at a picnic.

Reginald The Rocket stepped from behind a speaker holding a socket wrench and scratching his head. We locked eyes. He froze mid scratch. His orange jumpsuit made him look more like Reginald the Oompa Loompa than the flamboyant daredevil of his former circus life.

"I see you've picked up a new skill, Reginald. I guess there aren't many scooters to race in the pen, are there?"

"Gurble gurble yar, gurble."

I didn't even try interpreting his frustrated Reginald speak and made a point of looking at the tan canvas stretched above our heads. "At least you're back under the big top."

Reginald tossed his wrench onto a folding chair and left.

"So much for conversation."

I crossed the dance floor to the stage. The tent housed more than a sound system. Spot lights, color filter wheels, fog machines, and all sorts of projection equipment suggested a big finale for the picnic. Looked like the inmates tried to put together some kind of trendy dance club, not that I'd want to go to one, especially after all of that Pink Flamingo nonsense. I placed my hat on a speaker and claimed one of the folding chairs.

This is useless. We should be staking out the old strip club.

The tinker entered the tent. "Hey, Jimmy. I thought you'd be over by the food trucks."

"Well, I'm not."

A man wearing khaki's, a button-down, and a walkie-talkie clipped to his belt walked beside him. The man extended his hand to me.

I stood. "You must be Warden Penn. This is quite the shindig."

The warden shook with a firm clasp, a handshake of strength and conviction. "Your friend here said I had to meet the one and only, Jimmy Grits."

The tinker put his hand on my shoulder. "No reason to have another."

"Thanks. Anyway, warden, since we have a moment, I'd like to talk to you about the recent—." The prison yard speakers interrupted me with an announcement for all guests and inmates to make their ways to the main tent.

"Maybe later, Mr. Grits." The warden pulled some folded papers from his pocket, stepped onto the stage, and arranged his notes on the podium. "It's almost twelve, and the inmates asked me to MC the afternoon's events."

Ocean Mist's law enforcement and inmates filed into the tent. The tinker and I took seats near the stage. Badges filled the folding chairs to our left and right. The inmates gathered around the warden like a jump-suited choir.

The warden tapped his microphone. A bit of feedback screeched through the speakers. He began to speak, but a strangely familiar smell, really faint but enough to steal my attention from his words, reached this detective's highly tuned nostrils.

"Hey," I leaned toward the tinker, "do you smell that?"

"Sorry, I couldn't resist the chili."

"No, I mean—."

The smell became stronger. The inmates on the stage bolted. Guests stood looking to the warden for an explanation. I recognized the smell and moved to chase the inmates, but Patches' wacky tobaccy smoke spewed from the fog machines in thick clouds overtaking everyone in seconds. Even I wasn't fast enough.

Prison Break

Part 2: Under the Big Top

I opened my eyes, lifted my chin from my chest, and shook my head. Images came and went. Hot dogs. Shorts Lady. Reginald with a socket wrench. More hot dogs. The warden starting to talk. The wacky tobaccy fog.

I sat in the middle of the dance floor unable to move my hands. Rough rope tied my wrists. My metal chair's seat felt strangely cold. I looked down at my bare legs. The scumbags had taken my pants, coat, tie and shirt, but they at least dignified me by leaving my briefs, dress socks, penny loafers, and I could feel my fedora pushed down on my head. I yanked at my bindings, which looped around a tent pole tight against my chair's back.

I heard a groan behind me.

"Hey," I tried to turn in my seat, but more ropes pulled against my chest, "someone there?"

"Yeah, Jimmy. It's me." The tinker sounded groggy.

I wiggled enough slack in my bindings to look over my shoulder and saw him tied to a chair and the same pole as me. "Can you move?"

The pole shook. A ripple passed through a thousand square yards of canvas above our heads.

"Not really."

Having been tied up more than a few times in my career, I knew cords and knots could be worked loose over time, so I set at it twisting and moving my hands back and forth. "Have any idea where everyone went?"

"Not a clue. I saw you stand, then there was a bunch of smoke, and the next thing I know I'm here in my underwear."

"Start working at your ties. Keep your hands moving. See if you can get any play out of your knots." The pole didn't seem very sturdy, and the more we tried to free ourselves, the more it moved with us. "Any luck?"

"Not really. These are tight."

"Okay, we can't keep doing this all day. I have an idea."

"Is it a good idea?"

"I'll tell you in a minute." I rocked my chair back and forth.

"Jimmy, you're shaking the pole."

"That's the idea."

"It's not a good one."

My chair started to tip.

"Wait, Jimmy. I think we're tied together."

We crashed in a heap of ropes and aluminum chairs. Our combined weights yanked the pole out of its stand, tore it free from the canvas above us, and sent it clanging onto the dance floor.

I still couldn't see the tinker. "You okay?"

"No, why didn't you warn me?"

"Next time we're tied up under a tent pole in a prison yard, I will." I took a few breaths and moved my legs to try and get some feeling back into them. "Can you worm your way to the end of the pole? Once we're free of it, we should be able to untie our hands."

"Jimmy—."

"What?"

"The tent."

"What about it?" I looked up and found the canvas sagging more than my pants without a belt. One by one, other poles ripped free of their ties, toppled, and banged onto the dance floor until we found ourselves in darkness under a heavy blanket half the size of a football field.

"I told you it was a bad idea."

"Can you get to the end of the pole?"

"I'm trying." The tinker grunted and shuffled under the canvas. "Okay, I'm off."

I felt the pole against my back and inch-wormed my way along it. The canvas pushed down all around me, and the air underneath became hot and thick with dust. I couldn't get my breath and started to wheeze.

"Easy, Jimmy. Take slow, long breaths."

A bit of light spilled through a line of grommets. I could see the tinker struggling to prop the canvas around us with a chair.

"You won't be able to get it up onto its legs," I said. "Turn it sideways and pull it closer to us."

Some weight lifted from my back, and the chair gave me just enough room to free myself from the pole, undo the cords around my hands, and pull my legs up under me.

The tinker could barely speak between his huffs and puffs. "How are we going to get out of this one?"

"We'll just crawl under the canvas."

"Have you tried lifting this thing?"

I reached above my head and pushed. Might as well have been the ceiling of a parking garage. Trading being tied to a chair for laying in the fetal position, in my underwear, in the dark, and under a ton of fabric just didn't seem like progress. "Think we can cut through this?"

"You keep a pocket knife in your briefs?"

I moved my face closer to the grommets and took a deep breath. "Did you see the other chair?"

"I think it's over there by your foot."

I reached around until I found a cool aluminum tube, pulled it toward me, then ran my hand over the chair's parts until I found a loose screw holding a brace to a leg. Didn't take much effort to remove the screw. I ran its point back and forth on the canvas.

"That's going to take you forever."

"You got a better idea?"

The tinker held the chair seat and yanked on the disconnected brace bending it more and more with each pull. "This tubing is pretty flimsy. If I can just break it where it's flattened near the leg—." The brace snapped. The break looked pretty sharp. "Try this."

The broken aluminum worked better than the tiny screw, but we still had to take turns for at least an hour before we got a good rip going in the fabric and made a hole big enough for the tinker to push himself through. I poked my head out, grateful for better air, but didn't have enough room for much more than a shoulder.

The tinker scrambled around the prison yard searching grills, tables, and boxes. "You'd think there would be a knife or scissors around here somewhere."

"This is a prison. You won't find any sharp tools." I kept working at the rip's edge with the now dulled chair brace. "Go get some help."

"There's nobody around." The tinker stood with his hands on his hips for a moment, rubbed his jaw, and made his way to the hotdog table where he smashed a relish jar on the ground. Using a rag, he picked up a glass shard, came back to the canvas, and held the shard with the rag while cutting to expand the rip. "This isn't much better than that piece of aluminum."

The relish-slicked glass slipped from the rag and fell into the dark under the canvas.

"I think you cut enough." I wiggled my other shoulder through the rip, but the opening pinned my arms to my sides, and I got stuck just below my collar bones.

"Come on, Jimmy. You can do it!"

I tried to get my legs underneath me.

"That's it, Jimmy. Remember to breath."

A prolonged push and sustained grunt did nothing.

The tinker crouched down next to me. "Ten quick breaths then push."

I gained an inch, but the canvas cinched around my chest.

"I can see both elbows. Just a little more. Push!"

"I am pushing!" I bellowed and shoved my body a little more through the gap.

"Almost there, Jimmy. Really bear down. Ready, one— two—three!"

The canvas gave way on my right with a ripping sound, and I popped out kneeling half-naked and glistening in the midafternoon sun. I reached back into the rip, pulled out my fedora, and reshaped its crown. "Where did everybody go?"

The tinker pointed to a picnic bench propping the steel door into the prison. "Probably through there."

The air-conditioning just about froze my sweat-soaked underwear to my skin. Pulling up my dress socks and crossing my arms didn't help much.

We found the security booth controlling the yard entrance abandoned. A tan-painted cinderblock hallway led us to an intersection and another abandoned security station where a half-eaten hamburger and slab of cake sat on a scarred and badly-chipped wood desk. I placed my hand on the burger.

"You're not going to eat that, are you?"

"Of course not." I took off the top bun and felt the meat. "I'd say it's been off the grill for about an hour and forty minutes."

"How do you know?"

"I'm a detective, remember?"

A real heavy feeling grew in my gut. Every one of my private eye instincts told me I wouldn't find Ocean Mist's inmates all cozy in their cell block cots. Didn't think I'd find my pants any time soon, either.

The tinker craned his neck to the right and down the hall. "You hear that?"

We followed banging sounds to the visitation room, its benches and tables all bolted to the cement floor and vacant. Plastic vases on the tables held wilted flowers. Bands of sunlight entered through barred windows.

The banging came from my left, and I turned to find Ocean Mist's finest peering at us through plexiglass panels from the wrong side of a steel-framed wall lined with chairs and phones. They switched from banging on the plexiglass to yelling when they saw us, but I couldn't make-out their words. I figured *get us out of here* was a fair guess and took a seat, lifted a receiver, and everyone went quiet.

A woman with a really tight pony tail, thick glasses, and too much lipstick lifted the paired phone. "Ocean Mist Emergency Services. What is the nature of your emergency?"

I knew the voice right away. "Are you kidding me?"

"Oh, it's you."

I put the receiver against my chest and took a breath. Of all the people to pick up the phone, it had to be Ocean Mist's dispatcher.

The tinker leaned in and whispered. "You want me to talk to her? You know, because of your history?"

"No." I moved the receiver toward my face. "Keep your mouth shut."

"Look, Mr. Grits—."

"I didn't mean you."

The tinker leaned in again. "Jimmy meant me. He has this thing about phones."

"I bet he does."

"What do you mean by that, lady?"

"You're sitting in front of us in your underwear and that stupid hat. Do you really need to ask?"

"Just— okay— how did all of you get in there?"

"We woke up in here. Get us out."

"Where are the inmates?"

She shrugged.

"Okay, how do I open the doors?"

"Did you find any of the keys at the security stations?"

I put the phone against my chest and turned to see the tinker rearranging flowers in a plastic vase. "Hey, stop that. Did you see any keys back there?"

The tinker shook his head.

"We didn't see any keys, doll."

The dispatcher rolled her eyes and sighed. "Okay Mr. Grits, you need to get the spare master key."

"Where do we look?"

"Go back out the main entrance and lift the welcome mat."

The master key got us all the way to the lock-up where the prisoners had corralled Ocean Mist's law enforcement. Within moments, every cruiser, van, and armored SWAT vehicle in the prison's lot made beelines for town with sirens blaring leaving the tinker and me alone on the prison's doorstep.

Prison Break

Part 3: You Can't Go Home

The tinker trailed me on the long walk to the parking lot. Sweat rolled off my brow and down my back despite my lack of clothes, and the weight of a world flooded with criminals rested on my shoulders. The Studebaker came into view. My heart broke.

"Look what they did to my car!" Someone had written *Shrimp and Grits* in large white spray-painted letters across my girl's shiny black hood.

The tinker stopped in his tracks and propped his fists on his hips. "Who are they calling a shrimp?"

I circled the Studebaker and found the same words on the doors and trunk. "No one appreciates classics, anymore." Fortunately, they didn't find my key hidden in the visor. That trick never failed.

"Now what, Jimmy?"

"I've got some spare clothes back at the office."

The Studebaker made quick work of Highway One, but a Delaware State Trooper still overtook us on the off-ramp to Ocean Mist. Followed by another. Their sirens made my head hurt. We crossed the canal bridge and found Washington Avenue crammed with Ocean Mist's fire and medical vehicles, their emergency lights a late-afternoon fireworks display. A column of black smoke rose into the hot cloudless sky.

A cruiser blocked traffic. An officer stood at the bumper waving traffic into the side street. I pulled up next to her, leaned out my window, and opened my mouth, but she cut me off yelling above the sirens.

"Detective Grits, go on through!" She stood aside giving us just enough space to squeeze by her car.

"Oh no, Jimmy."

Flames licked skyward from the building housing my office. Waves of smoke broke over the Studebaker's hood. Mist from firefighters' hoses spotted the windshield. Stepping from the car felt like walking on jelly, and my mind blanked until I reached the sidewalk where someone said something about not getting any closer.

All of my files. A lifetime's collection of photos, recordings, transcripts, notes, profiles, interviews— all of it gone.

"Jimmy," the tinker said, "we should go."

"Who would do this?"

"Think about it. The prison is empty. It could be any one of a hundred people. Or all of them. We need to go."

I felt Ocean Mist's eyes on me. The town's residents, tourists, and business owners all bearing witness to this attack on decency and justice. All looking to me for what to do next.

"Jimmy, come on."

"This is a crime scene. I have to question witnesses. Collect evidence." If the prisoners had not taken my phone, I would have recorded video and taken photos capturing as many faces as possible.

"No, Jimmy—."

"Can't you see what's happening? Why are you in such a hurry?"

"We're standing on the sidewalk in our underwear."

"What?"

The tinker slid back into the car.

Can they put out the fire? Save some of my office? Some of my work?

The tinker honked the horn.

Underwear.

I got behind the wheel, backed away from the curb, and stopped. The mayor stood twenty feet away on the sidewalk— hard to miss the miscreant Abraham Lincoln doppelgänger. His expression surprised me. I expected satisfaction, maybe glee, but saw panic.

"You can't go home, Jimmy."

"What?"

"You're still not thinking right. You can't go home."

"Why not?"

"They might be waiting for you there."

"Then we can get them all at once."

"Listen to what you're saying." The tinker shook his head. "Let's just go to my house."

I STOOD IN THE TINKER'S SHOWER EMPTYING his hot water tank. The water couldn't wash away the anger in my chest or the image of my burning office from my mind, but the minutes of isolation and quiet helped me take stock of my situation.

Ocean Mist's badges could scoop up the little fish, the shoplifters, petty scammers, and everyday ruffians, but they would leave the big ones for me. Big-league criminals for the big-league player: Reginald, the pick-pocket lady, Frankenstein, Skee-Ball Granny, her grandson, Paddy the stroke specialist, Gilmer Aitkens, Bumper, and Patches to name a few. Fortunately, The Mime had put himself out of commission and lay under guard at the hospital.

I stepped from the shower, leaned on the vanity, and stared into the fogged mirror. Master chess players sometimes reexamined opponents' openings to predict future moves. No different from what this master detective needed to do.

The cake stunt might have gone bad for The Mime, but it created a distraction for Patches posing as the doctor, nurse, or whatever. He then smuggled wacky tobaccy gas into the prison— probably in the balloon tanks— for the big escape. The main event.

I never doubted The Mime was a fool, but the tinker had a point. *How his fellow inmates managed to convince him to try that hair-brained scheme—.*

Something the tinker had said when we stood outside my burning office replayed in my mind. *The prison is empty. It could be any one of a hundred people. Or all of them.* Hearing those words again started my wheels turning.

It can't be all of the prisoners.

One is still in custody.

Patches still has a loose end.

We need to get to The Mime first.

I wrapped a towel around me, poked my head out the bathroom door, and heard a wooden clunk, a ball rolling up a ramp, and beeping coming from the living room. "Hey, you playing Skee-Ball?"

"It helps me think."

I shook my head. "You got something I can wear?"

The tinker plodded down the hallway in big-eared dog slippers, stepped into his bedroom, and came out holding a pile of clothes. "How about these?"

"Cargo shorts and a Hawaiian shirt?"

"You expected something else?"

The thread-bare ensemble felt like rags in my hands. "How am I supposed to fit into these?"

"Suck it in. Make the best of it. It's all I got." He patted his back pocket. "What are the chances we get our wallets back?"

"Are you serious?"

"All my credit cards, Jimmy."

"You actually think they'll return your wallet? Do you know how criminals work?"

"Well, do you?"

"Yes!"

"Good, when do you think I'll get it back?"

I took a breath. "Yes, I know how criminals work, and no, you're not getting your wallet back. How many cases have you worked with me?"

He stuck out his thumb, looked at the ceiling, and extended one finger at a time.

I left him counting in the hallway and used the bathroom to squeeze into his rags. "We'll just have to use cash or checks."

"Checks?"

"Yes, checks."

"You're one of those guys always holding up the grocery line, aren't you?"

"Just call your credit card companies and cancel your cards, but make it quick."

"Online is faster."

"Whatever, just do it."

"I have some money in my top dresser drawer stuffed in the Scooby Doo socks. It's not a lot, but it'll help until the banks open in the morning."

"We'll make it work."

We climbed into the Studebaker and made for the hospital. Strobing reds, whites, and blues lit the Ocean Mist night. Sirens rose and died so frequently, I couldn't tell where one emergency started and another ended.

My town. My home I had sworn to keep free of crime and degenerates. My life's work gone with a single picnic.

I rubbed my face. "I need coffee."

The tinker managed a weak grunt.

The Ocean Mist Diner brewed twenty-four hours, and I needed a familiar haunt to remind me at least some parts of my world remained intact.

Only a few cars in the lot. The mayhem in town is probably keeping away the usual night traffic.

I started on my well-tread path toward the counter but stopped outside the diner's small gift shop. "Wait a minute."

The tinker just about smacked his face into my back.

Over-priced conveniences filled racks and shelves, but I only needed a moment to find the rack of burner phones, the kind just about every miscreant I had collared over the years had carried in their pockets. "Can you spring for a couple of those along with the coffee?"

"Good idea. You got the cash."

The diner's worn vinyl booths, chrome walls, and whiffs of greasy bacon called to me, but duty called much louder. Only enough time to grab a couple paper cups filled with black gold before hitting the road hoping to reach The Mime before Patches or his minions.

Caffeine and the hospital's brightly lit parking lot gave me a second wind. We hurried through shushing automatic doors for the trauma unit, an easy find given how many crooks I had sent there. An Ocean Mist officer planted on a small plastic chair in the hallway helped us pinpoint

The Mime's room. The way the officer rose, jittery and wiping his palms on his tactical pants, told me as much about our desperate and strained situation as the embroidered CADET patch on his breast pocket.

"You here by yourself?"

He looked us up and down then asked me, "Are you Detective Grits?"

"Today, I'm not so sure, kid."

The cadet smirked. "Do you two always dress alike?"

"Does the department always assign a Cub Scout to watch a convicted felon?"

He lifted his hands. "Okay, easy Mr. Grits. Everything is fine, here."

I threw a thumb toward the empty desks behind us. "Is that why there's no hospital staff on duty?" I pointed my chin at the trauma bay's large observation window and took a step in that direction. "How about why The Mime's curtains are pulled?"

The cadet moved into my path. "The nurse is with him. Besides, he ain't talking."

"He never does."

I shouldered past the cadet and opened the door. Nothing I saw surprised me: plastic burn tent, beeping and blinking equipment, a fishing show playing without sound on the television, half-eaten cafeteria meal on a rolling table, oversized Styrofoam drinking cup— everything one would expect to find in a hospital room dedicated to a prisoner, except the prisoner.

The tinker and cadet crowded behind me in the doorway.

The cop wanna-be's breath passed my cheek hot and heavy. "That's not possible. He was right there."

I spoke over my shoulder. "How long ago did the nurse come in here?"

"Fifteen, maybe twenty minutes ago, but no one came out. Where could they have gone?"

"The open window solves your mystery, cadet."

"But, we're three stories up."

I pushed between the cadet and tinker, took a breath in the hallway, turned for the trauma unit's exit, and pounded linoleum. "Maybe now you can hit the streets with the big boys."

THE TINKER HUNG A RIGHT TOWARD THE parking lot but stopped when I took the left.

"Jimmy, the car is this way."

"We're not leaving. I need to see a friend." I stopped at a door marked *Security* and pushed a buzzer button under a camera.

The door's latch clicked, and I pulled the big metal handle. "What do you say, Moose?"

My big-headed schoolmate swung his swivel chair away from a wall of monitors and smiled. "Always good to see you, Jimmy."

Half-inch thick spectacles made his eyes appear twice normal size but still not large enough to be in proportion to his head. Protruding ears and an elongated jaw rounded-out features leading to his childhood nickname. I had called upon Moose for a few cases needing a master of electronic surveilance, but he never seemed keen on leaving his stuffy little security room where at least fifty screens irradiated him on a daily basis.

The tinker, entranced by the wall of techie geekdom, walked past Moose and his desk to bask in the monitors' blue light. "I bet you can see a lot with this configuration."

Moose sat back in his chair and interlaced his fingers across his chest. "Oh, I see everything." He looked each of us up and down. "Aren't you two cute? Twins, and all? How did you get Jimmy to ditch his coat and hat?"

I turned Moose's chair to face him toward his terminal and pointed to one of the monitors. "See anything outside the trauma ward?"

"Nothing unusual."

"I'm talking about outside the hospital. You have any parking lot cameras picking up the trauma ward's side of the building? Like, the third floor specifically?"

Moose clicked around on his keyboard. Screens blinked from one vantage point to another. He fiddled with a joystick, and I watched a monitor way up on the wall where a small image of the hospital grew into a fuzzy set of windows. "We're maxed out with the optical zoom, but I might be able to get a little closer and clean up the image digitally."

"You keep recordings?"

"Of course."

"Can you go back about an hour?"

"I've got a full month for your viewing pleasure." Moose used his joystick to scrub through the past forty-five minutes.

"Wait," I pointed at the monitor and walked around Moose's desk to get closer to the wall, "do you see that?"

The tinker moved beside me. "Looks like two people standing in the window."

"Moose, can you go back and slow-motion forward?" The overhead fluorescents caused a glare on the monitor, and I bobbed and weaved a bit to get a clear view. "Stop! Right there. Now, slow motion forward."

One person opened the window. The other, moving stiffly and mummified with bandages, leaned over the sill, looked down, and shook his head vigorously.

"That's got to be The Mime. I bet the other is the person the cadet took for a nurse."

The nurse fussed next to the window and ducked out of view.

The tinker scratched his head. "What are they doing?"

"I think we're about to find out."

The Mime leaned way out of the room, tried to catch himself on the sill, then reached back for the window frame but couldn't bend his bandaged arms enough to grab anything. The nurse reappeared in the window holding The Mime's legs and let go.

I can't say I had ever really felt bad for criminals. They broke laws, and I made them face the music. What happened to The Mime, though, really challenged my street-hardened sensibilities. He fell, spinning like an unspooling yo-yo, one end of his bandage having been tied to something inside the room. The unwinding slowed his descent, but only so much.

"Pause it there, Moose."

The Mime froze mid spin.

"Okay, now zoom out."

The window image shrank making room for the hospital wall and lawn below it where clowns encircled an inflated crash mat.

The tinker tapped my arm with the back of his hand. "Hey, that's Reginald's gang."

"What gave you that idea? Okay Moose, hit play."

The Mime struck the crash mat dead-center, and its edges fluttered skyward. Two clowns dove into the enveloping nylon to drag The Mime free. They tried standing him up a couple of times, but he kept wobbling around and falling on his face. A big clown carried him off camera while the others folded the mat and packed their gear.

"Can you save this recording for us, Moose?"

"You bet."

The tinker looked at the floor and rubbed his neck. "We already knew the prisoners worked together to escape, but Reginald, his clown friends, and The Mime cooperating on the outside? And, with everything going on in Ocean Mist? This isn't making sense. The escapees should be scattering to all corners of the country."

"This all makes sense to them. We just don't see the big picture, yet." I put my hand on Moose's shoulder. "Thanks, old friend. We'll be in touch."

The hospital parking lot's harsh white lights washed-out the colors from sagging arborvitae, weeping pines, and drooping flowers in small mulch islands afloat in the asphalt. The lights washed-out the colors from the few cars scattered in the lot. The lights washed-out my dashboard. The lights washed-out my life.

Even the tinker and his endless optimism couldn't muster a *what's next, Jimmy?* There just didn't seem to be a next.

I sat staring out the windshield listening to the sirens filling Ocean Mist and undid a few more buttons of my borrowed Hawaiian shirt. *I need to get some real clothes.*

I put the old girl in gear and eased out of the lot. "We need help. Reinforcements."

"What I need is sleep."

"Okay, back to your place for a couple of hours' shut-eye then we work the phones."

"You have an idea?"

I didn't have enough energy to have an idea. Only knew we couldn't work alone. We drove to the tinker's house in silence hoping for some rest.

The tinker got out of the Studebaker, started up his front walk, but came back and opened the passenger door when he noticed I didn't get out and follow him. He leaned into the car. "What's wrong?"

I groaned, took a slow breath, and extended my pointer finger from the steering wheel. "Take a look at your bay window."

Glass shards ringed the window's gaping frame like shark's teeth.

The tinker slammed the car door and clenched his fingers in his hair. "I can't believe it! When will this all end?" He stomped into his lawn and looked into his living room. "They took my Skee-Ball machine! My Skee-Ball machine, Jimmy!"

A faint orange glow rising over the roof caught my eye. I got out and walked toward the back of the house until the crackle of flames stopped me from rounding the corner. Raising clenched fists into guard position, bending my knees slightly for mobility, and taking a moment to allow adrenaline to awaken exhausted muscles, I readied myself for whatever might greet me and sprung into the backyard to find the tinker's Skee-Ball machine alight on his patio.

"Hey," I called over my shoulder, "I found your game."

First time I had ever witnessed the tinker cry. My heart broke seeing him kneeling on the edge of his patio watching the flames through his tears. We shared a moment, I guess, and I reached deep into one of my short's cargo pockets for the burner phone. "I'm calling Angela. Get whatever you need and can carry. We can't stay here."

She didn't pick up for the unidentified number— I had taught her well. She would answer eventually, though, if the same number kept appearing. "Yeah, doll. It's me. I lost my phone. We need a place to lay low. You mind?" Heat from the burning Skee-Ball machine roasted my cheeks. I stepped back. "Do you still have my spare change of clothes? Great. Yeah, we can meet you at the library." I dropped the burner back into my cargo pocket and made my way to the garden hose.

Prison Break

Part 4: The Gang's All Here

The patched and frayed couch in the periodicals section never looked so inviting. I flopped onto the cushions half grateful for the chance to rest and half knowing I wouldn't be able to shut my eyes for more than a few minutes. Sirens rose and fell from cruisers crisscrossing the town beyond the library's windows where criminals carried-out their night-long benders.

How could I have missed all of this? A picnic for law enforcement appreciation? Really, Jimmy? Balloons and a bouncy house in a prison yard? I'll certainly know for next time.

Angela came out from behind the circulation desk. "Thanks for coming here, Jimmy. I just didn't want to leave the collection with everything going on out there."

"Sure thing, doll." *What would anyone want with all of these books?* Then I remembered Bumper and Patches had once answered that question for me. *I guess everyone has their thing.* "Thanks for getting my spare clothes."

She nodded. "I thought maybe you forgot I had them."

I loved it when she pouted. "Never, doll." I pulled my fedora down over my forehead to cover my eyes.

"The two of you look terrible." She pointed her cute little chin at the tinker. "He's just sitting in the nonfiction aisle rocking in a chair, and you look like you haven't slept in a week."

The library's front picture window shattered.

Something struck me in the gut, and I sat upright finding a heavy red brick on my stomach.

"Get away from the window!" I jumped to my feet crunching glass under my penny loafers, spun against the wall, and leaned just far enough to look out to the street. No one there.

Angela pressed against the wall across the broken window. "There's a note, Jimmy."

I retrieved the brick from the couch and opened the paper folded around it. *Get out!*

The tinker rushed from the nonfiction aisle. "Now what?"

"We need to leave," I said, "through the back!"

"Where are we going to go?" The tinker folded his arms. His glare challenged anyone to move him from his spot. "They're following us everywhere!"

Angela moved behind the circulation desk, retrieved Joey, the forty-five-magnum-looking date stamper she had used to threaten Patches so long ago, cocked the hammer, and thumped the desk with the heel of her hand. "I'm not leaving the books. Let them come."

"What are you going to do? Stamp their foreheads?"

Another crashing of glass, but this one came with the whooshing sound of an erupting Molotov cocktail. Then another and another until flickering oranges and reds filled the periodicals and fiction sections.

I took Angela by the shoulders. "Look doll, there is nothing we can do. If you don't leave, I'm going to carry you out."

"With your bad back?"

The fire spread quickly across the carpet and up the shelves.

The tinker shouted over flames. "Are you two coming?"

We filed out into the alley behind the library, turned to see the building fill with flames, and decided to keep running as a forest-worth of wood pulp turned to ash behind us.

The tinker stopped at the end of the alley, bent, and leaned on his knees. "Wait, I can't run anymore."

That's usually my line.

Angela buried her face in my chest and gripped the lapels of my sport coat. "Why are they doing this, Jimmy? Why burn all of our books?"

I took her cheeks in my hands and looked down into her eyes. "Those books can be replaced. It could have been worse." She knew what I meant. The archives lay safely within the stone room on the lighthouse island.

"Book burnings are all about control," the tinker said just above a whisper. "Control and the fear of free-thinking."

Maybe, but this time, it's about something else. I stepped away from Angela, walked into the street, and looked out toward Washington Avenue. A pink Cadillac crept away from the front of the library. *This time, it's about me.*

ANGELA STARED OUT THE PASSENGER WINDOW AT the passing street lights and darkened store fronts, but I knew all she could see was the library in flames.

"Where are we going?" she asked.

The same question had come to me ten blocks behind us. We could only circle Ocean Mist's streets for so long. "I don't know, yet."

The tinker lay across the back seat. "Back at my house, you said we needed to work the phones. What were you thinking?"

I took in a deep breath, held it, and let it out slowly. "I don't know."

"Sounded like you had an idea, or at least the start of one."

"I wish I did, but no."

Angela rung her hands in her lap. Kept her eyes fixed out the window. "We don't need ideas. We need a list. A list of every escaped prisoner you think could have done these things, and we hunt down each one."

"Hunt down each one, huh? You're talking about a list spanning my career."

"So?" Angela cracked her knuckles— one at a time. "We start at the top and work our way down one-by-one. No cops. No trials."

"Just take a breath there, doll."

"I know," came from the back seat, "let's throw them a picnic."

Even the Studebaker's engine sounded angry. The old girl pulled to the left when we approached the intersection with First Street. Seemed to want to take us somewhere. She carried us way out into the morning dark, and I eased her to a stop at the dead-end overlooking the marsh and lighthouse.

"Work the phones," I said. "Make a list. Start at the top. Throw them a picnic."

"What did you say?" The tinker asked.

"I have an idea."

I HEARD THE ELEVATOR DESCEND THEN STOP. Edward entered the island's underground room, his crown of stringy hair swaying with his stride, and joined the tinker, Angela, and me around a folding table.

Chicken Neck Nellie trailed Edward. Her tight jean cut-offs and t-shirt didn't have any stains, and her muck boots shined green.

Nellie must've taken the day off to help us.

She stopped halfway to the table and peered down the aisles of book-shelves, crates, chests and honeycombed racks of document tubes stretch-ing well beyond the gray limits of the single fluorescent light dangling above our heads. "What's all of this?"

Angela barely looked up from the table. "Temporary storage for the library. Don't go poking around."

I whispered in Angela's direction. "Easy, doll. She's here to help."

"Uh-huh." My librarian still didn't look up from the notes scattered in front of us.

The tinker leaned in close to me. "Those two still at it?"

"I heard that." Nellie resumed her walk to the table.

"So did I," Angela said.

I frowned at him.

"Why's it so dark?" Nellie asked.

Angela folded her arms and didn't change her stare. "We barely have enough solar for climate control. Any more questions?"

Edward lifted a dehumidifier's power cord and followed it back into the dark. "Give me a few more days, and I'll give you more juice."

"Not now, Edward." I waved him to the table. "The wiring can wait."

Nellie leaned against the table and into the light. She could never quite shake the odor of old chicken necks and marsh water, but her chis-eled and tanned body never disappointed me.

Angela elbowed my ribs. "Eyes on the problem, Jimmy."

"I'm not sure how I can help," Nellie said, "but I'll do whatever I can. It's like the inmates have taken over the asylum."

I rapped my knuckles against the table. "The streets may look crazy to the regular Joe, but there's something more controlled and sinister at work."

"You think someone's coordinating all of this?" asked Nellie.

I nodded. "I'm sure Bumper and Patches planned the escape, whatever is happening out there right now, and whatever will happen tomorrow."

The tinker propped his elbows and leaned on the table. "They're going after you, Jimmy. They're destroying everything you've built in Ocean Mist. You're business, your reputation—."

"And my friends. They've already come for you. Burglarized your house. Set fire to Angela's library." I looked into the faces of those around me, everyone I knew best. "I suspect they'll come for Nellie and Edward, too. That's why we need to give this scum what they want before they destroy all of our lives and burn Ocean Mist to the ground."

The tinker chewed on one of his nails. "What do you mean, Jimmy?"

"You said it, yourself. They want me. That's how we'll get them."

Angela said, "You're not making sense."

I gave her the once-over. "You feel like dancing?"

"What?" Angela would have laughed any other day. "You don't dance."

"He did once," the tinker said. "Ocean Mist has never been the same."

"Well," I took off my fedora and smoothed my hair, "it might be time to dance again."

The tinker leaned way into the light. "Are you talking about White Vinegar and Chow-chow?"

I took a deep breath and let his question hang in the air. "We need to do something big. Sucker them like they did to us with the Ocean Mist Law Enforcement Appreciation Picnic. Lure Bumper, Patches, and their friends with something they can't ignore. Make them think they've won. Wrap me up in a bow."

The tinker rubbed his chin. "That would have to be a big bow."

I reached across the table and swatted him with my hat. "Anyway, we reopen the Pink Flamingo. New ownership. Better than anything Bumper ever did. Make it known the club is doing business again, both legitimate and otherwise."

Edward jumped up and down and clapped his hands. "I love this idea. Can I be the D.J.? I've been taking beatbox lessons." He cupped his hand over his mouth and made huffing and spitting noises like an overworked horse.

Nellie stared into the floor and bit her lip.

"What are you thinking?" I asked.

She spoke without looking at me. "Let's say we pull this off— reopen the nightclub and draw in all of these criminals wanting you dead. Then what? How do we keep them from killing you?"

"You're right. They outnumber us, but, when it comes down to it, they're idiots. So, we outsmart them. Make it look like they're getting what they want then turn the tables on them."

My red-haired librarian leaned over the table making it hard for me to focus on what she said. "You mean turn the Pink Flamingo into a monkey trap like farmers use on the Asian subcontinent?"

Edward tugged on the tinker's shirt and spoke into his ear, but we could all hear him. "Asian farmers use nightclubs to catch monkeys?"

"I don't follow," I said.

Angela continued, "A farmer hollows-out a gourd, drills a small hole in it, weighs it down with sand, and inserts nuts or a piece of fruit. A monkey comes along, sticks its hand inside, grabs the fruit, and can't pull out its hand because grabbing the treat forms a fist, which is bigger than the hole. The monkey is trapped because it's too greedy to let go of the fruit."

"Yeah," I said, "something like that. Once the trap is sprung, and we have them, we call in the cavalry. Ocean Mist's P.D."

Angela nodded. "I see where you're going with this, but what about the capital to renovate? Even if we get that kind of money, we can't just take over an abandoned building. A lease takes weeks to negotiate, and to set up a business—."

"I happen to know Bumper's silent partner," I said. "Bumper ran the Flamingo, but the property belonged to someone else. Public records list the mayor as the deed holder, and the mayor has lots of money."

The tinker rubbed his eyes and lowered his head. "So, we need the mayor's help?"

I didn't like that part, either, but I couldn't think of an alternative.

"From the look on the mayor's face at the fire, he's worried about the sudden surge in competition. He'd probably give us a blank check to thin the herd of crooks shouldering in on his business."

The dehumidifiers' hums filled the silence while everyone considered my idea.

Nellie strummed her fingers on the table. "I know hard work, and this is going to take a lot of it."

I think they're with me.

Angela placed her hand on my cheek. "Crab lady is right. We can't do all of this by ourselves."

The tinker pulled out his burner phone and walked into the dark aisles. "I've got that covered. I'll be right back."

"So, it's settled, then. We have a plan." I hiked up my pants. "It's time for me to see the mayor."

Nellie took off a muck boot, reached inside, pulled out a pebble, and flicked it. "I can take you and your little friend across the marsh. I saw where you parked your car."

The tinker spoke to her from the dark. "I thought you only had room for one. You got a new boat?"

Nellie took a few steps toward his voice. "Oh, yeah. That's how I brought Edward here. Outboard engine and trolling motor. Titanium rudder. Customized racks and winches for my traps. I can even use re-claimed cooking grease as an alternate fuel."

"Nice! The future for biofuel is wide—."

"Hey," I banged the table, "can we get back to saving Ocean Mist, please?"

Angela squeezed my forearm. "Everyone, just wait a minute." The overhead light accented lines deepening across her forehead. "Jimmy, you can't go back into town, especially march into the mayor's office. That's like sticking your hand into a hornet's nest. We can't protect you there."

"Jimmy Grits doesn't need protection, doll." I straightened, and Angela stepped back. "Now isn't the time for men to be hiding under-ground and tip-toeing around in the shadows. I have to be out there. Seen. Feared."

The dehumidifiers filled the silence, again.

Edward cleared his throat. "Well, that was inspirational. How about this? Nellie can deliver a message to the mayor setting up a meeting on the boardwalk. You'll be in the open and on neutral ground. We'll all be nearby, if you need us."

"I like it," I said, "but I go alone."

NOT-SO-HONEST ABE APPROACHED A LITTLE stooped and a bit wary of the dark spots between the boardwalk's lights.

"Mr. Mayor."

"Grits."

"You look a little nervous."

The mayor gestured to an access ramp leading over the dunes and onto the beach. A dark 2:00 in the morning deserted beach. "Let's talk over there."

"Why? Afraid some of your constituency will see you talking with me?" I walked up the ramp, stopped, and leaned on a post not quite through the dunes. "Far enough?"

"You wanted to talk. Make it quick, Grits."

"That's the only way I know."

"I've heard."

"We both have skin in this game."

"Game? I don't know what you're talking about."

"You're feeling the pinch from the sudden competition. Maybe even seeing your godfather status slipping away from you?"

He offered an unconvincing chuckle. "I don't think so."

"If I'm wrong, you wouldn't have come here."

"What are you proposing?"

"I've got a plan to restore balance to Ocean Mist. Back to our old, *you put 'em on the street, and I take 'em off the street,* relationship." I looked out over the black rolling waves in the direction of a seagull's call. "Until, of course, I take you down."

The mayor gave a more convincing chuckle. "Let's say I'm curious. What do you want from me?"

"Money and a liquor license."

"What, no hitmen? How much money and when do you need the license?"

"I need the money tomorrow morning. Early. Enough to remodel a property off of Route One— at least, give it a lipstick-on-a-pig facelift. The liquor license, the day after tomorrow."

"What property?"

"The Pink Flamingo. You own it, don't you?"

"I thought we were talking about catching convicts, but you want to open a strip club?"

"Male review."

"What's the difference?"

"Ask the tinker."

"What does he—?"

"You ever hear the story about an ape from Asia trying to get its watch out of a pumpkin?"

"What?"

"The club is the watch, and the convicts are apes."

"You lost me."

"We're going to lure the convicts by reopening the Flamingo, make them think they got back their church of crime, and offer me as their first sacrifice."

"Too many metaphors, Grits. Just tell me what I get out of all of this."

I stepped back from the fence post and hooked my thumbs in my waistband. "You get to continue as the underworld's mayor and a remodeled Pink Flamingo."

"If I'm paying for it, you bet the club is mine."

"Does that mean you're in?"

The mayor laughed. "I want to make sure I understand what you're asking me to do. You want me to help you catch criminals by financing a forty-eight-hour remodel of a nightclub and by greasing palms to get a back door liquor license?"

"That about sums it up."

The gulls cried to each other over the beach. The tide must have been high, because the waves sounded close.

"Look, mayor, I'm all ears if you have a better idea."

The mayor's eyes lingered on me for a moment. He knew I held back one more want. "What else, Grits?"

"I need you to deliver a message."

"Yeah? What kind of message?"

"An invitation, really. Get word out on the street we'll be having a grand reopening."

"On top of everything else, you want me to burn my reputation by helping you set the trap? Using my property, fine. Money, you can have. A liquor license, I can get that, but my name— my name is my empire."

"Right about now, your empire looks like it's built on sand."

"No, I can't do it."

"Can't or won't?"

"Both."

"You've built this empire, as you call it, from the shadows, mayor. You've always known you'd have to step out into the light, some day. That day is here." A new chorus of sirens rose from the town, drifted over Happy Land, and floated into the ocean's dark. I couldn't have asked for a better way to punctuate my point.

The mayor looked at his feet, moved some sand around with the toe of his shoe, and scratched his cheek. "You got an account number?"

I pulled a deposit slip from my sport coat's pocket. "I opened it this afternoon."

The mayor took the slip. "The club stays mine."

"I certainly don't want it."

"If this doesn't work, you, me, and everyone in Ocean Mist are going to a place we can't come back from."

I tapped the top of a fence post, turned for the boardwalk, and didn't look back.

Prison Break

Part 5: Primping a Flamingo

The Pink Flamingo leered at the tinker and me in the rising sun's yellow light. We stood in the parking lot taking a moment to appreciate our complete underestimation of the building's decay, while the others went inside to chase out rats and pigeons through propped doors and broken windows.

I drained my coffee and crushed the cup. "So, where's the help you said was coming?"

"They'll be here."

"What makes you so sure?"

"That's them." The tinker pointed to a bulbous van laboring down the post-apocalyptic road in front of the Flamingo. "I'm surprised they're late. Last night's game must have been a doozy."

"You've got to be kidding me." I closed my eyes hoping I'd see something different when I opened them.

A minute later, the Mother of Pearl Pinochle Club limped and waddled one-by-one from the bus's door. Each elderly lady waved to us, and the one with pinwheels clipped to her walker blew a kiss to the tinker.

"Okay, this is your show," I said. "I'm going to the bank. Once I see the money come through, I'll send you a text."

"Got it. Then we place the hardware order, and Edward hits the electronics stores."

"I'll swing by town hall and the water department from the bank. I know a guy, and we'll have water and sewer by lunch."

The tinker extended his arms and gave the Pinochle club a gameshow host smile. "Good morning, ladies. Thank you so much for coming on such short notice. Let's go inside, and we can get to work."

I NEEDED SOME TIME TO MYSELF, EVEN if I spent it driving from errand to errand through the downward spiral of Ocean Mist. Roving packs of shifty no-good-nicks had taken the place of families migrating to the beach. The library and my office nothing more than burned-out shells. Here and there shopkeepers swept broken window glass from sidewalks. Blight smacked me in the face with every corner I turned.

Hard for me to be positive with so little going in my favor, but I tried to focus on the last twenty-four hours' successes: the mayor's money waited in the new account, the power company promised a work truck on site by the close of the business day, and my guy at town hall rushed the water and sewer hook-ups—responsiveness I didn't expect even by pulling strings. I guessed staying busy kept the good people of Ocean Mist from having to face the mayhem unfolding around them. Except for me, of course. I couldn't afford the luxury of distraction. Ocean Mist's future lay squarely on my shoulders.

I pulled into the Pink Flamingo's parking lot, navigated a trash-scape of piled water-stained ceiling tiles, broken furniture, and ragged bits of torn-out wallboard, found an open spot, shifted into park, leaned back in my seat, closed my eyes, and let out a long breath preparing for what might wait beyond the propped front door.

Putting one foot in front of the other took me into a cinderblock theater filled with a surreal freak-show of actors playing the parts of hyperactive construction workers. Grandmotherly ladies, three to each pneumatic screwdriver, drove fasteners into the block walls for studding. Their thick safety goggles dangled from pearl string lanyards, and their hardhats sat perched atop tight gray perms. The tinker, a pencil behind his ear, leaned over sawhorses and cut wallboard with a long serrated knife. Edward teetered on drywall stilts. Nellie hammered plywood to a frame for a new bar. Angela tap-danced between workstations holding hand drawn plans at arm's distance from her nose.

I stood watching the bizarre construction site—particularly amazed at how even coveralls and a coating of gypsum dust couldn't hide my librarian's amazing curves—and wondered if any of us really knew what we were doing.

Angela rolled up her plans and marched over to me. "You look awful."

"Thanks, doll."

"No, really. Just terrible. You need some sleep."

"We all do."

The tinker tossed his pencil onto a piece of uncut wallboard, cradled and arched his back, and held his stretch for a moment. "What do you think, Jimmy?"

A pneumatic drill's whine stopped with a bang, and I turned toward several Pinochle club members near the wall. One lady wrestled off her knit cardigan while yelling at another using language making my cheeks flush.

Angela stood on her toes and spoke into my ear. "You should've heard some of the things coming from their mouths before I told them to tone it down."

The tinker propped his hands on his hips. "We owe them big. They framed all of that this morning."

I tilted back my hat and scratched my forehead. "By themselves?"

"Of course." The tinker watched the women work. "It's right down their alleys."

"What do you mean down their alleys? What does framing have to do with Pinochle?"

"More than a few of them were Rosie Riveters."

"Wait a minute." I did the math. "That was World War II. Over seventy-five years ago. How's that possible?"

"The Greatest Generation," the tinker said. "The Greatest Generation."

Angela put her hand on my cheek. "Jimmy, you're right. We all need some sleep. There are some cots in the back. How about I show you where?"

The muscles in my neck and shoulders turned to jelly. The feeling spread through my body as she took my hand and led me down hallways to the left and right then left again through the hodge-podge of interconnected trailers and additions making-up the Pink Flamingo. She opened the door to a small room with a chair and two cots, which she pulled together, then took the sport coat from my shoulders and untied my tie.

"Lay down."

"Yes, ma'am."

She slipped my penny loafers off my feet, nestled in beside me on the neighboring cot, and draped her arm over my chest. "Try to get some rest. You deserve it."

I OPENED MY EYES FROM A SLEEP seeming to be nothing more than a blink, and when I reached to stroke Angela's hair, I found myself alone.

How long?

Even this seasoned private eye couldn't tell. My sleep, whether minutes or hours, did nothing to ease my aches and knots. Every muscle I knew and some I met for the first time hurt when I swung my legs off the cot and pushed into a stand.

Angela had folded my tie and reshaped my fedora leaving both piled neatly on the chair with my sport coat hung over its back. I suited up and checked my phone. Four hours. Exactly three and a half hours too long.

Construction sounds helped me retrace my steps through the Flamingo's maze of hallways to the main room. The Mother of Pearl Pinochle Club's departure had tamed the remodel activity, but the tinker and Angela still chugged away— a new layer of gypsum dust covered every inch of my girl turning her red hair white.

"You two still at it? When did you take your last break?"

The tinker didn't look up from his tape measure. "We're okay, Jimmy."

"Have either of you heard from my brainiac nephew?"

Angela brushed her coveralls creating puffs of white. "He got here about an hour ago. He's setting up some equipment in the back."

The tinker marked his wallboard. "Glo should be here, soon." He smiled when saying her name. "She's about a half an hour out on Highway One."

Angela moved between the tinker and me, turned her back to him, and said just above a whisper, "He's been calling her every ten minutes."

I nodded and folded my arms. "Glad I could teach him something about dames."

Angela used her *your books are way overdue* voice on me. "Dames? Why don't you go back and say hello to your nephew?" She pointed to a hallway.

I took a few steps, looked back, and she hoisted a new sheet of drywall onto some studs.

Women, just when you think you understand them.

Something long, thin, and squirmy dropped across my shoulders from the dark recesses above my head. I jumped sideways. A chill shot down my spine spreading like icy fingers into my arms and legs.

Edward straddled a joist about ten feet over my head. "Sorry, Jimmy." He clenched a bunch of cables with one hand and what looked like wire-strippers in the other. "One got away from me."

I straightened my hat. Adjusted my coat. "Let a guy know when you're crawling around up there."

He turned his face into his shoulder to wipe his brow with his t-shirt. "We can use a lot of the old club's wiring. I should have the new circuits run and connected to the service box in another hour or two, but we can't install any hardware until the drywalling is done. Too much dust."

"Yeah, too much dust."

"Did Angela tell you what we found behind the kitchen?"

"Bodies?"

"The Pink Flamingo's old mirror ball. You know that huge one they used to spin above the dance floor?"

"Can't say I'm acquainted."

"Well, I think we can use the ball, and your nephew seemed really interested in it."

A lifetime spent chasing criminals, making the streets safe, and I'm having a conversation about a mirror ball.

I shook my head, made my way into the hallway, and stopped to lean against the wall. My pulse should have slowed after the falling cable kicked me into action, but my heart pounded so hard I heard it.

All of my friends' work. All of the money. So much riding on this plan.
I couldn't catch my breath and took a knee.
Ocean Mist. My responsibility.
The hallway turned on its side. The floor's cold tile pressed against my forehead.
Is this a heart attack? No pain in my chest. This detective has the ticker of a mule. Poisoned! I've been poisoned! I tried to remember the last time I ate or drank anything. *Can't be poison. Or, could it be? You're fine Grits. Get up and shake it off. You're almost there. This plan will work.*
"Get yourself together, Jimmy," I said.
The world righted as I used the wall to pull myself back to my feet. A quick look over my shoulder. *No one saw me.*
I pulled my hat down over my brow and soldiered toward beeping and humming noises I could only attribute to my nephew. He sat in a closet-sized room on a rickety office chair. A multi-colored spaghetti of cables lay at his feet. Gizmos and whizbangs surrounded him. The dim blue glow of a laptop's monitor lit his face.
"Hey, kid." I tussled his wild curly red hair. "What's cooking?"
"Hi, Uncle Jimmy."
"Thanks for cutting your summer camp short. You, ahh, have fun fishing, making fires, and sleeping under the stars? All that camping-type stuff?"
"It wasn't that kind of camp, Uncle Jimmy."
"Oh?"
"Some retirees in Lewes started a community group to promote engineering with teenagers. They held the camp."
I tried to picture what an engineering camp would look like, but it just didn't click with me. "Engineering group, huh?"
"Yeah, the Future Engineers Community Association of Lewes."
"So, it's FECAL Camp?"
"Well, I guess it is."
"Thanks for cutting it short."
"Not a problem. Your friends told me what you want to do. I have an idea, but I'm going to need a pretty big power source. You think your friend Gloria will be able to help?"

"She works for the Nuclear Regulatory Commission. Big power is her thing. What's your idea?"

My nephew picked up a plastic band, the kind snapped on your wrist when entering a nightclub, and tossed it to me. "Put that on."

"This is kind of heavy for a wrist-band, don't you think?"

"It's the nickel-iron core."

"Right. Nickel-iron."

He turned some dials on a small box, which made a high-pitched whine. The wrist-band vibrated against my skin. He frowned and turned the dial some more. The plastic band tore free of my wrist, flew across the room, and stuck to a metal post in the corner.

I rubbed a red abrasion. "Isn't that something?"

"There's still a problem with the clasp. I'm thinking a micro titanium-wire-hook-and-loop fastener should do the trick."

"You tell me what you need, and I'll make it happen. Just as long as it happens the day after tomorrow."

"Talk about a time crunch."

"You ain't kidding, kid. You ain't kidding."

Glo arrived in a black SUV followed by an unmarked van. The vehicles pulled into the parking lot. The air around us seemed to change. It vibrated. Buzzed.

The tinker ran to the SUV. "I'm so glad you're here!"

Our friendly nuclear scientist threw her arms around him. Glo deserved a lot of credit. I could smell him from where I stood.

Glo touched noses with the tinker. "As soon as you explained the situation, I knew exactly how I could help." She leaned to the side and waved to me. "Hi, Jimmy."

The tinker pulled away from her and circled the van, as if he could see through its sides and study its cargo. "Is this it? All in one van?"

"You bet, and this will be its first field test."

"Field test?" My heart skipped a beat or two, and I began to feel like I did in the Pink Flamingo's back hallway. "What field test?"

Glo bounced over to me, folded her hands under her chin, and spoke softly through a smile like a thirteen-year-old inviting me to a surprise party. "It's our country's first completely portable thermonuclear fusion generator."

"First one?" I scratched the back of my neck and looked at the van then back at her. "What about Shuga's taffy machine? That's been around for decades."

The tinker opened the van's back doors. "The taffy machine is run by a nuclear fission generator. This is fusion. A million times more efficient and much more powerful."

Glo giggled. "That's okay, Jimmy. It's a common mistake." She clenched her fists at her sides and did a twisting dance-like motion on the balls of her feet. "Isn't this exciting?"

Exciting? My breathing became shallow. *Not again. No now.* I willed myself to take slower, deeper breaths. "What, exactly, do you mean by field test?"

"This is the first time we've taken it out of the laboratory."

The tinker called to us from inside the van. "Can you get Edward? We need to get this beauty hooked up to the service box. Oh, and let your nephew know we got his juice!"

"I'll go and do that." Leaving sounded like a good idea.

An Ocean Mist patrolman met me at the Pink Flamingo's entrance. The twenty-something needed a shave and a nap. Maybe a vacation.

"Officer."

"You Jimmy Grits?"

"I'm afraid so."

"I thought I recognized you from the picnic. Best potato salad I've had in a long time."

I reached for a manilla envelope in his hand. "That what I think it is?"

"Don't know. I was just told to bring it to you."

"I need you to give a message to your chief."

"Don't you have a phone?"

"Yeah, but your dispatcher and I don't get along. Tell your chief we're on schedule. No changes in plan." I tipped my fedora.

The patrolman climbed into his cruiser, and he was gone.

I opened the envelope, unfolded the type-written list of escapees, and groaned. I recognized more than half the names, just about every crook I had put away during my career. The next forty-eight hours would determine whether my legacy, my life, meant something or not.

I POINTED TO THE BOLD LETTERING ON the announcement draft and asked the tinker, "Do we really need the dance thing?"

For One Night Only, White Vinegar and Chow-chow Return To Ocean Mist's Premier Nightclub— The Pink Flamingo!

"Our target audience will need to know you'll be here."

"How will they know I'm White Vinegar?"

"You're not. You're Chow-chow."

"Well, how will they know?"

The tinker put his hand on my shoulder. "Trust me, they know."

I sighed, circled a couple of spelling errors and a dangling participle, and handed the invitation back to the tinker. "Can you get these printed and to the mayor's office before five?"

The tinker recoiled. "I'm not going there alone."

"Why not?"

"Remember what happened last time we went there?"

"Of course, but what did you expect? You were dressed like a bionic marshmallow."

"That was official NRC-issued personal protective equipment with a state-of-the art detection and containment system."

"Okay, an official bionic marshmallow. Take Nellie with you. No one will mess with you if she's within reach."

The reborn Pink Flamingo eclipsed every speakeasy known to this gumshoe: a polished parquet dance floor, hand-buffed and waxed oak-top bar, speakers the size of refrigerators, spot lights, a state-of-the-art disco laser light system, and the Pink Flamingo's original six-foot diameter mirror ball hanging high above it all. Two chrome poles broke up an otherwise spacious stage, but I couldn't complain. The ramshackle building must have had more than a few support issues.

Angela rubbed puffy eyes. Heavy lids hid some of the redness. "They did this for you, Jimmy." Her voice, little more than a whisper, wrapped around and warmed me. "You know that, right?"

I nodded. Looked at my watch. "Eight hours before opening, doll." I raised my hat into the air and crossed the dance floor. "Listen, everyone—."

The room went quiet and all heads turned in my direction. I pressed my hands onto the stage, jumped, and almost got my gut up over the edge but dropped back onto the dance floor. I pushed downward with my palms while tossing my leg onto the stage, but I couldn't get my hip high enough to roll onto my side and slid back to where I had started.

The tinker, standing behind the bar, dried his hands on a towel and draped it over his shoulder. "Want some help, Jimmy?"

"No, I don't want any help."

Third time was a charm.

I stood, brushed off my coat, straightened my tie, and strolled to centerstage. "Listen everyone, get some rest. We all need to be sharp and ready. More ready than we've ever been. You know what to do, so I don't think we need to run through our plan, again. Everyone, meet here at five. Not a minute later."

I scanned the room. The faces of everyone I cared about in the world looked to me for guidance, inspiration, and hope for a future Ocean Mist. They needed me.

I needed a cheesesteak and a bottle of Jack but had to settle for a deep breath. "The Pink Flamingo opens at six. Sharp!"

Prison Break

Part 6: Jimmy the Party Man

My nephew sat behind a bunch of monitors, keyboards, and switch panels all Christmas-treed together with a mass of wires and little boxes he called hubs. I kept my hands in my pockets and my distance half afraid the whole system would short circuit if I even breathed in the wrong direction.

"Our first guests are here." He pointed to a screen showing an array of camera angles from the parking lot. "Looks like some bikers."

"At least we know the mayor got the word out."

"Unless the *Satan's Darlings* on their jackets is the name of their book club, I think you're right, Uncle Jimmy."

The walkie talkie on my belt chirped. "Big Edward to Fat Boy, come in Fat Boy."

I pressed the talk button without unclipping the unit from my belt. "What do you want, Edward?"

"We got some hogs rolling up on us at the door."

"Yeah, we can see them on the monitor." I leaned in to count how many bikers crossed the parking lot. "Looks like quite a few."

"I copy, Fat Boy."

"Stop calling me that. Nellie, can you hear me?"

My nephew pulled back with a parking lot camera. Edward stood outside the main door. Nellie sat nearby on a high-seated bar chair behind a podium.

"Fat Boy, this is Chicken Neck. I'm all ears."

"I said, stop—. Look, just make sure those wrist bands are on good and tight. If anyone complains, tell them no booze without the band."

"10-4 Fat Boy."

My nephew put on a headset then sorted the rap sheets emailed to him from the prison. "Chicken Neck, this is Young Red. I got eyes on our guests. Can you delay them long enough for me to capture stills so I can cross reference?"

"You got it, Young Red."

I leaned over my nephew's shoulder. "When did all of you come up with these names?"

"Fat Boy, this is Big Edward. It's time for me to start up the beats."

I sighed into my walkie. "Okay, Edward. You can head inside."

"Uncle Jimmy, look," my nephew pointed to a still of a biker, "he's on the list of escapees."

"Stay sharp, everyone. We have the first name from the list." I asked my nephew, "What's the tinker's name?"

"Handle."

"What?"

"Handles, not names."

"Okay, what's his handle, then?"

"Little Man."

"Hey, Little Man. Are we ready for the main event?"

Like so many of history's great battle strategies, ours relied upon distraction. A distraction coming from the stage. Without a doubt, a job for the tinker.

"Being cool on the stool and ready for the party, Fat Boy. Come on back."

"Come back where?"

"No, Jimmy, that means it's your turn to talk."

"Why didn't you just say that?"

"I did."

"Look, everyone just speak English."

My nephew pointed to the screen. "A car just arrived."

"Pink Cadillac?"

"No, it's a compact. An old Volkswagen Beetle."

"Can you see who's getting out?"

He clicked some switches and fiddled with a small joystick. "A clown? Make that, three clowns. No, five. Six clowns—."

"I'm sure that's Reginald's gang. This could go on for a while."

I still needed to hear from Angela, our librarian turned bartender. Her being exposed in the club, interacting with those hooligans, and Glo waiting tables didn't thrill me, but it was their idea.

I tapped my nephew on the shoulder. "You're young Red, right?"

He nodded.

I clicked my talk button. "Old Red, this is Jimmy."

Radio silence.

I tried again. "Old Red, you out there? Over."

My nephew moved his hands away from his keyboard and looked slowly over his shoulder. "Uncle Jimmy, you trying to get Angela?"

"Yeah, why? What's the problem?"

"Old Red isn't her handle."

"FAT BOY, this is BOOKWORM, what do you want?"

"Uh, yeah there, Bookworm, making sure you're okay and ready behind the bar."

"Why wouldn't I be, FAT BOY?"

"Just checking." A deep bassline shook the walls, and I felt vibrations through the floor. Edward really hit the ground running. "I should have given Edward some records from my collection."

"Your polka collection? No, Uncle Jimmy, you shouldn't have." My nephew fiddled with the camera controls. "We're packing them in, now."

"How many on the list?"

"At least ten, so far."

"Okay, time for me to go backstage."

"Don't be seen. Not yet, anyway."

"Yeah, I know kid."

The Flamingo's maze of hallways kept me well away from the dance floor and kitchen, and I found the tinker backstage peeking through a heavy curtain.

"What's it look like out there?" I asked.

"This place is hopping." The tinker stepped back from the curtain, put his hands on his hips, spread his legs, and did a deep lunge. "Two years. I've been waiting for this moment for two years." He pulled out of his lunge and rolled his head to the left then right.

My turn to peek through the curtain. No exaggeration from the tinker. A crowd around the bar. Most tables filled. Some on the dance floor jumping up and down and gyrating to Edward's music. Our trollish friend stood behind his sound board, pressed a headphone cup against an ear, and moved his head forward and back like a spastic woodpecker.

I lifted my walkie. "Where are we with the list?"

"Fat Boy, this is Chicken Neck, we've gone through a lot of the wristbands."

"This is Young Red. We're only missing seven from the list."

The tinker put his hand on my shoulder. "All but seven? That's great! More than we expected."

Yeah, but which seven? "Anyone see Bumper or Patches?"

"That's a negative, Fat Boy," said Nellie.

"I didn't see them, Uncle Jimmy, and the parking lot is quiet."

I white-knuckled the walkie. "Edward, we need to stall."

"I have just the thing, Fat Boy."

The techno music stopped suddenly. A rumbling from the crowd took the place of the throbbing base and synthesized drums.

"Whatever you're doing, Edward, make it quick." Club-goers banged on tables, and I heard more than a few bottles and glasses shatter. "Edward?"

"I'm working on it, Fat Boy."

The speakers crackled then delivered a mono-recording of a highly-skilled accordionist's rendition of "The Chicken Dance."

Finally, some quality music.

A cheer rose from all corners of the Flamingo and the number of dancers tripled.

I pressed the talk button. "Hear that, Young Red? Now, that's music."

"Some things just can't be explained, Uncle Jimmy."

I let out a breath I didn't know I held. "Alright, everyone, that should buy us some time."

Despite the pre and post prison-break cooperation between Ocean Mist's scum and lowlife, our invitees kept to their own on the dance floor. Satan's Darlings grouped to the stage's right. They contributed rhythmic chain jangling when shaking their tail feathers. Gilmer and his stroke specialist had apparently reconciled and stood together flapping their wings. Reginald's clowns claimed territory to the left, preferring to raise and squeeze their horns for the clapping parts. I spied The Mime dead-center, conspicuous in his beret, black and white striped shirt, and nylon pants. His re-mummification—fresh bandages peeking from his shirt cuffs—made his dancing more of a stiff rocking motion than his signature pantomime used to sucker marks. The Frankenstein guy involved in the bandstand heist showed some pretty smooth moves for being an oil drum with legs. Skee-Ball Granny needed her grandson's help getting up from the knee bends, but she was a natural with the waddles. The whole thing turned out to be some twisted episode of *This is Your Life, Jimmy Grits,* only all of the guests wanted to kill me.

I pressed my talk button. "Any sign of Bumper and Patches?"

Angela locked eyes with me from the bar and picked up her walkie. "No, but a bird in the hand, Fat Boy. We already have more than we thought we would."

The tinker stood on one foot, propped his other against his inner thigh, and folded his hands in front of his heart.

"Now what are you doing?"

"Yoga. It helps center me. We're going on next."

"Yeah, I know."

I scanned the crowd again. No blonde beehive. No pipe smoke I could see. Or smell, for that matter. "The Chicken Dance" drew to its end. My heart raced.

The tinker grabbed the stage curtain's rope. "You ready?"

"Well," I loosened my tie, "the show must go on, right?"

The house lights dimmed.

Edward switched back to throbbing techno, and his voice rose over the music. "For our grand reopening of the Pink Flamingo, the new management is proud to present, for tonight only, White Vinegar and Chow-chow!"

I glanced at the tinker. "Let's get this over with."

The curtain opened, and a roar rolled up from the crowd hitting me like a wave on the beach, almost as strong as the wave of nausea in my gut. We moved to center stage. Edward pointed at us, bobbed his head up and down, and pushed buttons frantically with his other hand.

The tinker put his fists on his hips, jerked his head upward pointing his chin to the rafters, and thrust out his crotch. The crowd's roar became thunder shaking the building. He hopped from one foot to the other and kicked out his feet, swinging one foot to the left and the other to the right while working his knees. His upper body remained pole straight, and his sneakers clicked and clacked against the stage.

I stepped away from him and stared at his feet.

"Sneaker tacks, Jimmy. For Irish Dance." He finished a combination of moves, folded his arms, and nodded toward me as if to say, *your turn.*

I skipped forward and back, spun around, clapped my hands, and shook both in front of me.

"Come on, Jimmy. You've got to feel the music."

"I'm feeling sick."

The tinker switched styles moving more like he did during our last performance. Smooth and sultry. He swung his hips and unbuttoned his shirt.

"Okay," I said, "that's enough." I took off my belt and swung it in circles over my head. The signal.

Nothing happened.

I turned my back to the audience and faced the tinker.

"What's going on?"

"How should I know? Shake your butt."

"What?"

"You've got to do something." He tossed his shirt into the audience. "Just wiggle your butt."

"I'm not wiggling my butt."

"You need to keep their attention, and it's your biggest asset." The tinker shot past me, slid to the front of the stage on his knees, and leaned way back reaching with both hands toward the ceiling so the strobing lights flashed off of his alabaster and slightly concave chest. "Shake that money-maker, Jimmy!"

I put my hands on my hips, took a few gulps of thick air, and yelled over the crowd, "Edward, for crying out loud! Pay attention!"

He looked up from his soundboard, dropped his earphones around his neck, and craned an ear in my direction cupping his hand around it as if it would make a difference with the chaos between us.

I waved my belt around my head again, balled it up in my hands, and hurled it at the D.J. booth. For some reason, this inspired many on the dance floor to do the same. They bombarded Edward who dropped to the floor fearing for his safety. He raised both hands above the sound-board in surrender, stood when the volley ended, and gave me a sheepish thumbs-up.

Now, for the big finish.

Edward kicked the smoke machine into overdrive. Every laser fired at the mirror ball spinning above our heads turning the club into a huge kaleidoscope. The ball spun faster and dropped like the object of a New Year's Eve countdown. Dancers parted from the floor's center while moving, grooving, and engulfed in the throbbing, pulsing, flashing, sweaty, frenetic, and hedonistic dance club atmosphere. Exactly my plan. Exactly what I needed. Not an eye cast in my direction.

I slipped off-stage and into the wing to grab my walkie. "You watching, Young Red?"

"You bet, Uncle Jimmy."

"Pull the trigger in 3-2-1." The mirror ball just about touched the floor. "Now!"

The hairs on my arms, chest, and the back of my neck stood on end. Glo's fusion reactor in the parking lot charged the magnets hidden within the ball. Our VIP guests, the convicts wearing the iron-nickel core bands with my nephew's specially-made titanium hook and loop closures, flew across the room and slammed wrist-first into the spinning ball.

"It's working," I yelled through my walkie. "Time to call in the cavalry."

Nellie responded. "Police are on the way, Fat Boy."

Desperate cries drew me from the wing back to center stage where I watched escaped inmates magnetically joined to the mirror ball get dragged in circles around the dance floor. Some cried for help, some begged for the ball to be stopped, others cursed in ways I had not thought possible, and Reginald's clown posse honked their horns with reckless abandon.

I pressed my walkie's talk button. "Uh, Young Red, I think that's enough power."

Electricity arced in blue flashes from the ball's top to the ceiling's metal joists making loud buzzing and popping sounds. The chlorine-like smell of ozone filled the room.

"Young Red, you really need to cut back on the power."

Edward's soundboard exploded showering sparks over his booth and the bar. He screamed into his walkie, "Turn it off! For the love of God, turn it off!"

Guests without the nickel-iron wristbands climbed over one another to escape through the fire exits.

The mirror ball spun faster lifting the magnetized inmates by centrifugal force. Their legs and free arms flailed like the strands of a mop spun on its handle.

The tinker clenched his salt and pepper mange and jumped from the stage. "Oh, the humanity!" He inched along the wall toward the burning soundboard and said into his walkie. "Edward, are you okay? If you can hear me, but you can't speak, click your talk button once. Click twice if you can't hear me."

My nephew joined the yelling, his words almost incomprehensible through my small plastic handheld. "Uncle Jimmy, there's something wrong!"

"I can see that! Turn it off! Just, turn the whole thing off!"

"I tried, but it's not working!"

The tinker lifted Edward to his feet then said into his walkie. "Glo, what's happening?"

No response.

I crossed back into the stage's left wing, leapt down the short flight of stairs, kicked the side door's panic bar, and dashed into the parking lot. Electricity arced, crackled, and popped everywhere. A glowing blue spiderweb encircled the fusion reactor van, which emitted a red-orange light. I shielded my eyes, put more space between me and the government-vehicle-turned-solar-flare, and took shelter between the Volkswagen Beetle clown car and Edward's 1971 Gremlin.

"Jimmy!" Glo waved from the parking lot's edge and jumped up and down. "Jimmy!"

I said into my walkie, "Glo, what's going on?"

She just looked at me. No radio.

I ran to her. "What's going on?" I shouted.

"Too much power for the system."

"Tell me something I don't know!" Red and blue lights strobed from the street, but electricity arcing from the van and geysers of sparks shooting into the sky kept Ocean Mist's emergency vehicles from entering the lot. "You have to fix this, fast!"

"I have an idea." Glo squeezed my hand holding the walkie. "Tell Edward to meet me at the junction box."

I relayed the message and said to her, "I'll stay here to make sure none of the inmates give us the slip."

She skirted the reactor van, which had turned from red-orange to yellow, and ran into the club through the stage door.

I decided the clown car didn't provide enough protection, so I moved behind a station wagon and turned up the volume on my walkie. "What's going on inside?"

Angela responded. "We're pulling out every plug we can find, but the mirror ball is still spinning. Lights are exploding everywhere." Another of the tinker's *Oh the humanity!* outbursts drowned something else she said, but her question came through loud and clear. "Why can't anyone turn off the power?"

Hot air burned my lungs with every breath. I peeked over the station wagon's hood. The reactor van's yellow had become an angry violet-white. Paint on nearby cars curled into small ribbons and rose into the sky. Tires close to the reactor burst. One, then two, then three tires at a time. Officers scrambled in the distant street. The exploding tires must have sounded like a shotgun battle.

I dropped behind the station wagon. "Nellie, I need you to call our police contact. Tell them what's happening."

"Sure, Jimmy. I'll just tell them we have a bunch of criminals stuck to a spinning mirror ball and an experimental nuclear reactor about to melt down in the Pink Flamingo's parking lot!"

"Thanks, Nellie. I can always count on you."

The lot fell silent.

No more cracks, buzzing, rumbles—nothing.

I rose from my crouch.

No more arcing electricity or fountains of sparks. The van's colors slowly dimmed from the menacing shades of plasma to a dull red. Another car tire burst, which would have stopped my heart on any other day, but compared to the last fifteen minutes, the sound didn't even draw my glance.

I leaned against the station wagon, took off my hat, wiped my brow, and let out my breath.

Another disaster for Ocean Mist averted.

Never underestimate Jimmy Grits.

A hum filled my ears like a thousand giant hornets got really angry. A white flash and pop came from where the city's transmission lines connected to the Pink Flamingo. A rope-thick strand of white electricity zigged, zagged, and jumped from utility pole to utility pole toward the town.

I climbed onto the station wagon's hood and looked in the direction of Washington Avenue. Street lights flared then died in rapid succession. The big neon Shuga's Candy Shop sign ejected a shimmering stream of greens and blues into the night sky. Electric Armageddon had moved from the Pink Flamingo into Ocean Mist.

My heart thumped against my ribs.

Flashes near the bandstand spread into the residential neighborhoods appearing faster and more intense with each passing heartbeat until the overload-inspired discharges of the entire power grid reached a crescendo— Ocean Mist's transfer station erupted like an energy volcano.

No July Fourth celebration could have rivaled the pyrotechnic spectacle I witnessed against the backdrop of a dark and silent ocean. Charged and burning materials of every imaginable substance left the ground as if launched from mortars. Some burst into blossoms of sparks and crackles. Others simply dared to touch the stars. The show ended when the transfer station ceased to exist. The only light from an otherwise darkened town came from pockets of flames licking at the sky.

We just blew up Ocean Mist.

I clicked my radio, tried to speak, but my throat had dried and cinched shut. I swallowed a couple of times, licked my lips, and tried again to speak. "What— just— happened?"

Edward came across the air waves like a lottery winner. "We're in the clear, Fat Boy! I redirected the excess juice back into Ocean Mist's grid!"

Ocean Mists' police officers, every last one of them, crept into the Pink Flamingo's parking lot, some with their guns drawn, some behind their partners, and all with their eyes locked on the smoldering burnt-plastics-and-rubber-smelling van having returned to its original black.

The vehicle lurched, sending the officers scurrying backwards, then bounced on the rims of its popped tires, rocked back and forth, made horrible clanking noises, leaned, and crashed onto its side.

"I think it's dead," I yelled to the officers.

They stared at me.

I climbed down from the station wagon.

The Flamingo's main door opened.

I raised my fists, bent my knees, and turned my dominant shoulder toward the door ready to meet the army of criminals released from the mirror ball.

Jimmy Grits doesn't roll over for anyone.

The army came forth, but it did so staggering, stumbling, falling over itself, and vomiting a night's worth of nachos, chicken fingers, and alcohol.

I yelled again to the officers, "What are you waiting for? Get them while they're dizzy!"

Prison Break

Part 7: Last Call

The tinker slid into my Down and Out Burger booth, inched across the red vinyl bench facing me, and draped his arm over the seatback. "You want to get something?"

"They're not open for business, yet."

"Looks like they got power."

"Just a generator."

"Oh." He sighed and drummed his fingers on my steno pad laying in front of him.

I pulled it away and wedged it with some folders between my potted fern and the wall.

"Nice of them to let you work out of here until you get a new office."

"Sure. I'll just hang my shingle over—."

"You have Shingles? Those are painful, Jimmy. My uncle got them one time—."

"I don't have Shingles!"

"Wow, you're pretty touchy for a hero."

"Hero, huh?"

"Jimmy Grits, savior of Ocean Mist, the man who captured a mob of escaped prisoners and put them back behind bars."

I reached into my fern and pulled out a metal flask. "Not all of them."

"Not all of who?"

"Not all of the prisoners."

"Well, most. You look horrible. You sleeping okay?"

I shook my head and took a belt of Jack.

"Any idea when you can move back into your apartment?"

"When it's rebuilt, along with the rest of the town. My office might be finished first."

"Are you sure you don't want to stay with me? Mi coucha es su coucha."

"Thanks, but no thanks." The tinker's plaid sofa still smelled of its previous three owners. My Studebaker's cramped back seat won out over his furniture's stench.

"Suit yourself." He picked up my stapler and played with it. "You still meeting the mayor tonight?"

I nodded and rubbed my forehead.

"I really think I should go with you. Cover you. Back you up. Watch your six."

I took the stapler from him. "I told you he's been around the block as many times as I have. He'd know you were there."

"I could—."

"No disguises. You stay out of this. Hear me?"

"Okay," he sighed and started drumming again, "what's this guy's real name, anyway?"

"The mayor?"

"Yeah, I don't think I've ever heard—." The tinker stopped drumming. Something seemed to occur to him. I could've sworn I heard the sounds of a slot machine's reels locking home, one after another, coming from his head. "What's my name?"

"Your name?" I put the stapler next to the plant. "What are you talking about?"

"Yeah, my name. All the cases over the past few years, and I don't think you ever—."

"Come on, kid. What's in a name? I know who you are."

No one passed my boardwalk bench for at least a half an hour. Of course, I didn't expect many strolling at midnight under a sky as black as my sport coat and only days after the Pink Flamingo fiasco. Most of the town remained dark even with city workers and locals scrambling to replace power lines and lights. Few residents braved late-night walks. Even fewer tourists ventured into Ocean Mist.

A wet blanket of hot humidity hung over the town. I loosened my tie and placed my fedora on the bench. Footsteps approached from a nearby access ramp, and I figured it would be the mayor. I pulled the Flamingo's keys from my pocket and played with them to make clinking noises like a dog whistle calling the king of Ocean Mist's underworld.

"Grits."

"Mr. Mayor."

"Those mine?"

"Yep."

"Everything in order?"

"You might need to get a new mirror ball for your dance floor."

"I heard." The mayor took a seat on the bench but not too close, and he didn't look at me when he spoke. "This means our arrangement has come to an end." He put out his hand.

I kept playing with the keys. "Two on our guest list didn't show. Have any ideas why?"

The mayor crossed his arms. "Maybe they were busy."

I shook my head. "Our little shindig had everything they wanted—location, dancing—."

"And you? The great Jimmy Grits? Just say what's on your mind, Grits."

"Where are Bumper and Patches?"

"You got almost everything you wanted, and you still want more."

"Why did you warn them?"

"You can't expect me to part with all of my talent."

"So, they are yours. Why am I not surprised?"

"The keys, Grits." He put out his hand, again.

"I get it, now. You caused all of this, starting with that recipe book two years ago. You told Bumper and Patches about the library's special collections. Somehow, you even knew how to get into the archives."

"I know everything about this town."

"You lost control. You needed me to clean up your mess."

"The keys."

I made a fist around the shiny bits of metal before tossing them at his feet. "Don't think I'm giving you the keys to the city. Ocean Mist is my town."

"Well, Grits," the mayor bent for the keys, rose, and smoothed his shirt, "maybe the Ocean Mist you can see." He walked into the boardwalk's darkness. "Maybe."

NOIR Executive Offices
4221 Back Alley Way
Knuckles, Wisconsin 56271

Dear Mr. Cooper:

I am writing regarding *Jimmy Grits, Private Eye* featuring the character named Jimmy Grits. As president of the National Organization of Investigative Researchers, I wish to express my concern and disappointment with you having cast such a disparaging light upon a generation of hard-working literary private investigators.

If you had taken the time to interview a professional literary gumshoe of the 1940's and 1950's, had conducted a modicum of responsible research into the perilous lives of such investigators, I'm sure your storytelling would have been realistic and respectful. Perhaps, even meaningful. Portraying a literary private investigator of this era as overweight, oblivious, hard-drinking, and skirt-chasing does nothing but fuel an already unfair and inaccurate stereotype.

Additionally, don't be surprised if you receive similar letters from organizations representing the tinkers of our great nation. It seems you do not limit your hateful prose to one hard-working profession.

On behalf of NOIR members, I urge you to reconsider your approach to the character Jimmy Grits and to reflect upon the negative impacts of your more than questionable writing.

Sincerely,
Harold Hamfist, President
NOIR

Acknowledgements

Many people helped to bring Jimmy, the tinker, and their friends' adventures to these pages. David Bender, David Crill, and my father David Cooper, Sr. provided encouragement, insightful feedback, and much patience with my sometimes—often times—obsessive reengineering and rewriting of early drafts. Second-round readers Megan Quirk, Alyx Brehman, and my wife Judy Philips assisted me with conventions and identifying awkward scene changes. Philadelphia-based artist Aubrey Brown worked his magic to capture this book's whimsy and absurdity in beautiful cover art. Salt Water Media of Berlin, Maryland helped to assemble all of the pieces and to get Jimmy's tales into your hands. Finally, I am indebted greatly to the many dedicated public school teachers and college professors who provided me with the knowledge and tools necessary to create this work and so much more.